millie's fling

Jill Mansell

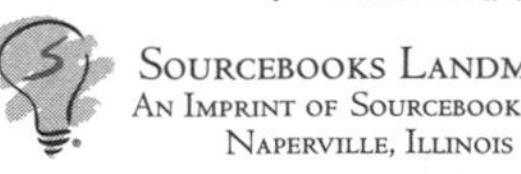

Sourcebooks Landmark™
An Imprint of Sourcebooks, Inc.®
Naperville, Illinois

Published by Sourcebooks Landmark, an imprint of Sourcebooks, Inc.
P.O. Box 4410, Naperville, Illinois 60567–4410
(630) 961–3900
FAX: (630) 961–2168
www.sourcebooks.com

Originally published in 2001 by Headline Publishing Group, London

Library of Congress Cataloging-in-Publication Data

Mansell, Jill.
Millie's fling / Jill Mansell.
p. cm.
1. Single women—Fiction. 2. Female friendship—Fiction. 3. Mate selection—Fiction. 4. Dating (Social customs)—Fiction. 5. Cornwall (England : County)—Fiction. 6. Chick lit. 7. Love stories. gsafd I. Title.
PR6063.A395M54 2009
823'.914—dc22

2009019076

Printed and bound in the United States of America
VP 10 9 8 7 6 5 4 3 2

For Lydia and Cory,
despite the fact that they are sick and tired
of having books dedicated to them.
Bad luck, here's another one.

Chapter 1

The view from where they were sitting was spectacular, but Millie Brady couldn't help wondering why Neil had driven her up here today to Tresanter Point. He wasn't normally the scenery-admiring type.

Next to her, in the driver's seat of his lovingly restored emerald green MG, Neil cleared his throat.

'Right, well, I've had a bit of a think about this, and we've been together for quite a while now.' Clasping her hand suddenly in his, Neil began to stroke it as if it were a nervous puppy.

All of a sudden Millie began to have an inkling as to what this might actually be about. Oh blimey, oh heavens, surely not… surely he wasn't gearing himself up to ask her to marry him…

'Not that long,' she put in hastily, 'not really. Only three months.'

'Still, we get on well, don't we? And the landlord's been dead funny about renewing the lease on our place. I think he wants us out of there.'

Since this was the flat Neil shared with four of his friends, Millie wasn't a bit surprised. The place was an indescribable pit.

'So what I thought was, what with the two of us being pretty much an item these days—Millie, hello, are you listening to me?'

'Mm? Oh, sorry.' Millie forced herself to pay attention; she had been distracted for a moment by the arrival at the cliff-top beauty spot of a gleaming burnt orange Mercedes. As it had screeched to a halt, Millie couldn't help noticing that the driver—a woman in dark glasses—had long, riotously curly hair the exact same shade of burnt orange as her car.

She was smoking a cigarette at a rate of knots. And not looking at all happy, Millie observed as the woman removed her dark glasses and began arranging a row of white rectangles along the dashboard, as if she were dealing out playing cards.

Pay attention now. Come on, concentrate. Millie gave herself an admonitory mental shake. If someone's asking you to marry them the very least you can do is listen; it's only polite.

'Okay, so how about if you jack in your place and we get somewhere of our own?'

Neil gazed at her in triumph, his hideous ordeal over. There, he'd done it. Said what he'd come here to say. Now all Millie had to do was swoon with happiness and say yes.

So he wasn't asking her to marry him, Millie realized with a rush of relief. There wasn't going to be any of that romantic down-on-one-knee business, followed by the production of a little velvet jeweler's box containing an engagement ring. No church, no honeymoon, no solemn vows, none of that sloppy malarkey, oh no. Neil was plumping for the cheaper, more down-to-earth option, basically because he was about to be evicted from his current abode and because he'd rather stick red-hot pins in his eyes than iron a shirt or have to do a spot of washing-up.

I'm only twenty-five. There has to be more to life.

Anyway, what *were* those white rectangles on the dashboard of the Mercedes? And shouldn't the woman with the chestnut hair—now out of the car—take a bit more care where she was going? The way she was wandering so close to the edge of the cliff was downright reckless, Millie tut-tutted; didn't she realize that if she slipped and fell on to the rocks two hundred feet below she could be *killed*?

'You're not saying anything,' Neil complained. 'I thought you'd be over the moon. No more having to share that poky little house with Hester—'

'It's not a poky little house,' Millie replied absently. 'And I like sharing with Hester.'

'But we'd be living together. That means I'm serious about you. We'd be, like, a proper *couple*.'

The wind was blowing the woman's red-gold curls around her face but when she put up a hand to sweep her hair out of her eyes,

Millie saw that she was crying. She also thought there was something familiar about the woman, but from this distance it was impossible to be sure.

Except something wasn't quite right here. The woman was still pacing up and down, smoking furiously, and pausing every now and again to peer over the edge of the cliff. Normally at a beauty spot you sat back on one of the benches thoughtfully supplied for the purpose and admired the stupendous view. This woman, Millie couldn't help thinking, was acting more like an Olympic high-jumper psyching herself up to make her third and final attempt at the world record…

'Okay, fine, if you don't *want* us to live together, that's up to you,' snapped Neil, abruptly letting her hand drop. 'Any normal girl would've been thrilled, but not you, oh no, I might have guessed you'd have to play hard to get. I mean, what d'you expect me to do? Beg?'

Oh good grief, she *was* psyching herself up to jump.

Only not upwards, Millie thought with a surge of horror. Belatedly she remembered that Tresanter Point wasn't just a renowned beauty spot. It also had something of a reputation as a lover's leap.

A haunt for would-be suicides.

This woman was planning on jumping *down*.

'Any normal girl would be flattered,' Neil was carrying on huffily. 'Any normal girl would have been chuffed to bits, I can tell you. Honestly, I can't believe you're being so ungrateful, what I don't think you realize is what a *catch* I am—hey! Where are you going? What d'you think you're playing at now?'

Millie was already out of the car, pelting hell for leather across the rough grass. The woman was currently standing with her back to her, engrossed in trying to light a second cigarette from the butt of the first. Her long indigo cotton dress flapped wildly around her legs, which were pale and bare. Her long copper hair, whipped by the brisk breeze, streamed behind her like a banner.

Screeching to a halt next to the Mercedes, Millie saw that she had been right. The white rectangles propped up on the dashboard were indeed envelopes, each one bearing a different name.

Either the woman was sending out invitations to a party or they were suicide notes.

Right, okay, mustn't panic, thought Millie. Panicking.

Now what?

BEEEP!

Startled, the woman at the edge of the cliff twisted round. So did Millie.

'What the hell do you think you're doing?' Neil yelled bad-temperedly at her from the MG.

'It's okay! I'm just, um, asking for a... light.'

Millie said the first words that sprang into her head. As Neil thumped the MG's steering wheel in exasperation, she turned her back on him and for the first time came face to face with the woman who was about to End It All.

Some instinct told Millie that if she stopped to wonder exactly *what* she should say, and whether whatever she was saying was right or wrong, she'd end up completely tongue-tied and too scared to say anything at all.

The only way to go, therefore, was to plunge right in.

'Well?' Millie gazed steadily into the other woman's puffy, sea green eyes. 'Have you?'

The puffy sea green eyes surveyed her as if she were mad.

'Have I what?'

'Got a light?'

'Of course I've got a light.' The woman inhaled irritably on her Marlboro and blew out a stream of smoke that was whipped into oblivion by the wind.

'So? Could I have a light?' Millie persisted.

'You could. But you don't appear to have a cigarette.'

'You have, though. Okay, so could I have a light *and* a cigarette?' Millie didn't dare wonder if she was sounding as completely ridiculous as she suspected she did.

The other woman sighed and flicked the Marlboro casually over the edge of the cliff. It sailed through the air, executing lazy somersaults as it went. Millie imagined a body doing likewise before crashing hideously on to the black, wave-lashed rocks below.

Oh help, she felt sick just thinking about it.

'Look, I know what you're trying to do here,' the woman sighed, 'and I appreciate the gesture, darling, really I do, but there's absolutely no need.' As she spoke, her green eyes filled with fresh tears. Her trembling fingers scrabbled with the flip-top lid of the Marlboro packet, and as she clumsily extracted another cigarette, the rest slithered out, bouncing to the ground around her feet like spillikins.

Millie helped her pick them up. The puffy eyelids and lack of make-up had effectively disguised the woman at first, but she recognized her now. Masses of red-gold hair, greeny-gold eyes, the Cartier watch, and that distinctive breathy voice… She was Orla Hart, one of the country's best-selling novelists. Now in her late thirties, she had been successfully churning out popular fiction of the glitzy kind for the last fifteen years, and earning herself a fortune in the process.

Click, went the lighter as Orla lit her third cigarette in seven minutes. Now probably wasn't the time, Millie tactfully decided, to warn her that smoking could seriously damage your health *and* cause those unattractive little vertical wrinkles above your upper lip.

'Look,' Orla gestured in despair over her shoulder, 'I was standing here, minding my own business, waiting for you and your husband to drive off. Couldn't you just go now?' she asked hopefully. 'I'd be grateful, really I would.'

'Oh brilliant,' said Millie, 'and where do you suppose that would leave me? In psychiatric care for the rest of my life, that's where. I mean, how would you feel if you left me here to jump off the edge of this cliff?' She raised her eyebrows inquiringly at Orla Hart.

Anguished, Orla shook her head.

'It's no good. You don't understand.'

'Okay, so you may as well tell me. Because I'm not going anywhere until you do.' Sinking to the ground cross-legged, Millie gave the grass next to her an encouraging pat. As she did so, they both heard the sound of an engine being started up and bad-temperedly revved behind them. Next moment, the MG had reversed sharply, turned back on to the road in an explosion of gravel, and roared off.

'God, I'm so *sorry*,' Orla groaned.

'Now I'm definitely not going anywhere.' Millie shrugged and patted the grass again.

'I feel dreadful.'

'Don't. He isn't my husband anyway. Just my boyfriend. Well,' Millie amended, 'probably ex-boyfriend by now.'

'And it's all my fault. Here, have a cigarette.'

Mortified, Orla knelt down next to her, opened the crumpled packet, and all but thrust a handful of Marlboros into her mouth.

'No thanks, I don't smoke. And I don't mind about him being an ex.' Realizing she couldn't let Orla Hart shoulder the burden of responsibility for what had happened, Millie smiled. 'Actually, you've done me a favor. It's quite a relief.'

'Lucky you. Not minding.' Orla pressed her lips together, her chin beginning to wobble.

Feeling suddenly brave—and prepared to rugby-tackle her to the ground if all of a sudden she tried to launch herself over the cliff edge—Millie said, 'So that's what this is all about, is it? Some man?'

'Some man,' Orla agreed wearily. 'Huh, that just about describes him. Oh Lord, what must I look like? I don't suppose you've got such a thing as a hanky?'

By a complete fluke, Millie had a clean tissue in her jeans pocket. Feeling braver still as Orla took the tissue and noisily blew her nose, she said, 'Husband?'

Orla had decimated the flimsy tissue in one go. Wiping her eyes on the hem of her indigo dress, she nodded.

'Not being funny, darling, but do you know who I am?'

For a brief moment Millie considered shaking her head. She would have done if she hadn't been the world's most hopeless fibber.

'Well, I didn't recognize you at first,' she admitted, 'but I do now.'

Orla summoned up a sad little smile.

'So you probably remember all that awful stuff in the press a few months ago about my husband having an affair.'

Cautiously, Millie said, 'Well… kind of.'

'With a younger woman, surprise, surprise. By the name of Martine Drew. She's twenty-seven.' Orla drew so hard on her cigarette she almost inhaled it whole. 'But I love my husband so I forgave him. I did everything I could to save our marriage, including moving out of London and buying the house down here. And Giles was happy to move. He said it was just a silly blip and she didn't mean a thing to him. He s-swore it w-was all over.'

'And it isn't,' Millie guessed.

'And it isn't,' Orla echoed, rubbing her pale, salt-stained cheeks. 'I was chatting away on the phone this morning to one of my old London friends and she told me she'd heard that Martine was living in Cornwall now.' The tears slid down Orla's face as she bit the knuckle of her right forefinger like a child. 'Well, that speaks for itself, doesn't it? Giles never did stop seeing her. It's obviously been going on the whole time. He's brought her down here, set her up in some *sweet* little cottage.' She spat the word out like a bullet. 'Oh yes, and you can bet your bottom dollar he's paying the rent with my money.'

Millie was so outraged on Orla's behalf that for once in her life she was speechless.

Noticing this, Orla sniffed and gave her another crooked, tinged-with-bitterness smile.

'I know, ironic, isn't it? Orla Hart, queen of the romantic blockbuster. I spend my life creating glorious love affairs and fabulously happy endings, and all the time my own marriage is a complete pig's b-b-bottom. Oh God, it's no good, I can't carry on any more. I'm so miserable I JUST WANT TO DIE.'

Yikes.

'Right,' said Millie, floundering a bit. 'Well, I can see why. So, um, have you made a will?'

Orla stared at her.

'What?'

'A will. You know, I hereby bequeath my worldly goods to the local monkey sanctuary and fifty thousand a year to my pet gerbil.'

'Of course I haven't made a will.' Orla shuddered. 'They're just morbid.'

'Oh well, that's handy then,' said Millie. 'So if you jump off this cliff now, your husband inherits *all* your money *and* your house, *and* he gets to keep his mistress in the lap of luxury for the rest of her life. I tell you what, why don't you just run over there,' she jerked her thumb over her shoulder, indicating the gleaming, burnt orange Mercedes, 'and tie a big shiny gold ribbon round that expensive car of yours, because your husband's girlfriend's going to have her sweaty little hands on that steering wheel faster than you can say Rest in Peace. She'll probably go with him to your funeral,' Millie rattled on, picturing it all in her mind, 'and the next thing you know, they'll be getting married!'

'Noooo!' howled Orla Hart, clutching her stomach and rocking to and fro in despair. 'He can't marry her, he *can't*.'

'You won't be around to stop him.' Millie shrugged. 'They'll be able to do whatever they like, because you'll be dead. And don't look at me like that,' she went on, 'because all I'm doing is being honest, stating the facts. Personally, I wouldn't kill myself, I wouldn't give the pair of them the satisfaction. I'd stick around and concentrate on making their lives hell!'

Miserably, Orla shook her head.

'You don't understand. I love Giles more than *anything*. I don't *want* to lose him.'

'Well you will,' said Millie, 'if you're dead.'

'God, you're brutal.' Heaving a sigh, Orla closed her eyes.

'Look, you've got a choice here. You can stay and fight for your marriage if that's what you want.' Privately, Millie thought she'd be mad to want to hang on to such a horrible-sounding man. 'Or you can kick your husband out and find yourself another one—bigger, better, and nicer in every way. That would really be having the last laugh.'

'Ho, ho,' Orla mimicked with a spectacular lack of enthusiasm. 'That is *so* likely to happen.'

'But it might.'

'You know what your trouble is? You've been reading too many trashy novels.'

'Oh come on, your novels aren't that trashy,' Millie protested.

'Thanks.' Miraculously, Orla's mouth began to twitch. 'But I wasn't actually talking about mine.'

Embarrassed, Millie flapped her hands in apology. The *faux pas* had always been a specialty of hers.

'Okay, sorry, but let's not change the subject. I still need you to promise that you aren't going to kill yourself. And you really mustn't, because all you'd be doing would be cutting off your nose to spite your face.'

Actually, if Orla were to throw herself off Tresanter Point on to the jagged rocks below, she'd be doing a lot more than cutting off her nose. There' d be body parts and internal organs splattered in all directions, followed by greedy seagulls shrieking with delight, swooping down, and snatching up ribbons of flesh in their beaks.

Millie wondered if she should point this out to Orla. Would it help or might it prove to be the final straw?

Luckily she didn't get the chance to find out.

'Okay, you win,' said Orla Hart. Drying her eyes on the hem of her dark blue dress, she shook back her hair and stood up. 'You're right. My marriage is worth fighting for. I *won't* let that grasping little tart spoil everything.'

Phew. Well, good. Millie, feeling her stomach muscles slowly unclench themselves, said encouragingly, 'You can do it, I know you can.'

When they reached the Mercedes—unlocked and with the keys still in the ignition—Orla scooped her hand along the row of envelopes propped up on the dashboard and shoveled them into the glove compartment. She looked across at Millie.

'Where do you live?'

'Newquay.'

'That's five miles away. How did that so-called boyfriend of yours imagine you were going to get home?'

Millie shrugged.

'That's why I had to make sure I changed your mind about chucking yourself off the cliff. So you'd be able to give me a lift.'

Chapter 2

OH WELL, SO MUCH for that theory, Millie concluded as she lay back in the bath and twiddled the plug chain with her toes. So much for the program she had watched three months earlier advocating the joys of the arranged marriage.

At the time it had seemed such a great idea. Millie had listened, transfixed, to the reasoning of the pretty young Muslim girl happily explaining why an arranged marriage was the only way to go. After all, look at the divorce rate among Westerners, who married for love. Disaster, absolute disaster. It stood to reason that what everyone *should* be doing was getting themselves matched up, forgetting all about this sexual-chemistry malarkey, and *gradually* allowing love to grow.

Since her last dozen or so boyfriends had all been unmitigated disasters, Millie had found herself nodding vigorously at the TV screen and agreeing with every word. And when, a week later, Hester had offered to set her up on a blind date with a friend of a friend because, 'I just know you two will get on,' she had said yes at once.

Upon meeting Neil, Millie had realized—also at once—that she didn't find him remotely fanciable. But that was all right, that was fine, because she wasn't supposed to. Fanciability was forbidden, remember? This time her love was going to blossom sloooowly, like a flower. All the things Neil did that irritated her beyond belief would—in due course—stop being irritating and instead become lovable quirks.

Apart from slurping his coffee like an industrial vacuum cleaner, which—Millie had to be honest here—was never likely to become a lovable quirk.

But the experiment hadn't worked. Three months down the line, Millie's flower was in no danger of blossoming. In fact, she suspected she'd been dealt a dud seed.

A very dud seed indeed.

'Tea and toast,' sang Hester as the bathroom door crashed open. Triumphantly she added, 'And I want to hear the whole story!'

'What story?' Millie surfaced and slicked her wet blonde hair away from her face, astounded by the sensitivity of her friend's antennae. How could Hester possibly know that she had spent the afternoon talking famous writer Orla Hart out of hurling herself off Tresanter Point?

'Don't drop it in the bath this time.' Dropping the lid of the loo seat down and settling herself cross-legged on it, Hester handed her the plate of Marmite on toast. 'Didn't you hear the doorbell just now?'

'No.' Millie guessed she'd been submerged at the time. Either that or singing in a loud and shamelessly off-key fashion. Gosh, she hoped it hadn't been Orla Hart at the front door.

Except that wasn't actually terribly likely, was it, seeing as Orla Hart didn't know where she lived.

'It was Neil. With your handbag.'

'Oh.' Millie nodded with relief. Her bag had still been in Neil's car when he had screeched off, abandoning her on the cliff top with End-It-All Orla.

'He practically threw it at me when I opened the door,' Hester complained. 'And he wasn't looking thrilled, I can tell you.'

'No. Well, I suppose he wouldn't.'

'Do you know what he said next?' Hester leaned forward indignantly.

'No.' To be helpful, Millie said, 'I was in the bath, remember?'

'He said he was bringing back your bag, not that you deserved it, and that you're a stuck-up spoiled bitch, a selfish cow who thinks you're sooo great, but you're not, okay?'

'Okay,' said Millie dutifully. 'Gosh.'

'Well, as you can imagine, I was shocked.' Hester gave her a severe look. 'I said, "Is this Millie Brady you're talking about? Are you *sure* it's Millie?"'

'And he was sure,' Millie guessed.

'He certainly was. What's more, it's over, okay? All over. He never *ever* wants to see you again, you're an ungrateful bitch, he wishes he'd never met you, you've got a *bloody* nerve thinking you're better than anyone else… oh, and by the way, that thing on your leg *isn't* attractive, in fact it's a downright turnoff and didn't you know only complete and utter floozies get themselves tattooed?'

'Oh. Well, I certainly do now.' Millie mustered a brave smile. She supposed she deserved it, jumping out of Neil's car at the crucial moment like that, without so much as a thanks-but-no-thanks. His feelings were bound to be hurt.

But the final jibe, the bit about the tattoo, hit home. Millie instinctively sank lower in the water in an attempt to conceal the decoration on her right thigh beneath a mound of bubbles. Getting herself tattooed in a moment of recklessness had definitely been something she'd lived to regret.

It was bad enough knowing you had an embarrassing tattoo without having to hear that it made you look like an out-and-out floozy.

'So just a wild guess,' said Hester, 'but would I be right in guessing you aren't exactly flavor of the month with Neil?'

'Not unless you count pickled-maggot flavor.' Millie pulled a face.

'Why?'

'He asked me to move in with him.'

'And you said no?'

'I didn't say anything. Just got out of the car and legged it.'

Hester pinched a triangle of Marmite on toast.

'All over, then?'

'All over.'

'Tuh. Lucky escape if you ask me. I knew that Muslim thing was never going to work.'

Millie shrugged.

'It was worth a try.'

'Are you upset?'

Honestly, some people.

'Of course I'm not upset! If I'd wanted to live with him I would have said yes.'

'Still.' Hester sipped her tea and tried to look sympathetic. 'It leaves you at a bit of a loose end, doesn't it? What you need is a distraction.'

'What kind of distraction?'

'The cheering-up kind. I know, we can throw a party! A house-warming party.'

Millie rolled her eyes.

'Hess, we've lived here for two and a half years.'

'Really? Gosh, time flies when you're having fun. Okay, we'll go out then, have a good old Friday-night binge.' Hester leapt excitedly off the polished wood loo seat, splashing tea on the bath mat. 'We'll hit the town, celebrate you finishing with numb-brain Neil, chat up hundreds of gorgeous surfers, and have the best time ever… a night we'll never forget!'

Well, that had been the plan anyway. But then that was the thing with nights out, Millie reminded herself several hours later as she took off her too-tight shoes and stuffed them into her bag. You never knew what kind you were going to end up with. It was a completely random thing. You could stop off at the wine bar for just-the-one in your awful office clothes and with your hair a disaster, yet miraculously end up having a truly fabulous time.

Then again, at the other end of the scale, you could spend four hours getting yourself tarted up, finally set out with adrenalin racing round your body and your hopes sky high… and what happened?

Precisely. Bugger all.

Which was, of course, exactly what had happened tonight. Oh, they'd had a good enough time, touring all the trendiest, most happening bars in Newquay and meeting up with loads of people they knew. But it had been, ultimately, a disappointment.

Like delving into your stocking on Christmas morning and discovering a year's supply of ravishingly wrapped… socks.

The moral of the evening had definitely been that you could meet a good-looking surfer but you couldn't make him think.

It had been, Millie ruefully acknowledged, an evening sorely lacking in brain cells.

'Ouch, my toes.' Hopping along the pavement, clutching a postbox for support en route, Hester massaged her own feet. She knew from bitter experience that if she took off her shoes she would hurl them into the nearest hedge. 'Still, that guy with the dark curly hair in the Barclay Bar wasn't bad, was he? Did you fancy him?'

The guy with the dark curly hair in the Barclay Bar had punctuated every sentence with, 'Know what I mean, man, yeah?'

'No,' said Millie, 'I didn't. He was awful.'

'I thought he was cute.' Reaching a lamppost, Hester leaned against it and kicked off her four-inch heels. 'Ooh, bliss, that is sooo much better.'

'Don't take them off.'

'I have to, I have to.'

'Don't throw them,' Millie begged, though why she was even bothering she didn't know. Hester had done this a hundred times, chucking her shoes into the nearest hedge or garden rather than carry them home. Sometimes, the next day, she would retrace her steps in search of them. If the shoes were still there, she fell on them with delight and treated them like returning prodigal children. If they were nowhere to be found, she popped into the police station—where they knew her well—to see if any had been handed in. Not that they ever were, but Hester enjoyed flirting with whoever was on duty at the time. And the policemen always seemed to enjoy it.

And after that, of course, Hester had the perfect excuse to go out and buy herself a new pair.

'You like those, they're your favorites.' Millie tried to stop her, but it was too late—Hester was already in mid-fling. The first red and black patent leather stiletto sailed into the air, gleaming in the light from the street lamp. As it somersaulted back to earth, Hester hurled the second stiletto, letting go of the heel too soon. It shot like a guided missile into the bush next to them and—

'MIAAOOWWW.'

'Oh God,' Millie's hands flew to her mouth in dismay, 'you hit a cat!'

Hester, equally horrified, gasped, 'I didn't mean to! It was an accident—oh please don't tell me I've killed it…'

Unable to look, she clamped her hands over her eyes as Millie crawled beneath the bush.

'Is it dead? Is it dead?' wailed Hester behind her. 'I don't believe this, I've murdered a cat, oh help, I feel sick…'

The next moment there was a rustle of leaves and a white cat snaked towards Millie, investigating her with elaborate caution before rubbing his head against her outstretched fingers and beginning to purr.

'You're okay, the cat's here, he's fine,' Millie called out. No blood, no broken bones, no apparent concussion; the noise he had made appeared to have been nothing more than a yowl of alarm.

'Phew, thank goodness for that.' Hester breathed a huge sigh of relief. 'I thought I'd murdered it.'

The cat was now busy licking Millie's hand. He was definitely unhurt. Aware that she was kneeling on a damp, mulchy carpet of leaves, Millie began to wriggle out from under the bush bottom-first. As she did so, her left wrist brushed against something smooth.

'White cotton knickers,' Hester complained behind her, evidently having recovered from her shock. 'You came out tonight wearing plain, white cotton knickers. Honestly, no wonder you didn't meet anyone nice.'

Scrambling to her feet, Millie tugged her skirt down and shook damp leaves out of her hair.

'I wasn't actually planning on showing anyone my knickers.'

'That's not the point. It's a state of mind. Wear sexy underwear and you automatically *feel* more attractive, so men will automatically *find* you more attractive, and before you know it you'll have hordes of them panting at your heels—'

'Unlike you, because you've just thrown your heels away,' Millie pointed out. 'Anyway, never mind my knickers. Look what I found under the hedge.'

As she held out the wallet she had knocked with her hand, Hester fell on it with a squeal of delight.

'Wow! What if it's stuffed with cash?'

'Hester, *no*.' Appalled, Millie wrenched the wallet back from her. 'You can't steal someone else's money.'

'Can't we?' Hester's face fell. 'Okay, I suppose not. Tuh, you and your scruples.' She tugged invitingly at Millie's arm. 'Just think, there could be *loads* in there. Imagine if you opened it up and there was a hundred thousand pounds. And who would ever know we'd found it?' She gestured around the dark, deserted street. 'We could buy a Ferrari and still have plenty left over for new shoes.'

Millie pressed the wallet to her cheek. The soft, well-worn leather was cold and damp and smelt of leaf mold; the wallet had clearly been lying there for a while.

'We'll take it to the police station,' she announced firmly.

'No!' Hester let out a groan; the police station was in the opposite direction. 'My feet hurt… they're on fire… oh please, I can't *bear* it.'

A mental image of Hester crawling on her hands and knees all the way back through the town flashed through Millie's mind. Not only crawling, but whingeing nonstop. Never mind the surfing championships; if Newquay ever decided to host the world whingeing championship, Hester would win it hands down.

Tucking the wallet into her bag, Millie said, 'We'll take it tomorrow.'

Chapter 3

By the time they arrived home it was midnight and Hester was still fantasizing happily about how *she* would spend the contents of a wallet if *she* were ever lucky enough to stumble across one containing a hundred grand.

Except by now she was going to need twenty times that amount.

'And a holiday, of course, have to have a holiday, maybe Florida, I've always fancied a trip to Disneyland… ooh, and a ring!' She clapped her hands together with delight at the idea. 'One with a massive diamond the size of a ping-pong ball, so heavy I can hardly lift my arm.' As she spoke, Hester was pulling a bottle of Chenin Blanc out of the fridge, miming the impossibility of lifting the bottle *and* wearing the world's biggest diamond. 'God, this is hard work, I don't know *how* I'll manage to drive my Ferrari, the weight of this ring's going to keep dragging my hand *right* off the steering wheel…'

'Oh dear. Bump,' said Millie, who was leaning against the microwave.

'What?'

'You. Crashing back to earth.' Having opened the wallet, she now waved it at Hester. 'Fifteen pounds.'

'Fifteen?' Hester's face fell several storeys. 'Is that all? Are you *sure*?'

Millie wasn't only sure, she was relieved. Hester could be horribly persuasive when she set her mind to it. And they were both deeply broke.

In the sitting room, over a tumbler each of white wine, they pored over the contents of the wallet.

'Ha! And his name's Hugh! Perfect for you!' Hester exclaimed, wagging a delighted finger at Millie. Then, peering at the full name on the driving license, she tut-tutted in disgust. 'Fifteen *pounds*. Hugh Emerson, I hope you know you're nothing but a lousy cheapskate.'

'But a kind-hearted lousy cheapskate,' protested Millie, ignoring the dig and leaping to his defense. 'Look, organ-donor card. Only nice people carry organ-donor cards. That makes up for him having no money.'

'Speak for yourself. *Nothing* makes up for having no money.'

'Petrol card, AmEx card, Barclaycard,' chanted Millie, flinging them down like a poker hand. 'Don't get excited, he'll have canceled them by now.'

'Video card,' Hester shuffled on through the pack, 'railcard, receipt from Computerworld… Good grief, Hugh, you're a total geek! Get yourself a life, man! You're how old?' She checked the driver's license again. 'Twenty-eight, for heaven's sake. You should be carrying condoms, not railcards. What kind of twenty-eight-year-old doesn't keep a condom tucked away in a corner of his wallet?'

'Um, the married kind?' Millie had found the photo tucked between two petrol receipts. She held it up for Hester to see.

'Good grief.'

'Hmm. So what's the final verdict on wallet-man? Not quite so nerdy now?'

Together they peered more closely at the couple in the photograph. The girl, in her twenties, was startlingly beautiful. Her dark hair swung around her face as she laughed into the camera, her eyes sparkled with fun, and she had the figure of a model. She was wearing three things: a bikini, a scarlet hibiscus flower tucked behind one ear, and a ring on the third finger of her left hand. Her right hand, meanwhile, was busy making bunny ears behind the head of her companion. Hugh—it had to be Hugh—sported an emerald green beach towel slung around his hips, a pair of dark glasses concealing his eyes, and windswept, streaky blond hair. Unaware of the bunny ears poking up behind his head, he was grinning broadly and holding a tropical-looking drink up to the camera. His other hand was around the girl's slender waist.

'Yuk,' Hester groaned. 'The picture of happiness. Doesn't it make you want to be sick?'

'But you can't call him a geek. You have to admit, he's gorgeous.'

Phew. Realizing she was in danger of drooling, Millie sat back on the sofa. Hugh might be wearing dark glasses, but there was no disguising those looks.

'Fancies himself,' Hester snorted. 'Those kind always do—think they're God's gift. I bet he sleeps around.'

'You are such a cynic,' Millie complained. 'You don't know, they could be the happiest couple in the world. They *look* as if they're the happiest couple in the world.'

'Men like that are never faithful. They don't know the meaning of the word.' Hester gave her a pitying shake of the head. 'They cheat on their wives for the sheer hell of it, just because they can.'

'In that case, why hasn't he got any condoms tucked away in his wallet?'

'Ha, probably just used the last one.'

Millie looked at the address on the driver's license.

'He's from London. He must have lost his wallet while he was down here on holiday.'

'Good,' said Hester. 'Serves him right for being unfaithful.'

Millie took another look at the photo; reluctantly, she decided that Hester was probably right. She had leapt instinctively to Hugh's defense because she so wanted to believe he was devoted to his wife and utterly faithful.

But it was like wanting to believe in the Loch Ness monster. You could believe all you liked, but the chances were, such a thing didn't exist.

As she knocked back the last of her wine, it occurred to Millie that she actually knew quite a bit about Hugh Emerson… the charming, cheating, silver-tongued bastard.

But still kind-hearted, she reminded herself. Otherwise he wouldn't be prepared to pass on any useful secondhand organs in the event of his death.

'Never trust a man with better legs than yours, that's what I say,' Hester declared. To listen to her, no one would ever think she had a perfectly good boyfriend of her own. Nat was lovely in all respects, his only drawback being the punishing restaurant hours he worked as a chef.

Plus, of course, the fact that the restaurant in which he worked happened to be five hundred or so miles away, in Glasgow.

Idly, Millie turned over one of Hugh Emerson's business cards. There was his mobile phone number. And right here, by amazing coincidence, was their phone.

'What are you doing?' said Hester.

'Seems polite to let him know we've found his wallet.'

'So why are you trying so hard not to snigger?'

Millie gave her an innocent look.

'No reason, is there, why we can't have a bit of fun first?'

It was half past midnight but the phone was picked up on the second ring. Anyway, Millie reasoned, good-looking twenty-eight-year-old Lotharios were hardly likely to be tucked up in bed and fast asleep by twelve o'clock on a Friday night.

In bed maybe, but definitely not asleep.

'Hello? Hello?' she breathed when she heard a male voice at the other end of the line. 'Hugh, is that you?'

'It is. Who's this?' The voice was deep-pitched and undeniably attractive, betraying a hint of amusement. That was the thing about silver-tongued bastards; they always had seductive voices with which to charm the knickers off you.

So long as they weren't sensible, white cotton knickers from Marks and Spencer, Millie silently amended. Even the most dedicated charmer might draw the line at that.

'Oh Hugh, thank goodness I've tracked you down at last! It's Millie here, remember? We met at that party in Fulham.'

'Millie.' As he repeated her name, she could practically hear him frowning. 'Sorry, you've lost me. Whose party are you talking about?'

Ha, of course he couldn't remember, he went to so very many parties. Probably three or four a night.

'It was five months ago, just before Christmas. You must remember,' Millie insisted. 'I was the one in the red dress with sequins down the side. We chatted for a while, then you took me upstairs and we—'

'I'm sorry,' Hugh Emerson interrupted with a smile in his voice. 'You've got the wrong man here.'

'Hugh, please, don't say that!'

'I'm serious. I don't know where you got this number, but it certainly wasn't me.'

'Your name's Hugh Emerson and you live in Richmond Crescent. You're twenty-eight years old,' Millie recited, slightly hysterically, 'and you have blond hair and great legs.'

'But—'

'And a birthmark on your stomach, just to the left of your belly button,' Millie announced triumphantly as Hester pointed it out in the photograph.

Clearly startled, Hugh Emerson said, 'Look, there's definitely been some kind of mix-up here.'

'Don't try and deny this,' Millie protested. 'You can't pretend it didn't happen, Hugh, because it *did*. I was at the party with my friend Hester and you were there with your wife or girlfriend or whatever she is... pretty girl, long dark hair, I can't remember her name...'

'Now hang on a minute—'

'No, Hugh, you listen to *me*.' Millie hurried to get to the punchline before she burst out laughing. 'You took me upstairs and seduced me, and I won't let you try and wriggle out of it. I'm pregnant, Hugh, I'm expecting your *baby*.'

This information was greeted by a suitably stunned silence.

Finally, Hugh said, 'Look, I really am sorry, but you're not.'

'Oh, I might have known you'd do this. You complete bastard,' Millie wailed. 'First you cheated on your wife, and now you're doing the dirty on me! Tell me, does she *know* what you get up to when her back's turned?'

Another pause.

Then, 'Is this Louisa you're talking about?'

'That's the one.' Millie beamed at Hester in triumph. 'Yep, that was her name, Louisa.'

Hugh Emerson's voice changed in an instant. All the initial warmth had gone out of it. Now it was as if a freezer door had been blasted open.

'Okay, I don't know who the hell you are, or why you're doing this. But for your information...'

'I can't hear,' Hester whispered frantically as his voice dropped further still. Tugging at Millie's elbow she hissed, 'I can't hear a thing. What's going on?'

CLUNNKKK. Millie slammed down the receiver. White-faced and appalled, she stared at Hester.

'What? What?'

Millie couldn't speak, she was too busy cringing all over. Her skin was actually crawling with embarrassment.

'Stop looking at me like that,' Hester complained. 'What did he say?'

Millie felt sick. She hung her head in shame.

'He and Louisa haven't been together for the last eight months.'

'Ha, what did I tell you? They split up because he was unfaithful to her.'

'Not quite,' said Millie. 'They split up because she died.'

Hester gave Millie a hug before she went on up to bed.

'Oh come on, cheer up, you didn't *know* she was dead.'

Millie shook her head.

'I'm such an idiot.'

'It was only meant to be a joke,' Hester consoled her.

Oh yes, and what a great joke it had turned out to be.

'I'm so ashamed. *So* ashamed.'

'I'm just glad you had the sense to use Number Withheld,' Hester said lightly. 'At least he's not going to be able to track us down and come after us with a shotgun.'

She went on up to bed but Millie stayed downstairs, hideously aware that she wouldn't be able to sleep. She couldn't stop thinking about the phone call. Every word was playing and replaying in her brain on an endless loop. The way Hugh Emerson's manner had changed so abruptly—and who could blame him?—sent shudders of mortification down her spine.

Since there was no way in the world she could bring herself to hand the wallet in at the local police station, Millie scribbled a quick note on a blank (i.e. totally unincriminating) sheet of paper.

Dear Hugh,

A million apologies for the phone call. We found your wallet and attempted a joke that went horribly wrong.

Yours,

Bitterly Ashamed.

P.S. Sorry, sorry, sorry…

Before she could start agonizing over whether the note was sufficiently apologetic, Millie parcelled it up with the wallet and all its contents, wrote Hugh's address on the front and plastered her entire emergency stamp supply across the top of the parcel.

At two o'clock in the morning, desperate to rid the house of evidence, she ran barefoot to the end of the road and shoveled the parcel into the postbox.

Chapter 4

A WEEK LATER, HESTER reeled home from work in a state of shock.

'You're not going to believe this.'

'Richard Branson came into the market, saw your stall, and hired you on the spot,' Millie hazarded. Hester, who sold earrings of the cheap, cheerful, and sometimes downright eccentric kind, was never going to be voted Businesswoman of the Year. 'He wants you to head up his new jewelry empire, Virgin Baubles.'

'Oh ha ha. Guess again.' This time, helpfully, Hester clutched both hands to her chest, miming palpitations.

'You're going to clean the windows and shampoo the carpet and do my share of the washing-up.'

This was yet more merry banter; Millie didn't seriously expect it to happen.

'Pay attention, will you?' Hester cried. 'This is a swoon. A swoooon. See? Look at me.' She rolled her eyes dramatically, like Rudolph Valentino. 'I'm swooning here, like I've never swooned before.'

'Okay. You just bumped into Jim Davidson in the street and he said, '"Ello there, 'Ester my darlin,' do us a favor wouldja, I'm covered from 'ead to toe in warm chocolate and I'd be *ever* so grateful if you'd just lick it all off."'

Hester had an inexplicable crush on Jim Davidson. *The Generation Game* was the highlight of her TV viewing week.

'Wrong,' said Hester. But with the merest tinge of regret.

'Okay then, I give up.'

'He's back.'

Who? Arnold Schwarzenegger as The Terminator?

The next moment, Millie guessed. The slight but unmistakable emphasis on the word He gave it away. She looked at Hester, who was all but jigging up and down on the spot.

'Oh God.' Millie's heart sank; she couldn't help it. 'It's Lucas, isn't it? Lucas Kemp.'

When it came to serious crushes, Lucas left Jim Davidson in the shade. In the shade with a droopy mesh tank top on. During Hester's hectically hormonal growing-up years, Lucas Kemp had been the big love of her life. Most of the time he had treated Hester with amused disinterest. But occasionally, when the mood took him and he was between girlfriends, he would pay her a bit of attention, dance with her at parties, walk her home afterwards, and snog her senseless, that kind of thing.

This, of course, had only made Hester love him more. The very fact that Lucas could treat her so casually proved beyond all doubt that he was better than she was and that she didn't deserve to be with someone so fabulous.

Lucas Kemp was wild and charismatic, with laughing green eyes and a provocative tilt to his mouth. In those days he had worn his wavy dark hair long and his jeans tight. The aura of danger about him had been—as far as Hester was concerned—impossible to resist.

Then again, Millie thought, that had been a good while ago now. It was six years since Lucas had left Cornwall for the more glittery lights of London. He could be paunchy and thinning on top these days, he might work in a bank and play shuffleboard in his spare time, and possess all the charisma of a tub of Vaseline.

Well he *might*, thought Millie.

Although it was unlikely.

'You are allowed to speak.' Hester was sounding miffed. 'Some kind of reaction would be nice.'

Fine.

Millie gave her a long look.

'What about Nat?'

'Oh!' Hester exclaimed in disgust. 'I might have known you'd say something like that. You just have to drag him into it, don't you?'

Being sensible didn't come naturally to Millie, but she knew she had to be the voice of reason here. Hester had plainly lost control of the reins.

'Come on, sit down.' She patted the battered sofa next to her. Hester, still jigging from one foot to the other like a toddler in need of the loo, wasn't a restful sight. 'Nat's lovely, you know he is. You waited years for someone like him to come along. Don't mess it up now.'

Hester stared at her.

'Who says I'm going to?'

'Hess, just look at the *state* of you.'

They had been friends for too long, that was the trouble. Millie knew her inside out. Hester, sitting down with a bump, sighed and said, 'Okay, okay, I know it's stupid, but I can't help the way I feel.'

'Nat's so nice,' Millie reminded her. 'He's good for you.'

'Ha. You mean like salad and steamed chicken and a glass of fizzy mineral water? But you can't *live* on that stuff, can you? Sometimes you just have to have something wicked and gorgeous like a bucket of crème brûlée.'

What with Nat working as a chef this was apt, even if it was also unfair. Then again, the fact that he was so ambitious didn't help matters. Leaping at the chance to work as a commis chef at L'Amazon in Glasgow hadn't exactly smoothed the path of true love.

In theory, Hester had understood why he'd needed to go, agreeing that it was necessary for Nat's CV and a fabulous chance to gain experience working at one of Scotland's finest restaurants with its two Michelin stars and dazzlingly arrogant head chef.

Oh yes, she'd been absolutely fine about it, really. In principle.

But Hester's principles had begun to take a bit of a battering in the last couple of months. She missed Nat dreadfully. He was working ludicrous hours, six days a week. And, rather like God, on the seventh day, Nat crashed out and spent the day in bed fast asleep. Her last trip up there to see him had been an expensive and deeply frustrating waste of time.

Basically, Hester had discovered, you could love someone to bits but still want to hit them over the head with a heavy alarm clock when they were lying next to you at two o'clock on a Sunday afternoon snoring their head off.

Whereas Lucas was both here in Cornwall *and awake*.

'You're right, I know you're right,' Hester admitted. 'I don't want to lose Nat.'

She didn't, she truly didn't. Nat was funny, easygoing, loyal, and great in bed. When he wasn't asleep.

Damn, why had Lucas had to come along now?

'Okay,' said Millie, 'how much money can you really not afford to lose?'

'Two pounds fifty.'

'I'm serious.'

'Twenty pounds.'

'Not enough. Two hundred.' Millie was firm.

'Are you *mad*?' Horrified, Hester cried, 'I definitely can't afford to lose two hundred pounds!'

'Great, that's the whole point. Better not lose our bet then.'

'A bet? What kind of a bet?'

'Between you and me.' Millie was delighted with her spur-of-the-moment idea; since she was currently off men in a major way, this wasn't a problem. 'No sex in Cornwall. Whoever gives in first, loses the bet.'

'That's not fair!' Hester let out a squeal of alarm. 'What if Nat gets a weekend off?'

'He's not going to. You know that,' Millie patiently reminded her. 'But if you go up to Glasgow again, you're allowed to sleep with him there,' she added generously. 'That's why I said no sex in Cornwall. For either of us. And no zipping over the border into Devon either. If you do that, you still have to pay up.'

Hester giggled.

'What are we going to call it, the Celibet?'

'Call it whatever you like. But,' Millie wagged a finger at her, I'm telling you now, I'll hold you to it.'

'Okay, deal.' Maybe, Hester decided, this was the threat she needed, the impetus to keep her on the straight and narrow. Besides, if she and Lucas did do it, how would Millie ever find out?

Reaching for Millie's hand, Hester gave it a firm, you-can-trust-me shake.

'No sex in Cornwall.'

'And don't even think of trying to lie to me,' Millie warned, 'because I'm telling you now, I'll always know.'

All this palaver and Hester hadn't even clapped eyes on Lucas Kemp yet. The news that he was back in Cornwall had been relayed—as far as Millie was able to make out—via one of the girls who ran the market stall next to Hester's, who had heard it from her hairdresser, who knew for certain that it was true because her brother's friend's girlfriend worked at one of the local property agencies as a letting consultant. And Lucas Kemp was currently leasing a pretty spectacular house somewhere in town, though nobody seemed to know quite where.

Since Lucas had been broke when he'd left Newquay six years ago, this was a promising development as far as Hester was concerned. He'd clearly done well for himself. She couldn't wait to casually bump into him and see for herself if he was as gorgeous as she remembered.

◈◈◈

'That's a staggering amount of make-up you're wearing for a quiet Monday morning on the stall.'

Millie couldn't resist pointing this out the next day when Hester made her appearance in the kitchen. As a rule, Hester favored the bare-faced look teamed with jeans and the first T-shirt to fall out of the tumble dryer. Today, by way of contrast, she had chosen leather ankle boots, black velvet trousers, and a white lacy top. She also appeared to be wearing the contents of a small Rimmel factory on her face.

'I just felt like dressing up for a change.' Hester attempted nonchalance without much success.

Millie raised an eyebrow over the rim of her coffee cup.

'In case Lucas Kemp happens to wander through the market in search of a pair of dangly sequinned earrings?'

'Oh don't be so mean,' Hester cried. 'I can want to look my best, can't I? Just because I'm not going to have sex with him doesn't mean I want him to see me looking a mess.'

Millie privately wondered if Lucas would want to see Hester looking like Dame Edna. She really was wearing an awful lot of mascara.

'Coffee?'

'I couldn't. Too nervous.'

The letterbox rattled at that moment, making Hester jump.

'Electricity bill,' said Millie, returning from the hall.

'Yuk, don't open it.'

'And a postcard from Nat.'

Millie thought it was a wonderfully romantic thing to do. By the time Nat finished his shifts at L'Amazon, it was the early hours of the morning, too late to ring Hester. So he'd taken to scribbling brief messages—affectionate or funny—on postcards and posting them to her instead.

This one had a picture on the front of a worried-looking cat clutching a tennis racquet. Underneath was written, 'It Takes Guts.' This appealed to Millie's sense of humor but all Hester did was glance at it and sigh.

'Lot of use a postcard is to me. What am I meant to do, stay in every night reading the stupid thing?'

'Hess, be fair. It's only for six months.'

'Sometimes,' Hester sounded fretful, 'six months feels like an awfully long time to be abandoned.'

Feeling brave, Millie said, 'Lucas Kemp abandoned you for six years.'

'That's hardly the same thing.' Hester was indignant. 'It's not as if he asked me to wait for him.'

'It's not as if he sent you any postcards either, is it? Or birthday cards or Christmas cards? He just disappeared.' He hadn't even been Hester's boyfriend, Millie was on the verge of pointing out, but at this rate she was going to end up being horribly late for work. She held up her hands instead, signaling a truce. 'Look, this is mad, we're arguing already, and there's absolutely no point. Because you're not *going* to be sleeping with Lucas Kemp.'

Hester opened her eyes wide, the picture of innocence.

'Of course I'm not.'

Naturally she was lying through her extra-thoroughly-brushed teeth.

'Besides,' said Millie, 'who says he's still single? He could be settled down by now with a wife and a Labrador and four kids.'

'Noooo!' Hester let out a wail of dismay. This hadn't so much as crossed her mind. Lucas *couldn't* be married.

Millie shrugged and picked up her bag.

'Just a thought. Not that it makes any difference to you either way.'

Hester summoned up some pride. 'Of course not.'

'Then again,' Millie added mischievously, 'he…'

'What? *What?*'

'He could be gay.'

Chapter 5

Fleetwood's, the small independent travel agency where Millie had worked for the last year, was run by husband-and-wife team Tim and Sylvia Fleetwood. They needed another member of staff but that didn't mean they had to be nice to them. On her first day, Millie had learned from the woman in the bakery next door that no one ever lasted there longer than a couple of months. Tim and Sylvia were the ultimate joined-at-the-hip couple. They wore matching coats, drove matching cars, and ordered identical meals whenever they ate out.

As far as Millie was able to figure out, they simply couldn't bear the intrusion of having someone else present in the office with them. All they really wanted was to be alone together in their own private world so they could canoodle and talk baby-talk to each other without being interrupted. Millie, who loved her work—it was Tim and Sylvia who made her feel slightly nauseous—was happy for their wish to be granted. As soon as a vacancy cropped up in one of the other travel agencies in Newquay, she'd be out of there faster than you could say Eurostar.

In the meantime, however, a job was a job.

'We'll just have something light for dinner.' Sylvia stroked the back of Tim's neck as she spoke. 'Steamed chicken and salad, that sounds nice, doesn't it? Then when we've done the washing-up we'll set off for our keep-fit class.'

Pretending not to be listening, Millie concentrated madly on her monitor.

'Salad? Why don't we have broad beans?' Tim gave his wife's waist a loving squeeze. 'We like broad beans, don't we?'

'Ooh yes, we love broad beans. That sounds wonderful. And shall we have pudding afterwards or not?'

'I think we'll give pudding a miss. We could always have a peach yogurt later if we feel like it. Millie, could you put out the new *Touring Cairo* brochures? Can I make you a cup of tea, sweetheart, or would you prefer coffee?'

'Darling, how kind, coffee would be great.' Millie beamed at Tim. This was her little joke, her attempt to lighten the atmosphere by a degree or two.

Well, it was always worth a try.

'Ha ha.' Tim's smile was perfunctory. 'Just get on with the brochures, Millie. There's a good girl.'

'Tea, sweetheart, I think.' Sylvia was gazing out of the window, smoothing the pleats of her navy gabardine skirt over her trim hips. 'I say, guess who's just pulled up outside? Tims, come and take a peek.'

Tims obediently went and took a peek. None the wiser, he said, 'Nice car but I don't recognize her.'

Sylvia looked pained; she hated it when they didn't both know the same things.

'You must, I've read all her books! It's Orla Hart, the novelist. Don't you remember, we read that article in the *Guardian* about her moving down to Cornwall? She's the one with the husband who can't keep his trousers zipped—oops, back to the desk, she's coming in!'

The door clanged as it was pushed open. Back behind the desk in record time, Sylvia patted her sprayed-rigid hair—making sure it was still the texture of concrete—and plastered a welcoming smile across her face.

'Orla Hart, what a treat, how marvelous to see you here!

Welcome to Fleetwood's, I'm Sylvia Fleetwood and this is my husband Tim, we're both *so* thrilled to meet you.'

Millie, kneeling on the floor with the hideous navy knife-pleated skirt of her uniform spread out around her like a… well, like a hideous navy knife-pleated skirt, felt a sudden rush of understanding for Hester this morning in her knock-'em-dead outfit. Not that she had a thumping great crush on Orla Hart or anything like that, but she still wished she could be meeting her for the second time dressed in something that made her look a little less like the comedy version of a nineteen fifties middle-aged spinster.

Behind her, Millie heard yet more effusive greetings being exchanged. The tips of her ears began to burn with a mixture of embarrassment and amazement that Sylvia and Tim could behave in quite such a starstruck manner.

Then again, they didn't exactly get much practice—their celebrity clientele to date consisted of a manic bearded fellow who was occasionally allowed to read the weather forecast on local TV and a giggly girl who had once been on *Blind Date*. When the boy on the other side of the screen had asked, 'What gives you the edge over the other two girls?' she had replied:

'If you pick me, number three,
You'll soon see it was meant to be
'Cos I'm a sexy blonde Aquarius born in Februareee
And I'm really good at poetry.'

The poor lad had turned pale with horror and promptly chosen number one instead.

'I do a fair amount of traveling,' Millie heard Orla explaining now. 'Research, you understand, for my novels.'

'Of course, of course,' Sylvia murmured reverently. 'We'd be delighted to help you with your travel plans. My husband and I have a *wealth* of experience which we'd be more than happy to put at your disposal!'

'Marvelous.' Orla sounded delighted. 'Now perhaps we could—'

'Excuse me,' Tim murmured, cutting in and swiveling round in his chair. 'Millie, *off* the floor if you don't mind. Do something useful and make the coffee. *Proper* coffee,' he added, drawing a chair up to the desk and patting it invitingly, gesturing for Orla to make herself comfortable. 'I'm sure we'd all like a cup.'

A minute ago it had been tea, but tea evidently wasn't glamorous enough for a mega-selling celebrity author. Thinking dark thoughts about Tim, because he was the one who had told her to get down on the floor in the first place, Millie stood up and began brushing wiry brown carpet fibers from her bare knees. It was that kind of nasty cheap carpet, and as usual, she'd ended up looking like a cavewoman with unshaven, deeply hairy legs.

'Millie, good heavens, it's you!' Orla exclaimed, her eyes like saucers. 'Oh, this is completely amazing, I thought I was never going to see you again…!'

Millie found herself being thoroughly hugged and kissed on both cheeks. If looks could kill, she'd have slumped back on to the carpet in a flash; rays of absolute fury were zapping like laser beams from Sylvia's narrowed eyes.

She's mine, her outraged expression told Millie. *You just leave her alone.*

If Orla was aware of the deadly hate-rays she blithely ignored them.

'This is brilliant,' she declared, her expression joyful. 'You can deal with all my travel arrangements—from now on, you'll be my very own personal organizer! Right, let's get on with it, shall we? I'm interested in Sicily—oh, and did someone mention coffee just now?' Beaming across at Sylvia she said, 'I'd *love* one. White with no sugar, thanks. And how about you, Millie—will you have one as well?'

◈◈◈

Orla finally left the shop forty minutes later, clutching an armful of glossy brochures. Thanking Millie effusively for all her help, she added over her shoulder to Tim and Sylvia, 'Oh, and thanks so much for the coffee.'

'You just had to be the center of attention, didn't you?' snarled Sylvia the moment the door had swung shut. 'Oh yes, I bet you really enjoyed that, sucking up to her just because she's famous, thinking you could lord it over us, treating us like minions, and acting as if this were *your* business!'

Minions? Startled, Millie took a step backwards.

'But—'

'How *dare* you treat us like that?' The higher Sylvia's voice rose, the more pronounced the tendons on her neck became. 'This is *our* business, you hear? You won't get away with this—'

'Come on now, darling,' Tim murmured in an attempt to placate her. Sylvia swung round to face him, her fists clenched at her sides. If he'd wanted to, Millie realized, he could have plucked her straining tendons like a harp.

'Oh, don't tell me she's wormed her way around you too! What did she do, make sheep's eyes at you, is that how she won you over?'

All this talk of worms and sheep's eyes was putting Millie right off her lunch. She was also horrified by what Sylvia appeared to be implying here.

'Oh yes, I've seen the way you look at her,' Sylvia hissed as though Millie was no longer there. 'Don't think I haven't noticed.'

'Sylvia, stop it.' Tim shook his head. 'She means nothing to me.'

'Look, this is stupid—'

'Stupid? Is that what you think?' Sylvia rounded on her in a flash. 'First you steal my client, now you're trying to steal my husband. Don't you UNDERSTAND?' she roared, her angry mouth inches from Millie's face. 'I CAN'T STAND YOU BEING HERE.'

Okay, enough was enough.

'Well, that's what I call a happy coincidence,' said Millie.

'Tourists tourists everywhere,' Hester announced, slamming the front door behind her, 'and not a sign of Lucas Kemp.' Reaching the living room, she threw herself down on the sofa and kicked off the instruments of torture on her feet—otherwise known as four-inch spike heels. 'Honestly, it's like trying to track down some exotic rare species... you know he's out there somewhere... other people keep telling you they've spotted him... but it doesn't matter how hard you look, it just doesn't happen.'

'Could be the shoes,' Millie suggested. 'You don't see David Attenborough in high heels.'

Ignoring this, Hester glanced at her watch. 'Anyway, you're home early. What's up, are you ill?'

'Nope.' Millie beamed at her. 'Actually, I'm ecstatic. I handed in my notice today—well, that's the polite way of putting it.' She spread her arms with relief. 'Then I walked out. And I'm never *ever* going back.'

'Really? Crikey. Well done, you.' This stopped Hester dead in her tracks. 'So what brought this on?'

'I couldn't stand working for them a minute longer.'

'Not surprised.' Hester was filled with admiration; much as she might long to, she knew she didn't have the nerve to make such grand, dramatic, stick-your-lousy-job gestures.

Particularly since she was self-employed.

'Plus,' said Millie, 'according to Sylvia, I'm just panting to have an affair with her gorgeous husband.'

Hester rocked with laughter.

'Pass the sick-bucket. And are you?'

'Well, of course, I'd jump at the chance, but I don't think I could bear all that jogging in matching track suits.'

'Imagine.' Screwing her nose up in sympathy, Hester said, 'The nerve of that woman, thinking you'd go for someone like him. He's ancient, for crying out loud.'

'In his forties,' Millie agreed. 'Almost as old as my parents. Last week a button came undone on Tim's shirt,' she continued, 'and all these awful white chest hairs popped out.'

'Eeeuugh. And he fancies you!' Hester's expression was triumphant. 'You wicked little home wrecker you.'

'He doesn't fancy me though, that's the thing! It's just Sylvia having one of her freak-outs. Anyway, I'm glad I left.' Millie shuddered with relief, 'Life's too short. You know, I honestly didn't realize how much I hated working with those two until I stopped.'

'You'll have to find something else to do.'

'No problem.' Millie's smile was bright, but this was undeniably the downside. Newquay in the summer season might be able to offer plenty of opportunities for employment but most of the jobs were awful.

Hard work and so poorly paid they made the wages of a Victorian chimney sweeper's boy look good.

Still, it wasn't the end of the world.

Millie ran herself a bath while Hester tried ringing Nat in Glasgow. Within seconds she was barging into the bathroom.

'Hmm. According to his flatmate, Nat's in the shower.'

Kicking off her knickers and wrapping a towel around herself, Millie said, 'It's this new-fangled thing called keeping clean. All the best people are doing it these days.'

'Okay, but what if it isn't true?' Hester looked fretful. 'What if I'm having a miserable time being faithful to Nat and in return he's out shagging his way round every waitress in Glasgow? How do I know he isn't making a fool of me?'

Exasperated, Millie poured half a bottle of Body Shop banana bath foam under the thundering taps.

'Because Nat would never do that. He just wouldn't, trust me.'

'Trust you? Ha, that's a good one. You're the shameless trollop who spends her days making cow's eyes at her ancient married boss.'

'Sheep's eyes,' Millie corrected her, testing the water with one toe. 'And stop getting your knickers in a twist about Nat. He'll ring back in a minute and everything'll be fine.'

'You've got your agony-aunt voice on,' Hester complained. 'All melty and soothing like a New Berry Fruit. Anyway, that's the other thing I came up to tell you. I'm just off out, so if Nat *does* bother to ring back, tell him I've gone to the gym.'

'The gym?' Millie, about to submerge herself in the bath, was astonished. 'But you haven't been to the gym for months!'

'All the more reason to go now, tone myself up a bit.' Hester patted her flat stomach with the faintly smug air of someone who knows she doesn't need toning up. 'Can't let myself go to seed just because Nat isn't here, can I?'

It didn't take a genius to work out that this was excuse-speak for, 'Can't let myself go to seed now Lucas is back in town.' Plus, Millie recalled, he'd always been a bit of a gym fiend himself. Hester was probably hoping to bump into him there, completely by chance of course, their eyes suddenly meeting across a ferocious-looking abdominal cruncher...

'Right, don't want to be late,' Hester chirruped, before Millie had a chance to open her mouth. 'See you when I get back!'

Nat phoned twenty minutes later. Millie, patting her wet hair with the towel slung around her neck, explained where Hester had gone.

'This is the opposite of a dirty phone call,' she told Nat. 'I've just had a bath; we couldn't be cleaner if we tried.'

'I can't believe she's gone to the gym,' Nat marveled. 'I thought she'd given up on all that.'

'Ah well, you haven't seen the state of her. In the last three weeks she's put on about six stone,' said Millie. 'Her boobs have dropped, her bum's like a sack of turnips. It's a horrible sight.'

'But she looked like that before. Why else d'you suppose I left?' Then Nat grew serious. 'How is she really?'

'Fine,' Millie assured him. 'Not fat at all.'

'You know what I mean.' Nat hesitated. 'I miss her, Millie. Being apart from Hess is the hardest thing I've ever had to do.' Another pause, then half laughing he said, 'God, listen to me. Cue the violins. I suppose I'm just asking if Hester misses me too.'

Millie's freakish ability to cross her toes had always caused howls of revulsion. Luckily there was no one around to witness the display as she crossed them now.

'Of course she does. She never stops talking about you. You're the best boyfriend she's ever had.'

'You always know the right thing to say.' Nat sounded as if he were smiling. 'Look, tell Hester I rang and give her my love, will you?'

'In a non-physical way,' Millie assured him as the doorbell rang. 'Ooh, have to go, someone's at the door.'

'And I need to get back to work. I'll try phoning again tomorrow night. Off you go,' said Nat. 'Speak to you again soon.'

'Bye.' Millie wondered if Hester realized how lucky she was. Why couldn't everyone in the world be as lovely as Nat?

Chapter 6

Orla Hart was shivering on the doorstep in a hopelessly impractical pink lace shirt, long floaty skirt, and silver sandals. The weather had taken an abrupt turn for the worse and raindrops were spitting ill-temperedly from a slate grey sky.

Standing next to Orla on the step was a stone statue of a young girl clutching a bowl.

Temporarily lost for words, Millie said, 'I didn't even know it was raining.'

'Well you do now. Okay if I come in?'

Millie stepped to one side and Orla staggered past her into the narrow hallway with the statue in her arms. Panting slightly, she lowered it to the ground, before turning to face Millie.

'Okay. Now last time I gave you a lift back to Newquay, you wouldn't tell me where you lived.'

'That's because you kept insisting you wanted to buy me something as a way of saying thank you,' Millie reminded her.

'But you saved my life!'

'All I did was sit and talk to you for a bit. I didn't want a reward.'

'Well, too bad.' Orla's smile was unrepentant as she patted the carved stone head of the statue. 'I saw her this afternoon and knew at once I had to buy her for you. Isn't she heavenly? Think how gorgeous she'll look in your garden!'

She probably would, thought Millie, if only we had one.

'She's great.' Praying she could bluff her way through this—maybe by some miracle Orla Hart wouldn't notice that all they possessed was a tiny backyard—Millie said, 'But you didn't need to do this.'

Orla shook her wet hair out of her greeny-gold eyes and fixed her with an earnest gaze.

'Remember on that cliff top, you said you couldn't walk away because your conscience wouldn't let you? You told me you'd end up a basket case if you left me there to jump.'

'Sort of.' Tightening the belt of her dressing gown around her waist, Millie wondered if she had post-bath panda eyes from where her mascara had run. She hoped Orla wouldn't think she'd been crying.

'Well, now it's my turn to have you on my conscience. Shall we go through?' Tilting her head, Orla indicated the living room, which Millie knew for a fact was in a mess.

Luckily Orla didn't appear to mind. Her bright eyes darted around the room, taking everything in. But in a nice rather than a critical way, Millie was relieved to note.

Unlike her own mother.

'You've been sacked,' Orla told Millie, perching on the arm of their old bottle green chesterfield sofa.

'Actually, I resigned.'

'Really?' Orla didn't sound convinced. 'I went back there this afternoon and that owner-woman said they'd had to let you go.'

'I definitely resigned,' Millie assured her.

'Oh. Well, good. I think.' Orla paused, looked anguished for a few seconds, then blurted out, 'Okay, but you have to be completely honest now, did it have anything to do with me?'

'Nooo!' Millie exclaimed, so dramatically that they both knew at once that it had. If you wanted to sound believable, Millie remembered—too late, as usual—you had to sound normal, verging on the deadpan. Never ever overdo it.

Except, of course, she always did.

'It wasn't really to do with you,' Millie rushed to explain, 'I promise. You just somehow ended up getting dragged into it.'

'I knew it.' Orla sounded distraught. 'That awful woman with the huge wart on her nose. She was behaving really oddly with me.'

Millie frowned. 'Sylvia? Sylvia doesn't have a wart on her nose.'

'She's mean, like an old witch,' Orla declared impatiently. 'She looks as if she should have a wart on her nose. And I practically had to twist both her arms off before she'd give me your address. So go on then, why did you leave?'

Since Orla had now slid off the threadbare arm of the chesterfield and was making herself comfortable on the sofa itself, Millie fetched a bottle of red wine from the kitchen, unearthed two glasses that actually matched, and told her.

'You're allowed to smoke,' she added, detecting the signals of nicotine deprivation as Orla fiddled frantically with her many bangles.

'Are you sure? I could always go and stand in the garden.'

The clothes-airer was currently up in the yard, which meant there wouldn't be room for Orla too. Lord, that carved stone statue was going to look as out of place there as Victoria Beckham in a betting shop.

Millie said generously, 'It's raining. Anyway, I don't mind. Just flick your ash in that plant thingy behind you.'

Hugely relieved, Orla kicked off her flat silver sandals and lit up. Her toes actually curled with pleasure, Millie noticed, when she inhaled.

'So the old witch thought you were after her husband,' Orla marveled when she'd heard the whole sorry story. 'She must be one of those super-jealous types who imagines every female under the age of eighty is panting to get their hands on her man. I hope you told her you'd rather have sex with Jabba the Hut. Actually, it would jolly well serve her right if you *did* have an affair with that awful husband of hers, or gosh, better still, I could have an affair with him! Ha, that'd teach her a lesson, wouldn't it?'

Heavens alive, Millie goggled in alarm, was this what all novelists were like? One teeny germ of an idea and they were off and running with it like a relay baton, getting more and more carried away?

Not to say it wasn't an entertaining idea in theory...

'Except Tim would never have an affair with anyone,' she told Orla gloomily. 'He and Sylvia do everything together. He probably goes along to the bathroom with her when she wakes up in the night needing the loo.'

'I can't bear those kind of couply couples!' Orla exclaimed with passion.

'They wear matching sweaters.'

'Well that kind of behavior is just *laughable*.'

'And they go to the same aerobics class.'

'Pathetic. People like that,' Orla declared, 'make me want to be sick.'

'They were never friendly towards me anyway, so it's not as if I enjoyed working for them.' Millie gave her a reassuring look. 'Actually, walking out on that job has quite cheered me up.'

'Oh, but I still feel horribly guilty.' Having smoked her way down her cigarette at a rate of knots, Orla swiveled round and stubbed it out in Hester's neglected azalea plant. 'And I forgot to ask you this morning how it turned out with your boyfriend after he stormed off last week.' She looked hopeful. 'Did he forgive you for jumping out of his car and saving my life?'

'Um... actually, no. But it doesn't matter,' Millie went on hurriedly. 'I told you before, I didn't even want to be with him. Really, it was all for the best.'

'Oh Lord, this is terrible,' wailed Orla, 'I'm a complete walking disaster. Here's you, a lovely, kind girl who's never done anyone any harm. And now, you're left without a job *and* a boyfriend—for pity's sake, one way or another I've managed to single-handedly destroy your life.'

'Will you stop this?' Millie's eyebrows shot up in disbelief. 'You're doing it again, getting carried away, making a drama out of a... blip. For a start, Neil wasn't the love of my life. Secondly, I *can* find myself another job.'

'But—'

'And I'm not always a lovely, kind person either,' Millie assured her. 'Sometimes I can be completely vile.'

'Well I'm sorry, but I don't believe that for one moment. I mean, look at you,' Orla declared, spreading her hands, 'with your ripply blonde hair and those great big eyes... you're an absolute angel! Yes, that's exactly what you look like, an *angel...*'

Millie had always yearned to be tall and angular with sticky-out cheekbones, poker-straight black hair, and a haughty manner. Her ideal woman was Lily Munster. Desperate to convince Orla, she said, 'But that doesn't make me a nice person!'

'I bet you are.' It was no good, Orla's mind was made up. 'I bet you've never done anything thoughtless or mean in your life.'

So Millie was compelled to prove it, mentioning no names of course, by skimming through the story of Hugh Emerson's wallet, the ensuing phone call, and the stomach-churning moment when she realized she'd committed one of the all-time great faux pas.

'So you see,' Millie concluded five minutes later with just a smidgen of triumph, 'I can be as awful as the next person.'

'Except you didn't know this chap's wife was dead. Sorry,' said Orla briskly, 'but that doesn't count at all. Anyway,' she went on, 'you've gone bright red just telling me about it, which only goes to prove what a sweetheart you are.'

It was hopeless. For a fraction of a second Millie was tempted to announce to Orla that one of her hobbies was pulling the wings off butterflies and that she was also partial to a spot of kitten-drowning in her spare time.

But what with being so lovely, of course, she couldn't bring herself to do it.

Changing the subject instead, Millie said, 'So how are things going with you and your husband?'

And promptly prayed that Orla wouldn't burst into tears, rush up to the bathroom, and start glugging down the contents of a bottle of bleach.

She didn't. Phew.

'Giles? Oh, we're fine, absolutely fine, it was all a mad, mad misunderstanding.' Between lighting up another cigarette and dropping her heavy silver lighter back into her bag, Orla flashed her a dazzling smile. 'I'm just so glad you were there on that cliff top to stop me killing myself.'

'You wouldn't have killed yourself,' said Millie. 'Not really.'

Orla shrugged.

'I've wondered the same thing myself, lots of times. But I was pretty desperate.' She paused, then added with a wry smile, 'I'm still glad you happened to be around.'

'What was the mad misunderstanding?'

Millie was amazed she dared ask such an outrageously personal question, but she had to know. Anyway, Orla had already dragged pretty much her entire life story out of her; a spot of counter-nosiness surely wouldn't go amiss.

'Oh, too silly for words! There was me thinking that Giles had installed Martine down here… and he didn't have the faintest idea she was even *in* Cornwall! It was all her fault,' Orla explained, wafting smoke in all directions. 'Giles finished with her but she refused to accept it. Typical scorned-mistress scenario—she kept ringing him and begging him to take her back, but Giles was brilliant, he just kept saying no. So in the end, out of sheer desperation, the silly girl moved down to Cornwall and rented a little cottage completely off her own bat. Giles didn't have anything to do with it. When I confronted him he was absolutely gobsmacked!'

'Oh.' Millie swallowed. 'Well, um, good.'

'So there we go, all that silly worrying for nothing,' Orla declared. 'Of course, we can't physically evict her from the county, but she isn't a problem anymore. She's still there in her sad little cottage, but I can deal with that. I've got my husband back and I'm happy.'

Orla was telling the truth, Millie decided. She genuinely believed what she was saying. In which case...

'That's brilliant,' she told Orla warmly. 'I'm so pleased for you.'

'Oh God,' Orla let out a wail of dismay, 'you really *are*. I've jack-booted my way into your life, crushed it to smithereens, and *you're* still pleased for *me*!'

All this guilt, she had to be a Catholic.

'I love that word,' Millie sighed, tucking her bare legs under her and idly winding the belt of her dressing gown around one hand. 'Actually, I *really* love it. Smithereens. I wonder if it's Irish?' Clutching an imaginary microphone, she announced with a flourish, 'And now, ladies and gen'l'men, we are proud to present on stage here tonight... the Smithereens!'

'Can you sing?' asked Orla abruptly.

'Er... not really.'

'What does that mean?'

Here she goes, off again, thought Millie, asking a load of questions that make no sense at all.

'I'm not great and I'm not bad.' She decided to humor Orla. 'Just average.'

'Dance?'

'I've got legs, haven't I?' Millie wiggled her toes. 'Anyone with legs can dance. After a fashion.'

'And you're not shy,' Orla went on, slopping red wine over her skirt as she delved into her bag. 'I may have just the thing for you... hang on, I know it's down here somewhere... ah, here we are.' She pulled out a business card and waved it triumphantly at Millie. 'This fellow could be right up your street.'

'Oh God, don't tell me,' Millie groaned, 'it's Andrew Lloyd Webber and he's going to pester me to star in his next West End musical.'

'No, no, I'm serious. We met briefly at a party the other night and he's looking for girls just like you.'

'Brilliant,' said Millie. 'He's a pimp, desperate to recruit new hookers to replace all the ones who've been carted off to the cells.'

'Will you pay attention?' Orla scolded good-naturedly. 'This fellow has just set up a kissogram service here in Cornwall.'

Oh for heaven's sake.

'A *what*?'

'No need to look so shocked, there's nothing sleazy about it. The whole thing's completely above board,' declared Orla. 'It's just a bit of fun... you can book Chippendale-types for hen parties, Granny-grams, roller-skating gorillagrams—oh, that would be a big plus, if you can roller-skate—even juggling clowns on uni-cycles...'

'I don't think it's really my kind of thing,' said Millie, feeling a bit mean when Orla was so clearly filled with enthusiasm.

'Okay, I know it's not exactly your run-of-the-mill office job, but according to this chap the pay's not bad. I mean, why work for eight hours pushing a load of paperclips about when you could earn almost as much money in one and a half hours?'

'Roller-skating around in a gorilla suit?'

As it happened, Millie *could* skate. Rather well, in fact.

'Just a thought,' said Orla. 'You don't have to. Pretty dishy chap, though, running the company.'

She winked, gave Millie an encouraging nod and pressed the business card into her hand.

Millie turned it over and studied the blurb on the front.

'Single too.' Orla sounded pleased with herself. 'I checked.'

'Kemp's,' read Millie. 'Kissograms to make your parties go with a scream. Prop: Lucas Kemp. Tel: 01637 blah blah blah.'

Oh, terrific.

Aloud she said faintly, 'Well, thanks.'

Chapter 7

TYPICALLY, IT TOOK HESTER no time at all to unearth the card.

'What's that awful statue doing in the bathroom?' she demanded the following morning.

'Orla Hart gave it to me. She blames herself for me being out of a job. It's her way of making up for it,' Millie explained.

'Well, next time she feels guilty, tell her we'd prefer shoes. Bugger.' Hester gazed down in frustration at her bare legs, which were decorated with strips of loo paper stuck on with blood. When she moved, the loo paper fluttered in the breeze.

'Never shave your legs in a hurry.'

'I wasn't in a hurry, I was nervous. Today could be the day I bump into you-know-who. Oh, this is hopeless,' Hester groaned as a trickle of blood slid down the back of her calf. 'Why won't it *stop*? I look like I've been attacked by a plague of rats.'

'Wear jeans,' Millie called over her shoulder as she disappeared into the bathroom.

When she emerged ten minutes later, Hester was standing in the middle of the living room with an odd look on her face.

'What?' demanded Millie. 'Honestly, are you still waiting for your legs to stop gushing? You're going to be so late for work.'

'My jeans are in the washing basket,' Hester announced.

Heavens, Orla Hart wasn't the only drama queen around here. What was Hester hoping, that this would make the front page of the *Cornwall Gazette*!

'So I thought I'd wear tights instead,' she went on.

Phew, never mind the *Cornwall Gazette*, thought Millie, put me through *this minute* to the editor of the *News of the World.*

'But I didn't have any without holes in them,' Hester continued, her tone conversational, 'so I thought you wouldn't mind if I borrowed a pair of yours instead.'

Oh.

Oh bum.

In fact, massive bum.

'I've got some opaque black ones,' Millie said hopefully. 'They'd hide the cuts on your legs.'

'And while I was going through your knicker drawer, I happened to come across… this.' Hester held up the business card with Lucas Kemp's name on it. 'How could you do this to me? That's what I don't understand. I've spent the last three days in a complete *tizz*, wondering if I'm ever going to track him down, and all the time you knew exactly how I could do it, because you had *this* card with *his* number on it, HIDDEN IN YOUR FLAMING KNICKER DRAWER.'

It probably wasn't the moment, Millie decided, to make a feeble joke about her inflammable knickers.

'Okay, now listen, I haven't had this card for days. Orla Hart gave it to me last night and I needed time to think. I was going to tell you this evening,' she pleaded, 'but you know what you're like. The last thing you need is to go hurling yourself at Lucas Kemp, drooling all over him like a besotted bulldog, and letting him think you're a complete pushover, there for the taking.'

Hester stepped back as if she'd been slapped across the face.

'A besotted… bulldog? Is that what you're saying I look like?'

She sounded so hurt. Guiltily Millie shook her head.

'Of course not. I just couldn't think of anything else that drooled.'

'Labradors drool,' Hester announced stiffly. 'My auntie's

Labrador drools all the time. And St. Bernards drool. You really didn't have to say bulldog.'

'Sorry.'

'Anyway, I wouldn't throw myself at Lucas! I have no intention of letting him think I'm a pushover.'

'Of course you wouldn't. Sorry,' Millie repeated, her tone humble. Even though she knew, just *knew* without a doubt, that Hester had already learned the phone number on the card by heart.

Mollified, Hester said, 'Why did Orla Hart give you Lucas's business card anyway?'

'He's looking for people to do the kissograms. Orla thought I might be interested. She was just trying to help because she feels so responsible for—'

'Ohmigod!' In an instant Hester forgot all about being stroppy. She clapped her hands like an excited child. 'This is *brilliant.*'

'But I told her it wasn't my kind of thing.'

'You could do it!'

'I'm a travel agent,' Millie protested.

Well, kind of.

'An unemployed travel agent,' Hester pointed out.

'Yes, but singing telegrams! They're so… so…' Millie floundered; they were definitely so something, she just couldn't explain what.

'Would you have to take all your clothes off?'

'No!'

'Do it then,' Hester ordered.

'I don't know if I want to.'

'Excuse me, but *is* your name Victoria Beckham?' Hester rolled her eyes. 'No it isn't, so you can't exactly afford to be fussy, can you?'

'I was thinking more of a bar job,' said Millie.

'Oh don't be so mean,' Hester pleaded. 'At least ring him and fix up an interview.'

Millie feigned puzzlement.

'Why?'

'Because then you can meet up with him and have a lovely chat about the good old days, and that'll give him the chance to ask you all about me and you'll be able to tell him how gorgeous and popular I am, and before you know it he'll be desperate to see me again and that's when you'll say, "Hey, why don't the three of us meet up for a drink tonight?" and he'll say, "Millie, that's a *fantastic* idea," and it'll all happen in a really easy, natural way. Bingo. Not a besotted bulldog, not a ribbon of drool in sight!'

'And no sex either,' Millie reminded her.

Hester looked shocked.

'Absolutely not.'

'Good. Okay.'

This is what Orla means about me being nice, Millie realized. I hid the card from Hester for her own good, and she's managed to make me feel so guilty I've ended up agreeing to do the one thing I really didn't want to do.

Well now I'm going to be mean and it jolly well serves her right.

Smiling like a dutiful wife, she stood at the front door and waved a deliriously happy Hester off to work. Still minus any tights and with the long-forgotten strips of loo roll like tiny red and white banners flip-flapping around her legs.

Nobody picked up the phone when Millie rang the number on Lucas Kemp's business card. Her conscience clear once more—ah well, at least she'd tried—she decided to make the most of her unexpected freedom and pay a visit to her father instead.

When Millie's parents had split up five years earlier, it had been at the instigation of her mother. Adele Brady had yearned for more; she had her heart set on a glittering metropolitan lifestyle.

And in due course, a refined metropolitan husband to match.

'Cornwall just isn't *me*,' Adele had told Millie at the time. 'It's sooo parochial. I need glamour, I need opera, I need… oh God… Harvey Nichols!'

'See? She's got her eye on some other fellow already.' Millie's father, Lloyd, had winked at Millie. 'Mind you, I wouldn't have thought he'd be her type… an overweight ex-showjumper famous for his two-fingered salute. Can't imagine he'd be much of a one for the opera.'

Millie had grinned, because she knew her dad was teasing her mother.

'Pathetic, completely pathetic,' Adele had hissed back, not getting it at all. 'I could do *so* much better than you.'

'Jolly good.' Lloyd wasn't bothered; he was too used to his wife's endless criticisms. At first, the fact that he and Adele were polar opposites had been a huge novelty. But after twenty years, it had well and truly worn off.

'I'm going to be happy,' Adele had declared with utter confidence.

'What, with this Harvey Nichols chap?' There was a mischievous twinkle in Lloyd's eyes. 'Quite sure about that, are you? Because you need to watch these horsey-types, you know. They're known to have a bit of a thing about pointy spurs and a whip.'

'A whole new life for myself.' Adele had gazed at him with contempt. 'A glorious new life and a glorious new man to share it with.'

'Ah well, each to his own,' Lloyd had said good-naturedly. 'Women? I give up on them. From now on, it's a bachelor's life for me.'

Famous last words.

For Adele, as well as for Lloyd.

Adele had spent the last five years racketing around London in a state of increasing desperation. She was a fifty-five-year-old Bridget Jones in Burberry silk-knits, constantly complaining that there were no decent men *anywhere* and that the only males who enjoyed opera were all homosexuals. In cravats.

Lloyd, meanwhile, had settled quite happily into his newfound bachelor lifestyle for all of three and a half months. Then, quite by accident, he had met Judy.

At a petrol station on the outskirts of Padstow, of all the exotic locations imaginable.

Lloyd had been about to pay for his petrol at the till when a female voice behind him in the queue had declared, 'Bugger!'

Lloyd, swiveling round to see who the Bugger belonged to, had smiled broadly at Judy.

Flapping her hand in half-hearted apology, Judy had pulled a face then grinned back.

And that, basically, had been that.

'I've just stuck twenty quid's worth of petrol in my car.' Judy showed him the contents of her well-worn handbag: a Mars bar, several dog biscuits, one lipstick, and a wrinkled Dick Francis paperback that looked as if it had been read in the bath. 'And I've come out without my sodding purse.'

A single lipstick. And no hairbrush. Lloyd was instantly enchanted.

'No problem, I'll lend you the money.'

He liked the way she didn't launch into a flurry of Oh-no-I-couldn't-possiblys.

'I might be a con-artist.'

'A con-artist,' Lloyd gravely informed her, 'would never say that.'

'Okay, you're on.' Judy nodded, accepting his offer and jangling her car keys. 'And I only live a mile down the road, so if you aren't in a tearing hurry you can follow me home and I'll pay you back.'

'I might be an axe murderer.'

'I've got my dogs at home,' Judy confided. 'Axe murderers don't scare me.'

Without meaning it to happen, Lloyd realized before the afternoon was out that he'd met his soulmate, the woman with whom he wanted—no, not wanted, with whom he *had*—to spend the rest of his life.

Judy Forbes-Adams had been widowed three years earlier. At fifty-three and with her children grown up, she too was satisfied with her life just the way it was. She loved horses and dogs and the Cornish countryside with a passion. On special occasions, she dashed on a bit of Yardley lipstick and remembered to brush her hair. She wouldn't have recognized a designer outfit if it leapt out at her screaming Chanel, although she had both the means and the figure to wear anything that took her fancy. And, best of all, she couldn't be doing with opera. Judy's idea of a good time involved listening to *The Archers* on Radio 4 while she planted out her pelargoniums.

It drove Adele insane that the good fairy had had the nerve to grant Lloyd the happy ending.

'It's so unfair,' she complained. Frequently and extremely crossly.

'You'll find someone else,' Millie tried to placate her. Frequently and with an increasingly weary edge to her voice.

'How your father can be content with a woman who spends her life in denim jeans is beyond me,' Adele sniped. 'Jeans, I ask you, *and* she's nearly sixty.'

'Don't ask me to say bitchy things about Judy. I like her.'

'Ha. Next you'll be telling me she's a better cook than I am.'

Adele liked to spend hours preparing tremendously ornate meals that she painstakingly arranged on plates so they ended up looking like mini-scaffolding.

'She's nothing like you in the kitchen,' Millie said truthfully. She was fairly sure Adele had never stood gossiping at the stove waving a cigarette in one hand and stirring gravy with the other. Judy was, in fact, a terrific cook but Millie had learned—for the good of her health—to be diplomatic. 'She does shepherd's pies, steak-and-kidney puddings, stuff like that.'

'Great piles of stodge. No wonder your father's happy. Peasant food,' Adele snorted. 'That kind of thing's right up his street.'

Chapter 8

Peasant food was right up Millie's street as well. Lunch with Judy and her father was always a treat.

Today it was sausage-and-onion casserole, rich and gloopy and piled over butter-drenched baked potatoes. Lloyd uncorked a bottle of Shiraz and Millie began to bring them up to date with all the gossip, kicking off with how she had come to be unemployed.

'But that's just appalling!' Judy exclaimed. 'Honestly, couples like that make me *shudder*. And now you're jobless… well, we can give you some money if you're desperate, just say the word.'

'I'll be fine.' Millie was touched by the offer, but she shook her head. 'Finding work isn't a problem. In fact, there's one job Hester's really keen for me to go for.' Pulling Lucas Kemp's business card out of her back pocket, she showed it to them.

'Darling, a strippogram!' Judy clapped her hands in delight. 'What a *scream*.'

'If I stripped, people would definitely scream. Either that or complain loudly and demand their money back. I wouldn't have to take my clothes off,' Millie explained.

'They want all sorts, like people who can sing, dance, and roller-skate. Anyway, it's just an option. I'll probably end up waitressing or working in a bar.'

'You could juggle,' Judy declared with enthusiasm. 'That would be fabulous! Who could resist a singing, roller-skating jugglogram?'

'Except I can't juggle,' Millie pointed out.

'No, but I can.' Jumping up from the table, Judy grabbed five satsumas from the fruit bowl on the dresser and began tossing them into the air. Deftly, she juggled them then caught them and executed a modest curtsey.

'Five years,' Lloyd marveled. 'Five years we've been together and I never knew.'

'Just one of my little secrets.' Judy raised a playful eyebrow at him. 'International woman of mystery, that's me.'

'Did you run away as a child and join the circus?' Millie was enthralled.

'What else can you do?' said Lloyd. 'Walk tightropes? Tame lions? Balance a ball on the end of your nose?'

'When I was nineteen, I spent the summer traveling with a boyfriend. When we ran out of money we learned how to juggle. Then we busked our way around Europe.' Judy shrugged as if it were the most normal thing in the world. 'And once you know how to do it, you never forget. Like riding a bike. Now there's a thought.' Eyes alight, she turned to Millie. 'You could be a unicycling, singing kissogram, that'd really stop the show!'

Millie burst out laughing at Judy, standing there before her in her loose white shirt, faded jeans, and espadrilles, with her messy shoulder-length fair hair and her hands full of satsumas.

'Don't tell me you know how to unicycle as well.'

'Of course I don't know how to unicycle. We could never have afforded a unicycle! Heavens, we were so broke we could barely afford the paraffin for our flaming clubs.'

When they had resumed eating, Lloyd frowned at the business card on the table.

'Why does this fellow's name sound familiar?'

'He's the one Hester spent her teenage years pining over,' Millie reminded him. 'The DJ, remember, who moved away to London?' She pulled a face. 'Now he's back and Hester's come over all hopeless and besotted. That's why she's so keen for me to take the job. Poor Nat. I just hope she doesn't do something incredibly stupid and make an idiot of herself.'

'I was keen on a girl once,' Lloyd idly recollected. 'I used to cycle past her house, peering up at her bedroom window. Then one day I saw her there, watching me. I was so excited I crashed my bike into her father's car.'

Judy grinned and sloshed more wine into their glasses.

'Oh well, if it's embarrassing moments you're after, I was once *mad* about this boy in St. Ives. One day a crowd of us went down to the beach for a swim and there he was. So we stripped off our clothes—we were all wearing our swimsuits underneath—and I decided to be really brave. I sauntered up to him in front of all his friends and asked him if he knew the time.'

'And?' Millie held her breath.

'He said, "Yeah, darlin,' about time you got your knickers off." And when I looked down I realized I still had my awful pink underpants on over my swimsuit. It's not *funny*!' Judy protested. 'Imagine the trauma. Took me years to live it down.'

Emboldened by the urge to compete—and by her third glass of red wine—Millie immediately launched into her own embarrassing story, the one about the Wallet and the Phone Call.

When she reached the hilarious punchline ('For your information, my wife is dead'), Judy groaned and clapped her hands with a mixture of horror and delight.

'I know, I know, I'm *so* ashamed.' Millie shook her head and felt herself going bright red again; it happened every time she even thought about it.

Lloyd patted her arm and said cheerfully, 'My daughter, the diplomat.'

'Dad, I was mortified! I just hung up.'

'Maybe it wasn't true,' Judy suggested. 'My darling husband

always had atrocious taste in sweaters, but as soon as anyone made fun of them, he'd look distraught and say, "This was the last thing my mother knitted for me before she died."'

It was a nice thought, but Millie knew she couldn't allow herself to hang on to it.

'This chap wasn't joking,' she said sadly. 'He really meant it. He was disgusted with me. Up until then he'd seemed so nice… he had this really warm voice.'

'Oh well, that's men for you.' Judy waved a dismissive arm. 'So what did you do with the wallet?'

'Posted it off to him. I scribbled a quick note saying sorry, but the guilt won't go away. You'd think it would have started to wear off by now but it hasn't, in fact it's got *worse*.' Millie shuddered just thinking about it. 'Whenever I remember that phone call I get these awful icy shivers whooshing down my spine. Sometimes it's like standing under a *waterfall*—'

'Darling, write him another letter!' Judy exclaimed. 'A proper one this time. Then you can grovel and apologize to your heart's content.'

Millie wilted; she only wished she could.

'I can't remember his address. Too embarrassed, I expect. It's wiped from my memory. Gone.'

'Oh well then, put it out of your mind. Just forget it.' Judy's tone was consoling. 'Life's too short.'

'Certainly was for that fellow's wife.' Lloyd winked at Millie across the table.

'Dad! That's a terrible thing to say!'

'I know. Can't think where I get it from,' said Lloyd.

'One, two… bum.'

'One, two, three… bugger.'

'One… oh fuck it!'

From the living-room doorway, Hester said, 'I'd ask you what you thought you were doing, but it would be a dumb question.'

'Oh, hi.' Bending down, Millie retrieved the satsumas that had rolled under the table. She'd dropped them so many times they were now as soft and squishy as breast implants.

'You're juggling,' Hester said accusingly.

'I'm not, am I?'

'No, actually, you're not. You're trying to juggle.'

'I've spent the whole afternoon trying to juggle… one, two, three… *damn.* Judy's been teaching me. She said it was easy,' Millie wailed, 'and it's not, it's bloody impossible!'

'Stop, then. Don't do it.'

'Two, three, four… sod it. And no I *won't* stop.' Millie doggedly picked up the dropped satsuma. 'I'm not going to let this beat me.'

'You even left the post sitting on the mat,' Hester complained, waving the sheaf of letters like a poker hand. 'I stepped on them when I opened the door. Oh yuk,' her lip curled up in disgust as she leafed through the unexciting collection, 'now I know why you didn't pick them up. Water rates, phone, scary bank statement, gas bill… nightmare.'

'There's a letter from Nat.' Millie recognized the handwriting on the final envelope.

'If it was stuffed with cash I might be excited,' Hester said fretfully. 'Did you phone Lucas?'

She really was a hopeless case.

'No,' said Millie. 'Although I thought I might write to Nat, keep him up to date with… everything.' Meaningfully, she waggled her eyebrows.

'Honestly, you have no idea how unscary that is.' Hester broke into a grin. 'You *know* you'd never do that.'

'I might,' Millie protested. 'Nat's my friend too.'

'And that makes no difference at all.' Hester was smug. 'Because I'm your *best* friend.'

'I could always demote you.'

'You never would though. You love me too much. Will you phone Lucas tomorrow?'

'I might.'

'Pleeease?'

'I'll think about it.' Millie heaved a sigh. 'And while I'm thinking about it, you might like to make me a cheese and Marmite toasted sandwich and a lovely big mug of tea.'

The penny suddenly dropped several hours later. Hester was out again, pounding the treadmill down at the gym and no doubt carefully patting her face with a hand towel every couple of minutes so her make-up wouldn't run. Millie, having wallowed happily in the bath and caught up with the goings-on in *EastEnders*, wandered through to the kitchen in her dressing gown in search of biscuits. With no Hester around, it looked as if she was going to have to make her own tea.

Idly rolling the end of her dressing gown belt into a Catherine wheel, Millie ate a biscuit and waited for the kettle to boil. There were the bills that had arrived today, thrown down on the worktop waiting to be filed away.

In the bin, where all bills that didn't have FINAL DEMAND printed in menacing red letters all over them were meticulously filed.

Steam began to billow from the spout of the kettle. Millie, counting under her breath, tried to guess the exact moment it would automatically switch itself off.

(The words Get a Life sprang to mind, but it was a harmless enough game and she enjoyed it.)

'Three, two, one… *now*.'

Click, went the kettle.

And *dinggg*, went the penny as it suddenly, finally dropped.

'Oh!' Millie exclaimed aloud, her heart pounding away like Hester on her treadmill.

Scrabbling at the bundle of bills, it took her no time at all to find what she was looking for.

I am such a *jerk*, thought Millie. Why on earth didn't I think of this before?

There, on the itemized phone bill, was the mobile phone number she had rung at half past midnight on the third of May.

Simple.

Four minutes and thirteen seconds, Millie noted. That was how long she and Hugh Emerson had spoken to each other. Funny how much chaos and damage you could inflict in four minutes and thirteen seconds. Not to mention pain and embarrassment and shame and bitter regret.

Chapter 9

Needing time to think, Millie helped herself to a handful of biscuits and made herself that cup of tea.

Okay. Right. Clearly she needed to phone the man and apologize properly, because the awful guilt wasn't going to go away of its own accord.

Then again, she wasn't exactly looking forward to hearing those disdainful, icy tones the moment she told Hugh Emerson who she was.

I want to be spoken to in that lovely warm voice, Millie thought sadly. It was strange, but she actually *yearned* to hear him talk to her in that easy, friendly way again.

Okay, granted, he'd only sounded friendly for about twenty-five seconds last time, but… well, those twenty-five seconds had made a lasting impression.

The next moment, Millie's bare toes began to tingle and curl up with excitement as the germ of an idea crept into her mind.

Hugh Emerson would be far more likely to be nice if he didn't know it was her he was speaking to.

It took another fifteen minutes of mulling over the possibilities, fine-honing her plan, and giving it a few trial runs before Millie plucked up the courage to dial the number.

Ring ring.

Ring ring.

Of course, he might not be there. He could be out—

'Hello?'

Eek, it was him! Clamping the phone to her ear, hanging on to it for all she was worth, Millie took a huge breath and launched into the spiel she had, in true *Blue Peter* fashion, prepared earlier.

'Joe? Och, thank goodness you'rre therre, ah'm having the worrrst time o' it herre, you just hafty help me beforre ah goa arround the twist. Ah'm stuck on this terrible crossword, it's drrivin' me *mental*, now listen, it's seven letterrrs—'

'Hello, sorry,' Hugh Emerson finally managed to get a word in edgewise, 'I'm afraid you have the wrong person here.'

Millie feigned delight. 'Och, Joe, dinna mess arround, ye canna fool me!' Oops, accent beginning to slip a bit, have to keep it going. Think Scottish, think Sean Connery, think Billy Connolly. 'Listen to me noo, here comes the firrst clue… seven letters… are you ready, Joe?'

'I'm ready, but I'm still not Joe.'

Millie heard the amusement in his voice, knew he was shaking his head at her mistake. The delicious tingly feeling in her toes whooshed up to her knees.

'Och no! Is that *rreally* not you, Joe?' Indignantly she said, 'So in that case who *are* you, and what are you doing answering Joe's phone?'

Hugh laughed, then said nicely, 'I think you must have dialed the wrong number.'

'No! Have I? Och, I'm so sorrry!' Millie laughed too, in what she hoped was a convincingly Scottish fashion. Think *Local Hero*, think Mel Gibson in *Braveheart*, think *Taggart*.

'Not a problem,' Hugh Emerson replied easily.

'Och, you must think I'm a complete *haggis*, rrambling oan like that. Well, I suppose I'd better leave you in peace…' Millie allowed her voice to trail away, signalling regret.

'Look, you may as well ask me now you're here,' said Hugh Emerson. 'Seven letters, did you say? What's the clue?'

Yesss! Falling back on the sofa in ecstasy, Millie kicked her feet in the air like a beetle. That was the truly brilliant thing about crosswords, nobody could ever pass up the opportunity to show off.

'Okay, it's the title of a Humphrey Bogart film, *The* something *Falcon*." Oops, accent alert; in her excitement she'd completely forgotten about being Scottish. To make amends Millie added hastily, 'Och, it's verra verra harrrd, I havnae a clue maself.'

'*Maltese*,' said Hugh Emerson.

Bugger, too easy. Clearly a man who knew his Bogart.

'Fantastic!' Millie exclaimed. 'Now, eighteen across is two words, five and eight letters… och, I can't take up your time like this, you must be busy, I really shouldna trrouble you.'

'It's okay. Fire away.'

Millie stiffened; now he sounded faintly patronizing, as if she was just a silly girlie who couldn't be expected to know the answer to a simple question.

'He wrote the nineteen fifty-four film *The Seven Samurai*… oh wait, hang on, that was… ooh, whats his name, Akira somebody… yes! Akira Kurosawa!'

'That's right. Well done.' To Millie's delight, he sounded surprised. Impressed, even. Ha, all of a sudden she wasn't quite so thick after all!

More crucially still, she'd drawn level.

One all.

He was a man; she knew he wouldn't be able to resist it.

His tone extra casual, Hugh Emerson said, 'Any more?'

Oh, he sounded so lovely, so charming, so… *nice*.

'If you're sure,' Millie said playfully.

'Fire away.'

'Okay. The actor who played Tonto in *The Lone Ranger*… ooh, actually I think I *do* know this one…'

'Jay Silverheels,' Hugh said promptly.

And with a hint of triumph.

'Yes!' Millie exclaimed, 'It *fits*. Well done. Golly, you must be ancient if you can remember *The Lone Ranger*.'

He laughed. 'Thanks a lot. Haven't you ever heard of reruns?'

'Oh, feeble excuse.'

'Actually, I'm twenty-eight.'

I know, thought Millie, her whole body zinging and tingling, I know exactly how old you are. I even know your date of birth.

'Oh well, if it's reruns we're talking about, I was more of a *Munsters* girl myself.'

'And I bet you wished you could have long black hair like Lily Munster.'

'I did! I did!' shrieked Millie, beside herself with amazement and delight. 'I used to spend *hours* practising her glidey walk and plastering my mouth with red felt-tip pen because my mum wouldn't let me borrow her lipstick.'

'Bet you can't remember the theme tune.'

'Ha, but I can,' Millie retorted happily. 'I love that music, it's practically engraved on my heart!'

'How's the sickness by the way?' said Hugh, before she had a chance to draw breath and launch herself with gusto into the theme tune.

'Sickness? Let me tell you, there's absolutely nothing wrong with being a *Munsters* fan! Now being a fan of *Star Trek*, I agree, *is* a bit weird—'

'I meant morning sickness.'

Millie frowned. Was this *a Munster joke* she'd failed to get? For a couple of seconds she was stuck for a reply.

'Are you not suffering from it?' Hugh Emerson inquired. 'I thought most pregnancies involved some degree of morning sickness.' He paused, allowing the significance of what he was saying to sink in.

Millie, certainly feeling sick now, stammered, 'I d-don't… I d-don't…'

His tone cool, he went on, 'You are the girl who rang the other week, aren't you? To tell me you're expecting my child?'

That was the trouble with holes in the ground: they were never around when you most needed them.

Bugger, just when she'd been enjoying herself too.

Deep, deep, *very* deep breath.

'I'm sorry, I'm more sorry than I can say. That's why I was ringing you, I promise, to let you know how awful I still felt.' Millie just blurted the words out, any-old-how. 'I wanted to write but I didn't keep your address, and then this morning our phone bill arrived and there was your number and I felt as if I'd been given a second chance... but I couldn't bear to tell you who I was straight away, in case you yelled at me and slammed the phone down, and I was just so desperate to hear you sounding normal instead of like a bucket of ice cubes. I *was* going to confess,' she concluded her breathless tumble of apology, 'I swear I was, but then we started talking and you were being so lovely... I was just having *such* a nice time, I kept putting it off and off.'

'There never was any crossword.' Hugh Emerson spoke without emotion.

Millie heaved a sigh. 'No.'

There was a lot to be said for embroidering the truth—gosh, in the past she'd been known to embroider whole tablecloths—but now she felt she owed it to him to be honest.

'Akira Kurosawa,' he said in disbelief. 'How did you know that?'

'It's my dad's favorite film,' Millie confessed. 'I bought him the video last Christmas.'

'And the truly abysmal Scottish-Welsh-Irish accent. Where did you get *that* from?'

'I'm sorry.' Millie sagged back against the sofa cushions in defeat. 'Accents have never really been my thing.'

'I should say not. You sounded like Russ Abbot.'

Honestly, it was like auditioning for a starring role on Broadway. Did he have to be *quite* so critical?

'I was aiming for Billy Connolly,' said Millie.

Hugh Emerson, now sounding exactly like a bored casting director, replied, 'Allow me to let you in on a little secret. Scottish people do not begin every second sentence with the word Och.'

'Right.' Millie was humble. 'Sorry.'

'So you keep saying.'

'But I *am*. I told you, I rang to apologize.'

'To clear your conscience, you mean,' Hugh Emerson drawled.

He certainly wasn't making things any easier. Determined not to shout something petulant and slam the phone down, Millie was nevertheless glad he was two hundred-odd miles away in London.

'To clear my conscience? Okay, yes, that too.' She heard her own tone of voice switch gear, from grovely to curt. 'So accidentally making a faux pas has never happened to you, is that what you're telling me? You're a stranger to embarrassment. You've spent your whole life doing and saying *exactly* the right thing.'

Curt with a hint of accusation.

'Absolutely,' Hugh Emerson replied.

'Oh well, in that case, congratulations. You are *officially* the luckiest man alive.'

The millisecond the words were out of Millie's mouth she regretted them. If her tongue had been long and curly enough, like an anteater's tongue, she would have flicked it out, scooped the words back in, and swallowed them.

Because he wasn't the luckiest man alive, was he? His wife was dead.

So much for her puny attempt at sarcasm. Now he could really lay into her.

Not daring to breathe, Millie braced herself for the blistering riposte.

'Except, actually, now you come to mention it...' Hugh Emerson sounded thoughtful. 'There was the time I said to a girl, "You've been eating biscuits, brush those crumbs off your face." And she said, "They're not crumbs, they're warts."'

'No!' Millie let out a shriek of delight. 'You didn't do that! I don't *believe* it.'

'True,' he admitted.

'But you apologized to her.'

'Well, I tried,' said Hugh. 'But I don't know if she heard.'

'Why ever not?'

'My six friends were making a bit of a racket, banging the table and yelling, "Nice one, Hugh," and roaring with laughter.'

Millie laughed too, elated that she wasn't, after all, about to be slaughtered. He had let her off the hook, and the relief was monumental. In fact, he was in definite danger of sounding almost human again.

'By the way, thanks for posting my wallet back to me,' said Hugh. 'Out of interest, where did you find it?'

'Here in Newquay. Under a hedge in Furness Lane.' Because he was a tourist, Millie added, 'It's one of the roads leading away from the seafront.'

'I was carrying my jacket.' He sounded rueful. 'It must have dropped out of the inside pocket.'

'You men, I don't know how you cope without handbags, I really don't.'

During the pause that followed, Millie wondered if she'd put her foot in it again. As the silence lengthened she envisaged—with mounting horror—the cringe-making possibilities. Maybe his wife had died tragically as a result of getting her handbag strap accidentally twisted around her neck?

Maybe she'd been dancing round her handbag when she'd tripped over the strap, lost her balance, clunked her head on the edge of a table, had a brain hemorrhage, and died?

Or maybe she'd been attacked by a mugger who'd tried to snatch her handbag, and when she'd hung on to it, he'd pushed her under the wheels of a passing bus?

Heavens, there were any number of ways a handbag could kill you, it was practically a deadly weapon.

James Bond, Millie decided, could do a lot worse than give up his Walther PPK and start carrying a handbag instead.

But when Hugh finally spoke, there was no mention of handbags. Nor were there any signs that she had committed yet another hideous faux pas.

'Okay, listen, say no if you don't want to, but I'd like to buy you a drink.' He paused. 'To thank you for returning my wallet.'

'Blimey, that *is* mad.' Millie shook her head. 'All the way from London to Cornwall for a drink with a total stranger.'

'I lost that wallet two months ago. I don't live in London any more.' Sounding amused, he explained, 'The post office is forwarding my mail.'

Oh. *Oh.*

'Oh,' said Millie, startled. 'So where are you now?'

'Just outside Padstow. I've bought a house not far from Constantine Bay.'

Oh my giddy aunt, not far from Newquay either.

I've got a date, thought Millie, putting the phone down shortly afterwards in something of a daze. I've been and gone and got myself a date with a complete stranger. I've never met him, but the sound of his voice does weird things to my insides and his laugh makes my toes tingle.

Does that *count* as a real date?

The phone rang again five minutes later, while Millie was in the kitchen shaking chilli sauce over a bowl of Kettle Chips.

'Look, it's me again.' Hugh Emerson had evidently phoned 1471. 'I forgot to ask if you're married or single.'

Gulp.

'Oh.' Millie shivered with pleasure, licked chilli sauce from her fingers—wow, *hot*—and said, 'Well, actually, single.'

Shame about the promise she'd made to Hester, but never mind. What a mad idea that had been anyway.

'Boyfriend?'

'Nope, no boyfriend,' Millie said gaily. 'Nobody. Absolutely no one at all!'

'Right. Well, I just wanted to make myself clear. This isn't a date, okay? I'm buying you a drink, to thank you for returning my wallet. A drink, that's all.'

'Um…' Millie's heart sank. '… okay.'

'It's not a date. You do understand that, don't you? Not *a date* date.'

'Not a date. Fine, absolutely, couldn't agree with you more.' Millie's heart had by this time reached her boots—well, it would have done if she'd been wearing any. And her toes weren't curling up anymore, either. They were lying there, looking sad and dejected on the kitchen floor.

'Dating isn't on the agenda,' Hugh explained kindly. And fairly unnecessarily, under the circumstances. 'Since my wife. I just needed to make sure you understood. I don't… *do* dates.'

A little voice in Millie's head—Hester's voice, actually—whispered triumphantly, 'Ha ha, serves you right, ha ha haHAHA.'

'Don't worry,' Millie declared with as much cheerful sincerity as she could muster. 'I mean, I agree with you. Absolutely. Neither do I.'

Chapter 10

'WELL, WELL, MILLIE BRADY, come here and let me take a proper look at you.' Lucas Kemp held out his arms, greeted Millie with a kiss on each cheek, and gave her a long, leisurely once-over. Grinning broadly, he said, 'Gorgeous, gorgeous. You haven't changed a bit.'

'Neither have you.' Millie was smiling too; she'd forgotten what an incorrigible flirt he was. Well, not forgotten that he was a flirt—that would be like forgetting that bananas were yellow—it was the sheer *extent* of it that had faded from her mind over the years.

Lucas Kemp would chat up a kitchen table, so long as it was a female table. He was relentless.

Actually, Millie had to admit that Lucas was still looking pretty good himself. Especially considering the life he'd probably led. When he'd left Cornwall six years ago to seek DJ stardom in London, his hair had been shoulder-length, his sideburns long and pointy, and he'd cultivated that young Rod Stewart style of dressing that was so easy to mock. Particularly in Newquay.

Now his hair was shorter, the sideburns still there but less pointy, his hawk-like nose as big as ever. He was wearing a plain black sweater with the sleeves pushed up and black trousers. And no socks. No shoes either. All the better for stripping off in ten seconds flat and leaping into bed with his next conquest, thought Millie, stifling amusement.

Anyway, this was Lucas Kemp's office, on the ground floor of his home, and he could wear whatever he liked.

Well, preferably not a jockstrap and wellies.

'Right, down to business.' Lucas perched on the edge of his desk and gestured Millie towards the leather chair. 'So you think you could handle this kind of work?'

'I need a job, it sounds like fun, I can roller-skate, and I don't mind making an idiot of myself. What more can I tell you?'

'Perfect,' said Lucas cheerfully. 'How about stripping?'

Eek.

'Sorry,' Millie was firm. 'I don't mind dressing *up* in daft outfits, but there's no way I'm getting my kit off.'

'Shame. Stretch marks?'

'No! Bloody cheek!' Millie exclaimed before realizing he was teasing her.

'Plus,' Lucas was grinning again, 'you'll be needing a sense of humor.'

He spent the next thirty minutes listening to her sing, watching her dance, going over exactly what the job entailed, and explaining how the business was run.

Finally he said, 'Well, that's about it. Welcome to Kemp's.'

'You mean I'm in?' Millie was astonished. 'I've passed the test? You really want me?'

Oops, wrong thing to say. Lucas's green eyes crinkled at the comers in the knowing way she remembered so well. Not that he'd ever singled her out for such treatment; it was just how Lucas was. He did it to everyone. Kitchen tables included.

'I really want you.' The words were accompanied by a playful lift of his eyebrows. Holding out his hands, he went on, 'Hey, who wouldn't? With that figure and those eyes, not to mention the hair.' Lucas shook his head, apparently lost in admiration. 'You know what you've always reminded me of? The fairy on top of the Christmas tree.'

'Great, thanks a lot,' Millie groaned. When you'd spent your life longing to be Lily Munster, this wasn't a compliment.

'And how's the rest of it going? Married? Single? Steady bloke?'

Last night, Hugh Emerson had asked her the same question.

'Lesbian,' said Millie.

But of course this didn't put Lucas off, his eyes actually lit up.

'*Fabulous.*'

'Not really,' Millie said hastily before he started formulating plans for an all-singing, all-fondling kd langogram. 'And no, I'm not involved with anyone at the moment. Giving myself a break from men.' He was still smirking. 'Lucas, it was a poor joke, I'm really not interested in women. How about you?'

'Me? Oh, I'm definitely interested in women.'

'Enough to marry one?'

He looked appalled.

'No thanks.'

'Girlfriend?'

'Well, you know… I keep myself busy.'

Same old Lucas, thought Millie with a smile. That meant he had half a dozen on the go, girls he saw every now and again when it suited him and doubtless treated appallingly, just as he always had in the old days.

As if on cue, as he was showing her out of the house, Lucas said, 'How's Hester, by the way? Did you two keep in touch?'

'Oh yes.'

He looked pleased. 'That's great. What's she doing these days?'

Talking about you, mostly. That is, when she isn't racing hell for leather around Newquay trying to accidentally bump into you.

Aloud, Millie said, 'She's in the jewelry business.' Well, it sounded a bit more impressive than telling him Hester sold quirky earrings on a stall in Newquay market.

'Really? So where's she living now?'

Here goes.

'With me.' Millie turned and gave him an extra-stern look. 'And no, before you even think it, she isn't a lesbian either.'

Lucas laughed.

'Dear old Hester, she was always a good sort.'

Oh dear, thought Millie, that wasn't very promising. Hester was hardly likely to be flattered. Old *and* a good sort; it was an outrageous slur on her character.

Realizing that he was still talking, Millie said, 'Sorry, what was that?'

Lucas repeated casually, 'And is she still single as well?'

It was like a Pavlovian response, Millie decided, he simply couldn't resist asking the question. Some men could never have too many strings to their bow.

'Gosh no, Hester's got the most gorgeous boyfriend,' she told Lucas with enthusiasm. 'He's wonderful, they're the perfect couple, Hester's blissfully happy with him. Really, love's young dream.'

Millie wondered if maybe she'd overdone the praise, gushed a bit too much. Lucas was a thrill-of-the-chase man through and through... the thought that Hester might be happier with someone else than she had been with him could pique his interest.

The words bull and red rag sprang to mind. Oh Lord, he might regard it as an irresistible challenge.

But all Lucas did was shake his head and smile carelessly as he pulled open the front door.

'Dear old Hester. That's great news. I'm happy for her. Okay then, I'll see you at midday tomorrow and introduce you to the rest of the crew—damn, sorry.'

He answered his mobile as they made their way over to Millie's mud-splashed lime green Mini. She listened to Lucas charm and cajole someone called Darling into forgiving him for standing her up last night. As he did so, he winked at Millie and mimed good-natured despair.

When the phone was safely switched off she said, 'You haven't changed at all.'

'Actually, I have.' Lucas gave her shoulder a reassuring squeeze. 'I've got better.'

Millie looked skeptical.

'At what?'

'Sweetheart,' he lifted a playful eyebrow, 'trust me, everything you can possibly imagine.'

'Well?' demanded Hester, dragging her in through the front door so hard that Millie almost ricocheted off the wall. 'Was he fat? Was he bald? Did he ask about me?'

'All his own hair and teeth. And no, he isn't fat. And yes, he asked about you.'

Hester let out a whoop of joy.

'And what did you say?'

'I told him you were seriously involved with the loveliest man in the world.'

'Oh God no, you didn't! What did you have to say *that* for?'

'Because it's true. You are.'

Hester mulled this over for a couple of seconds. Finally she said, 'Maybe it'll make him jealous. Wonder what he could be missing.'

'Anyway, I got the job, thanks *very* much for asking,' said Millie. 'I'm glad you're so interested.'

'Really? Brilliant. Maybe I could do it too.' Hester perked up at the prospect of working for Lucas.

'Except you can't sing,' Millie reminded her. 'You have to be able to sing.'

'Bugger. Are you sure?' Hester looked hopeful. 'Couldn't I just whip my top off instead?'

❖❖❖

Orla Hart stood in the conservatory of her spectacular new home with its dazzling sea view and watched Giles, her beloved husband of over sixteen years, climb out of his car and wave up at her.

Oh Giles, are you doing it again? Are you?

Are you being unfaithful to me?

Orla pushed her long auburn hair back from her forehead, smiled, and waved back. A loving faithful husband, that was all she wanted. It wasn't too much to ask, surely? Giles had a marvelous life, they lived well—*very* well—and he was free to play as much golf as he liked.

So why did he have to go and spoil it all by getting himself involved in these ridiculous, meaningless relationships?

Thinking about it caused an almost physical ache in Orla's chest. She hated, absolutely *hated* having to be suspicious, always on the lookout for clues. It wasn't only depressing, it was exhausting too. She was exhausted now, for heaven's sake, and this was midday.

Still, at least today she had something else lined up to take her mind off Giles and whatever he might be up to behind her back.

Not quite yet though.

'Hi, darling! Did you get what you wanted?' Orla greeted him brightly as he reached the conservatory. Although this was something of a rhetorical question, since Giles always got what he wanted.

'Newspaper.' He waggled a copy of *The Times* at her, then held up a dark blue Fogarty & Phelps carrier. 'Truffle oil and Serrano ham from the deli. Box of cigars. Oh, and a couple more bottles of that tawny port.'

So, ten minutes' worth of shopping and he'd been out of the house for an hour and a half.

Orla's stomach was in knots. She didn't want to think like this. Oh God, why did her whole life have to be riddled with doubt?

As if reading her mind, Giles added carelessly, 'Plus a few other odds and sods. And the traffic was diabolical, of course. Whole town's crawling with bloody tourists.'

Well this much was definitely true. It *was*. Hating herself for doing it, Orla went over to Giles and gave him a welcome-home hug. As she did so she inhaled slowly, her senses on red alert for the faintest trace of perfume.

Any perfume, but particularly L'Heure Bleu.

But there wasn't, there wasn't, oh the relief! Hating herself this time for having doubted him, Orla blurted out, 'Do you know how much I love you?'

It would have been nice, at this point, if Giles could have responded in a romantic manner. But that was men for you, they never seemed to realize the importance of romance. Instead, Giles absent-mindedly patted her elbow and said, 'I'm starving… good grief, what is *that*?'

He was peering over her shoulder. Swiveling round, Orla saw that his attention had been caught by a geriatric, lime green Mini, a dust cloud billowing in its wake as it zoomed up the drive.

'Watch out, the hippies are in town.' Giles chuckled at the incongruity of the scene as the Mini screeched to a halt next to his gleaming white BMW. 'What's this all about, then? Want me to send them packing?'

'It's Millie,' said Orla, 'the girl I told you about.'

Well, half told him about. She hadn't mentioned the circumstances of their first meeting on the edge of the wind-ruffled cliff top at Tresanter Point.

'Oh. Her.' Giles's hand slid from the crook of her elbow. 'I can't imagine how you think this is going to work. It's a ridiculous idea.'

'Maybe. I'm still going to do it though.'

Famed for her cheerful, easygoing nature, Orla seldom put her foot down. But when she did she was unshakeable. Nicely, she said, 'Will you be joining us for lunch?'

Giles looked as if she'd just asked him to eat his own underpants.

'Why would I want to do that?'

'Millie's lovely. She's great fun. You'd like her.'

Orla didn't get her hopes up.

'Ha, and she could end up costing you millions. No thanks.' Giles mimed a shudder of horror. 'I'll sit this one out, if it's all the same to you. Spend the afternoon at the club.'

Chapter 11

If this was how best-selling authors lived, thought Millie, no wonder it hadn't occurred to Orla Hart that there were some people who couldn't afford the luxury of a back garden.

The house was incredible, vast, and hugely glamorous, and painted such a dazzling shade of white that it reminded Millie of Hollywood teeth. Ultra-brite white with a hint of *Baywatch*. But for all its modern angles, polished beechwood flooring, and endless sets of white-framed French windows, it wasn't unwelcoming. Orla had filled the cool, airy rooms with flowers, bright cushions, and an eclectic assortment of paintings and prints. The lighting was imaginative, the sofas inviting, and the views—it went without saying—terrific.

'And this is my study.' Having given her the guided tour, Orla now threw open the last door along the landing. 'Where I write.'

Millie still had no idea why Orla had invited her here today, but she was certainly enjoying herself. Lunch, Orla had said, and a kind of proposition. Since she knew Orla was feeling guilty about helping her to lose her job, Millie guessed she was about to be offered some form of part-time work—typing or filing, maybe—to make up for it.

The study was entirely functional, with a state-of-the-art computer installed in one corner. Filing cabinets lined one wall, bookshelves another. The blinds were drawn, shielding Orla from the temptation of gazing idly out at the view. The revolving chair in front of the PC was old and tatty, and looked deeply uncomfortable.

'I know,' said Orla. 'It's the lucky chair. Six pounds fifty, twelve years ago, and after half an hour sitting on it, your backside's gone numb. But it's my favorite chair for writing on.'

The bookshelves were stuffed with copies of Orla's novels; hardbacks, paperbacks, trade paperbacks, and foreign-language editions, hundreds of the things in every size and color.

'And this is how you plan out your work?' Millie peered up at the series of charts pinned around the walls. Every chart was covered in a mish-mash of names, arrows, and biographical details, and a different colored felt pen had been used for each of the characters. Beneath these descriptions, chapter headings were listed and cross-referenced, enabling the various plot lines to be meticulously followed and worked out.

'God!' Millie exclaimed. 'I had no idea. This is like a military campaign.'

She'd naively imagined that writers just sat down and wrote whatever came into their heads.

'I know, I know. That's exactly what it's like.' Orla heaved a sigh, 'Rigid, regimented, all planned out from the first paragraph, right the way through to the bitter end.'

Millie was still busy marveling at the fine detail.

'And there was me thinking you just made it up as you went along.'

'Good heavens. Be spontaneous, you mean?' Orla smiled slightly and lit a cigarette. 'Sit down each morning wondering what might happen next? Not having *the faintest idea* how the story might turn out?'

There was an unfamiliar edge to her voice. Thinking she must have offended Orla, Millie flapped her hands and said hurriedly, 'Look, I'm sorry, I'm a complete idiot and I don't know the first thing about writing a novel! Of *course* you have to plan it out—'

'But the thing is,' Orla cut in, 'I don't.'

There it was again, that edge. Millie looked at her, confused. She'd completely lost track of this argument.

'It's what I do,' Orla went on, 'because it's what I've always done. But it's not actually compulsory.'

'Oh. Right.' Millie nodded apologetically. She was beginning to wish she'd stayed at home and practiced her juggling.

'Look, sit down.' Abruptly pulling a sheet of paper from her desk drawer, Orla directed Millie on to the uncomfortable swivel chair. 'And take a look at this. Then maybe you'll understand.'

She stood in front of the window, smoking furiously and tugging at the cuff of her lilac, Bohemian-style shirt.

As Millie began to read the photocopied review of Orla's last novel, she shuddered in sympathy. The reviewer had stormed in with all guns blazing, criticizing the style and content of the book, and gleefully poking fun at the characters. The newspaper review was headlined, ORLA LOSES THE PLOT, and went dramatically downhill from that point. No critical stone was left unturned, and the agony didn't end there. Cruel references were made to Orla's personal life. She was selling out, writing on autopilot, churning out rubbish that was an insult to her fans purely for the money and probably in order to shore up her marriage.

'This,' the review scathingly concluded, 'is the very worst book I have ever read. But at least I was paid to read it. Unless anyone you know is prepared to pay you, I suggest you do yourself a huge favor and leave Orla Hart's latest apology for a novel firmly up there on the shelf.'

'My God,' Millie gasped, staring at Orla. 'That is so *mean*.'

'One way of putting it.' Orla's tone was casual but there were tears glistening in her eyes. Vigorously she stubbed out her cigarette.

'Do you know this man?' According to the byline, the reviewer was one Christie Carson. The accompanying photograph was of a bearded, thin-faced, sardonic-looking male in his fifties. 'I've never even heard of Christie Carson.' Outraged, she said, 'And he's so *ugly.*'

'The hairy weasel.' Orla was fiddling frantically with her cigarette packet, clearly desperate for her next fix. 'No, I've never met him. But I like to think he smells like a weasel too. Nasty, spiteful, jealous little man. He's one of the new Irish writers,' she explained, because Millie was still mystified. 'Forever banging on about literature and integrity and truth.' Her lip curled in disdain. 'Oh, he's a right smug intellectual, always being nominated for some award or another, but he doesn't make as much money as I do. They try and pretend they don't care but they're actually eaten up with envy.'

'But that's exactly why you mustn't let this upset you.' Millie rattled the photocopied sheet of A4 at her. 'Don't give him the satisfaction. Just ignore it!'

'And count my money,' Orla suggested dryly. She raked her fingers through her hair. 'Easy to say, not so easy to do. The next time you're ripped to shreds by a vindictive stranger in a national newspaper, why don't you ring me up and tell me how easy it is to ignore. Sorry,' she waggled her diamond-encrusted fingers in apology, 'but you have no idea how much it hurts. I worked bloody hard to write an entertaining book and this is what I get in return, some beastly little man telling me my plots are unbelievable, my characters far-fetched, and my writing style about six rungs lower on the ladder than Jackie Collins's.'

Trying to help, Millie said, 'But you must get nice letters as well, from people who've enjoyed your books.'

'I get *loads* of nice letters.' Orla's voice began to rise. 'But they don't *count.* It's nasty stuff like this that counts… *this* is what keeps me awake at night—'

'That proposition you said you had for me.' Millie intercepted her in mid-rant. 'Would it by any chance have something to do with this Christie Carson?'

'Funny you should mention it,' said Orla, puffing away on her next cigarette. 'Yes.'

'Do you want me to write rude letters to him? Gun him down in the street? Wait until he's gone away for a few days and post prawns through his letterbox?'

The faintest of smiles flickered across Orla's face.

'I wouldn't waste prawns on a man like that. Maybe rotten fish heads.'

Alarmed, Millie said, 'It was meant to be a joke.'

'You don't have to murder him.' Orla held open the study door. 'Come on, let's go downstairs. We'll talk about it over lunch.'

'Promise me I don't have to seduce him,' said Millie.

They ate poached salmon, baby new potatoes, and a roasted red-pepper salad.

'So you see?' asked Orla when she had finished outlining her plan. 'All you'd have to do is be yourself.'

'I don't get it.' If she did, Millie thought it was the weirdest idea ever. 'You want your next book to be the story of all the things that happen to me in the next... how long? Six weeks? Six months? Year?'

'No time limit. Just as long as it takes before we reach some kind of happy ending.'

Mad. Seriously mad.

'So that would make it like my autobiography?'

'Biography,' Orla corrected her. 'And no, I'd be writing a novel. The whole thing would be fictionalized. But I'd be paying you to provide the plot.'

'What if I can't?' Millie started to laugh, because the prospect was so ridiculous. 'I mean, it is quite likely, you know. I've no boyfriend, I've sworn to steer clear of men for the rest of the summer, and I have about as much social life as your average Pot Noodle. I hate to say this, but your novel wouldn't be exactly action-packed.'

Orla wasn't laughing. She shrugged and jutted out her lower lip.

'Maybe not, but at least no one would be able to call it fanciful and far-fetched and ridiculously over the top.'

Millie blinked.

'You're prepared to do all this because of one bad review.'

'Actually, I'm doing it for all sorts of reasons. First of all, I think you'd be great material,' said Orla. She held her glass of Frascati up to the light, admiring the way the sun glinted off it. 'Think how we met, for a start. Then there's your gorgeous wallet story… and losing your job… and getting another job working for the handsome guy your best friend has a mad crush on—'

'Okay, okay,' Millie said hurriedly. She wouldn't have called her wallet story gorgeous.

'Secondly, I'd be getting out of the planning rut. I wouldn't know what was going to happen next, simply because it won't *have happened* yet! So no need to agonize over the plot,' Orla said joyfully. 'And you have no idea how great that would feel. I'd be free!'

Orla was right; Millie had absolutely no idea how great that would feel—the last piece of fiction she'd written had begun, 'Dear Great Aunt Edna, Thank you so much for the lovely pair of shorts you knitted me…'

'Go on,' she urged Orla. 'What else?'

Orla flew into the sitting room, returning moments later with a copy of her latest paperback. Holding it face-out, so Millie could see the instantly recognizable cover, she said, 'See this? It's an Orla Hart blockbuster. Actually, it's the thirteenth Orla Hart blockbuster, and so far we've sold one and a half million copies. Which is fantastic, of course, for both me and my publishers. Because as far as they're concerned, I'm their star battery chicken. Every year they take it for granted that I'll just churn out another book.'

'Egg,' said Millie.

'Golden egg,' Orla corrected her with a faint smile. 'In fact, a jewel-encrusted, solid-gold Fabergé egg the size of a sofa. Which is why, when I wanted to change my writing style a couple of years ago, they wouldn't let me. They sweet-talked me out of it, in case I dented their precious profits. But this time I'm going to do it, I'm going to ditch the bonkbuster trappings, the clichés, the whole Orla Hart format. I'm going to write a proper *literary* novel, just to prove to all those bloody sneering critics out there that I can!' As she spoke, she jabbed viciously at the review she had brought downstairs with her. 'And sod anyone who cares more about the money than they care about me.' She paused, then added calmly, 'And that goes for Giles too.'

Blimey.

Millie nodded, impressed. Orla was using the opportunity to punish Giles for having had an affair. Maybe it was also her way of testing him. If this change of direction were to fail, Orla wanted to know if he would continue to support her.

For richer, for poorer, in sickness, and in health.

'You'd have to change all the names,' Millie warned.

'Darling, I know that. I thought we might call you Gertrude.'

'Still seems a bit drastic.' Millie gazed reflectively at the unattractive photograph of Christie Carson above his byline. 'Couldn't you just phone him up, shout "Wanker!" and tell him he's got a nose like a Jerusalem artichoke?'

He didn't, but Millie never let the facts get in the way of a good insult.

'Nose? Ha, willy more like. And don't think I haven't been tempted.' Orla poured them both some more wine before settling back in her white rattan chair. 'I hate that man, I really hate him for writing all that horrible stuff about me.' She paused, then fixed Millie with a look of weary resignation. 'But what I hate more is having to admit to myself that in some ways he's right.'

Before Millie left two hours later, Orla scribbled out a check for five thousand pounds and stuffed it into her hand.

Oh my giddy aunt. Five thousand *pounds*.

'Really, you don't have to,' Millie protested, not meaning it for a second. How awful if Orla said, 'No? All right then, I'll have it back.'

Happily she didn't.

'Rubbish.' Orla was brisk. 'This is a business arrangement. It's only fair.'

It was, Millie decided happily. It *was* fair. Except…

'I'm a bit embarrassed. What if you end up with a book where the girl spends her whole life watching *EastEnders*, shaving her legs, and trying to eat chocolate without getting it on her clothes?'

Despite years of practice, she'd never mastered the art of biting a Cadbury's Flake without crumbly bits falling down her front.

'Exciting things will happen,' Orla said soothingly. 'And if they don't, we'll jolly well *make* them happen.'

'Gosh.'

'All you have to do is report back to me once a week.'

There was no denying it; this was easy money. Easy peasy.

'And tell you everything?' asked Millie.

'Everything.'

'Do I have to be called Gertrude?'

Orla patted her arm.

'Darling, we can call you anything you like.'

'Oh well, in that case,' Millie brightened, 'could you also make me look like Lily Munster?'

Chapter 12

It was weird, getting ready for a date-that-definitely-wasn't-a-date. Millie felt it was only polite to have a bath before meeting Hugh Emerson. But she didn't dare dress up, in case he thought she was trying to impress him. He was a widower, a recent widower, and the very last thing he was interested in was getting hit on by some eager female desperate for a boyfriend.

Not that she was eager or a desperate Doris, but since they'd never met, Hugh wasn't to know that.

Damn, thought Millie, pulling a face at her reflection in the wardrobe mirror, this would all be so much easier if only I hadn't seen that photo of him in his wallet.

Or if I'd seen the photo and he'd been ugly.

Except then, of course, she might not have been seized with that shameful urge to ring his number and speak to him again.

His wife just died, his wife just died. Millie forced herself to run this cheery mantra through her brain as she pulled on a pair of white jeans, beige espadrilles, and a khaki tank top. Ha, see, *that's* how much I'm not bothered about making a good impression. Dragging a brush through her white-blonde hair, she hoped he wouldn't assume it was dyed. Oops, and whatever happened, she mustn't *mention* that word, the dreaded d-word.

Not much make-up. Just a bit of mascara.

Okay, and a quick once-over with the translucent powder.

Um, and some lipstick of course. Couldn't go without lipstick. Only pale pink, though, nothing mind-boggling.

Sod it. May as well slap some eye shadow on too.

Well, thought Millie, it was all very well not wanting to look like a desperate Doris, but then again it wouldn't do to have him thinking you were a complete dog.

She spotted him the moment she arrived at Morton's, one of the popular bars just off the seafront. Pretending she hadn't, Millie glanced around in distracted, will-someone-please-help-me? fashion and waited for Hugh Emerson to approach her.

It took him less than thirty seconds to do so. Which impressed Millie to no end.

As did Hugh himself. Gosh, he was even better looking than his photo.

'Is it you?' As he spoke, the corners of his mouth twitched with amusement.

'Och, well, maybe it is, and maybe it isn't,' Millie responded with a playful smile. 'But if it's a drink you're offairing, I'd love a pint of porridge. Shaken, not stirrrred.'

'Been practicing the accent, I see.' He nodded gravely. 'Excellent. They'll be signing you up as the new James Bond any day now.'

Millie beamed up at him.

'Fantastic, I've always wanted a license to kill, especially those teenage boys who try and run you off the street with their skateboards, or little old ladies who bash you from behind with their wheelie-shoppers, ooh, and people who stick their chewing gum under tables, they *really* deserve to die… um, hi, I'm Millie, sorry, bit nervous, can't think why, I mean it's not as if this is a date or anything.'

How could I? How *could* I have said the d-word, the one word I swore I wouldn't say? Mortified by her lapse into auto-babble, Millie prayed he hadn't noticed. Heavens, and what if his dead wife *had* been one of those people who parked their chewing gum under tables? Or went around bashing people's ankles with her wheelie-shopper?

In a fluster, Millie said, 'Look, I don't want you to think I'm a complete alcoholic or anything, but why don't we order that drink?'

Which of course meant he immediately would think she was a complete alcoholic. Not to mention a twit. Oh yes, wonderful, this was getting off to a flying start.

Bugger, why couldn't he have been ugly? Some men were just born inconsiderate.

'They don't serve porridge,' Hugh announced.

'No? Oh well,' said Millie, 'in that case I'll have a G and T instead.'

Sitting down, she watched Hugh Emerson ordering their drinks at the bar. He was pretty tall, six foot one or two. He also worked out, if the athletic look of his body was anything to go by… unless of course he'd been a big old tub of lard before, until grief had robbed him of the will to eat…

Oh stop it, stop thinking like this, for crying out loud. She'd seen the photograph of him and his wife, hadn't she? Of course he hadn't been fat.

But it was no good, Millie couldn't help herself. She'd never met a young widower before, couldn't begin to imagine the horror of what he must have been through.

Gosh, he had such a nice nose, practically the straightest nose she'd ever seen. And an excellent jawline. And fabulously long-lashed eyes the color of treacle toffee, and dark blond hair that curled over the collar of his blue and white hooped rugby shirt—

'Here you go, gin and tonic, loads of ice, slice of lemon.'

Millie seized it thankfully and took a sip. Bleeugh. That was the great thing about ordering a drink you weren't actually wild about; it meant you took your time over it and didn't get legless in twenty minutes flat. Besides, in these days of alcopops and blow-your-head-off designer cider, it was nice to be different. Gin and tonic always made her feel so Lauren Bacall.

'Here we are then, you've done your duty,' Millie said brightly. 'Bought me a drink as a thank you for returning your wallet. If you like, you can go now.'

Hugh smiled and leaned forward, resting his elbows on his knees. Jolly nice knees, she couldn't help noticing. Jolly nice elbows, come to that.

'I was intrigued, I admit.' His tone was good-natured. 'Two mad phone calls. How could I not meet you, put a face to the voice?'

'And?' Millie gave him a sympathetic look. 'Are you shocked? Did it never occur to you that I might be as ugly as this?'

'Don't worry, I braced myself,' said Hugh. 'I was prepared for the worst.'

'That's really kind. If you'd taken one look at me, turned green, and made a dive for the door, well, I'd have *died*—'

Oh God, oh God, I can't believe I *did it again*!

Millie buried her face in her hands, took a couple of deep breaths, then forced herself to look up again at Hugh Emerson.

'I'm sorry. Okay? I'm so, soooo sorry about this. You know how it is when you're trying desperately hard not to mention something? And it keeps popping out *because* you're trying so hard not to say it? Well, that's what's happening to me this evening and I really, *totally* apologize but I just can't help it.'

She knew she was bright red; her face was actually pulsating with shame.

'Right.' Hugh shrugged. 'Fine. That's perfectly okay.' He paused, then said, 'But I don't have the faintest idea what you're talking about.'

Millie stared at him. He *must* know. Was this a joke? Was he simply being ultra-polite?

Unless... oh God... he'd been stringing her along all this

time, pretending his wife was dead when all along he'd never even been married.

'Dead. Dying. Death. Deadly,' Millie recited. 'Those kind of words are the kind I've been trying to avoid. Because of your wife.'

Your so-called wife, anyway.

'Oh, I *see*. I didn't realize. Look,' said Hugh, 'it's fine, don't worry about it.'

Or, thought Millie, you do have a wife and she's still alive and well, in which case you're a complete and utter bastard.

'How did she die?' The more Millie thought it through, the more likely it seemed that her suspicions were correct. Which made it, all of a sudden, incredibly easy to ask the questions she'd never thought she'd be able to ask.

'Horse-riding accident.'

'What was her name?'

'Louisa.' He paused. 'I've already told you that.'

I know, thought Millie. Just double-checking.

Aloud she said, 'When did it happen?'

'Last October.'

'What date?'

For a second, Hugh stared at her in disbelief. Then, slowly, he shook his head.

'You're going to check this out, aren't you?'

Embarrassed, Millie feigned innocence.

'I don't know what you mean. I was just interested—'

'You think I'm making it up, spinning you a line.'

It was no good. He knew. And he wasn't sounding thrilled.

Millie fiddled with her glass and said awkwardly, 'Well you could be. These things happen. And,' she added with a flash of spirit, 'you don't look like a widower.'

'Maybe not. Then again—modesty aside—I don't *need* to go for the sympathy vote. Plus,' he went on coolly, 'this isn't actually a date, is it? I'm not interested in persuading you to jump into bed with me. I promise you, sex is the last thing on my mind.'

How completely infuriating. And what a stupendous challenge! For a moment Millie experienced a wild—and thankfully fleeting—urge to hurl herself on to Hugh Emerson's lap, plunge her hand down the front of his jeans, and find out for herself if he was telling the truth.

Instead, mentally supergluing herself to her chair, she changed the subject.

'So what made you move from London down to Cornwall?'

'I didn't need to be there anymore. We always loved it down here. And I work from home,' Hugh shrugged, 'so there was nothing to stop me. Anyway, I was sick of the city. Living by the sea beats the hell out of London.'

'What line of work are you in?'

'Software development. Designing websites, advising other companies, showing them how to maximize their potential… I'm just a hired gun, really. Or a hired nerd.' He grinned, clearly able to say this because he knew he was about as un-nerdy as it was possible to get. 'But I'm pretty good at what I do. And it pays well. Plus, I get to surf in my spare time.'

Millie immediately pictured him in a black rubber wetsuit, his wet, sun-streaked blond hair flopping over his tanned forehead as he raced down Fistral Beach and launched himself into the sea…

'How about you?'

Hugh's voice wrenched her back to reality.

'Hmm? Me?'

For a moment there, she'd quite lost track of the conversation.

'Career? Job? Do you have one?'

Hang on, was he speaking extra-slowly? Being the teeniest bit patronizing… again? The little hairs rose along Millie's spine and she said stiffly, 'Of course. I'm a travel agent.'

'Really? That's great. Which agency?'

'Um. Fleetwood's, in Baron Street.'

'I know it.' Hugh looked delighted. 'I was in there yesterday—you must have been on your lunch break.'

Bugger.

Why, thought Millie, do I always have to get caught out?

'Actually, I don't work there any more.' She pulled an it's-delicate face. 'Spot of bother with the Fleetwoods—not my fault, of course, but I chose to leave. It seemed best.'

All she'd been trying to do was impress Hugh, convince him that actually she wasn't as dippy and hopeless as he clearly thought she was.

For a second it crossed Millie's mind that she *could* tell him she was the heroine of Orla Hart's next novel. That sounded a little bit impressive, didn't it? A touch more glamorous and Liz Hurleyish and intriguing?

Then again, it could cause problems. Hugh Emerson, Millie sensed, probably wouldn't be impressed. In fact, he was likely to find the idea that this very meeting could end up in Orla's next million-seller deeply off-putting. If not downright insulting, both to him and the memory of his wife.

Best not to mention it, Millie decided with relief. She didn't want to scare him off.

Or get sued.

'So what are you doing now?' said Hugh.

Oh. Oh dear, throat-clearing time. He definitely wasn't going to be impressed when he heard about her new job.

Not that it should matter *at all*, Millie reminded herself, but somehow it just did, it really did.

She shifted uncomfortably in her seat, like a beauty queen asked to recite the periodic table.

'I'm... well, it's only temporary, just until something else in the travel industry comes up, because of course that's my *real* thing...'

'So in the meantime,' Hugh prompted, 'your unreal thing is...?'

'Um—WHAAA!'

Millie shot out of her chair as a warm hand caressed the back of her neck, then—like lightning—slid south. Pirouetting round practically in mid-air, she saw Lucas Kemp laughing down at her.

'Lucas!'

'Hi, Millie. A little jumpy this evening, aren't we?'

'You snuck up on me! Gave me the fright of my life.'

That wasn't all he'd given her, Millie realized moments later. She was experiencing a whole new sense of freedom... oh, for heaven's sake, he'd only gone and unfastened her bra.

'Lucas.' She gave him a look. 'It's what boys do when they're fourteen years old.'

His grin broadened. 'Ah, but you have to admit I'm good at it.'

With a sinking heart Millie realized it was introduction time. She was going to have to explain to Hugh Emerson that this grinning, bra-unclipping, leather-trouser-wearing example of the male species was, in fact, her new boss.

Wasn't it absolutely typical, though, that while Hester was dolling herself up and racing around town doing her damnedest to bump into him, Millie was managing it even when she didn't want to.

Opening her mouth to make the embarrassing introduction—oh, Hugh was going to be *so* impressed—Millie was beaten to it once again by Lucas.

'By the way, I need you in the office by ten o'clock tomorrow to try on the monkey suit. We've had the head dry-cleaned but the zip needs fixing, and if you want any seams taken in we need to get it done before Friday.'

'Friday?'

'Your first booking,' Lucas announced. 'One of the surgeons at Newquay General. The theater staff booked it for his fortieth birthday—they loved the gorilla angle because apparently this guy used to work with the VSO in Uganda. Come to think of it, these surgeon-types are pretty nifty with a needle—maybe you could get him to alter your suit.'

Thanks, Lucas.

Thanks a lot.

Chapter 13

'HUGH, THIS IS LUCAS, my new boss,' Millie said flatly. 'He runs Kemp's, the kissogram agency. On Friday I'm going to be a gorilla—'

'A roller-skating gorilla,' Lucas put in. 'They were mad about the idea of doing it on roller skates.'

'They want me to roller-skate into the *theater*? Won't the patient mind his operation being interrupted?' Millie began to look alarmed. 'And will I be expected to wear a mask and juggle surgical instruments?'

'You need to practice the juggling a bit more,' Lucas said kindly. 'And you wouldn't be allowed into the theater. They want you to do it in the staff coffee room.'

'Right. And this is Hugh,' Millie concluded. 'A friend of mine.' Ha, highly likely after this little episode. 'Well, kind of a friend.'

She'd done her best to pretend her bra wasn't undone but now both straps were sliding down her arms. Heaving a sigh—honestly, how juvenile a trick had that been?—Millie flicked the straps over each elbow, whisked the scarlet bra out through her left sleeve-hole like a conjuror and dropped it into her bag, lying open on the floor.

Lucas and Hugh Emerson, who had just finished shaking hands, gave her a brief round of applause.

God, thought Millie, they're going to become friends, I just know it.

'Let me get you a drink,' Lucas offered, eyeing their empty glasses. 'What are you two having?'

Millie hesitated. So did Hugh. To her horror she realized that he wanted to leave; he'd bought her a gin and tonic, done his duty, and now he'd had enough. The prospect of spending another thirty minutes in the company of an off-duty roller-skating gorillagram was more than he could stand.

'Thanks, but we can't.' Millie jumped to her feet, sending beer coasters frisbeeing in all directions. 'We have to be somewhere—gosh, actually we're late already! Okay?' Tapping her watch at Hugh, she jerked her head in the direction of the door. 'Come on, we'd better get a move on, the others'll be wondering where we've got to.'

As soon as they were outside on the pavement, Millie stuck out her hand and shook Hugh's surprised one.

'Thanks for the drink. It was nice to meet you. Right, well, I'll be off.'

'Hang on.' Hugh looked puzzled. 'What about the others—won't they be wondering where we are?'

Millie experienced a flicker of disappointment; somehow she'd expected better of him.

'It was just an excuse. To get us out of there.' As she spoke, Millie realized the joke was on her. Hugh Emerson had been on the ball all along.

'You mean the others aren't waiting for us?' His dark eyes glittered with triumph at having caught her out. 'Damn, that's a real shame. And I was so looking forward to meeting them.'

'Ha ha.' Dutifully, Millie smiled. 'Well, early start tomorrow, I'd really better be off. Bye.'

She was moving away from him now, walking backwards up the hill…

'Millie, stop—'

'Ow!' Having ignored his plea, Millie promptly cannoned into the lamppost behind her. Clutching her left shoulder and trying to pretend it hardly hurt at all—ow, *ouch*—she wondered why her life had to so closely resemble Mr. Bean's. What she wouldn't give to be sleek and chic and in control at all times.

'All right?' Reaching her, Hugh looked concerned.

'Oh, marvelous. The bone's shattered, of course, but apart from that everything's fine.' The words came out through gritted teeth as waves of pain whooshed up and down her arm.

'Look,' said Hugh, 'have I said something to upset you?'

'No.'

'So why the sudden rush to get home? Couldn't we go for something to eat?'

Millie gazed up at him, so surprised she almost forgot about her shoulder.

'I thought you wanted to get away. You looked as if you were desperate to escape. The way you hesitated when Lucas offered us a drink.'

'You hesitated too. I was waiting for you to say something,' said Hugh. 'I thought, as he's your boss, you should be the one to decide.'

They gazed at each other. Millie smiled first.

'How stupid is this? Go on then, you've twisted my arm.'

'Your arm? You mean this one here, with the multiple fractures and bits of bone sticking out? I wouldn't dream of twisting it.' He raised a teasing eyebrow at her, then indicated the restaurant behind her, its red, green, and white awning lazily flapping in the breeze. 'Okay, food. This place is supposed to be pretty good, isn't it? Italian okay for you?'

Millie had a sudden yearning for fresh air. The last time she'd eaten at Bella Spaghetti she'd been with Neil and half a dozen of his rowdily drunk friends.

'Actually, what I'd really love,' she told Hugh, 'is a bag of chips.'

❖❖❖

They took the coastal path away from the center of Newquay, headed east, and bought takeaway chicken and chips before making their way down to Fistral Beach. It was a warm evening, the tide was out, and an apricot sun hung low over the violet-tinted sky. The surfers had given up for the day and the beach was almost deserted. Millie and Hugh ate their chicken and chips, walked for what felt like miles across the wet sand, and talked nonstop.

In any other circumstances, it would have been romantic.

'So what happened to you, then?' Hugh picked up a flat pebble and skimmed it across the surface of the water. 'On the phone, when I told you I didn't date, you said that was fine, neither did you.'

'Oh, nothing really.' Millie was embarrassed; it was like breaking a fingernail and being consoled by some bloke with one arm and no legs. 'I split up with someone a few weeks back and decided I could do without the hassle of men.' A seagull, squawking as it wheeled overhead, sounded as if it were mocking her. 'I've taken a vow of celibacy,' Millie explained, picking up a stick and hurling it at the seagull, who dodged it with ease. 'No sex for the rest of the summer. Actually, it's quite liberating.'

Hugh said dryly, 'I'm sure it is, when you have the choice.'

'But everyone has that choice.'

He looked at Millie.

'You could meet someone tomorrow and fancy them like mad, but it's your decision whether or not you sleep with them.'

Millie, who was confused, said carefully, 'Ye-es.'

Oh God, could he *tell*? Did he know she fancied him like mad?

'I'm just saying you're lucky, that's all.' Hugh shrugged and kicked a tangle of seaweed out of his path. 'To be able to feel that kind of attraction. And fall in love with them, if that's what you want to do. Because I can't imagine it ever happening to me again.' He paused, his dark eyes bleak. 'And I wouldn't even want it to.'

Millie didn't know how to react to this. Being at a loss for words wasn't really her, but she was terrified of coming out with something irredeemably frivolous or hurtful or downright stupid.

Finally she said, 'It won't always be like that. It's only been eight months. You'll meet someone else one day.'

Cliché cliché cliché.

'Except I'd rather not meet someone else.' A small crab scuttled sideways out from beneath a rock as Hugh bent down to pick up a fresh supply of flat pebbles. Rapidly, one by one, he spun them into the breaking waves.

'Yes, but—'

'No buts. I've decided. Because I know, I really and truly *know*, that I never want to go through that horror again. I loved my wife,' he said simply, 'and she died. What if I *do* meet someone else in a couple of years' time? Who can guarantee she won't die too? It could happen. At any minute of any day, with no warning at all, it could happen again.' He shook his head. 'And I'm just not interested. It's not worth the risk. I'd rather stay single and unattached.'

Millie was finding this hard to accept.

'But people are widowed and they marry again! Sometimes they're widowed two or three times but they *still* don't give up.'

'Fine, if that's what they want to do,' Hugh said flatly. 'But I don't.'

A lone couple were making their way along the beach towards them. Millie, brushing her hair out of her eyes, watched them. The man's arm rested protectively across the girl's shoulders, while her own arm was curled around his waist. They were even walking in time, matching each other stride for stride. Laughing at something his girlfriend had said, the man planted a loving kiss on her forehead.

'How does that make you feel?' said Millie. 'Seeing those two together like that. Don't you envy them?'

Hugh shoved his hands into the pockets of his jeans.

'No. I feel sorry for them. Because by tomorrow one of them could be dead.'

'You can't go through life thinking like that!'

'Can't I? But you haven't been through it. You have no idea how it feels.' Pausing, narrowing his eyes as he gazed out to sea, Hugh said, 'Let me tell you about something that happens three or four times a week. I'm asleep in bed when the phone rings, waking me up. I reach out, pick up the phone, say hello. And then I hear Louisa's voice, and she's calling my name, and I can't believe it, because this means it's all been a terrible mistake—Louisa isn't dead after all, she's alive, and I'm just *so happy*—'

Abruptly, Hugh stopped. After a moment he said, 'And then I really wake up.'

Millie blinked and wiped the back of her hand across her eyes; how embarrassing, she was the one crying while Hugh was the one who'd lost his wife.

She shook her head.

'God, I'm sorry.'

'There's nothing I can do to stop it happening,' said Hugh. 'Being that happy, then waking up, and crashing back to earth… I can't begin to describe how it feels.'

'Awful,' Millie whispered, feeling hopelessly inadequate.

'Certainly no picnic.' Taking pity on her, Hugh nodded in agreement. His smile, brief and automatic, didn't reach his eyes. 'And the thing about recurring dreams is you can't control them. I just want them to go away.' He paused, then sent another pebble skittering into the waves. 'And I don't think they ever will.'

'Phwoaaar, definitely dishy,' drooled Hester, who had been lurking behind her bedroom curtain watching Millie get dropped off by Hugh. 'Great car, too. But you didn't kiss him! What's the matter with you, girl?'

Since this was the twenty-first century, Millie found it hard to believe that Hester was still using words like 'dishy.' Honestly, next she'd be saying 'far-out' and 'groovy' and 'cool dude.'

'It wasn't a date,' Millie wearily reminded her. 'And I definitely wasn't going to kiss him.' She shivered at the thought; Hugh Emerson had to be as off-limits as it was possible to get, 'Remember? His wife just died.'

Hester rolled her eyes.

'I don't mean a raunchy kiss—you don't have to launch yourself at him and stick your tongue down his throat! A quick peck on the cheek, that's all I'm talking about. Something sedate. Surely it's only polite.'

'We didn't even shake hands. Just said goodbye and that was it.' Millie pulled a face; to be honest, she hadn't been quite sure *how* to go about leaving Hugh Emerson. After getting on so completely brilliantly together, the end bit of the evening had been a bit awkward. She'd wondered if he was already regretting telling her so much about himself.

'So when are you seeing him again?'

'It wasn't a date, dipstick! We didn't arrange to meet again. He just drove off.'

Hester, who was draped across the sofa wearing her Ricky Martin T-shirt-cum-nightie, rolled on to her front and began flicking through the TV channels in search of hunky men.

Or even… bleeugh… *dishy* ones.

In the end, she was forced to settle for Gary Rhodes.

'Sounds like you had a fun evening. You must have been bored out of your mind.'

'It wasn't boring.' Instinctively, Millie leapt to Hugh Emerson's defense.

'Get your hair cut,' Hester shouted at Gary Rhodes on the TV, 'and stop poncing around making out you're so great.' Over her shoulder to Millie she added, 'Actually, that's a thought.'

Millie was busy levering the lid off the biscuit tin.

'What is?'

'How do we really know his wife's dead?'

'She is, I know she is,' Millie sighed.

'Yes, but you're ultragullible. You always give everyone the benefit of the doubt. '*You*,' Hester pointed out, 'think Gary Rhodes can't help looking like an overgrown back garden because his hair just naturally grows like that.'

'She was killed in a horse-riding accident,' Millie said defensively.

Hester waggled her eyebrows in a meaningful manner.

'Really? Or did he murder her?'

'Okay, maybe he murdered her. And this is a mad conversation,' Millie pointed out, 'because I shouldn't think I'll ever see him again anyway.'

'If he's an ice-cool con man who murdered his wife, he'll be in touch.' Hester nodded knowledgeably. 'He'll come up with some feeble excuse to see you again. You're probably already earmarked as target number two.'

'If he's an *intelligent*, ice-cool con man,' said Millie, 'he'll find himself a target really worth murdering. Someone with a lot more money than me.'

Chapter 14

'Bit big,' said Millie the next morning, 'but quite comfy.'

Having braced herself for the worst, she was glad it didn't itch.

Lucas was busy on the phone. Sasha, who had Olympic-sized breasts and platinum-blonde hair, was measuring how much the gorilla suit needed to be taken in. As well as being Lucas's strippogram, Millie gathered she was also his kind-of-girlfriend. Evidently she did a great Marilyn Monroe.

'Rather you than me,' Sasha said cheerily when the last pin was in place. 'Stuck inside that great furry thing… I'd get claustrophobic in no time flat!'

You don't say.

'Actually, it's not too bad.' Millie did a little dance to demonstrate. 'At least there's room to move inside.' Pulling a face she added, 'I'd feel a lot more claustrophobic trapped inside Lucas's leather trousers.'

'What's all this about you being trapped inside my trousers?' Lucas had finished his phone call. His wink encompassed both Sasha and Millie. 'I know how I'd feel and we're not talking claustrophobic. So, how's the suit?'

'Great. Never felt more glamorous.'

There were four types of kissogram and Millie suspected she'd be the one getting the most wear out of the gorilla suit. Sasha was the sex-bomb who was happy to strip down to a couple of tassels and a sequinned G-string. Eric, a mild-mannered history teacher by day, was transformed at the flick of a leopard-skin jockstrap into a lovable, roly-poly, wise-cracking Full Monty-type at night.

The fourth kind was the hen-night special when the handsome dark stranger swept the lucky participant off her feet, flexed his muscles, flattered her outrageously, and prayed the effort of having to lift fifteen stone of shrieking, flailing female wouldn't cause his leather trousers to split.

'What gave you the idea of starting up a kissogram agency?' Millie asked as Sasha began to peel her out of the gorilla suit.

'Spot of girlfriend trouble.' Lucas grinned and flicked the ring-pull off his can of Coke. 'One of them was refusing to leave my flat, another was turning into pretty much a full-time stalker. I couldn't be doing with the hassle anymore. And I'd had enough of the radio station, getting up at four-thirty every morning to do the breakfast show.' Generously, he offered Millie a swig of Coke. 'Anyway, a friend of mine had a load of costumes he wanted to sell. I bought them and decided to move back down here to Cornwall. For the summer, at least. We'll see how things go.'

The different costumes were hanging up on a rail behind him. Everything from the *Officer and a Gentleman* outfit and the policeman's uniform to Sasha's fabulously over-the-top Cleopatra get-up. Stacked on the floor next to them was a pile of cellophane-wrapped T-shirts with 'I've Been Kemped' printed across them and a crate of cheap sparkling wine.

And tomorrow I've got to do my bit, thought Millie, experiencing a sudden attack of stage fright. Sing, dance, make people laugh, and *not* fall off my roller skates.

'Don't worry,' said Lucas cheerfully, 'you'll be fine. The first time's always the worst. Just close your eyes and think of the cash.'

'If I close my eyes,' said Millie, 'I'll definitely fall off my skates.'

◈◈◈

The phone was ringing when she arrived home. Grabbing it, Millie said, 'Yes?'

'Three letters. Simply something.'

Her heart soared; she couldn't help it. She didn't even want it to soar, but when these things happen, they happen. It wasn't something you could physically control.

'Red,' said Millie. Gosh, there was a coincidence, that was currently the exact same color as her face. It had been so long since she'd fancied someone she'd completely forgotten about all this blushing palaver—in fact, she hadn't even realized you *could* blush in a room on your own.

'Excellent. Now how about: Item of female apparel of a conical nature?'

'Um… ooh, witch's hat!'

'Not quite, try again. Underwear, three letters.'

'Bra! Oh my hero, you found my red bra!' Millie let out a squeal of delight.

'In my car.'

'That is so *great*, it's my absolute favorite bra! When I got home and realized it was gone I thought it must have fallen out of my bag on the beach. I had visions of it being swept away, bobbing along merrily for weeks on end before ending up in America.'

She was gabbling. Okay, stop it.

'I found it this morning.' Hugh paused. 'Under the passenger seat.'

It was the pause that did it. Until that moment Millie had simply been delighted to hear from him again so soon and thrilled to discover she hadn't lost her very best bra.

But in that brief, all-too-significant fraction of a second between sentences, the horrid truth came crashing down like a slab of concrete. Millie went cold all over.

He thinks I did it on purpose. He thinks I deliberately hid my bra in his car, so I'd have an excuse to see him again!

God, it was exactly the kind of thing Hester would do. Millie wondered how on earth she could convince him that she absolutely *genuinely* hadn't had any idea she'd left her bra in his car and what's more she'd never dream of playing a dirty trick like that, never ever *ever*.

But of course, Hugh didn't know she wasn't that kind of girl. The sneaky Hester kind. He thought she had done it deliberately. And if she tried to tell him she wasn't like Hester and it had been a complete accident, honestly, Millie realized she'd only be making things worse.

Because, let's face it, her heart had definitely soared earlier. She'd been ecstatic when she'd heard his voice on the phone.

Oh dear, it was a horrible thought, but what if, subconsciously, she *had* left her bra under the passenger seat on purpose?

'Look, I've got an appointment in Newquay tomorrow afternoon.' Hugh's voice cut through her inner turmoil. 'If you're home around fiveish, I'll call by and drop it in.'

Millie squeezed her eyes shut, then opened them again.

'That would be great.' She forced herself to sound cheerful and enthusiastic and as if she hadn't noticed anything amiss. 'My little bra, back again! Hester and I might even have to throw a welcome home party for it. Oh,' she added as a seemingly careless afterthought, 'we'll both be out tomorrow afternoon, so don't bother trying the doorbell. Just shove it through the letterbox, okay?'

We love you James, we really do,
We love your ability
To perform anything from a brain transplant
To an appendectomy.

When it comes to surgeons you're number one,
We're especially keen on your gorgeous bum,
Far better than Alan's or Sunil's or Doreen's
And so tempting to touch in your surgical greens.

You're forty today and we all think
You definitely improve with age
Meet us tonight in the Crown for a drink
And let's get as pissed as... parrots.

Millie ran through the poem one last time. Honestly, what a heap of drivel.

Still, at least it wasn't her heap of drivel. The theater staff who had booked the gorillagram had faxed it through to Lucas's office yesterday and were no doubt delighted by their wit. All she had to do was recite it.

'Okay, he's out of theater,' hissed one of the scrub nurses. Grabbing Millie by the arm, she propelled her along the corridor and swung her to the right. 'Remember, he's the blond one with the droopy moustache.'

'Fine.' Millie lowered her gorilla's head into place.

'Ready?'

'Ready.'

'Can you breathe in there?'

'Not really, no.'

'Oh well, never mind,' giggled the scrub nurse. 'Come on, let's go!'

The job went off like a dream. James, the surgical registrar whose birthday it was, was a terrific sport. The forty or so hospital staff who had managed to cram themselves into the coffee room whooped and whistled and applauded on cue. Millie, feeling as if she was on stage, roller-skated her way around James as she recited the hysterically funny poem. Thankfully, the in-jokes meant a lot more to his co-workers than they did to Millie and everyone laughed themselves sick. Then a dozen or so cameras were produced and flashbulbs popped like fireworks as Millie presented James with his 'I've Been Kemped' T-shirt and bottle of cheap sparkling wine. She took off her gorilla's head and gave James a kiss on the cheek. He picked her up and twirled her around and told her he'd never seen a gorilla with blonde ringlets before. Then, back on terra firma, Millie led them all in a rousing chorus of 'Happy Birthday.'

More photos. More people told her she was great. They gave her a round of applause. She was no longer on any old stage, she was Shirley Bassey taking her curtain calls after a sell-out show at the London Palladium.

'It was my first time,' Millie happily confided in James as she was leaving.

'Don't worry,' James told her, 'we never tell our patients either.' He grinned. 'For some reason they prefer not to know.'

Back at home by four o'clock, still sky-high on adrenalin, Millie was oh-so-tempted to wash her hair (the gorilla head had flattened it completely), re-do her makeup, greet Hugh at the door with the news that she was back after all, and regale him with the story of her magnificent triumph.

But that was the kind of behavior he would expect of a girl who was so lacking in the art of subtlety that she deliberately left her best lace bra on the floor of his car.

It was the kind of thing Hester would do.

I must not open the front door when he gets here, Millie vowed.

Or the front window.

◈◈◈

Hugh was late. He wasn't coming. He'd realized he couldn't bear to be parted from her irresistible, underwired, dramatically padded red bra, Millie fantasized. Maybe he wanted to wear it himself.

At five-thirty, peering out from behind Hester's bedroom curtains, Millie spotted his car slowing to a halt outside the house. She instantly threw herself, sniper-style, down on the floor.

He rang the doorbell and waited. Checking first that she wasn't in. Just being polite, thought Millie. Mustn't, *mustn't* answer the door.

Scuttling crab-like across Hester's bedroom carpet, she crawled out on to the landing and watched, nose to the ground, as the metal flap was pushed open and a scarlet satin strap appeared through the letterbox. For a moment she imagined grabbing it and giving Hugh a fright. Heavens, having a tussle over her bra, how immature, the very *thought* of it.

The next moment, a flash of fuchsia pink appeared next to Hugh's dark outline through the frosted glass of the front door. Millie froze in alarm as she heard Hester say perkily, 'Well, hi! I know who you are!'

Bugger, bugger. It was half past five and Hester—with her customary hideous timing—had picked this moment to arrive home from work. Worse still—oh God—she was being *perky*.

'I know who you are too,' said Hugh.

The letterbox rattled, the bra strap twitched.

'And are you here stealing underwear,' Hester brightly inquired, 'or delivering it?'

'I wouldn't steal this bra,' Millie heard Hugh say gravely. 'It's not my size.'

'Oh, ha ha ha ha ha,' trilled Hester, overdoing it as usual.

'Millie left it in my car. It fell out of her bag,' Hugh explained.

'But isn't she in? It's half past five, she should be in!'

'I tried the bell. No answer.'

'Well you can't just post a bra through our letterbox and rush off!' exclaimed Hester. 'Millie was worried she'd never *see* you again!'

Up on the landing Millie let out a low moan and banged her forehead despairingly—but quietly—against the carpet.

'Anyway,' Hester rattled on, 'she'll be home any minute now, so why don't you come in and wait? Have a drink and a bit of a chat?'

No, no, noooo, Millie silently howled, even as she began to shuffle backwards along the landing. But the silent pleading didn't work. She might have known it wouldn't. Hester was too pushy and Hugh too polite. He simply couldn't bring himself to say no.

Back in Hester's bedroom, squashing herself out of sight in the gap between the bed and the window, Millie heard the familiar click of Hester's key turning in the lock. God, it was dusty down here, she hoped she wouldn't sneeze.

And she certainly hoped that Hester wasn't planning to take advantage of Hugh's inability to say no by dragging him up to her bedroom and reminding him what he'd been missing out on all these months.

Although *should* that happen, Millie thought, it would be great to suddenly pop up from nowhere, tap Hester on the shoulder and announce, 'I think you owe me two hundred pounds.'

Chapter 15

It was the longest twenty-five minutes of Millie's life. Terrified to move in case the floorboards creaked, she held her breath and listened to Hester merrily burbling away downstairs, so eager to keep Hugh there that she was barely letting him get a word in edgewise. It was probably better that she couldn't make out what Hester was actually saying to him—it didn't bear thinking about.

'Top of the stairs and to the right,' she heard Hester call out, and Millie's heart began to leap around her rib cage like a terrified gazelle. This was what Hester always told guests when they asked for directions to the bathroom, and of the two doors on offer to them, they invariably picked the wrong one.

Boing, Boing, BOINGGG went Millie's heart as the bedroom door was pushed open. For a second she knew Hugh was standing there in the doorway surveying Hester's bed. Millie squeezed her eyes shut and stopped breathing altogether. There was something tickling her nose but she didn't dare move…

Phew. Safe. The door closed again. She heard Hugh find the bathroom. Two minutes later he made his way back downstairs.

Shortly after that, he left.

Just as Millie was clambering out of her hiding place—yeugh, cobwebs—she heard Hester racing up the stairs. Quick as a flash she threw herself on to Hester's bed and closed her eyes.

'Bloodyhell!'

Feigning surprise, Millie blinked and rubbed her eyes and mumbled, 'What?'

'We thought you were out! Why are you asleep on my bed?'

'Huh? Oh, I was shattered. There was a fly buzzing around in my room so I came in here.' Looking bemused, Millie added, 'Who's *we*?'

'Your chap! Hugh Emerson! He's been downstairs, waiting to see you!'

'Really? Oh well, never mind.' Millie yawned and stretched, rather convincingly if she did say so herself. 'I've had a lovely sleep.'

'I came home and he was on the doorstep, feeding your bra through the letterbox. Your *best* bra,' Hester added, doing that Roger Moore thing with her eyebrows. 'Go on, admit it, you left it in his car on purpose.'

'You *would* think that.' Millie wished there was an on-off switch in Hester's back. Sometimes, like a Furby, she was just too much.

'Anyone with half a brain would think that. It's totally obvious. Especially when he's so dishy.'

Eeyurggh, that word again.

'And off-limits.'

'That only makes him dishier. We always want what we can't have.'

And you especially can't have him, thought Millie with a surge of extremely muddled emotions. If anyone around here's going to want him and not have him, it's jolly well going to be me!

Good grief, where had *that* come from?

Aloud she said, 'What about Lucas?'

'Ah,' Hester swooned with joy against the windowsill, 'he's still my number-one man.'

Poor Nat.

'What about Nat?'

'Oh stop giving me that shriveled-spinster look—I'm allowed to fantasize, aren't I? Nat *would* be my number one, if he was here. But that's the trouble,' Hester declared fretfully, 'he isn't here, is he? He's too busy searing scallops in sodding Glasgow.'

The doorbell went an hour later.

'You're a star,' Lucas told Millie when she opened the door. He broke into a huge grin. 'I was passing, so I had to drop by. One of the theater sisters rang me this afternoon and said you were fantastic. In fact, she was so impressed, she wants to book you for the day after tomorrow.'

'Oh wow.' Millie was delighted. 'Where?'

'The big supermarket on the outskirts of Wadebridge. Her husband's the manager. It's their silver wedding anniversary and she wants you to turn up at one o'clock. He'll be on his lunch break in the staff canteen.' Lucas handed her an envelope containing all the details. 'Bloody awful poem, so sloppy it makes you want to throw up, but hey, that's not our problem—'

'Ouch,' complained Millie as she was knocked sideways by a highly perfumed human bowling ball. Whoosh, the air in the hallway was suddenly thick with Estée Lauder's Dazzling.

'I thought I recognized that voice!' Hester exclaimed, clutching her bath towel around her and dripping water and bubbles all over the floor. 'Lucas, how are you? You haven't changed a bit—you're looking great!'

'Hello darling, so are you.' Bending down, Lucas gave her a warm kiss on each cheek. Then, because he simply couldn't help himself, he trailed an index finger idly along the line of her collarbone.

Hester trembled like a whippet. It was a wonder her tongue wasn't lolling out of her mouth.

'It's so good to *see* you,' she told Lucas, as if it weren't already screamingly obvious. And now she was stretching her neck, imperceptibly straining towards him, yearning—like a whippet desperate for affection—for him to stroke her collarbone again.

'Lucas just called by to give me my next booking,' said Millie.

'Oh, but you must come in for a drink.' Eagerly, Hester clutched his tanned arm. 'You *must*, we can chat about old times!'

The shame of it, Millie thought. Two hours ago Hester had lured Hugh into the house against his better judgment, and now here she was doing the exact same thing again. Honestly, she was like some insatiable Black Widow spider, preying on innocent young males.

Except Lucas, of course, was about as innocent as Peter Stringfellow.

'Sounds great,' he winked at Hester, 'but we can't stop. I'm driving Sasha down to St. Ives.' As he spoke he jerked his head behind him to the car parked outside the house. Sasha, dressed as a nun, was leaning against the hood smoking a cigarette and casually straightening the seam on one of her fishnet stockings. A couple of pensioners waiting at the bus stop a little way down the road determinedly didn't look shocked.

Hester's face fell.

'Is she your girlfriend?'

'We get on well enough,' said Lucas cheerfully. 'See a fair bit of each other, you know the kind of thing.'

Hester did. She could also guess which bits of each other they saw. Lucky Sasha, the mere thought of seeing Lucas's bits was enough to send Hester's insides lurching into a spin cycle of joy.

Lucky, *lucky* Sasha.

Tarty bitch.

'"A message from your loving wife,"' Millie read aloud, having opened the envelope. She cleared her throat and began:

Twenty-five years of wedded bliss
And never a day without a loving kiss.

My darling Jerry I want you to know,
I never realized it was possible to be as happy as this.

'God, you're right,' she told Lucas, 'this *is* awful.'

A lump had sprung into Hester's throat; she thought it was romantic.

'All you have to do is keep a straight face.' Flicking his dark hair out of his eyes, Lucas checked his watch. 'Right, better not hang around, can't keep the old boys at the Conservative Club waiting.' He winked again at Hester and briefly patted her on the head. 'See you around, sweetheart. Don't do anything I wouldn't do.'

'See? I told you he'd got fat and ugly,' Millie murmured as they watched Lucas saunter back to the car. Sasha, flicking her half-smoked cigarette into the gutter, gave them a wave goodbye and blew the pensioners at the bus stop a jaunty kiss.

'He patted me on the head,' Hester groaned. 'On the *head*. I mean, how unromantic is that?'

'It could be worse.' Privately, Millie felt it was the very best thing Lucas could have done. 'He could've given you a Chinese burn.'

'The first time I see him in hundreds of years and he treats me like a five-year-old!' To illustrate the unfairness of it all, Hester's voice rose and she stamped her foot. 'I thought jumping out of the bath would help. I'm wet, I'm naked, I've still got my make-up on... God, what more could he want?'

Millie thought of Sasha.

'Maybe a nun in a basque?'

Hester tried hard not to be irritated when Nat rang in the middle of *Coronation Street*. She'd told him a thousand times not to even think of phoning her between seven-thirty and eight—on *any* night of the week—but he always forgot. It had to be a man thing. Either that, Hester thought darkly, or they did it on purpose.

Just when it had got to a good bit too.

'I've got a five-minute break before all hell lets loose,' Nat said cheerfully. 'Jacques is convinced the guy booked for table six at eight o'clock is working undercover for the *Michelin Guide*. We're packed out, Danny's called in sick, and all the waitresses are crammed into the loo doing their make-up because table four's been booked by Sean Connery, except I don't think it's going to turn out to be the Sean Connery they'd like it to be.'

All of a sudden Hester wanted to cry. Millie was right, Nat was lovely. And she missed him dreadfully, she really did. The sound of his voice brought it rushing back to her, like the surf crashing on to Fistral Beach.

'Oh Nat, I wish you were here.'

She meant it. Nat loved her. He would never pat her on the head.

'Now that's a coincidence, because I wish you were here too. Actually, that's why I'm ringing.' Nat sounded pleased with himself. 'I've persuaded Jacques to let me have next Saturday off. You could come up on Friday night, we'd have the weekend together and you could catch the train back on Sunday night. How about it, wouldn't that be brilliant? A whole weekend!'

Hester's spirits rose for a nanosecond, then sank again. *In theory* it sounded brilliant. But in reality it would mean a knackering train journey, followed by both of them being absolutely shattered on Saturday. Saturday evening, okay, they'd have a ball. But Sunday would be miserable, both of them knowing that by mid-afternoon they'd be clinging to each other on the railway platform, having to say goodbye for another goodness-knows-how-many weeks. And then, she would have the return journey to endure, the ultimate in depressing, slit-your-wrist experiences. Apart, maybe, from having to trudge back to work the next morning knowing that that was what you'd spent the whole of last week getting so ridiculously excited about.

It would also mean closing the stall on Saturday, the most lucrative day of any market's week. And the train fare would cost a fortune she really couldn't afford right now.

'Hess? Are you still there?'

'Of course I'm still here.' Hester rubbed her forehead. Where else was she likely to be? 'It sounds great, but... I don't know, money's pretty tight, and the train journey's a pain... I just don't know if it's worth all that hassle for a Saturday night out.'

Brief silence.

'But at least we'd be together,' said Nat. 'I thought that's what you wanted.'

'Time travel, that's what I really want. A TARDIS I can step into, that'll get me up to Glasgow in three seconds flat.'

Another, longer silence.

'Shall I come down to you?'

'Oh Nat.' Hester's eyes filled with hot tears of shame. 'That'd be even worse. You don't finish work until midnight on Friday... you'd sleep all the way through Saturday... it's really not worth it.'

She heard someone in the background yelling at Nat.

'Okay. Just a thought. Look, I've got to get back to work, the Michelin guy's turned up.'

'It was a wonderful thought, Nat.' A tear rolled down Hester's cheek and she wiped it away with the back of her hand. 'But seeing you again just makes it harder to say goodbye, I can't bear it when the train pulls out of the station and—'

'Have to go.' More bawling in the background, instructing Nat to get his bloody arse into gear. 'Love you, bye.'

'Love you too,' whispered Hester. But it was too late, the line had already gone dead.

Millie came through from the kitchen with a consolation mug of tea.

'And a Snickers bar,' she produced the bar from behind her back with a flourish, 'to cheer you up.'

'Bugger,' said Hester as the familiar theme tune filled the living room. 'I even managed to miss *Coronation Street*.'

'It wasn't that exciting.'

'I still wanted to see it.' Fretfully Hester slurped her tea. 'Bloody Nat, why does he always have to ruin everything?'

'Oh come on,' Millie protested. 'You can't blame Nat, he phones whenever he has the time to phone. It isn't his fault.'

'Of course I can blame him,' shouted Hester, 'and it *is* his fault. If he hadn't gone away to Scotland I might *have* some kind of life, and then I'd never have stayed in every night like a sad old spinster and got hooked on bloody soap operas in the first place.'

Chapter 16

Millie began to feel as if she were embroiled in a soap of her own the following lunchtime when she answered the front door and found her mother, clutching a copy of the glossy magazine *The Opera Lover*, on the doorstep.

Even more bizarrely, Millie's ex-boss, Tim Fleetwood, was standing in the road behind her, panting slightly as he unloaded a set of tartan luggage from the boot of his slate-grey Renault Megane.

'Mum! What are you doing here? What's going on?'

Adele, as always ludicrously overdressed, this time in a turquoise Chanel-style suit and matching stilettoes—in Newquay, at one o'clock in the afternoon—enveloped Millie in a cloud of Byzance as she leaned forward and kissed her on each cheek.

Each cheek, Millie noted. Adele and her fancy city ways. She'd be switching to semi-skimmed milk next.

'I think I should be asking *you* what's going on.' Her mother wagged a finger at her. 'I *had* planned to surprise you, turning up at the travel agency. Imagine the shock when Tim told me you weren't working there anymore! You could have told me, darling—I felt a complete *ninny*.'

Hmm. No change there, then. Much as she loved Adele, Millie couldn't help wishing sometimes that her mother would stop wafting around the place like a genuine opera diva and just behave in a more normal fashion.

'I tried to ring you the other night,' she lied, 'but there was no reply.'

'And that was it? You couldn't be bothered to try again? Honestly, young people today, I don't know! Just pop them in the hall for me, Tim, would you please?'

Tim struggled past them with the suitcases. Having at first tried to pretend he hadn't noticed her, he was now forced to glance at Millie and say—a mite sheepishly—'Hi, how's it going?'

Of course he sounded sheepish. He was such a wimp he couldn't even stand up to his wife for long enough to tell her he wasn't having an affair, Millie reminded herself.

What a total woolly vest.

Aloud, she said, 'Brilliant thanks. I've got a terrific new job, the people I work with are really nice, and the money's fantastic.' Having made her point, Millie added sweetly, 'How's Sylvia?'

'Fine.' Tim deposited the last two cases on the floor—plonk, plonk—and straightened back up. 'Right, well, better get back to the shop.'

Where Sylvia will no doubt be waiting with her index finger poised over the timer button on her stopwatch, thought Millie with a bland smile.

'Tim, you're an angel, mwahr, mwahr.' Adele kissed him on both cheeks too, causing him to break out in a light sweat. The poor fellow was terrified, Millie realized, in a blind panic. Maybe Sylvia was waiting for him not with a stopwatch but with a machete.

'I thought I'd surprise you, whisk you away somewhere glamorous for lunch,' Adele explained over coffee. ('Oh God, darling, *please* not that awful instant stuff.' 'Mum, awful instant's all we've got.') 'There was nowhere to park outside the travel agency so I paid off the taxi. Imagine how silly I felt when I realized you weren't even there!'

'You should have phoned,' said Millie. 'Still, it was nice of Tim to offer to drive you over here.'

'Tsh, I had to drop enough hints first,' Adele snorted. But in an elegant way.

'So how long are you down for?' As she said it, Millie crossed her fingers behind her back.

'Oh, I don't know, maybe a couple of weeks. Just needed a change of scenery,' sighed Adele, who had been really quite keen on a merchant banker who had had the gall to dump her for somebody else. But that was by the by, and certainly not the kind of tale one would want to relay to one's daughter. 'London's so stuffy and bustly at this time of year—we're up to our eyes in tourists.' She shuddered dramatically. 'Awful. I couldn't bear it. Had to get away.'

And of course Newquay, the surfing capital of Europe, was so empty and tourist-free, Millie thought dryly. Man trouble, this was what this was all about, she'd bet money on it. Just as she knew the reason Adele never went anywhere without an 'intellectual' magazine tucked under her arm was because you never knew who you might bump into. Evidently, it was a wonderful icebreaker for fellow 'intellectuals,' announcing to the world in general—and potential husbands in particular—that you weren't a brainless airhead.

'Well, it's really nice to see you,' Millie said valiantly. 'You can have my room and I'll sleep on the sofa.'

Heaven knows what Hester was going to make of this alarming turn of events, but what else could she do? Hardly recommend a cozy B&B.

'Darling, how sweet of you, but I couldn't possibly stay here!'

Phew. Thank goodness for that. Even her mother was sensitive enough to realize she couldn't just turn up without warning and take up residence—

'In this poky little cottage?' Adele laughed at the very idea. 'Where there's no room to swing a cat and you don't even own a proper coffee machine? Lord, the very thought of it makes me shudder!'

Oh.

'Oh,' said Millie. It was a bit of a slap in the face, but actually the kind of slap in the face you didn't mind too much. This was good news, after all. And Hester would be relieved. 'Where are you staying then? A hotel?'

'On my alimony? You must be joking, darling.' As Adele sipped her coffee she pulled a good-grief-this-is-disgusting face. Then, recovering, she smiled brightly across at her daughter. 'I thought I'd stay with Judy and Lloyd.'

'You know what you are, don't you?' said Millie. 'Mad, that's what.'

They were sitting out in Judy and Lloyd's garden, sharing a bottle of wine, and enjoying the warmth of the sun. Upstairs, Lloyd was showing Adele to her room.

Judy shrugged and batted away a hovering wasp.

'Why, what am I supposed to do? Just say no?'

'Yes!'

'But then it would look as if I cared. And I don't care. Not in a jealous way, at least.'

'It must still feel a bit weird,' Millie protested.

'Not really. She isn't *that* bad. I mean, she's only your mother,' Judy reminded her. 'Not Pol Pot.'

'Hmm.' Millie wasn't so sure. 'She can be hard work, I don't know why Dad didn't put his foot down.'

'Yes you do. We all do. Because he's just too bloody nice to turn her away.'

'Okay, but if she drives you mad, let me know. Otherwise it's not fair on you.'

'Don't worry, I can take care of myself.' Judy sounded entertained. 'She's your father's ex, that's all. He was so good when I had dotty Aunt Sarah to stay for a month last year—and she was bedridden, poor old duck! So how can I kick up a fuss about having Adele to stay for a few days?'

Millie suspected it wouldn't be long before Judy began to wish Adele was bedridden too. Glancing back at the house, she watched her parents make their way across the garden towards them.

Adele was now clutching a fringed lilac shawl and a hefty hardback biography of Placido Domingo.

'Honestly, you're hopeless,' she was telling Lloyd. Turning her attention to Millie she said, 'I asked him what he thought of Andrea Bocelli and he said signing for Aston Villa had been a big mistake.' She rolled her eyes. 'He really is a *total* philistine.'

Lloyd, ambling along the path behind her, was chuckling good-naturedly to himself. He winked at Millie and said, 'That's great. What's a philistine?'

The supermarket on the outskirts of Wadebridge was packed with shoppers. Feeling pretty daft, aware that people were laughing and pointing at her as she skated through the main doors, Millie consoled herself with the reminder that she was earning money. And spreading a little happiness. Not to mention giving the manager a silver wedding anniversary gift he'd never forget.

Nobody was expecting her. Pat, the theater sister, had made her wishes plain to Millie this morning.

'His staff are great, just like one big happy family,' she'd explained over the phone, 'but I don't trust them to keep it to themselves. If just one person lets slip to Jerry, it'll all be spoiled. When you turn up I want it to be a fantastic surprise!'

A toddler in a stroller, spotting Millie, let out a wail of anguish and burst into noisy tears.

Oh well, can't win them all.

❖❖❖

As she skated past the newspapers and magazines, Millie realized she was attracting more and more attention. As if she was the Pied Piper, a number of children were starting to follow in her wake. Over to the left, the checkouts were all busy. To the right, a scrum of customers milled around the fruit and veg. A couple of teenage boys pummeled their chests and let out deafening Tarzan howls.

Spotting the inquiries desk *way* over to the left behind the line of checkouts, Millie tucked the T-shirt and bottle of sparkling wine under her arm and headed for it. Thanks to the turnstiles and inescapable one-way system, she was forced to navigate her way through pastas and sauces, cakes and biscuits, and cat food and dog chews (mmm, yum).

Finally, Millie squeezed past a huge woman bulk-buying biscuits and rolled up to the customer inquiries desk.

Three supervisors grinned at her.

'Monkey nuts? Aisle sixteen, love,' said one of them hilariously.

'I'm here to see the manager,' said Millie, a fair-sized crowd beginning to gather around her.

The manager?'

'Jerry Heseltine.' Why were the women giving each other odd looks? 'I do have the right supermarket,' Millie told them earnestly. 'His wife gave me exact instructions.' More wary expressions, a couple of nudges, and one smothered grin. 'She arranged for me to come here today as a surprise. It's their silver wedding anniversary.'

The tills behind her were beginning to fall silent. One of the young bag-packing assistants cackled with laughter. All eyes were fixed on Millie.

'Jerry Heseltine,' she repeated, beginning to perspire a bit inside the costume. 'He is your manager, isn't he?'

Golly, how embarrassing if he turned out to be a trolley collector who'd spent the last twenty years lying to his wife, telling her he was the boss.

'Oh, he's our manager,' said one of the supervisors, whose name-badge announced that she was Mavis. 'But he isn't around.'

'His wife said he'd definitely be here,' Millie wailed. God, was she supposed to *wait*! 'Look, where *is* he?' she pleaded. 'Do you know what he's doing and what time he'll be back?'

The two supervisors flanking Mavis began to snort with laughter. Mavis, casually consulting her watch, said, 'What's he doing? Well, it's four minutes past one, so having steamy sex with Doreen Pringle, I imagine.'

'Oooh nooo!' Millie put a hairy paw up to her mouth in horror.

'And he wasn't actually planning on being back,' Mavis concluded with an air of malicious triumph. 'They've both taken the rest of the afternoon off.'

'Hell's bells,' groaned Millie. 'This was supposed to be so romantic.'

'He's a selfish, cheating git,' Mavis announced. 'And she's an uppity cow. Works on the deli counter. Three lunchtimes a week they slope off together to her place. It's been going on for the last two years.'

'What a bastard.' Sorrowfully, Millie shook her gorilla's head.

'Doreen only lives down the road,' one of the other supervisors suggested helpfully, as supermarket supervisors tend to do. 'On the Lime Acres estate. You could always pop along there and do your bit on her front doorstep.'

'Thanks. But maybe not,' Millie sighed.

Practically everyone at the tills had heard every word.

As she skated wearily towards the exit, Millie marveled at the selfishness of men. That poor theater nurse had been so thrilled at the prospect of surprising her loving husband… how could she have been married to him for twenty-five years and have got it so horribly wrong?

She'd been right about one thing though, when she'd described the staff at the supermarket as one big happy family. Except it clearly hadn't occurred to her that her own husband might be off playing mummies and daddies in his lunch hour with Doreen from the deli.

Donk! Something ricocheted off the back of Millie's head, almost sending her careering into a bank of potted plants. Regaining her balance in the nick of time, she spun round and saw that one of the teenage boys had thrown a banana at her.

Killing themselves laughing, they jumped up and down and made whooping monkey noises.

For pity's sake. It was enough to put you off the opposite sex for life.

Back at the car, Millie removed her skates and placed the gorilla head on the passenger seat next to her. Phew, that was better.

What a complete bastard.

She saw him as she was pulling out of the car park thirty seconds later. He was unloading the contents of his shopping trolley into the boot of his car. Wearing white jeans and a sea-green polo shirt and looking even more gorgeous than ever.

Okay. Relax. Breathe normally. Just drive past and pretend you haven't spotted him.

Keep your eyes fixed on the road ahead. Don't look left. Don't look left, don't look left, don't look… *Bugger.*

Bugger and damn, she'd looked left. Just as Hugh Emerson finished loading the last carrier bag into the boot and glanced up.

He grinned, recognizing her at once. Millie immediately broke into a sweat, not helped by the fact that she was encased from neck to ankles in an eighteen-pound gorilla suit.

Okay, not the end of the world. Just nod and wave in a casual fashion, acknowledge his existence, then drive off. That's easy, no need to panic, you can do that.

And she could have done, if a skinny woman pushing a

piled-high trolley across the road in front of her hadn't lost control of it at that moment and slammed the front wheels into the curb. A packet of loo rolls and an untied bag of apples toppled to the ground. The woman, panicking, tried and failed to jerk the trolley back on course. Frantically, mouthing apologies, she bent down and began retrieving the scattered Granny Smiths, but the polythene had split and as fast as she collected them up and threw them back in the bag they tumbled out again.

The trolley was still blocking the road. There was no escape. This is exactly what would happen to me, thought Millie, if I'd just robbed a bank and was desperate to make a quick getaway.

My whole life is one great big hideous jinx.

Chapter 17

Taking pity on the skinny woman's predicament, Hugh strolled over and helped her pick up the escaped apples. The woman, Millie could tell, was both grateful and impressed. Next, he skillfully manuevered her trolley up over the curb and sent her off happily in the direction of her car.

Even more skillfully, he was back in front of Millie's lime green Mini before she had a chance to drive off. With a slight smile, he indicated that she should open her window.

Begrudgingly, Millie wound it down. She'd taken off the hairy gorilla hands in order to drive, of course, but they were still dangling by their velcro fastenings from her wrists.

Any monkey-nut jokes, Millie decided, and she'd be forced to run over his foot. Plus, he'd better not mention bananas.

Don't try and be witty, *please* don't try and be witty. Because I promise you, I'm not in the mood.

And a broken foot often offends.

'I always think golf buggies are the answer,' Hugh remarked. 'The first supermarket to give us golf buggies instead of unsteerable trolleys has to be on to a winner, don't you think?'

Millie smiled; she couldn't help it. Whenever she thought about Hugh Emerson—which was scarily often—she grew dry-mouthed and panicky. But as soon as they were actually conversing again, she mysteriously relaxed.

Any normal person, of course, would do it the other way round.

'Thank you.' She nodded gravely, like the Queen. 'For not making any banana jokes.'

'I don't know any banana jokes.' Hugh paused. 'Well, apart from one, which I couldn't possibly repeat.' Another pause. 'Not in front of a gorilla, anyway.'

'Would you do something for me?' coaxed Millie. 'Just put your foot under my front wheel for a moment?'

'Oh dear, bad day?' Hugh was laughing down at her now. 'And here on business, at a guess. Did it all go horribly wrong?'

Briefly, Millie told him.

'And *then*, as I was leaving, some scummy apology for a schoolboy hit me on the head,' she concluded indignantly. 'With a *sodding* banana.'

'You know what you need,' said Hugh. 'A drink.'

'You must be joking, I am *not* going back into that supermarket!'

'I didn't mean a cup of tea and a bun, I meant a proper drink. A huge vodka and tonic with plenty of ice and lemon.' The corners of Hugh's mouth began to twitch. 'And a bun.'

Hugh's house was only a couple of miles from the supermarket. Since he had bags of frozen stuff rapidly defrosting in the boot of his car, Millie followed him back to the detached Victorian property, high on the hill overlooking Padstow.

She was looking forward to a vodka and tonic.

And to seeing where Hugh lived.

Most of all though, she couldn't wait to help him unpack his supermarket shop.

You could tell *so* much about a man by the food he bought. As she pulled up on the driveway behind Hugh's car, Millie felt a squiggle of excitement mingled with panic. Yikes, this really was kill or cure. If he'd been in there bulk-buying frozen haggis and tinned meat pies or, worse still, *tofu*, she'd go off him in a big, big way.

She'd actually forgotten she was still in her gorilla suit until the woman next door popped her head over the wall, started to say something to Hugh, then spotted Millie and said, 'Oh!'

'Bang goes my street cred.' Hugh raised an eyebrow as the woman scuttled back into her house. 'Now I'll never get invited to Edwina's next dinner party.' He nodded at Millie's hairy outfit. 'Do you want to take it off?'

She feigned alarm.

'What, right here?'

'Oh, sorry.' Starting to laugh, Hugh unlocked the boot of his car. 'But you must have a change of clothes with you.'

Millie did, of course she did. An orange skirt and a white tank top, stowed in a carrier bag under the passenger seat of her own car.

But there was just something irresistible about borrowing someone else's clothes.

Particularly when they were someone you happened to have a bit of a girly crush on.

'I didn't think I'd need them, I was just going to do the job then drive straight back home again.' Opening her eyes wide, Millie shook her head. Then, rubbing imaginary beads of perspiration from her brow, she shrugged and said bravely, 'Doesn't matter, don't worry about me.'

'You're completely mad,' said Hugh. 'You do know that, don't you? Seventy degrees and you're driving around in a car, in a gorilla suit. You'll get heatstroke.'

'I'll be fine,' Millie protested. Feebly and wondering if she had the nerve to swoon.

Hugh was grinning. 'Come on. I'll lend you something of mine.'

Yay, result!

❖❖❖

The house was a renovated late-Victorian property, smartly decorated but clearly in need of a woman's touch. Millie was no Jane Asher but even she had an urge to fling a couple of cushions on to the window seat in the hall, hang a few pictures, and scatter brightly colored rugs over the polished parquet floor.

'I know.' Hugh followed her gaze. 'Kind of empty-looking. Doing the girly stuff was always Louisa's department.'

Left alone in the kitchen, Millie was surreptitiously investigating the contents of the supermarket carrier bags when he returned with a faded denim shirt and a pair of cut-off Levi's.

'They'll be too big, but better than nothing,'

Millie didn't think they'd be better than nothing; she'd actually much prefer nothing—but no, no, enough of that fantasy. Anyway, she wanted to wear his clothes. And they did smell gorgeous.

You couldn't fault a man who used Lenor.

'You go upstairs and change. I'll start unpacking this lot. Then we'll have that drink.'

The topaz and bronze bathroom was clean, tidy, and bereft of unnecessary toiletries in the way that only a man's bathroom could ever be. As she wriggled out of the gorilla suit it occurred to Millie that the opposite sex missed out on a lot. It must be so boring, getting up in the morning and not having sixteen different kinds of shampoo to choose from. How they could limit themselves to one bottle and use it until it was finished was completely beyond her. It was so sad! And only one bottle of conditioner, imagine! And one bar of soap!

Still, the denim shirt was as soft as chamois leather and so faded it was almost white. It must have been washed and ironed a million times. Millie, fastening the mother-of-pearl buttons, realized with a jolt that maybe this was a job that had been done by Louisa.

Instantly, she was awash with guilt. This was the shirt that Hugh's late wife had so lovingly laundered, and now it was being worn by a shameless hussy with designs on her husband...

I can't believe I'm even doing this, thought Millie, forcing herself to face her embarrassed reflection in the mirror above the basin.

Chastened, she stepped into the sawn-off Levi's and pulled the belt tightly around her waist.

Anyway, at least she had one thing to be grateful for. Shameless designing hussy she might be, but it was all quite irrelevant. Because Hugh had made it clear that he had absolutely no designs on her.

To punish herself, Millie didn't even borrow his hairbrush. Nor, on the way back downstairs, did she allow herself to peep into any of the bedrooms.

Well, maybe just the one. And the door was open anyway.

It was the room where Hugh slept. The double bed, with a navy and white duvet, was unmade. There were clothes hung over the chair, a stunning view from the window overlooking the river, and assorted computer magazines scattered on the bedside table.

Together with an alarm clock, one of those bendy-necked reading lamps, and a photograph, in a plain brass frame, of Louisa.

Well, what had she expected? Whips and leg-irons and a party-sized box of condoms?

'What's going on?' said Hugh, behind her.

'Oh!' Caught in the act, Millie spun round. How awful, now he thought she'd been snooping.

Mortified, she realized that she had.

Oh God, now Hugh was bound to conclude that she was turning into some kind of mad stalker. Heavens, what if he thought she'd deliberately followed him to the supermarket in order to engineer their meeting?

'Sorry, sorry, sorry,' Millie blurted out. 'I just couldn't resist a quick peep, but I absolutely *promise* I'm not a stalker.'

Hugh smiled.

'That's okay. Human nature.'

'What?' Millie was astonished. 'To *stalk*?'

'To look in other people's rooms. See how they live, find out more about them. Ever buy *Hello!* magazine?'

'Yeeurgh, no!'

'But you'll flick through it in the newsagents.'

'Oh, flick through it, of course.'

'There you go,' said Hugh.

Passionately grateful, but still squirming with embarrassment, Millie hugged the discarded gorilla suit to her chest and said, 'I didn't look in any other rooms, I promise.'

'Don't worry. I've got nothing to hide. Not even any naked slave girls chained up in the attic.'

He was smiling; he'd forgiven her for being a sneaky snoop. Millie relaxed.

'Or slave boys?'

'Oh well, slave boys, obviously. But apart from them, nothing at all.'

Downstairs, Millie helped him to unpack the carriers and put away the food. To her relief she approved of almost everything he had bought, especially the litre-sized carton of Rocombe Farm hazelnut ice cream. Apart from an apparent passion for pickled gherkins (bleeugh—was he *pregnant*?), they were astonishingly shopping-compatible. Happily, Millie loaded the fridge with unsalted Danish butter, free-range eggs, Cambazola, and fresh Parmesan. She was also pleased to see he'd chosen cherry tomatoes, posh loo rolls, new potatoes, and two bottles of Fitou wine. Definitely a man after her own heart.

No economy-sized tins of marrowfat peas, thankfully.

Or horrible pies made from dog meat masquerading as steak and kidney.

Or worst of all, prawn-cocktail flavored crisps.

◈◈◈

'Bloody men,' Millie sighed, wriggling her bare toes and admiring the way the ice cubes in her glass glittered like diamonds in the bright sunlight.

'I break open the vodka *and* a fresh bottle of tonic, and this is the kind of abuse I get,' said Hugh. 'Thanks a lot.'

They had been sitting out in his back garden enjoying the warmth of the sun and arguing about pickled gherkins when Millie had abruptly remembered what had brought her here in the first place.

'That poor woman,' she groaned. 'I must phone Lucas and let him know what happened. He'll have to tell her I turned up but her husband had been called away to an emergency meeting.'

'Cheer up.' Hugh looked amused. 'At least he isn't your husband.'

'But that's not the point,' Millie wailed. 'What I'm saying is, she thinks she's married to Mr. Wonderful and he's probably spent the last twenty-five years lying to her! How can anyone ever be sure they aren't being made a big fool of? It's so scary.' She pulled a face. 'I could meet someone gorgeous tomorrow and fall head over heels in love with them, but could I ever *really* trust them?'

Hugh shrugged easily.

'Have to go with your instincts, I suppose. That's all you can do.'

'Oh brilliant. Like my supermarket manager's wife.'

'I'll buy you a lie-detector kit for Christmas,' he promised with a grin.

'Oh God, do I have to wait that long?'

'Anyway, I thought you were off men for the summer. Didn't you declare yourself a sex-free zone or something?'

Millie tipped back her head and took a slurp of her drink. An ice cube and the slice of lemon landed on her nose. She was bored with the Celibet, but it was probably best not to announce this to Hugh. It didn't take a genius to work out that the fact that she was a sex-free zone was the reason he had been able to relax in her company.

It had made it possible for them to be friends without him having to worry all the time that she might be harboring some devious hidden agenda.

Like maybe ripping off his clothes with her bare teeth and—no, no, stop right there, don't even *think* that thought!

Safer by far, Millie decided, to make sure her shameful agenda stayed hidden. Under lock and key. Maybe in a safe. Or better still, a Swiss bank vault.

Nodding in agreement, she lied happily, 'No men, no sex, no hassle. Actually, I can't think why more people don't do it, it's the only way to live! Look, I really should tell Lucas what happened. Okay if I use your phone?'

'Feel free. When you've finished you can bring out another beer from the fridge.' Hugh grinned over at her. 'And one for yourself, of course.'

'I've got to drive home.'

'You could stay for something to eat. I do have food,' he reminded her. 'You may not believe this, but I've been to the supermarket.'

In the kitchen, as she dreamily uncapped two bottles of Becks, Millie wondered what it would be like to kiss Hugh Emerson, how it would feel to run her fingers through his floppy, sun-streaked hair, how his warm skin would feel sliding against hers.

Then, before she got completely carried away, she gave herself a brisk, back-to-earth slap on each cheek, picked up the phone, and punched out Lucas's number.

Chapter 18

Typically, Lucas roared with laughter when he heard what had happened.

'Sweetheart, don't get so het up! It's *okay*,' he reassured Millie. 'The woman paid in advance.'

For heaven's sake. Men, couldn't you just boil them?

'That's not why I'm het up,' Millie spluttered, 'The tosspot's having an affair! He's a complete lowlife! And you can't keep her money—we'll have to give her a refund.'

'Look, business is business,' said Lucas. 'We kept our part of the bargain. It's not our fault her husband's fooling around.'

'You're heartless,' Millie cried.

'Thank goodness for that. Better heartless than a total pushover.'

'God, I hate you.'

'I know you do. Never mind, I'm your boss. It's my job to have pins stuck into my effigy,' said Lucas.

He was grinning, she could just tell.

'You're on his side.' Millie wished she had a wax effigy handy now. 'You're a man, so you just think it's funny. Imagine how you'd feel if you were the one being cheated on!'

But Lucas was by this time openly laughing at her. There was such a thing as trying to stretch the imagination too far. No one had ever cheated on him in his life.

'Look,' he said good-naturedly, 'it's sweet of you to be so concerned—'

'Lucas.' Millie gave it one last shot. 'I always thought that maybe, deep down, you were a decent person.'

'Well I'm not. Heartless through and through, that's me. Sex and money, sweetheart, are what make the world go round. Anyway,' Lucas concluded cheerfully, 'this bloke's wife doesn't know she's being cheated on, does she? So where's the harm?'

'You should be ashamed of yourself.' Millie was filled with disdain. 'You are unbelievable.'

'God, you're beautiful when you're angry,' said Lucas, still laughing as he hung up.

'Here's your beer, sorry I was so long, my boss is a complete pig and I'm thinking of setting him up on a blind date with Lorena Bobbitt—oops, sorry!'

Millie skidded to a halt on the grass as she realized Hugh was no longer alone. Perched on one arm of the wooden garden seat, wearing a pink dress and hugging her knees, was a girl in her late teens with glossy waist-length hair the color of caramel, plenty of orange lipstick painted on her mouth, and a look of adoration in her eyes.

It was the kind of look you saw a lot of on the faces of the audience at a Tom Jones concert. Sort of dazed and gooey, like a half-chewed Jelly Baby. Until she turned, startled, in Millie's direction and said, 'Hugh? Who's *this*?'

The next moment a whole new scenario played itself out in Millie's mind. Hugh would laugh and say, 'Her? Oh that's just Millie, I invited her back here to have a drink with us. You remember, darling, Millie-the-gorilla, I mentioned her the other day. Millie, let me introduce you. This is Orange-Lips, my girlfriend.'

Or fiancée.

Or new wife.

Millie braced herself, her heart pounding away like Michael Flatley's feet.

'Kate, this is Millie, a friend of mine. Millie, this is Kate, Edwina's daughter.' With a brief nod in the direction of the stone wall, Hugh explained, 'She lives next door.'

Phew.

Well, semi-phew. It would have helped if the girl-next-door could have been less pretty.

'Mummy popped out earlier to remind you about dinner,' said Kate. 'She said you had someone with you dressed up as a gorilla.'

So he hadn't been joking about the dinner parties, Millie realized.

'That's right.' Hugh nodded, 'Millie works for a kissogram agency in Newquay.'

'How extraordinary. Poor you!' Kate turned briefly in Millie's direction before swiveling back to give her undivided attention to Hugh. 'But look, we can't wait to see you tonight, Mummy's doing rack of lamb... oh, and sooo much has happened at work, I've got *heaps* to tell you—'

'Kate, hang on, your mother didn't invite me over to dinner this evening.'

'I know she didn't. I asked you, remember? Last weekend!'

Hugh closed his eyes briefly.

'I remember you mentioning it.' He sounded resigned. 'But I didn't say yes.'

Kate's eyebrows shot up in alarm.

'Didn't you? Are you sure? I thought you did. Oh God, and Mummy's been slaving away in the kitchen *all* afternoon—'

'Look, I'm sorry.' Hugh was clearly embarrassed. 'But I've invited Millie to stay for something to eat.'

'Mummy's going to be dreadfully upset.' Kate's face began to crumble like a seven-year-old's. 'We were all *so* looking forward to seeing you.'

'Look, it's fine, absolutely fine, I have to get home anyway.' Millie plonked the two beers down on the wooden table, unable to bear the awkwardness for another second.

'Really? Oh well, it's been lovely to meet you.' Recovering in an instant—maybe she *was* a seven-year-old—Kate beamed at her, then reached over and picked up one of the condensation-covered bottles of Becks. 'There, all sorted out.' Happily, she clinked her full bottle against Hugh's almost empty one. 'Mummy will be thrilled.'

Oh Lord, thought Millie, don't say Mummy fancies him too.

'Sorry about this,' Hugh murmured as he walked Millie back to her car. 'She's the bane of my life. When you move house you make an effort to get along with the new neighbors, but what can you do with someone like Kate?'

Praying her nose wouldn't suddenly telescope forwards and scrape along the gravel drive, Millie said, 'She seems nice enough.'

Her nose didn't do it, thank God. Hugh cast her an impatient glance.

'Millie, come on, don't tell me you hadn't noticed. Kate's got a howling crush on me.'

Oh no, surely not, how truly appalling, what's the matter with the girl, thought Millie slightly hysterically.

Aloud she said, 'Of course I noticed.'

It takes one to know one.

'It's embarrassing,' Hugh groaned. 'I mean, she's so obvious about it and so determined. The last thing I want to do is upset her, but she won't take the hint. It's like trying to fend off a twenty-stone grizzly bear… she just can't seem to understand that this is the last thing I need right now.'

No, thought Millie, the last thing you need is *two* girls with crushes on you, competing for your attention.

Talk about undignified.

Fumbling with her key, Millie managed to unlock the driver's door. Through the car window she glimpsed the carrier bag containing her orange lycra skirt and white vest.

I am shameless, completely shameless, and I deserve to be punished, thought Millie.

'So we've still got the clothes thing going on.' Smiling slightly, Hugh touched her rolled-up denim sleeve. 'First your bra, now my shirt and shorts.'

'Don't worry, it won't happen again, I promise. I'll post them back to you. Right, I'll be off then, enjoy your meal—rack of lamb, yum, gorgeous—you have a nice time and keep the neighbors happy!' By now she was in the driver's seat revving the engine like Michael Schumacher.

'Millie—'

'Okay, see you around and thanks for the drink,' sang Millie as the car shot forward. 'Byeee!'

Millie was wallowing in the bath the next morning when the phone rang on the floor next to her. Oh hooray for cordless.

'I've got another booking for you. Or do you still hate me too much?'

'Well,' said Millie, 'the thing is, I do still hate you. But on the other hand, a job's a job.'

'That's my girl.' Lucas took the jibe in good part. 'In that case, I forgive you for calling me all those mean names.'

'Ha.' Millie prodded her plastic ducks with her toes, sending them bobbing off into a mountain of foam. 'That's nothing. You should have heard the names I called you after you'd hung up.'

'Ah well, when you're as irresistible to women as I am, you get used to it. In fact,' said Lucas, 'are you sure you aren't secretly in love with me yourself?'

'Damn, rumbled again. Meet me at twelve-thirty in the car park at Gretna Green,' said Millie. 'I'll be the one in the frilly white dress and veil.' She paused. 'Just out of interest, can you always tell when a girl's keen on you?'

'Course I can. Easy.'

'*Always?*'

'Always. No question.' She could picture his smirk as he replied. 'All girls are the same, just so easy to read. It's like they're holding a big flashing sign above their heads.'

'Okay, some girls go ahead and broadcast it, they don't care if you know,' Millie began.

'You mean like your friend Hester.'

Good grief, he'd only chatted to her on the doorstep for about thirty seconds.

'We-ell, maybe.' Millie was cautious.

'Come on,' Lucas jeered down the phone. 'Definitely. It's written up there in neon.'

'But what about girls who, um, don't want you to know? The ones who are doing their best to hide it. Can you still tell, even then?'

'Look, there's the eyes, the voice, the body language… there are a million tiny signals and no one can hide all of them. Take it from me,' said Lucas, 'you can always tell.'

Not what she wanted to hear.

Oh, thought Millie, wishing she hadn't asked now.

Actually, not *oh*.

Sod it, bugger, and fuck.

Chapter 19

Orla, wearing a long purple sundress with a fringed and zigzagged hem, smoked furiously, took copious notes, and jumped up every couple of minutes to scrawl some pertinent new detail on one of the many sheets of paper pinned around the walls of her study. Millie, providing a running commentary of the events of the past week, and doing her best to make them sound enthralling, sat on the lilac suede chaise longue and helpfully held up the different colored felt pens so that Orla, whisking past, could seize the right one for each character.

Well, a running commentary of *most* of the events of the past week. Millie had decided that Hugh shouldn't be included in any of this. She was feeling the teeniest bit guilty though, wondering if it was a deceitful thing to do. After all, Orla was paying her a great deal of money for the unexpurgated version of her life and here she was, leaving out the person who was currently having a fair old go at disrupting it.

Not that Hugh was aware of this, of course.

She sincerely hoped.

Millie went hot and cold all over again. It happened every time she mentally replayed Lucas's voice drawling, 'Trust me, it's like it's written up there in neon. You can *always* tell.'

All she could do was cling to the hope that it was a Lucas-thing, something he simply had a talent for detecting, like other people might be gifted musically or have an aptitude for languages.

Anyway, she wasn't telling Orla, and that was that. And it wasn't cheating, surely, to leave someone out. Inventing characters, making stuff up, pretending things had happened to you when they hadn't—well, *that* was cheating. That would be really deceitful, especially when what Orla was after was real-life stuff.

So that was okay, Millie reassured herself. She didn't have to feel guilty, she could just leave Hugh out.

And actually, Orla had heaps to keep her going, Millie marveled, watching her scrawl the supermarket debacle up on the wall in blood-red felt-tip. She'd already devoured the news about Adele moving in with Lloyd and Judy, Hester's continuing fixation with Lucas… and the discovery that Lucas not only knew all about it but was about as tempted as a vegan in a pork-pie shop.

'I love all this,' Orla declared, 'it's so real and down-to-earth! No glitz, no glamour, no celebrities, just ordinary people living mundane lives, wearing chainstore clothes, and cheap shoes…' Her eyes alight with joy, she waved her free hand in the general direction of Millie's pink flip-flops. 'But money or no money, we're all searching for the same things, aren't we? It doesn't matter who you are or how much money you have. Love and happiness, that's what it's all about!'

Ordinary people living mundane lives. In cheap shoes. Gosh thanks, thought Millie.

'Oh God, I'm sorry, it wasn't supposed to sound like that!' Guessing from her expression what she was thinking, Orla rushed over, gabbling, 'I just meant it's a whole new thing for me because I've never written about ordinary people before! Have I offended you? Oh please don't be offended, I meant it in the nicest possible way, truly I did!'

She was clearly mortified.

'It's all right, I know what you meant.' Millie had to stop Orla before she rocketed out of control and spontaneously combusted right there on the Persian rug. Orla Hart novels were a genre in themselves, jam-packed with millionaires, celebrities, and witty, jet-setting, beautiful people living out extraordinary, action-packed lives. The whole point of this new book was that it was going to be totally different in both style *and* content.

Not much happening at all, to characters who were poverty-stricken, boring, bus-catching, and so ugly it was no wonder they hardly ever had sex.

Apart from Lucas, of course.

Millie began to wonder if this had been such a good idea after all. Maybe she should apologize for being such a failure, admit defeat, and give Orla her five grand back.

Except, damn, she'd already spent some of it.

By sheer accident, of course. And only on absolute essentials, like dragging her car kicking and screaming through its maintenance test.

And buying chocolate biscuits.

And wine for the fridge. (Their fridge was extremely fond of wine.)

Oh yes, and a new stripey bikini… plus a few other clothes… and an mp3 player.

And shoes. But only cheap ones, naturally.

'Darling, I *love* all this,' Orla went on, gesturing with enthusiasm to the sheets of paper pinned up around the room, 'but we really do need you to have a love life of your own. Or at least someone you can be *interested* in.'

Don't blush, don't blush.

'I will, I promise,' said Millie. 'I'm just going through a bit of a lull at the moment. It happens,' she added with a shrug, 'that's real life for you.'

'Of course it is,' Orla declared, stubbing out her cigarette. 'But it's not allowed to happen in novels. You're beautiful, darling, you're twenty-five years old! What we want now is for something *zingy* to happen… we need someone to sweep you off your feet, put the sparkle back in your eyes, make your heart beat faster…'

Millie, her heart already beating faster, made a huge effort to banish Hugh Emerson from her mind. Instead she said brightly, 'I know someone who could do that. Jonathan Rhys Meyers.'

'Darling, what a shame, no celebs allowed in this novel. Otherwise of course I'd have arranged for you two to meet.'

Millie swallowed.

'God, *really*?'

'No.' Her greeny-gold eyes bright with mischief, Orla chucked the finished with felt-tips on to the desk. Raking her fingers through her wavy red-gold hair, she wandered over to the window and gazed out. 'But the world's full of possibilities.'

'Mundane possibilities.'

Millie was disappointed about Jonathan Rhys Meyers.

'Ah, but when you meet Mr. Right he won't be mundane, will he? Everything about him will thrill you and that's how you'll know he *is* Mr. Right!'

'Oh well,' said Millie, 'easy. No problem. I'll do that tonight then, shall I? Just pop down to our local wine bar and pick someone up?'

'You could, of course you could.' Orla was bubbling over with enthusiasm. 'Anything's possible, isn't it? That's the beauty of this whole scheme! But wine bars aren't the only places to meet men. I mean, for example, come over here and take a look out of this window…'

Mystified, Millie untangled her legs and slid off the chaise longue. Orla, beaming with delight, moved to one side and put her hands on Millie's shoulders, pointing her in the direction of the shrubbery to the left of the velvety sloping lawn.

Below them, stripped to the waist and lifting rocks into a wheelbarrow, was a tanned, dark-haired man Millie had never seen before in her life.

'Who's he?'

'His name's Richard,' Orla announced with pride. 'He's our new gardener. So, what do you think?'

Millie was incredulous.

A set-up?

'Did you hire him specially for *me*?'

'Darling, don't be silly, of course not. We've got a *huge* garden. Giles hates doing that kind of thing and I don't have the time to do it. So there you go, we needed a gardener.'

Millie turned and gave her a long look.

'Okay, fine, you needed a gardener. So what happened, you looked up "Gardeners" in the *Yellow Pages*, picked one completely at random... and when he turned up he just happened to look like that?'

Orla grinned and lit another cigarette.

'Well, not quite.'

'Go on then,' said Millie. Tell me.'

'I rang up eight gardeners and invited each of them over for an interview. They were all terribly *nice* of course,' Orla explained, 'and they all had heaps of gardenery-type qualifications.'

'And?'

'Well, some of them were old, and some were ugly, and two of them were... shall we say, rather attractive.' Orla took an unrepentant puff on her cigarette. 'So I casually asked them about their personal circumstances, you know, home life and such, and one of them turned out to be married with three children and a Rottweiler.'

'Really,' said Millie.

'And the other one was single! He did have a girlfriend but they broke up a year ago. And he seems *so* charming and he has stomach muscles like you wouldn't believe... ooh, and his favorite author's Salman Rushdie, isn't that marvelous? I thought you'd like a man who knew how to read.'

Salman Rushdie? Oh please.

'This,' said Millie, 'is shameless.'

'No it isn't, it's human nature,' Orla brightly assured her. 'Why hire an unattractive person to work for you when you can hire a pretty one? I'm telling you now, show me a man with an ugly secretary and I'll show you a man scared to death of his wife.'

'But you're matchmaking.'

'Absolutely not!' Orla spread her arms wide. 'Darling, I'm just... broadening your horizons. Giving you the opportunity to meet more people.'

'More men.'

'And why not? Why's that so terrible?'

'It's cheating,' Millie protested.

'It's not cheating at all. It's called making the most of a situation, setting the ball rolling, then sitting back, and seeing what happens. It might work, it might not, but what do you have to lose?' Orla gestured enticingly out of the window. 'I mean, look at him! Crikey, if I were fifteen years younger I'd be down there chatting him up faster than you can say riding mower.'

Millie followed her gaze.

'His hair's too short.'

'Hair grows.'

'I don't believe the book thing for a minute. How can *anyone's* favorite author be Salman Rushdie?'

'Okay, but he's still lovely,' Orla insisted. 'I promise you.'

Millie looked again at the man Orla was intending—metaphorically—to hurl her at. This was beginning to feel alarmingly like being bundled into an arranged marriage. She wondered how Richard-the-new-gardener would react if he knew about it.

Poor chap, and there was he thinking Orla had hired him purely on account of his dazzling horticultural techniques.

'Well?' Orla prompted eagerly. 'You're the important one. What do *you* think?'

Oh dear, what can I say? He has a great body, thought Millie, and a nice neck, and he definitely knows how to handle a wheelbarrow.

But he just doesn't make my heart go zinggg.

'I don't know.' Millie was reluctant. 'I'm not sure—'

'Of course you're not sure! Good grief, you haven't even spoken to him yet! We'll go downstairs in a minute, invite him to join us for a drink on the terrace, then I'll introduce you properly. And there's no need to look at me like that,' Orla scolded as the phone on her desk began to ring, 'I'll be perfectly discreet. Yes, hello?'

Millie moved away from the window in case Richard-the-gardener happened to glance up and discover he was under surveillance.

Okay, being blatantly ogled.

'JD, how lovely to hear from you.' Winking at Millie, Orla perched on the edge of the desk and mouthed 'my publisher.' Then with a mischievous grin, she reached across and pressed the hands-free button. Immediately JD's voice boomed out of the phone.

Orla waggled her eyebrows in just-listen-to-this fashion.

'Darling, the finance boys are tearing their hair out, we really need to get this new contract drawn up, I can't keep them hanging on any longer.'

'JD, it's sweet of you to be so concerned, but I really don't feel I can sign a new contract just yet,' said Orla. 'Not when I haven't the faintest idea how long it's going to take me to deliver the next book.'

'And that's another thing—you still haven't told me what it's about! I mean, it's not as if we're after a full synopsis,' JD pleaded over the speakerphone, 'but at least give us a clue.'

Some poverty-stricken girl with cheap shoes and no boyfriend, who leads a very mundane life, thought Millie. Oh yes, that would go down a treat.

'You see, there you go again,' Orla told him cheerfully. 'Nag, nag, nag, always *pressuring* me. Well I'm sorry, JD, but I don't have anything to show you yet, it's still very much at the planning stage. So you'll just have to wait.'

Gosh. Millie gazed at Orla in admiration. She knew nothing about the world of publishing, but she couldn't help thinking you had to be an awesomely successful author to be able to speak to your publisher like that.

JD, clearly also reminding himself of this fact, began back-pedaling madly. 'Darling, of course, of course, take as much time as you want.'

'What a liar,' Orla mouthed fondly across at Millie. Still perched on the edge of the desk, she crossed one leg over the other, jiggling a metallic violet sandal as she eased another cigarette from her packet. The sandal dropped to the floor and Millie saw that it was a Manolo Blahnik. No cheap shoes for Orla Hart, it went without saying. Each strappy violet sandal had probably cost more than a portable color television.

'So how's Cornwall?' JD was being extra-jovial now, changing the subject. 'Settling in all right? Enjoying the peace and quiet after London? And all that stunning scenery! You know, I envy you. When I was a lad, my parents always used to take us to Cornwall, glorious place, haven't been down there for ooh, must be twenty years.'

'It's still glorious,' said Orla. 'You and Moira must come down and stay with us, we've got heaps of room… How's Colin, by the way? I heard something a while back about him having a spot of bother with his girlfriend.'

'His son,' Orla mouthed to Millie by way of explanation.

'Oh, that's all over. Didn't work out.' JD's tone grew over-casual, as if he were trying to convince himself it couldn't matter less. 'Boy's not bothered. Just one of those things.' He waited. 'Moira's disappointed, of course, she's longing to see him settled down. Especially now he's turned thirty. Still, what can you do?'

Millie watched Orla have an idea; she actually saw it happen. It was like when Tom thought of a terrific new way of catching Jerry and a light bulb flashed on above his head. In similarly cartoony fashion, Orla's green eyes widened with delight and her mouth began to stretch into an unstoppable Tom-type smile.

'Actually, JD, you really *must* come down and see us! Look, we're having a party, um, a week on Saturday, and we'd love you to be here. You and Moira, *and* Colin of course! Make a long weekend of it, how does that sound to you?'

Millie knew how it sounded to her. You didn't need to be a rocket scientist to work out what Orla was up to. Clearly, a thirty-year-old single bloke who'd just been dumped by his girlfriend would be the perfect match for a boyfriendless, mundane twenty-five-year-old who wore cheap shoes.

We can wear matching windbreakers and corduroy slacks, thought Millie, getting a vivid mental picture of the pair of them shyly holding hands. In her mental picture, Colin wasn't exactly George Clooney.

'... Oh yes, huge.' Orla was carrying on happily without her. 'A housewarming party for all our friends, old and new. So how about it, do we have a date? Yes? And Colin too? Fab! Yes, of course there's room in the garden to land a helicopter... okay, great, I'll speak to you again in the week.'

'You're barmy.' Millie shook her head as Orla at last hung up.

'Darling, it's an inspired idea! We need a party anyway to cheer us all up—don't think for one moment I'm doing this just for you.'

Not thinking for one moment that Orla was telling the truth, Millie said, 'So who else are you going to invite? Just people from London?' Slightly suspiciously she added, 'You don't know anyone down here yet.'

'All the more reason to throw a party.' Orla was delighted with her plan. 'If you want to make more friends, what better way?'

❖❖❖

Downstairs, Giles was back after his morning game of golf. In a good mood ('Went round in seventy-four, not bad eh?'), he made coffee for them while Millie explored the contents of the biscuit tin and Orla sat at the kitchen table excitedly jangling her many bracelets as she compiled a list of people to invite.

Entertained by the look of growing incredulity on Millie's face as the list progressed, Giles explained, 'What you have to understand about Orla is, she collects new friends like other people collect stamps. It's her hobby.'

'Only *lots* more interesting.' Unrepentant, Orla added Colin's name to the list with a flourish. 'Anyway, what's wrong with that? I'm a writer. If I didn't meet people, I wouldn't be able to do my job, would I? Especially now,' she glanced across the table at Millie, her smile mischievous, 'with this latest project. I want your flatmate Hester to come, for a start. And your mother. And of course I've just *got* to have Lucas-the-leather-clad-stud!'

Millie said, 'Just so long as he doesn't decide he has to have you.' She watched Orla scribble down a lot more names. 'Fogarty and Phelps? The delicatessen on the High Street? Are you asking them to do the food?'

'No.' Orla looked surprised. 'I was just going to invite them to the party. We buy loads of stuff from there.'

Millie wondered who else Orla was thinking of adding to the list—the girl from the petrol station, maybe? The post boy? The chap from the Gas Board when he called to read the meter?

'... the Westlakes, of course.' Orla was practically talking to herself now, engrossed in lengthening the list. 'Ooh,' she glanced excitedly up at Millie, 'and your father and Judy.'

'But, they don't know you,' Millie wavered. 'All these people you're inviting that you've never even met... how do you know they'll turn up?'

Orla, lighting a cigarette, exchanged a glance with Giles before giving Millie a dazzling smile.

'They just will.'

Giles, standing behind Orla and resting his hands on her shoulders, said with evident pride, 'This is Orla Hart we're talking about. Of course they're going to turn up.'

Chapter 20

GILES WAS RIGHT, NEEDLESS to say. Millie realized how idiotic she'd been to worry. Enthralled to have been invited, two hundred guests RSVP'd that they'd be delighted to attend Orla's party. Her usual London firm of party planners duly rolled up the next Saturday morning to erect the marquee on the east-facing lawn, organize the music and the food, and generally do all the donkey work while simultaneously exclaiming over the beauty of Orla's house, the fabulousness of her grounds, and the to-die-for views.

Millie, having driven over at lunchtime at Orla's request, marveled at the activity surrounding them.

'I have to tell you, this is nothing like the bring-a-bottle parties Hester and I have at our place.'

Even the flower arrangements in the portaloos were spectacular. This party had to be costing Orla an absolute fortune. Millie wondered if the fact that it constituted research for the next book meant it was tax deductible.

At least the weather was perfect, hot and sunny with only the lightest of breezes skittering in off the sea.

'Lucas has a booking at eight, but he'll come straight over as soon as he's finished.' Millie was following Orla upstairs to her room. 'What happened to your publisher and his wife? I thought they were coming down for a long weekend.'

'Oh, he was caught up at some do last night. They're arriving this afternoon.' Winking over her shoulder at Millie, she added, 'With Colin.'

The mental image was still firmly fixed in Millie's mind of some nerdy, bumbling, good-hearted lad with sweaty palms and a pudding-basin haircut. For the first time, she plucked up the courage to say, 'Look, this Colin bloke, you aren't going to force him on me, are you?' Another mental picture began to take shape, of him clutching a plate of vol-au-vents and spending the whole evening shadowing her. Every time she turned round, there he'd be, grinning toothily and offering her a nibble.

While hovering at a discreet distance, Orla and JD and Mrs. JD nudged each other with pride, whispered that it was all going frightfully well and didn't they just make the *sweetest* couple?

'Force him on you?' Orla looked shocked. 'I'm not forcing anything to happen—the whole point of this book is that you live your own life! All I've done is invite Colin down here. You might love him to bits or you might decide you can't stand him. But it's entirely up to *you*.' She grinned. 'Darling, don't panic, I'm not a pimp.'

'So what's he like?' Reluctantly, Millie decided to give her the benefit of the doubt. 'Does he have a job?'

She had privately concluded that Colin—with his Christmas-present sweaters and placid manner—was a bit simple.

'Well, I suppose you could say he's between jobs at the moment.' Orla gestured in that airy way people do when they're talking about someone a bit simple. 'Taking a bit of a break, that kind of thing.'

Millie nodded, understanding.

Right, a total no-hoper.

They had reached the master bedroom by this time, a vast expanse of deep blues and greens and endless mirror-fronted fitted wardrobes. Hanging from one of the wardrobe doors was a Dolce & Gabbana bag, which Orla unhooked and passed to Millie.

'Wow, is this what you're wearing tonight?' Reverently, Millie pulled out the honey-colored shift dress fashioned from fine, butter-soft suede. It was scoop-necked, sleeveless, and very elegant, the kind of thing supermodels slunk along catwalks in. It was also absolutely tiny.

'No, you are.' Looking pleased, Orla threw herself on to the bed. 'I chose it. For you. Isn't it great?'

Dolce & Gabbana? If they'd just opened a shop in Newquay, this was the first Millie had heard of it. Stunned, she said, 'How?'

'I spotted it in a fashion piece in the *Sunday Times* last week. Phoned up, ordered one, it was delivered yesterday.' Orla shrugged as if it were obvious.

How the other half shop.

'Right. Of course,' said Millie.

'Go on then, try it on!'

Millie looked at her.

'I'm sorry, this is a beautiful dress, and it's really kind of you to buy it for me. But I can't wear it.'

'Why not?' Orla bounced upright on the bed. 'Because it's suede? But you aren't a vegetarian!'

'Not because it's suede.' Even as she said it, Millie was running her fingers regretfully over the bodice of the dress. 'Because it's Dolce and Gabbana, and it cost a fortune, and it wouldn't be *me*. It's cheating. Everybody would automatically assume I was a Dolce and Gabbana kind of person and I'm just not. I'm a chainstore girl, I buy clothes from Top Shop and Miss Selfridge and Dorothy Perkins.'

And I wear them with cheap shoes...

'But it's a present, and you'd look so great in it,' Orla pleaded.

'You want me to be Cinderella,' said Millie, 'but *Cinderella*'s a fairy tale. And you want your book to be real. I mean it. Designer labels might be you, but they aren't me.'

'The label's on the inside,' Orla explained. 'Nobody would know! If anyone asks, you can tell them you bought the dress in Top Shop... then they'd think how fabulous you looked and be even more impressed!'

'That's cheating even more.' As Millie spoke, someone tapped on the bedroom door.

Giles stuck his head round.

'JD just rang to say they're running late. Colin's been held up at some interview thingy so they'll be here around six.'

Millie frowned.

Interview thingy? On a Saturday afternoon? Colin had to be applying for the position of assistant lettuce-washer in McDonald's.

'Oh, JD warned me about it yesterday, said this might happen.' Diamonds the size of frozen peas glittered as Orla flapped her hand. 'The MTV thing. I suppose bloody Madonna kept everyone waiting for hours.'

Madonna?

Did she just say Madonna or McDonald's?

Mystified, Millie said, 'What?'

'Oh darling, didn't I mention it? They're rumored to be doing a film together… then again, you know what these movie people are like, it might never come off.'

'A film? *Colin?*'

Orla was grinning now; she'd held out as long as she could.

'Although they'd be brilliant together, no question about it. And now he's finished his run in the West End he's looking for another project, something new and a bit different.'

Making a film with Madonna… fair enough, that counted as something a bit different.

'Okay,' Millie demanded. 'Who is he?'

'Well, just darling Colin as far as we're concerned.' Orla was smiling fondly as she spoke. 'But I suppose you'd know him as Con Deveraux.'

Millie's stomach did a quick swish-swish spin. She gulped. Con Deveraux was the all-singing, all-dancing star of the dazzling new show that had taken the West End by storm.

He was sex on legs.

Oh good grief, thought Millie, and Orla's only gone and invited him down here to meet *me*!

'This is definitely cheating,' she told Orla. 'You said no celebrities.'

Orla looked indignant. 'It's not cheating at all. I've known Colin since he was fourteen years old. He might be a celebrity to you, but to me he's just JD's little boy.'

'So what are you up to this evening? Off anywhere nice?'

The phone was sandwiched between Hester's left ear and shoulder as she painted her nails bright orange. She knew she didn't need to lie, Nat had never minded her going out and having fun. All she had to do was tell him about Orla Hart's party. He'd be delighted, he'd ask her what she was wearing and encourage her to have a great time.

But that was the trouble. What she couldn't tell Nat was that Lucas Kemp was going to the party as well. And there was a chance she might end up having a truly great time. Just not the kind Nat would want her to have.

'No, I don't feel like going anywhere.' Basically, it was simpler to fib. 'I just fancy a quiet night in.'

Bugger, now she'd messed up a nail. Nat certainly picked his moments to phone.

'Come on,' he sounded amused, 'it's Saturday night, you'll have changed your mind by nine o'clock.'

Hester was indignant. What was he saying, that she was weak-willed or something?

'I will not be changing my mind.' She flapped her wet nails as she spoke, uncurling her legs and splaying her toes in preparation for their second coat. 'Definitely *definitely* staying in.'

'Money's running out,' said Nat, who was calling from the payphone in the restaurant. Above the sound of the pips he called, 'Love you, speak to you soon, bye.'

'Love you too,' Hester began, but he'd already hung up. Well it was six o'clock. Back to work, rush rush, chop chop, slave slave. She could picture it only too clearly, the heat and chaos of the kitchen, everyone yelling at each other, the head chef threatening to sack anyone who sliced the wrong thickness of star fruit...

It was almost insulting, Hester decided, that Nat would rather be up there in Glasgow enduring all that torture than down here with her.

Right. Toes. Second coat of Orange Dazzle.

She'd make sure somebody appreciated all the effort she was putting in, if it killed her.

And hadn't orange always been Lucas's favorite color?

Orla and Giles had pulled out all the stops. Or rather the party planners had. As Millie and Hester rattled up the drive in Millie's car, they saw that as well as the artful flood lighting around the house, the trees had been swathed in glittering white fairy lights. The marquee, like a giant wedding cake, occupied the east lawn. Music was spilling out from the marquee and guests milled around the garden in the deepening twilight. The sky was marbled yellow and purple like a bruise, the air warm and still. There were also some extremely smart cars parked along the driveway and, behind the house, Millie glimpsed the rotor blades of a helicopter silhouetted against the skyline. Thankfully there were a few other unsmart cars there too. Squeezing the Mini in between a gleaming black Jag and a much-abused blue van with 'Water, I need water' scrawled across its dusty rear doors, Millie switched off the ignition, spotted Orla amongst the crowds, and wished for the hundredth time she hadn't worn the dress.

'How do I look?' she asked Hester, who was straining forwards, frantically elongating her eyeliner in the rear view mirror.

'What does it matter how you look?' Hester's hands had by this time begun to shake, which wasn't doing her any favors, eyeliner-wise. 'I'm the one meeting Lucas—you should be telling me how great I look.'

Chapter 21

'STUNNING. GORGEOUS,' ORLA DECLARED with all the told-you-so satisfaction of a bride's mother. She hugged Millie again. 'You look terrific. I'm *so* glad you changed your mind about wearing it.'

Millie wasn't, she was consumed with guilt. She felt like a vegetarian caught guzzling a bacon sandwich.

At home she had tried on practically the entire contents of her wardrobe in search of the perfect party outfit. But all the time she'd been able to hear the D&G dress whispering silkily, 'Go on, wear me, you know you want to.'

Even though it was inside its carrier bag, stashed behind the bedroom door, Millie hadn't been able to block out the sound of that hypnotic voice, breathing encouragement. 'Hey, why not? I'm here now... and you *know* I'll make you look great

Millie had done her best to ignore the dress. She had scruples, didn't she? If she was going to be the role model for the main character in Orla's book, she had to be real, she had to be *herself.*

In her own clothes.

No matter how cheap they might be.

The trouble was, after an hour of trying on, it was jolly hard to have scruples when everything else looked awful and the most fabulous dress in the world was peeking provocatively over the top of its carrier bag, winking, and murmuring, 'Hi sweetie, I'm still here.'

So in the end—of course—she'd been *forced* to wear the bloody thing, just to shut it up.

'And you must be Hester,' Orla went on, greeting her with an enthusiastic kiss on each cheek. 'Looking wonderful too, of course. I've heard all about you, it's fantastic to meet you at last! Thank you *so* much for coming.'

Hester was instantly won over, as people invariably were, by Orla's charm and warmth. Now she understood how Millie had become so friendly with her so soon—and how Orla was able to invite a whole load of people she barely knew to her own party.

Not that Hester would have dreamed of staying away. After all, hadn't Lucas been invited along too?

'Are my parents here yet?' Millie thought how weird it sounded, lumping her mother and father together when in fact they comprised a strained menage à trois with Lloyd and Judy as the couple and Adele the loose cannon.

'Absolutely.' Orla's greeny-gold eyes twinkled. 'Your mother's carrying a volume of Sylvia Plath's poetry. I think I blotted my copybook when she asked me which writers I most admired and I said Stephen King.'

'Blimey!' Hester exclaimed.

'Oh darling, are you dreadfully shocked? I know people always say their favorite writers are Tolstoy and Proust, but I just can't do it,' Orla agonized. 'And I'm sorry but Stephen King *does* write brilliant books—'

'Ahem.' Millie cleared her throat. 'Actually, I don't think it was that kind of blimey.'

Glancing over her shoulder, following the direction of Hester's wide-eyed gaze, Orla relaxed and said, 'Oh, you mean Colin.'

Con Deveraux came over, carrying something rectangular and gift-wrapped.

'A little something I thought you might like,' he told Orla as, exclaiming with delight, she began to tear away at the blue and gold paper. 'Hot off the press. A friend of mine works for the company that's printing them up.'

'Eeurgh.' Orla yelped and jumped back in disgust when she saw what it was. Holding the offending item at arm's length—like a box of maggots—she said, 'Am I allowed to burn it?'

Hester was still quietly goggling at Con Deveraux in his cream linen trousers and exquisite pale green shirt. What he may have lacked in conventional good looks, he more than made up for in charisma. Exuding testosterone and star quality, he looked as if at any second he might burst into one of the spine-tingling dance routines featured in *ZaZoom*.

'What is it?' Millie peered over at the cover of the book dangling from Orla's disdainful fingers.

'A proof copy of Christie Carson's first novel. The snide, weasel-faced little megalomaniac who gave me that diabolical review.' Orla pulled a face at Con. 'I can't *imagine* why you think I'd want to read this.'

'Anyone here know any black magic?' Millie said brightly. 'We could cast a spell, turn it into the worst-selling book of all time.'

Con grinned down at her.

'You're Millie, right?'

Aware that Hester, next to her, was panting like a Yorkshire terrier, Millie said, 'And you must be JD's son?'

He laughed.

'Orla told me to look out for you.'

Why, why, thought Hester, *why* couldn't Orla have told him to look out for me instead? Why did all the good stuff always have to happen to Millie? Okay, so Lucas would be here soon, but that was beside the point. Crikey, Hester silently marveled, if anyone could give Lucas a run for his money in the gorgeousness stakes, it was Con Deveraux.

'And I'm Hester,' she told Con, in case he secretly fancied her rotten but was too shy to ask.

'I didn't get it for you so you could do that.' With an apologetic smile in Hester's direction, Con turned and seized control of the book. Orla, who was busy waggling her fingers in a witch-like fashion and sticking imaginary pins into the cover, said, 'But it's what I want to do!'

'We've already decided. I put the idea to the old man on the flight down and he's all for it. You're going to review the book,' Con explained. 'For whichever paper will give you the biggest coverage. Everyone knows what Christie Carson did to you—'

'Bloody hell, I should think the whole *world* knows about that.' Orla shuddered at the memory, then brightened as she realized what Con was getting at. 'You mean I can get my own back on Mr. Nasty-Beardy-Weasel-Face? Slag him off and give his grotty little book the worst review ever in the history of the whole wide world? Darling, you are completely brilliant!'

'Well,' said Con, 'you could do that. It'd make you feel better and everyone else would pat you on the back. They'd say well done and that it jolly well served him right for being so horrid to you in the first place.'

'Which it would,' Orla declared with immense satisfaction. Then, catching the look in Con's eyes, she wailed, 'Oh what *now*? There's a *but*, isn't there? You're going to say something beginning with But.'

Con winked at Millie. Noticing a waiter gliding by, Millie snaffled Hester and herself a couple of drinks.

'*But* my friend gave me this proof copy yesterday.' In an aside, Con briefly explained to Millie and Hester, 'Proof copies come out ahead of publication, for reviewers and people in the book trade.' Turning back to Orla he added, 'And I spent the whole of last night reading it.'

Orla held up her hands, warding him off. 'Don't tell me. I don't want to know.'

'It's very, very good.'

'Oh God,' Orla cried in disgust.

Con shrugged.

'I'm sorry. But it is.'

'I can still trash it though,' she said eagerly. 'I can still rip it to shreds.'

'You could. Although everyone would know exactly why you'd done it.'

'She's got to go completely the other way!' Millie exclaimed. Her eyes locked with Con's. 'What she has to do is give the book a *wonderful* review.'

'Precisely.' Con grinned at her once more. 'Spot on. Tit for tat isn't going to win anybody any brownie points.'

'You just have to rise above it,' Millie told Orla. 'Prove to everyone that you haven't a spiteful bone in your body. You had the perfect opportunity to retaliate... but you didn't. Because you're a better person than that, and you'd never dream of stooping so low.'

'Actually,' said Orla, 'I would. I'm dreaming of it right now.'

Across the daisy-splashed lawn, Millie spotted her mother. Adele was deep in flirtatious conversation with a man in his early sixties.

'Um...' she tapped Orla on the arm, 'who's that chap over there?'

God, how embarrassing, Adele was showing him her Sylvia Plath.

'Where? Talking to your mother, you mean?' said Orla.

Con Deveraux, following the direction of their gaze, said, 'That's my dad.'

The car might not be new but it was performing like a star. Nat, whose own ancient Ford Escort had taken to breaking down at practically hourly intervals in recent weeks, had persuaded Julio, one of the waiters he shared a flat with, to lend him the little Renault for the trip down.

Thank God, Nat thought now, otherwise he'd still be stuck on the outskirts of Carlisle.

It had taken nine hours, but at last he was here. Back in Cornwall. Back in Newquay. The smell of the sea through the car's open windows filled his nostrils, exhilarating and familiar at the same time. God, it was good to be home.

He couldn't wait to see Hester again. Couldn't wait to see the look on her face when she pulled open the front door and saw him there.

Nat pulled into Hester's road, packed with cars as usual, and managed to squeeze the custard-yellow Renault into a space just a couple of houses up from Hester and Millie's. Climbing out of the car, he realized just how much he ached. Since ringing Hester from the Michaelwood service station on the M5, his joints had seized up even more.

But he didn't care. Nothing else mattered now. He was here, and every muscle-numbing minute of the journey from Glasgow had been worth it. Hester was about to get the surprise of her life.

After knocking the knocker and ringing the doorbell several times, Nat realized his great plan had gone somewhat pear-shaped. Hester wasn't there. She had changed her mind after all and gone out.

Oh well, it wasn't the end of the world, Nat reminded himself. Disappointing, but not entirely unexpected.

Although the whole point of asking Hester where she was going tonight had been so he could surprise her when he turned up there too.

Never mind, they had the rest of the weekend ahead of them.

Stretching his aching shoulders, Nat made his way back down the street, threw his overnight bag into the boot, and locked the Renault up for the night. He'd walk into town from here, trawl a few bars, see if he was able to track Hester down one way or another.

And if he couldn't, he'd just come back here at closing time and wait for her to come home. He knew Hester well enough to know that if she was tired, she wouldn't be late.

Millie and Hester, investigating the marquee, were realizing that they actually knew quite a few of the other guests, or at least recognized them enough to say hello to. Richard, the gardener Orla had been so keen to set Millie up with, was looking incredibly spruced up in a neatly pressed khaki safari suit.

'God, no wonder I didn't fancy him,' Millie murmured to Hester. 'Can you imagine going out with someone who wears a safari suit?'

'He wants to be David Bellamy when he grows up.' Hester gave her a nudge. 'Ooh look, don't Fogarty and Phelps look different out of their striped aprons!'

Tom Fogarty and Tim Phelps, joint owners of the best delicatessen in Cornwall, were there with their wives. A group of men in garish clothes—surely Giles's cronies from the golf club—were roaring with laughter at some joke. People were already starting to dance, among them Lloyd and Judy, Millie noticed.

'There's Jen and Trina,' Hester pointed out, spotting two coltish young blondes she recognized from Newquay's trendier nightspots. Remembering, she said, 'Of course, they live up here, I gave them a lift home once from Freddie's Bar. They must be Orla's neighbors.'

It was nine o'clock now, and the marquee was filling up fast.

'Do I look okay?' Having drained her glass, Hester struck a pose. 'Hair all right? Lipstick still on? No bits of food stuck in my teeth?'

'You're fine.' Millie knew what had prompted this. Lucas would be here any minute now.

Basically, Hester was a lost cause.

'Oh God,' Hester squeaked suddenly, like a bat. 'There he is!'

He was indeed. Standing at the entrance to the marquee with his dark hair ruffled, his leather trousers gleaming in the dim light, and his bottle green eyes not missing a trick. Spotting Jen and Trina in their skimpy crocheted day-glo tank tops and shorts, he grinned in recognition then waved and nodded at several other people he knew. Finally—when *everyone* had noticed him—he made his way over to Millie and Hester.

'Good turnout,' Lucas approved, seizing a drink from one of the waitresses who had promptly beelined towards him and flashing a friendly smile at Hester. 'Hess, you're looking great, love the shoes.'

Hester, her heart spinning like a Catherine wheel, peered down idiotically at her feet to see which ones she was wearing. Oh yes, silver strappy mules sprinkled with pink glitter. Now they were her absolute favorites—hooray for glittery mules!

'How did the hen night go?' Millie asked. 'Got away in one piece, then.'

'The hen was sloshed.' Lucas grinned. 'She wanted to call off the wedding and run away with me instead. She tried to persuade me to go to Antigua with her instead of her husband.'

Hester knew how the girl felt. Eagerly she said, 'So what did you do?'

'Dragged her into the ladies' loo and gave her a good seeing-to.'

'My God, you didn't!'

'No.' Lucas winked. 'Hess, I'm shocked. You don't seriously think I'd do something so crass?'

Crass? Good grief, it was her most cherished fantasy come true! Hester's toes were tingling at the mere *thought* of being royally ravished in a toilet cubicle—

'Here she is, here she is!' Materializing at Millie's side, Orla gaily drew her round to come face to face—once more—with Con Deveraux. 'We wondered where you'd got to! I was mentioning your juggling skills to Con and he's *deeply* impressed.'

Standing next to Lucas was playing havoc with Hester's adrenalin levels. As another waiter moved past, she grabbed two glasses of wine from the tray.

'Do you remember Lucas?' Millie innocently asked Orla. 'You met briefly once before.'

As if anyone could forget meeting Lucas Kemp.

'Of course I remember,' Orla gushed.

'Hi again.' Lucas bestowed his most dazzling get-your-knickers-off smile upon Orla. 'Thanks for inviting me. By the way, I love your shoes.'

No! No! Wrong, wrong, wrong. Hester, unable to believe her ears, stared at Lucas. You don't love *her* shoes, you love *mine*.

'And I can see why you're such a wow with the girls,' Orla told him cheerfully.

'Oh dear.' Miming apology, Lucas winked at her. 'Did I forget to do up my flies?'

Chapter 22

Lucas was flirting with Orla. Feeling left out, Hester wandered off in search of another drink. On the edge of the dance floor she bumped into Jen and Trina, shimmying away like nobody's business and causing the band's eyes to boggle almost out of their heads.

'Hey, Hess! What a laugh, eh? Not a bad bash, considering it's full of oldies!' Trina, writhing energetically, seized Hester's glass and drained it in one thirsty gulp.

'Mind you, can't see it lasting too long.' Jen pulled a face. 'We reckon they'll want tucking up with their mugs of cocoa by midnight.' Trina and Jen were eighteen and twenty respectively.

'I don't want to be tucked up with cocoa by midnight.' Hester was alarmed by the prospect. Although she wouldn't mind being tucked up with Lucas.

'So, fancy coming on out with us? We're planning to hit a few clubs later,' panted Trina.

'Why not? Could do.'

'Yeah, it'll be a laugh.'

'Okay,' said Hester. 'Well, see how things go here.' It was hard to give up the Lucas fantasy entirely.

'She's still got it then.' Jen gave Trina a nudge as Hester made her way back to the bar.

'Got what?'

'Stonking great crush on Leg-Over Lucas.'

Trina looked surprised. 'I thought she was still seeing that chef guy.'

From her lofty position as elder sister, Jen rolled her eyes and said, 'God, you're so *young*.'

'I don't know whether or not you've noticed this,' Con Deveraux's tone was conversational, 'but there does appear to be some serious matchmaking going on.'

It was the fourth time in less than an hour that Orla had deftly engaged the two of them in conversation then flitted off.

'I spotted it too,' said Millie. 'I'm really sorry.'

'Don't be.'

'Just so long as you don't think I asked Orla to keep hurling you at me.'

He looked amused.

'It's all right, I don't.'

'Smile,' Millie prompted, 'we're being watched.'

Con's mother and Orla were observing them from a discreet distance.

'Spied on, you mean.' His tone was one of good-natured resignation. 'It's okay, I'm used to this. My mother won't rest until she sees me settled down with the perfect girl.'

'Why? It's not as if you're ancient.'

God, I'm getting old, thought Millie. He's thirty and I don't even think that's ancient.

Con shrugged. 'It's her mission in life. Nice dress, by the way. That color really suits you.'

Glancing over, Millie saw that Moira Deveraux and Orla were huddled together, deep in conversation. Spotting her, Moira instantly stopped talking and pretended to be busy admiring one of the flower arrangements.

'It must matter to her a lot,' said Millie.

'Believe me, it does.'

'Wouldn't it be easier just to tell her you're gay?'

One minute Millie was standing there in the air-conditioned marquee sipping her drink and chattering happily away. The next moment, faster than you could say bolt-from-the-blue, Con had snatched the glass from her hand and swept her outside.

Millie couldn't even feel her feet touching the ground... his arm was clamped like a steel girder around her waist... goodness, he was strong...

When they were out in the garden, Con still didn't release his grip. He kept on going, threading his way through the clusters of guests on the lawn until they reached the back of the house.

But even that wasn't good enough for Con Deveraux. Patting the back pocket of his trousers with his free hand, he pulled out a couple of keys and steered Millie over towards the helicopter, crouched on the dry grass like a prehistoric bird of prey.

Millie, gazing up at it in amazement, said, 'Good grief, are you planning to kidnap me?'

If he was, Paris would be nice.

'We need to talk. Without being overheard.' Sliding open the passenger door, Con gave her a brief leg-up. Then, striding round, he hopped in the other side.

As soon as both doors were closed he turned to Millie. 'How did you know?'

'I didn't. I didn't, I swear.' Not for the first time Millie wished she wasn't blessed with the ability to always say the wrong thing to the wrong person at the wrong time. 'It was a joke, that's all. I just thought it would be a great way to stop your mother nagging you about girlfriends. I'm sorry,' she pleaded. 'It's not even funny. But I *promise* I didn't know!'

Con's gaze was unwavering. It was like being eyeballed at close range by a bird of prey.

'You're sure?'

'Absolutely.'

He breathed out.

'Okay.'

'But I know now,' Millie ventured, feeling brave. 'So doesn't the same answer apply?'

Con shook his head.

'You mean come out? Admit to the world that I'm gay? No, it doesn't apply. I can't do that.'

Millie thought about this for a while.

'Why not?'

'I just can't.'

Gosh, he was stubborn,

'Give me one good reason,' Millie insisted.

'You don't understand,' Con replied flatly. 'It would kill my mother.'

In the distance they could hear the party carrying on without them. But here, locked in the intimate bubble of the helicopter, Millie felt she could say anything.

'Look, this isn't going to go away, is it?' She kept her voice gentle; it clearly meant so much to him. 'And it wouldn't kill her, you know. She might be shocked and upset for a while, but she'd come round in the end.' Ooh, listen to me, I sound lovely, like that warm cuddly therapist on *Richard and Judy*. 'She's your mother, she *loves* you,' Millie carried on, 'and if she cares that much for you, she'll accept it! You *can't* spend the rest of your life living a lie.'

In the darkness, his profile was taut. This, Millie realized, was a completely bizarre conversation to be having with a near stranger. But she couldn't help thinking she knew best.

'Maybe not,' said Con, 'but then again, maybe I won't have to.' He turned his head and looked directly at Millie, the expression in his eyes bleak. 'Maybe I just need to spend the rest of *her* life living a lie.'

Millie pictured Moira Deveraux in her mind: a slim, well-dressed woman in her fifties with a bright smile, and extremely bouffant blonde hair.

'My mother has a malignant brain tumor,' Con went on evenly. 'It's inoperable. They tried chemotherapy but the tumor's too entrenched. According to the doctors, she has anywhere between six and eighteen months to live.'

'Oh God.' Reaching out, Millie touched his white-clenched knuckles. 'I'm so sorry.'

Now she realized why her gaze, earlier, had been repeatedly drawn back to Moira's immaculate, carefully styled hair-do. It was a wig.

'I know my mother. I love her more than anything.' For a moment Con's voice broke. 'Almost as much as she loves me. I was going to tell her, for all the reasons you listed just now. But she fell ill. And now I can't. It would devastate her, and she wouldn't have time to get used to the idea.' He stopped, his eyes glittering with tears. 'So that's why she mustn't find out. If she has to die, I want her to die happy.'

Millie squeezed his hand. No wonder he'd overreacted to her glib suggestion earlier.

'I'm sorry,' she repeated in a whisper. 'You're right. Absolutely right.'

Con managed a brief smile.

'Thanks. Don't tell Orla, okay?'

'Of course I won't.'

He gave her a hug.

'And if I were straight, I promise you, I'd fancy you like crazy.'

Half laughing and half crying herself, Millie hugged him back.

'If my mother could see us now,' Con murmured against her hair, 'she'd be in seventh heaven.'

Sniffing back tears—not very elegantly—Millie said, 'Orla would too.'

◈◈◈

'Oh wow, *look*.' Overwhelmed, Kate nudged Hugh as they rounded the side of the house. 'How cool is that? Keeping a helicopter in your back garden, can you *imagine*?

Hugh glanced over at the turquoise and white Bell Jet Ranger. He'd visited the house on a number of occasions and never seen a helicopter here before.

'I don't think it's Orla's,' he told Kate. 'Probably belongs to one of the guests.'

'Cool,' sighed Kate, dragging him towards it. Then, excitedly, she whispered, 'Ooh, there's someone in there. Look, look, they're all over each other—in a *helicopter*—that is so wild!'

Kate was practically tugging the sleeve off his shirt. Hugh didn't mean to look, but he couldn't help it.

Nor could he help recognizing the girl in the passenger seat, locked in a passionate embrace with the man next to her.

He might not recognize the dress she was wearing, but there was no mistaking that rippling silver-blonde hair.

Something went clunk in the pit of Hugh's stomach. Next moment, the man with his arms around Millie looked up and saw they were being watched.

Hugh saw him smile briefly and tap Millie on the shoulder, drawing her attention to the fact that they had an audience. Millie, laughing and peering round him, gazed out through the Perspex bubble into the dimly lit garden…

'Blimey!' Kate exclaimed, boggling back at her and turning to Hugh in amazement. 'You know who that is, don't you? Whatsername… thingy… gorilla-girl…'

'Millie,' said Hugh.

◈◈◈

'Oh my giddy aunt!' In the helicopter, Millie was so stunned she almost toppled right off her seat.

'Surely not.' Con kept a straight face. 'She's not old enough to be any kind of aunt, let alone a giddy one.'

'Bugger,' Millie gasped as Hugh pointedly turned away.

'You know her, I take it?'

'Well, sort of.' Millie was wondering what on earth Hugh was doing here. Did this mean he knew Orla?

More to the point, she thought with a surge of jealousy, what was he doing here with his gushing, besotted, teenage next-door neighbor?

'Him, then,' said Con as Hugh and Kate disappeared from view. 'It's him, isn't it? Who is he? Boyfriend?'

Huh, Millie thought, some hope.

Aloud she said, 'God *no*.'

Chapter 23

Lucas was nowhere to be seen. Neither was Trina.

'Where is she?' Hester asked Jen.

'No idea. Loo, I expect.' Jen looked vague. 'She's been gone ages.'

Oh brilliant, thought Hester, this is all I need.

As she backed away she collided with one of the bar staff who was carrying in a fresh crate of wine. Actually, now there was an idea. This, Hester decided, was what she *really* needed.

Seizing an opened bottle from the crate, she murmured 'Emergency,' to the startled barman and headed outside.

It was dark now, but the fairy lights illuminating the trees gave the place an unseasonal Regent Street feel. As she meandered around the garden in search of Lucas and Trina, Hester tried to imagine what she would say if she caught them in flagrante.

Then again, what could she say? She had no claim on him. Because he wasn't hers, was he?

Hester wandered on, investigating the tree-lined path that led away from the back of the lawn. When she heard the sound of splashing, she realized that this must be where the swimming pool was hidden. Millie had mentioned it earlier.

And, pretty obviously, someone else had found it.

Clutching the frosty, condensation-dusted bottle of Fleurie to her chest, Hester crept along the narrow path praying she wasn't about to find Lucas and Trina joyfully cavorting together in the water.

When she reached the clearing in the trees and saw what

was happening in the luminous, underlit pool, her eyes filled with tears.

Of relief.

Lucas wasn't with Trina. He was here, alone. Just swimming. On his own. Oh thank you God, thank you. Beaming uncontrollably, Hester was just glad that Lucas was currently under the water—otherwise he might be able to hear her knees clackety-clacking together.

Making her way—unsteadily—around the edge of the pool, Hester came across the rustic bench with his discarded clothes slung across it. She touched the soft white Ralph Lauren cotton shirt, ran her fingers lovingly over the… mmm… still-warm leather trousers—

'Hester!' Lucas's dark head popped up out of the water like a seal. Grinning, he said, 'I hope you weren't about to run off with my trousers.'

'Ha ha,' said Hester merrily—goodness, the very thought—'are you supposed to be in there?'

'I asked Orla. She said it was fine.'

He was wearing dark blue boxer shorts. The water, lapping the sides of the pool, looked almost as inviting as his body.

Lucas, treading water, said, 'What are you doing?'

Dopey question. Hester unzipped her dress and stepped out of it.

'Joining you.'

He swam lazily backwards.

'I was about to get out.'

'Not yet. Stay and keep me company,' said Hester, diving in.

The moment she hit the water her bra shot up over her breasts. By the time she surfaced it was floating in front of her chin, pale and lacy and clearly not up to the task of containment in a diving situation.

Luckily, several glasses of wine ensured that Hester didn't care.

What was the big deal, anyway? People these days went topless on the beach all the time.

'Oh dear.' Lucas was laughing. 'Mascara.'

Bugger, she'd forgotten about that. To stop him laughing, Hester flicked water at him.

Being wet, needless to say, suited Lucas and his mascara-free lashes no end.

He splashed water back at her. Gasping with simulated outrage, Hester swept a great wave of water over him. Oh yes, this was brilliant, just like one of those Rock Hudson, Doris Day movies where Rock and Doris bickered endlessly but you knew that deep down they fancied each other like mad.

'I'm going to duck you,' Hester cried joyfully and Lucas flashed her his wickedest grin.

'I've got water in my ears—I'm sorry, did you just say duck or…'

Hester let out a squeal of fake-indignation and launched herself at him. Laughing, he grabbed her arms. Hester instantly stopped squealing and gazed with unconcealed longing at his mouth. His hands were clutching her elbows and her body had gone all zingy. Closing her eyes she allowed herself to float forwards gently, until her mouth brushed against his stubbled chin—

'I'm getting out now,' said Lucas.

Hester kept her eyes closed. This wasn't at all the kind of thing Rock would say to Doris.

'Don't,' she murmured, her heart racing as her breasts brushed against his chest. 'Don't get out yet.'

You're not even *in* yet!

'Hester, look at me. This isn't right.'

Damn right it isn't right, Hester thought frustratedly. This wasn't supposed to be in the script at all. I'm Doris Day, remember, and you're Rock Hudson…

'You're a great girl,' Lucas went on kindly, 'but you're spoken for. Millie told me all about your boyfriend. She told me how perfect for each other the two of you are.'

Oh fantastic. Thanks, Millie. Thanks a lot.

'He's in Scotland,' Hester muttered. What was going on here anyway? Lucas was a stranger to guilt; he wouldn't recognize a scruple if it jumped up and wrapped its legs around his neck.

'You still shouldn't cheat on him. That would be a rotten thing to do.'

'But he wouldn't know about it,' Hester pleaded. 'How can it be rotten if he never finds out?'

Lucas, his hand gentle, pushed a strand of wet hair out of her eyes.

'You can't guarantee he wouldn't. It's too big a risk to take.'

'Can't I be the one to decide that?'

'I promise you, I'm not worth it. Come on,' he winked and pulled away, 'race you to the side. We've got a party to get back to. Millie will be wondering where you are.'

'Are you sure you don't mind this arm business?'

'Feel free,' Millie said generously. Con had one arm draped around her shoulders and his other hand was affectionately stroking her wrist. Across the dance floor, pretending not to have noticed, Moira Deveraux was beaming away like a halogen lamp.

'We're making my mother very, *very* happy.'

'Good.' Millie smiled at him. 'Any time you need a stooge.'

'Millie Brady, I can't leave you on your own for five minutes,' an amused voice drawled behind her.

It was Lucas, damp-haired and grinning from ear to ear.

'Lucas! You're all wet.'

'I've been swimming.'

'Have you seen Hester? We can't find her anywhere.'

'We had a swim together.'

Oh God, thought Millie.

'Just a swim,' Lucas mockingly tut-tutted. 'Honestly, what a mind you've got. She'll be here in a minute—she just had to repair her make-up.'

Men, they really were hopeless optimists, Millie decided. If Hester had been for a swim she'd be repairing her make-up for an hour at least.

'So that's your boss,' Con remarked when Lucas had headed over to the dance floor. 'I suppose he's straight?'

'As a spirit level.'

'Thought so. Shame,' murmured Con.

'Just as well.' Millie gave him a reproving nudge in the ribs. 'That's hardly the way to impress your mother.'

'I'm so glad you two like each other,' Orla told Millie when Con had gone in search of fresh drinks. Delightedly she added, 'I knew you'd hit it off.'

Yikes, give Orla an inch and she'd take a ten-mile route march. She'd be down at the local church before you could say confetti, flirting with the vicar and putting up the banns.

And Moira would probably start knitting bonnets and booties…

'He's great,' Millie agreed, 'but I don't know if we're talking the romance of the century.'

'No? Shame. Oh well, never mind.' Orla shrugged. 'Lucky I got you a choice then.'

'A choice…?' Millie blinked. Was this why Orla had invited Hugh along to the party? Except if that was the case, what was Kate doing here superglued to his arm?

'Richard,' Orla chided, nodding across the dance floor to where Richard-the-gardener was roaring with laughter, probably at some hilarious gardening joke.

Millie nodded, disappointed.

'Right.'

'And Miles Carter-Buck, from the golf club. You haven't met him yet, he's a stockbroker.' Hurriedly Orla added, 'But I promise you, he's really nice.'

No mention of Hugh. Millie couldn't see him anywhere. Nor could she bring herself to ask Orla what he was doing here, because Orla's antennae would be twitching and buzzing in a flash. She'd be unstoppable.

Instead, to change the subject, Millie said, 'Who's that girl talking to Giles?'

Who indeed? Orla had never seen the girl before, but the familiar little knots were already tightening themselves in her stomach. Not that there was any particular reason to be suspicious, but that was the trouble with an unfaithful husband. If he'd done it once, he could always do it again. Once the trust was gone, you were never able to relax completely. You could never check the pockets of clothes before they went into the washing machine without mentally bracing yourself for the discovery of some incriminating scrap of paper, either a receipt or a phone number, capable of making your heart go thud-thud-thud.

But that way led to endless pain and misery. Orla knew she had to give Giles a chance to redeem himself, to prove he'd turned over a new leaf. Apart from anything else, she knew only too well that endless suspicion and jealousy on her part could destroy their marriage just as effectively as infidelity on his.

The affair with Martine was over. She had to, *had* to believe this. And just because he'd done it before didn't necessarily mean he'd do it again.

'I don't know who she is.' Orla plastered on a bright smile. 'But this is a party, isn't it? Why don't we go over and find out?'

Chapter 24

'Sweetheart, hi.' Giles slid an affectionate arm around Orla's waist. 'Say hello to Anna, from the golf club. She lives in Perranporth.'

'Lovely to meet you.' Warmly, Orla shook the girl's hand. Anna had a firm grip—well, you'd expect that in a golfer—clear grey eyes, and chin-length hair cut in a glossy, magenta bob.

'You too.' Anna smiled. 'It was so nice of your husband to invite me along tonight. I'm pretty new to the area, so I don't know all that many people down here yet. Having a huge party like this is a great idea.' Shyly she added, 'You have a beautiful house.'

'Well, you must come to dinner one night.' Orla spoke with characteristic enthusiasm. Superstitiously, she had already decided the nicer she was to this girl, the less likely Giles would be to start up an affair with her. Or, at any rate, the girl might have enough principles to say, 'Oh no, I *couldn't*, your wife is so lovely. I couldn't possibly do anything to hurt Orla.'

'Anna was just telling me, she's a dressmaker,' said Giles.

'A dressmaker, how fabulous! In that case I must come and see you,' Orla burbled. 'I'd absolutely love to be one of your clients—did you make that gorgeous outfit yourself?'

'Excuse me,' murmured Millie, catching a glimpse of Hugh and Kate through the crowd. 'I'll catch up with you later, there's someone I'd like to say hello to.'

Con had been dragged on to the dance floor by two of the brash, anything-for-a-giggle wives from the golf-club set. Dancing good-naturedly with the pair of them, he winked at Millie as she made her way past.

What am I going to say to Hugh? What am I going to say to him?

Millie didn't get the chance to find out. A mere six feet separated her from Hugh and Kate when she was unceremoniously ambushed by Richard-the-gardener wearing a broad grin and his shirt unbuttoned, Tom Jones-style, almost to his waist.

A few beers, evidently, and Richard shed his inhibitions faster than you could fell a small tree,

'MillieMillieMillie, a little birdie tells me you wouldn't say no to a dance,' he crowed happily—and appropriately—as both arms closed around her like a vice.

Thanks, Orla.

'Maybe later.' Millie didn't have to look over to know that Hugh and Kate were watching.

'No time like the present,' bellowed Richard, hauling her—like a recalcitrant wheelbarrow—on to the dance floor. 'Come on now, don't be shy, I know you fancy me!'

'Actually, I—'

Don't, Millie had been about to say, politely, but she was too slow. Richard's eager mouth fastened limpet-like over hers and all she could do was let out a throaty gurgle of protest.

Uh oh, serious suction…

'Okay, now listen to me,' Richard announced when he came up for air. 'Basically, I know I'm a bit pissed, otherwise I'd never have had the nerve to do that. But I think you're bloody gorgeous, and when Orla started dropping hints… well, I realized she was letting me know you felt the same way about me.'

Millie winced. That was the trouble with Orla's hints, they were the size of lawn mowers. The Rolls-Royce, sit-on kind.

'So how about it?' Richard was gazing at her in earnest.

'How about what?'

'You and me! Getting it together. What d'you reckon, eh?'

Oh dear, the seduction technique was a trifle lacking. Could explain why he's still single, Millie thought. Maybe he should consider taking up evening classes in Beginner's Finesse.

'Well—'

'Millie, seen Hess anywhere? Oops.' Jen stifled a grin. 'Sorry to interrupt your big snogging session, but she said she might be up for a trip into town and now we can't find her.'

Gratefully, Millie extracted herself from Richard's grasp. Quite a firm grasp, actually, as if she were a stubborn tree root he was determined to pull up.

'I'll come and help you look.'

Outside, Jen pulled out her mobile and rang for a taxi. Trina said, 'We're going to hit a few clubs. Fancy coming with us?'

'I can't. Giving my mum a lift home.' Millie pulled a face. 'Look, I'll see if Hester's in the house, you search the gardens. She's here somewhere.'

Hester wasn't in the house. By the time Millie reemerged there was no sign of Jen and Trina. Either they'd found Hester and bundled her into the cab with them or, by a process of elimination, she was back in the marquee.

She wasn't. So that was it, Hester had definitely gone. Con Deveraux, greeting Millie's reappearance with delight, said, 'My darling, you've been away for ages, some dreadful shrieking women have been chucking me around the dance floor like an old floor-cloth… you have no idea how much I've *missed* you.'

'Let me guess,' said Millie as he ran a flirtatious index finger along the line of her collarbone, 'your mother's watching us.'

'Like a hawk. A very proud and happy mother-hawk, at that.' He grinned down at her, his hand affectionately rubbing her shoulder. 'I'll have to introduce you to her in a minute, before she bursts.'

'Okay, but let me have a word with someone first.' Millie, busy scanning the marquee, had—at last—spotted Hugh and Kate. They were still here and she knew she had to speak to them. 'Back in a sec.'

The band had done a terrific job of getting everyone up on to their feet; the air reverberated to the sound of 'Hi Ho Silver Lining' (no wonder Jen and Trina had been so keen to escape) and the dance floor was as packed as the M25. Millie, fighting her way through the hordes of arm-waving, heel-banging forty-somethings, saw that Hugh and Kate were now talking to Orla.

Oh dear, not ideal.

Millie hung back for a few moments, waiting for their conversation to end, while the dancers swirled and stamped around her.

Hugh kissed Orla. Kate, giggling and starry-eyed, kissed Orla as well. Then Orla kissed and hugged them both in return… and now all three of them were laughing together…

Honestly, what was going *on* over there? Anyone would think they'd just got engaged.

Millie abruptly felt sick. Good grief, oh no, *surely not.*

By the time she'd finished battling across the floor, Orla was on her own. Hugh and Kate had vanished.

'Hi. Um, where did those, um, people go?' Skidding to a halt, Millie did her best to sound as if she were making polite conversation, merely interested in Orla's welfare.

'Home.' Orla was waving at people she knew, beckoning a waiter over, and tapping her feet in time with the music. 'Got an early start tomorrow.'

Clunk, went Millie's heart, dropping into her boots. Thanks to her feverishly overactive imagination, an early start could mean only one thing.

Gretna Green.

Her voice came out all high and squeaky, very Minnie Mouse. 'Uh, who are they?'

Orla took one look at her and started to laugh.

'Oh, right, you mean the devastatingly good-looking guy who was just here? You're wondering if by any chance he's another of the possibles I lined up for you tonight to take your pick from? Sorry, sweetie, but he isn't a contender.'

Millie was glad of the multi-colored lights swirling over the dance floor, camouflaging her pink cheeks.

'I wasn't wondering that at all. I just asked you who they were.'

'Hugh Emerson. Hot-shot computer consultant. Gorgeous,' said Orla with a naughty grin, 'but not for you.'

'Oh.' Her heart banging away, Millie said, 'His girlfriend seems quite… young.'

'Not girlfriend, just some neighbor. Hugh installed my computer. His wife died a few months ago.' Orla was having to shout to be heard above the music. 'Tragic, tragic. Absolutely heartbreaking. And the very last thing you need. Rebound relationships.' She shuddered theatrically. 'The very worst kind in the world. Doomed to disaster, darling, don't even consider it!'

Just some neighbor. Not his girlfriend, not his fiancée, Millie thought ecstatically, just some neighbor, *hooray*.

'No, no, you concentrate on darling Con.' Orla gave her arm an encouraging squeeze. 'He's lovely and he's single.'

Yes, thought Millie, but I'm a *girl*.

Nat made his way along the street, praying the lights would be on in Hester and Millie's house. A trawl of the bars and nightclubs had turned up several old friends but no Hester. Now it was midnight and he was shattered; the five-hundred-mile drive down from Glasgow had really taken it out of him.

There were no lights on, but Nat rang the doorbell anyway. Maybe they were asleep in bed.

He rang again, then banged on the door with his clenched fist.

Nothing, no response, still no one at home.

Hess, where *are* you?

Crouching on the doorstep, using the pen in his jacket pocket, Nat scribbled a note on the back of a flyer advertising special rates for pizza deliveries.

> *Hess. Surprise! See the yellow Renault parked outside between the white van and the dark blue Jag? Now look inside...*

Smiling to himself, Nat pushed the note through the letterbox. Then, yawning uncontrollably, he made his way back to the borrowed car. At least it was a warm night. He'd sleep until Hester arrived home and found him. Knowing her, the moment he closed his eyes she'd be back, covering him with kisses, shrieking with delight, and waking everyone in the street.

Hester blinked up at the canopy of branches spread out over her head. Through the gaps between the leaves of the cherry tree she could see stars glittering in the indigo velvet sky.

When you wish upon a star... Hester thought groggily, clutching the empty wine bottle to her chest and realizing that she must be very drunk indeed if she didn't even care that wiggly insects could—at this very moment—be crawling through her hair and heading straight for her ears.

She didn't even care that the ground was spectacularly uncomfortable, her mouth was dry, and her eyes were sore from crying. At least it was peaceful out here. All she could hear was the gentle slip-slop of the water lapping at the sides of the pool and the raucous strains of the party carrying on in the far distance.

Earlier—how long earlier?—she had heard Jen and Trina calling her name. Then they'd stopped. After that, only a couple of wild rabbits bouncing across the grass had briefly disturbed her, before loping off once more into the undergrowth.

Together.

Gone to get laid, no doubt. Lucky old rabbits.

God, I made a fool of myself tonight, thought Hester, holding the bottle up to check it really was empty. I'll be the laughing stock of Newquay when this gets out.

And it's all Nat's fault. If he'd been here, none of this would have happened.

Her eyes filled with fresh tears as she realized how unfair she was being, blaming Nat.

It's no good, I'm just a horrible, horrible person. I don't deserve a lovely boyfriend, Hester decided wretchedly.

But it still wouldn't have happened if only he'd been here.

Hester closed her gritty eyes. Eeeuurgh, now her head was spinning like a… like a spinny thing. Okay, just ignore it, maybe rolling on to her side would help… ooh yes, that was *much* better…

Within seconds, Hester was asleep.

Chapter 25

A PUBLISHER, AN ACTUAL literary giant. Now this was more like it!

Adele, thrilled to be engaged in conversation with an intellectual, was doing her level best to impress JD—Jasper Deveraux, what a name—with her knowledge of the great poets.

It would have been nice though, if he could have shown a bit more enthusiasm in return.

'Sylvia *has* to be my favorite, of course.' As she spoke, Adele deftly slid her copy of Sylvia Plath out of her bag and whisked it in front of his startled eyes like a flashcard. 'But one can't ignore Christina Rossetti, such *awesome* power and grace...'

Poetry wasn't JD's thing at all; nothing sent him off to sleep faster than a couple of sonnets. Unless there was a punchline to look forward to, a guaranteed laugh at the end. Pam Ayres was far more up JD's street than Sylvia face-like-a-wet-weekend Plath.

Who was this Christina Rossetti anyway, with her awesome power and grace? Sounded like an Olympic gymnast.

In a valiant attempt to change the subject, JD nodded vigorously and declared, 'You're absolutely right, of course. So tell me, have you managed to get away yet this year?'

God, listen to me, I sound like a *hairdresser*.

About to launch into something moving and profound by Rossetti, Adele was abruptly halted in her tracks. Holidays, holidays, now what could she say that would impress this wealthy, powerful, erudite man?

'Not yet, but I certainly will,' Adele trilled. 'Monte Carlo and St. Tropez are my favorite places to visit,' she confided prettily. 'How about you?'

'Oh, we have a villa in Tuscany. Marvelous food, wonderful wine, just the place to get away from it all,' JD enthused. Then he laughed. 'That is, until you realize everyone you know is out there getting away from it all too!'

Tuscany. Tuscany. As she watched him chuckle to himself, Adele suddenly realized two things. Tuscany, also known as Chianti-shire, was where influential, intellectual, artistic, and literary types took their holidays. The glitterati. BBC executives. Actors. Writers. Opera singers. Good grief, why had it never occurred to her before that Tuscany would be *the* perfect place to vacation and meet glamorous, intellectual people on exactly the same wavelength as herself?

The second thing Adele realized was that although she'd read endless newspaper articles about Tuscany and the kind of people who holidayed there… gosh, even the Blairs… she didn't actually have the faintest idea where Tuscany was.

Give her a map of Europe and a pin and she wouldn't have a clue. Spain? France? Italy? She had an inkling it was in the *middle* of somewhere, but that was all. Could be any of them.

How incredibly embarrassing. Chianti-shire. But when you weren't a great drinker of wine that was no help at all. Was Chianti a Spanish wine or Italian or French?

First thing tomorrow, Adele silently vowed, she would find out everything there was to know about Tuscany, every tiny last detail.

Including which country it was in.

Aloud, she said vivaciously, 'Of course, my great love is opera. I'm a huge fan of Andrea Bocelli.'

JD, more of an Andrea Corr man himself, decided the time had come to make his escape. Touching the back of Adele's hand he said genially, 'Why don't I go and find you a drink?'

Much as he shared his wife Moira's wish to see his son happily settled down with the right girl before she died, he couldn't help hoping that girl wouldn't be Millie.

Being condemned to a lifetime of in-law-dom with Adele Brady would be more than he could bear.

'You have a fabulous daughter,' Orla told Lloyd Brady as they said their good-byes at the end of the evening. Turning to Judy, who was holding Adele's pink cashmere wrap while Adele made a production of kissing JD and Moira, she added in an undertone, 'And you have the patience of a saint.'

'I do.' Judy nodded cheerfully. 'Then again, I also have a secret stash of cyanide.'

Moira Deveraux whispered in her son's ear, 'You don't have to stay here at the house with us, you know. Nobody would mind if you… disappeared.'

Con grinned at the way his mother raised her penciled-in eyebrows delicately in Millie's direction as she spoke.

'Mother. I can't believe you're even suggesting it.'

'We're only down here for one more day.' Moira tapped her watch. 'Sometimes, darling, you simply can't afford to hang around, you just have to go for it.' Her expression softening, she went on fondly, 'Your father and I had a whirlwind romance, you know. He swept me right off my feet and we were engaged within a week.'

'You mean he tried it on with you the first night and got lucky.' Con looked scandalized. 'Mum, I'm sorry, but that is disgraceful. I'm deeply, *deeply* shocked.'

Unperturbed, Moira said serenely, 'The spark was there. When the spark's there, you can't ignore it. And,' she smiled over at Millie, 'I saw it there between the two of you tonight.'

'Okay.' Con held up his hands in defeat. 'I already tried it. I said I wanted us to spend the night together and she turned me down. She told me she wasn't that kind of girl.'

So Millie had standards, morals, a healthy respect for her own body. Happily, Moira said, 'Now I like her even more.'

It was two o'clock in the morning by the time Millie arrived home after first dropping off her mother, her father, and Judy. Now, parking a little way up the street, she passed a white van, a Renault the color of Bird's custard, and a dusty dark blue Jaguar.

The house was silent and empty. Yet another flyer advertising pizza delivery had been pushed through the door; Millie kicked it to one side and headed on up the stairs. Hester wasn't back yet. Still, if she was out with Jen and Trina that was hardly a surprise.

Exhausted, Millie peeled off the fabulous Dolce & Gabbana suede dress, skittishly didn't bother removing her make-up, and was asleep within seconds of falling into bed.

Something was ringing. On and on, in a horribly persistent fashion. Millie groaned, rolled over, and pulled the pillow over her head. If it was Hester leaning on the doorbell because she'd forgotten her key she would be forced to kill her.

But it wasn't the doorbell, her confused brain finally managed to figure out. The ringing was too rhythmic for that.

It was the phone.

Urrgh, no, go *away*.

Buried beneath the pillow, Millie kept her eyes closed and prayed for it to stop. But whoever was calling was certainly persistent; they were showing no signs of giving up.

Then again, it could be a genuine emergency, Millie realized as she padded downstairs to answer the phone.

Hester, desperate to come home but so drunk she couldn't remember where she lived. Ha, that had happened before.

Or Adele, panicking because she couldn't find her precious volume of Sylvia Plath poetry and ringing to find out if she'd left it in the car.

Or even Con Deveraux, calling to tell her he couldn't sleep for thinking about Lucas in his tight leather trousers and begging her for Lucas's phone number…

Hm, maybe not.

In the living room, Millie picked up the phone.

'Hello?'

'Are you alone?'

'What?'

'Is he there with you?'

In her muddled, just-woken-up frame of mind, Millie couldn't place the voice at the other end. Well, that wasn't strictly true, she *thought* she could place the voice because it sounded exactly like Hugh Emerson's voice, but since the logical, slightly-less-befuddled part of her mind told her it couldn't possibly be Hugh, she knew she must be wrong.

'Is who here with me?'

'I don't know. Any of them, take your pick. Just say yes or no.'

Lord, now it sounded even more like Hugh's voice. Startled—and by this time pretty much awake—Millie said, 'Nobody's here. I'm on my own. Why?'

A pause. Followed by a sigh. Of relief?

'I just needed to find out.'

Millie, her heart racing like a greyhound, whispered, 'Why?'

'Come on.' This time his tone was wry. 'I think you know.'

Millie couldn't speak. The greyhound in her chest was hurtling around the track. In a daze, she glanced at the clock on the mantelpiece and saw that it was three-thirty.

Three-thirty, in the morning…

'Millie? Are you still there?'

'I think so.'

'Open the curtains.'

'What?'

'Go on.'

Was this actually happening? Or was she really still upstairs in bed with her pillow clamped over her ears?

Oh well, if it was a dream, where was the harm in letting it carry on?

Crikey, Millie thought, this was in danger of turning into the best dream she'd had in years.

Making her way over to the window, she pulled open the curtains.

Hugh was out there, on the pavement, illuminated by the pool of orange light from the streetlamp overhead. He had changed into a white denim shirt and jeans.

Speaking into his mobile, he said simply, 'I needed to see you.'

Oh good grief.

But like this?

Millie wished she wasn't wearing her saggy purple Harry Enfield T-shirt; the picture on the front of *Kevin the Teenager* wasn't what you'd call seductive. She also wished—illogically—that she'd had the presence of mind to brush her hair before staggering downstairs to answer the phone.

'You needed to see me? Why?'

'I just did.'

Making a feeble stab at humor, Millie said, 'Bet you wish now you hadn't bothered.'

'No.' Deadpan, Hugh replied, 'I've always had a thing about Harry Enfield.'

Pause. Millie couldn't speak.

'Right,' said Hugh. 'Well, we can carry on like this for the rest of the night, or you could think about whether you might like to open the front door.'

'Two minutes,' said Millie shakily. 'I'll be back in two minutes.'

'Where are you going?' He half smiled. 'Upstairs to tip some bloke out of bed and squeeze him like toothpaste out through the back window?'

'Surprisingly close,' said Millie. 'Actually, upstairs to clean my teeth.'

Chapter 26

When Millie opened the front door two minutes later she said, 'I wasn't expecting this to happen.'

'Neither was I.' Hugh walked her gently backwards through to the living room and gazed down at her, the expression in his dark eyes unreadable. 'That chap I saw you with… the one in the helicopter… are the two of you…?'

'No.' Millie was trembling. 'No.'

'What about the other one? In the marquee?'

'He's Orla's gardener. He was just out of his tree.'

'Well, that's appropriate.' Hugh waited. 'And there's definitely nothing going on between you and your boss?' Lucas!

'Definitely nothing going on,' Millie whispered. 'Absolutely definitely not.'

'Right. Well, good.' As Hugh pushed his sun-bleached hair back from his forehead, Millie saw that his hand was unsteady. 'I couldn't sleep, you know,' he went on. 'Couldn't stand the thought of all those men hanging around you tonight. It made me realize… God, *so much*.'

'And?'

'I had to come and see you.'

Feeling brave all of a sudden—ah well, what the hell, it might still be a dream—Millie raised one eyebrow a fraction and said quizzically, '*See* me?'

He reached out and touched her face, his warm fingers tracing the outline of her pale pink mouth.

'Okay. Kiss you.'

Too slow, too *slow*. By this time, tormented beyond endurance, Millie flung her arms around his neck, pressed every available cell of her body against him, and whispered, 'Right, well, better get on and do it then.'

The kiss, when it happened, sent everything spiraling out of control. Millie, feeling as if she were on fire, wouldn't have been the least bit surprised if her *Kevin-the-Teenager* nightie had suddenly burst into flames. There was enough electricity zapping through her body to light up the Trafalgar Square Christmas tree. It was simply beyond belief that one mouth, one pair of lips, and one tongue could be capable of having such a staggering effect on… well, *all* of her.

This was kissing as Millie had never known it before, such a dazzling experience that she actually did stagger. Her knees had gone, and she was forced to open her eyes just to get her bearings. Dazed and blinking, she realized that while the rest of her had been dizzily reveling in the glory of Hugh's mouth on hers, her shameless fingers had been busy pulling his shirt out from his jeans, unfastening buttons like nobody's business, and roaming frantically over his chest…

Oh well, nothing like playing it cool, keeping them guessing, maintaining that enigmatic facade—

'*Ouch*.' Hugh winced. 'What was that for?'

'Oh God, sorry, sorry. I needed to make sure I wasn't dreaming.' Millie agitatedly rubbed the red mark on the back of his hand. 'I was pinching myself. Except no wonder I couldn't feel it,' she apologized. 'I pinched the wrong hand.'

He held her face, his mouth a tantalizing half-inch away from her own.

'I've dreamed of doing this for weeks. I haven't been able to stop thinking about you. I swore to myself nothing would ever happen, but tonight was too much. I just couldn't stay away.'

Millie was so happy there were tears swimming in her eyes.

'I'm glad. I mean, me too. Thinking about you all the time, wishing something could happen.' Drunk with exhilaration, she was having trouble stringing together a sentence that made sense; the glorious smell of his bare skin alone was enough to reduce her to gibberish. 'I was so jealous, seeing you there with Kate. I thought you were going to elope with her to Gretna Green. And now you're here, you came all this way to see me, well, kiss me… you really are an excellent kisser, by the way, I can't imagine how you got to be so good, but if you ever fancy a part-time job I'm sure Lucas would hire you in a flash…'

'Millie, you're wittering.'

'Gosh, am I? Surely not. Not me, I promise you, I never ever witter when I'm nervous.'

'Are you nervous?' Hugh smiled down at her. 'Why?'

Why? Why? Was the man *mad*!

'Because you drove over here to kiss me and now you've kissed me and you're still here,' Millie blurted out, 'and I may not be the shiniest shell on the beach, but I think even I can guess what might be about to happen next.'

While she'd been babbling away, Hugh had been holding her head between his hands, gently stroking the ultra-sensitive skin just beneath her earlobes. Now he took his hands away and began rebuttoning his shirt.

'I didn't come round here to make you do anything you don't want to do. If I'm making you nervous, I'll go.'

'Nooo!' Letting out a squeal of dismay, Millie grabbed him before he could disappear. 'I didn't mean it like that. I want you to stay, more than anything. I'm just scared I'll be a disappointment. You might think I'm rubbish in bed.'

Hugh looked as if he was trying hard not to laugh.

'Why might I think that?'

Millie hadn't the foggiest. She just knew, suddenly, that it was a horrible possibility.

'Well, it's like Richard-the-gardener, at the party earlier.' Shaking her head, she tried to explain. 'He kissed me, and it was awful, completely awful, like being attacked by an Aquavac. But he doesn't know he's a useless kisser, does he? He probably thinks he's *brilliant*. So how do I know I'm not as bad at… you know, *thingy*… as he is at kissing?'

Hugh's mouth was starting to twitch at the corners.

'You don't kiss like a sink-plunger, I can promise you that. Besides, it works both ways. I might be useless in bed.'

'Seriously?'

'No. Actually, I'm spectacular.'

'Now you're definitely making fun of me.'

As he put his arms around her, Millie could feel his shoulders shaking with laughter.

'I'm not. I just think we should risk it, that's all. You can give me marks out of ten if you like.'

Millie smiled. She began to relax, just a fraction. She was pretty sure she wasn't hopeless in bed.

Oh God, it's going to happen, she shivered, it's actually going to happen.

Best of all, evidently having decided to crash out at Jen and Trina's house, Hester wasn't here.

I can have my wicked way with Hugh, Millie thought joyfully, and she'll never know! Hooray, I won't have to pay her two hundred pounds!

Before she knew it, Hugh was kissing her again. Unbelievably, the fireworks were almost more dazzling this time. Even more astonishingly, her fingers—completely of their own accord—were now engrossed in undoing the zip of his jeans.

'The curtains are still open,' Hugh murmured.

'We'd better go upstairs,' Millie whispered back, tingling at the erotic contact of his mouth against her ear.

'Are you sure?'

'I'm sure. How about you?'

'Daft question. I drove over here at half past three in the morning, didn't I?'

Millie took a deep breath. She didn't want to say the next thing, but it had to be said.

'How about… you know… your wife?' Pause. 'Louisa.'

Instantly she wished she hadn't added the last bit. As if he may have forgotten his wife's name.

'I'm here,' Hugh repeated, brushing a stray tendril of hair from her cheek. 'I don't want to talk about Louisa.'

Good, thought Millie, because I don't either.

'But you're sure?'

Lifting her up into his arms—eek, no knickers!—Hugh carried her effortlessly towards the staircase. Amused by her futile attempts to pull down her nightie and keep herself decent—for the next ninety seconds at least—he said, 'I'm sure.'

It had been magical. Millie, her eyes closed and her limbs comfortably interlaced with Hugh's, decided that there was no other word for it.

Just magical.

'And now the scores please, from the judging panel,' intoned Hugh. 'First, marks out often for content.'

'Well, that's easy.' Millie's eyelashes fluttered and she peeped up at him. 'Two.'

'Style.'

'One.'

'Star quality.'

'One and a half.'

Hugh shook his head and tut-tutted like a plumber being asked to give an estimate.

'Oh dear, harsh scoring from the British judge. Does she realize, I wonder, what she's let herself in for…?'

'Aaargh, no!' Millie let out a shriek as he began to tickle her rib cage; within seconds she was a squealing, writhing heap, hopelessly tangled up in the sheets. 'Ten, I meant ten! Absolutely ten out of ten… perfect!'

'For which category?'

'All of them!' gasped Millie.

'Even star quality?'

'Sixteen out of ten for star quality!'

'Excellent.' Nodding with satisfaction, Hugh stopped the onslaught. 'Ladies and gentlemen, the British judge has sensibly reconsidered the scores she awarded earlier, and I have to say, this is much more like it.' Pausing, he went on, 'I also have to say, the British judge wasn't half bad herself. She participated in the proceedings in a highly satisfactory manner.'

There then followed the kind of Hollywood moment that made the breath catch in Millie's throat. For several seconds she and Hugh gazed at each other, saying nothing but each silently acknowledging that what had just passed between them had been *meant* to happen.

Finally, Hugh bent his head and pressed a row of kisses around the base of her throat.

'Thanks.'

'Don't mention it. Any time,' Millie said half jokingly. 'My pleasure.'

'I'm serious.' Hugh's dark eyes softened. 'You're amazing. I haven't been able to stop thinking about you. I thought I was hallucinating at first when I saw you at Orla's party. Except,' he added ruefully, 'if it had been an hallucination you wouldn't have been kissing some other chap in a helicopter.'

'It wasn't kissing. Just a hug. He was upset about something,' said Millie. 'Anyway, you were there with thingy.' She wriggled her head into a more comfortable position in the crook of Hugh's shoulder and slung one leg carelessly over his. 'I still can't believe you know Orla as well.'

'I designed a website for Fogarty and Phelps,' Hugh explained. 'People order customized gourmet baskets from their deli to be delivered all over the world... it's boosted their business by three hundred per cent. Anyway, Orla picked up a leaflet about it in their shop, got chatting—the way she does—and told them how desperate she was for someone to put together a new software package for her. It's not what I normally do, but you know what Orla's like. She phoned up and begged me to help her out... and basically I couldn't refuse.' He smiled. 'How about you?'

'Through the travel agency. We just seemed to hit it off,' said Millie, almost completely truthfully. 'But what I don't understand is why *you* were there at the party with your next-door neighbor.'

Hugh rolled on to his side, ruffling his hair and propping his head up on one elbow.

'I wasn't going to go. I haven't been to a party since Louisa died. But Kate came over to borrow some milk—'

'*Milk?*' Millie's eyebrows shot up in disbelief. 'Couldn't she have gone to the corner shop for milk? You know, the corner shop at the end of your road, less than fifty yards from your front door?'

'Evidently not.' Wryly Hugh said, 'She finds some excuse or other to pop round most days.'

'Tart.' Millie was indignant.

'Anyhow, she spotted the invitation on the kitchen table and practically wet herself with excitement. She couldn't believe I wasn't planning to go. Kate's a huge fan of Orla's books, and the invite said to bring along a guest. After that she went on and on at me until I gave in. I didn't have the heart to disappoint her.'

'You are a soft touch,' Millie declared. 'A great big fluffy marshmallow. And *she* is a complete tart,' she added, dropping kisses on his hard, deliciously brown chest. 'Do you realize, that girl would jump into bed with you at the drop of a hat? Honestly, talk about shameless, couldn't *possibly* be like it myself.'

'Perish the thought.' Smiling, Hugh traced his fingers along the curve of her hip. 'Anyway, I'm not interested in jumping into bed with her. I was the perfect gentleman this evening, I'll have you know. Took her along to the party, dropped her home again, pretended not to notice that she was waiting for a good night kiss…'

'At the very least,' Millie cried. 'The hussy!'

'Basically,' Hugh went on, 'all I could do was think of you. I couldn't sleep, I was so jealous. Wondering just how involved you were with Helicopter-man, dreading what you might be getting up to, imagining him whisking you off to London…'

'No,' whispered Millie, her eyes filling with tears of happiness for the second time that night. 'And no, and no. This is all I want. You're the only one I want. And now that it *has* happened...'

'What?' Hugh pulled her into his arms.

'I just want it to happen all over again.'

He grinned. 'Excellent idea. That is, if you're not too tired.'

The cheek of it!

'What do you think I am, some kind of wimp?' Outraged by the slur, Millie rolled him over on to his back and pinned his arms to the bed. 'Let this be a warning to you, neither of us are going to get *any* sleep tonight.'

Rrringgg, rringg, rrrrinngggg.

Jerking awake, Millie sat bolt upright and flung herself across the bed to switch off the alarm clock. But instead of empty space, she encountered warm flesh. Milliseconds later, the wondrous events of the last few hours came flooding back.

Hugh, blinking and rubbing his eyes, said, 'It's not your alarm clock.'

Oh. Oh no, so it wasn't. The clock was silent, its hands indicating that it was six-thirty. By Millie's reckoning, they'd managed a whole three quarters of an hour's sleep.

So where was that awful piercing noise coming from?

'Doorbell,' murmured Hugh. 'Hurry up, Cinderella. Your helicopter awaits.'

'Don't make fun.' Millie pulled a face. 'It could be your next-door neighbor, come to challenge me to pistols at dawn.'

Her Harry Enfield T-shirt-cum-nightie was draped over the dressing-table mirror where she had so impatiently flung it last night. Covering her nakedness with her white towelling dressing gown, Millie fumbled with the belt as she staggered along the landing. Muscles she hadn't used for a long time were now making their presence felt—hooray, we got laid last night!—each step causing her to wince with a mixture of pain and remembered pleasure.

Hester's bedroom door was still open, her bed unoccupied. It had to be Hester ringing the doorbell, arriving home happy and exhausted after a completely riotous night out.

Happy and exhausted and about to become happier still, Millie realized, when she discovered Hugh upstairs. Oh well, so Hester would win the Celibet and become two hundred pounds richer.

What the hell. With a soaring heart and an uncontrollably smug smile, Millie decided that some bets were simply worth losing. In fact, this one had turned out to be the bargain of the year.

Chapter 27

'Oh my God!'

Millie experienced acute head-rush when she saw who was standing on the doormat.

Nat?

Nat!

'Sorry.' Nat managed a repentant grin. 'Sod's law, you always get the wrong person out of bed. Did I wake you up?'

'It's six-thirty in the morning. It's Sunday,' Millie babbled helplessly. 'Of course you woke me up! Nat, I can't believe this, what are you *doing* here?'

'Drove down last night to surprise Hester. But she was out so I waited in the car. Then fell asleep. Hess was supposed to wake me up when she came home, I put a note through the door…' As he spoke, Nat's eyes traveled down Millie's body, all the way to her bare feet. There on the floor, squashed beneath her left heel, lay the pizza delivery flyer with his message scrawled across the back.

'Oh.' Apologetically, Millie bent down and peeled it off the sole of her foot. 'Sorry.'

'My fault. Anyway, I'm here now.' Nat might be looking pretty disheveled from his night in the car but he sounded cheerful enough.

'I'll go on up, shall I? Surprise her.'

Oh dear. There was a lot to be said for cloning, thought Millie. If she could have fobbed Nat off with an artificial reproduction of

Hester—and had a fighting chance of getting away with it—she would have done it without a shadow of a doubt.

For a mad moment she even considered claiming that Hester had got up early and already gone out. For an invigorating jog maybe, or a dawn raid on the gym.

But since that was never going to work either, Millie took a deep breath and said, 'The thing is, Hester and I went to a party last night and a couple of girls we know persuaded Hess to go on with them to a club, then stay the night at their house, so she isn't actually home yet, she'll still be out for the count at Jen and Trina's, fast asleep and snoring like a St. Bernard, you know what Hester's like after a night on the ti—um, town.'

Not tiles, definitely not tiles. Although from the way Nat was looking at her she might as well have said on the tiles.

Might as well have said 'After a night of lust in another man's bed,' frankly. Nat had by this time gone quite white.

The really frustrating thing was, she was making a hash of the explanation and it might actually turn out to be true.

But Millie couldn't help thinking that somehow, one way or another, it wasn't terribly likely. She had a sneaking suspicion that Hester had met up with Lucas after the party and was at this precise moment lying wrapped around him in his bed.

'I rang Hester last night,' said Nat. 'And she told me she wasn't going out.'

Helplessly Millie shrugged. 'She changed her mind.'

'Can I still come in?'

'Um… well…'

Nat looked at her.

'She's here, isn't she? Upstairs, with some other bloke.'

'Of course she isn't! Nat, I swear to you, she's at Jen and Trina's… if I knew their number I'd ring them right now and prove it!' As she spoke, Millie prayed that Nat didn't have their number.

'I've been such an idiot.' Nat shook his head.

'Come in and search the house.' Nobly Millie stepped to one side. 'I promise there's no one else here. I'll make you a cup of tea,' she added, feeling sorry for him. 'And breakfast, if you like. I can do a bacon sandwich.'

Poor Nat. He had driven down from Glasgow to Newquay, for this.

'No thanks.' He rubbed his hand distractedly over his bristly black crewcut. 'I'll let you get back to sleep.'

'Nat! You can't just leave.' Millie tried to tug him inside but he shook her off his arm.

'I think you'll find I can. Sorry if I woke you up. When Hester gets back,' Nat's jaw was taut with misery, 'tell her I'll be in touch.'

'Who was that?'

'Hester's boyfriend, Nat. He drove five hundred miles to see her and she isn't here so now he's going back! What are you doing?' Confused, Millie realized Hugh was already wearing his jeans. Now he was pulling on his shirt, fastening the buttons she had so joyously unfastened earlier. 'You don't have to get dressed.'

'Sorry, there's some work I need to get sorted out.' Hugh wasn't looking at her. He was busy tucking his shirt into his jeans, combing his hair with his fingers, searching for his shoes.

'Work?' As Millie echoed the word, her stomach began to go into free fall. 'At ten to seven on a Sunday morning?'

'Look, thanks for last night. But I really have to go.' She stared at Hugh in disbelief. He had never looked more devastatingly handsome, or more distant. And everything had appeared to be going so well. This wasn't meant to happen at all.

'I thought you couldn't stop thinking about me.' Oh dear, *oh dear*, not what the experts advise in their fifty fail-safe-ways-to-keep-your-man books. But Millie couldn't stop herself; she had to at least *ask*.

'That was because I wanted to sleep with you.' Hugh was patting his pockets, searching for his car keys. 'Now that's out of the way, everything should be fine.' He shrugged. 'Back to normal.'

'I don't understand.' Humiliated beyond belief—because she simply hadn't expected this to happen—Millie heard her own voice slide up a couple of octaves. Oh terrific, now she sounded like one of those squeaky rubber toys dogs play with. Then carelessly cast aside, the moment the novelty's worn off.

'Yes, well.' Hugh's tone was distant. 'That's because it's a man thing. It's what we do.'

'But—'

'Millie, we had sex. That's all.' He paused in the doorway, his expression softening. 'And it was great, really it was. But it isn't going to happen again. It can't happen again. I told you before, didn't I? I don't want a relationship.'

This was true, Millie acknowledged. But she'd thought he'd changed his mind.

Gullible, that's what I am.

She didn't bother trying to explain. Gullible was a girl thing.

Instead, thankful that at least she wasn't sobbing wildly, wrapping her arms around Hugh's legs, and screaming at him to stay, she nodded jerkily.

'Okay, right, I understand.'

Hugh looked relieved.

'Are you sure?'

'Oh yes, absolutely. Fine by me.'

You bastard, and I thought you loved me!

'Good. Well, I'd better make a move.'

Millie climbed back into bed, pulling the rumpled duvet up to her chin.

'Can you find your own way out?'

'I should think so. I'm not sure where I left my—'

'Keys? On the coffee table. Next to your phone.'

The one you rang me on last night, when you drove over here and stood outside my window.

'Right. Well, thanks again.'

'Don't mention it. Glad to be of service.'

This was so, so, *so* much worse than being told you wore cheap clothes. Stuffing the corner of the duvet into her mouth, Millie listened to Hugh's footsteps on the staircase. Next she heard the clinking of keys, then the sound of the front door opening and slamming shut.

Maybe it was a trick. Maybe Hugh was only pretending to have left. At this very moment he could be creeping back up the stairs, about to burst into the bedroom with a broad grin on his face and a triumphant, 'Ha! Only joking! You didn't believe me, did you?'

But there was a limit to even Millie's endless supply of gullibility. She didn't lie there seriously expecting this to happen.

Which was just as well, because it didn't. Instead she listened to a car engine starting up outside, followed by the sound of the car being driven off down the road.

Looking on the bright side, at least Hester wasn't here to demand her winnings.

As it turned out, sleeping with Hugh Emerson hadn't been worth two hundred pounds after all.

At nine o'clock, Giles brought Orla a cup of tea in bed.

'What's it like?' He nodded at the book she was leafing through, the infamous proof copy of Christie Carson's novel.

Orla heaved a reluctant sigh. 'Very Irish. Jaunty, but at the same time profound. It's actually quite hard to be objective,' she admitted, 'when all you can think about is how much you'd like to be sticking hot pins into the man who wrote it.'

'Will you do a hatchet job?'

Melting inside, Orla watched him stir her tea before handing it over. She loved it when Giles did that for her, he could be so caring and thoughtful when he wanted.

'I'd love to do a hatchet job,' she announced fretfully. 'But JD thinks I should give it a glowing review. Ha, set fire to the thing, that'll make it glow.' Throwing the book down, she stretched and held out her arms. 'Anyway, you don't have to be up yet. Come back to bed.'

Giles was standing at the window with his back to her. The next moment his shoulders stiffened with surprise.

'What the…?'

'What?' demanded Orla, sitting up. 'What the *what*?'

'USO.' Giles started to shake with laughter. 'Heading this way.'

Orla looked bemused. 'USO?'

'Unidentified Staggering Object. Christ, ha ha, she'll be lucky to make it across the lawn.'

Hopping out of bed, as incapable as ever of resisting a bit of intrigue, Orla followed the line of his pointing finger.

Emerging unsteadily from the trees at the back of the garden, carrying an empty wine bottle in one hand and a pair of silver mules in the other, was Hester.

Looking bedraggled and distinctly the worse for wear.

'Hi. Okay, um, I'm really sorry about this.' As she stumbled over the words, Hester belatedly realized she was covered in bits of twigs and grass. 'But I fell asleep in your garden. Down by the pool. I don't suppose I could use your loo?'

God, talk about embarrassing. Her brain felt as if it were two sizes too big for her skull, she ached all over from lying all night on the rock-hard ground, and her bladder was threatening to explode. It didn't help that Giles, who had flung open the kitchen door, was wearing a canary-yellow cashmere sweater, Rupert Bear golfy-type trousers, and a gallon of Kouros.

Not to mention a king-sized smirk.

'Darling, so *that's* where you were. Millie was looking everywhere for you last night!' Orla, in a turquoise silk robe, bustled forwards and gave her an enthusiastic hug. 'You poor thing, you look dreadful. Whatever happened?'

A hug was the last thing Hester needed; the slightest pressure around her waist and she might wet herself.

'Nothing. Just drank too much and crashed out.' Pleadingly she said, 'Where's your bathroom?'

'Top of the stairs, turn left, fourth on the right. Tea or coffee?' Orla began to fill the kettle at the sink.

Acutely aware of how she must look with her wrinkled dress, bleary eyes, and shiny face, Hester was already making a bolt for the staircase.

'Um, tea would be great.'

Bursting into the bathroom at warp speed, Hester had almost reached the loo and was already fumbling with the waistband of her gold lurex knickers before she realized she wasn't alone.

Con Deveraux, naked and dripping, stepped out of the shower.

'Aaarrgh!' Hester yanked her knickers back up again so fast she almost garotted herself.

'Oh come on, I'm not that ugly,' Con protested, laughing as he reached for a green and white striped towel. 'Sorry, I thought I'd locked it.' He nodded in the direction of the door. 'This is always happening to me. You see, there's a kind of left-handed lock on the bathroom door in my flat, it turns the opposite way, so now I—'

'Out, OUT!' shrieked Hester, giving Lady Macbeth a run for her money. Desperation made her reckless and she found herself manhandling Con Deveraux out of the bathroom before he even had a chance to fasten the towel around his waist.

Oh, the luxury, the utter *bliss* of finally being able to wee uninterrupted. Her skin actually prickling with relief, Hester let out a low groan and surrendered herself to the moment, not even caring that Con Deveraux might still be outside the bathroom door, able to hear everything that was… er, going on.

He was, too. When she'd finished splashing her face with water and had feebly attempted to comb her hair with her fingers into something approaching a style, Hester opened the door and found him leaning, arms folded, against the wall opposite.

Grinning, naturally, like a Cheshire cat.

'Better now?'

'Sorry about that. I was desperate.'

'You're not kidding. Still, I'm sorry too, if I gave you a fright back there.' The grin broadened. 'I didn't realize you'd stayed the night.'

Since there were probably still assorted bits of garden in her hair, Hester guessed he was being polite.

Ruefully, she said, 'I didn't realize I'd stayed the night either. I fell asleep outside.'

Chapter 28

'Stop apologizing,' Orla scolded, shoving a mug of tea and two ibuprofen into Hester's trembling hands. 'A party's not a party without guests crashing out in peculiar places. Now drink this, swallow these, and see if you feel up to a spot of breakfast. And will Millie be worried about you? Should we give her a ring and let her know where you are?'

The ibuprofen went down a treat. Happily glugging back the hot tea, Hester shook her head.

'She'll still be asleep. No point waking her up. If I could borrow your phone, though, I'll order a taxi.'

'Darling, you don't need to do that. Giles can drop you back!'

Giles, glancing at his watch, pulled a face and said, 'That's pushing it a bit, we're teeing off at ten sharp.'

He was distraught, Hester could tell.

'No problem, I'll give her a lift home,' announced Con, coming into the kitchen fully dressed. He looked inquiringly at Orla. 'If I can borrow your car?'

'Of course you can.' Beaming with delight, Orla declared, 'And don't think I don't know what this is all about!'

Giles, busy practicing tee-shots with an imaginary nine iron, said, 'Why? What is it all about?'

'Romance, darling, *romance*.' As Giles stared in disbelief at Hester—a fine fellow like Con surely couldn't be interested in someone so bedraggled—Orla went on triumphantly, 'Con's pining already—he can't wait to see Millie again. Oh, when Moira wakes up she's going to be so thrilled!'

Hester was feeling so miserable and sorry for herself that all it took on the journey home was one idle question from Con—'So how did it go last night with you and that Lucas guy?'—and in no time at all the whole sordid story had come tumbling out.

'I was out of my tree,' Hester concluded, still hating herself but feeling surprisingly cleansed for having told Con everything—gosh, confession really *was* good for the soul, no wonder Catholics made such a big thing of it. 'I threw myself at him and he threw me right back,' she rattled on. 'And you have no *idea* how humiliating *that* is! I mean, this is Lucas Kemp we're talking about, not Cliff keep-it-zipped Richard. Lucas has a reputation like you wouldn't believe… he'll sleep with anyone, *anyone*." Hester shook her head in despair, then added crossly, 'Just so long as it's not *me*.'

'Anyone?' Con's tone was mild.

'Anyone with a detectable pulse. Oh, and they do have to be female. This is really kind of you,' said Hester as they approached the house. 'It's on the left, further down, number forty-two. Bloody holidaymakers hogging all the parking spaces as usual… ooh, hang on, there's someone pulling out.'

While Con waited for the car to move he said easily, 'But you still have your boyfriend, that's something. Or have you lost interest in him now?'

'Nat?' At the thought of Nat, a marshmallow-sized lump expanded in Hester's throat. 'Of course I haven't *lost interest* in Nat.'

Con shrugged.

'So how do you feel about him?'

Was he about to give her a big telling-off?

'I love him.' Hester's voice began to wobble. 'I really do. But he's not here, is he? He hasn't been here for *months*. And this business with Lucas… well, that started years ago, before Nat and I ever met. When I heard that Lucas was back in Newquay, I just had this uncontrollable urge to see him again, to find out if those feelings *were* still there… it was all so unfinished, you see. And of course the feelings were still there, like the world's biggest sherbet dip,' Hester concluded miserably. 'But only on my side, not his.'

Con smiled.

'You'll get over it.'

'I suppose. Sod's law,' she announced wryly as he pulled into the just-vacated parking space. 'Serves me right for being a complete bitch and trying to cheat on Nat in the first place. I throw myself at Mr. Never-Says-No and he turns me down flat. It's like a punishment from God. What do they call it, divine something or other?'

'Divine Retribution.' Con raised an eyebrow. 'I always think it sounds like a great name for a drag-queen.'

He'd managed, against all the odds, to cheer her up. Hester, still laughing as she climbed out of the orange Mercedes, slipped her arm companionably through his as they headed for the house.

'You know, it'd be brilliant if you and Millie got together.'

Con didn't tell her that it would be more than brilliant, it'd be a miracle.

'If she has sex with you, she'll owe me two hundred pounds,' Hester confided happily. 'Oh by the way, could you be an angel and not mention the Lucas thing to Millie? She'll only call me a shameless trollop and lecture me, and I'm really not up to it.'

'I promise not to mention the Lucas thing,' Con solemnly assured her.

'Come here.' Reaching up, Hester planted a big sloppy grateful kiss on his cheek. 'I love you. You are… *gorgeous*.'

◈◈◈

When Nat had driven off earlier, he had got as far as the outskirts of the town before turning round and heading back. He was being ridiculous, he'd told himself. Overreacting. It was perfectly possible that Hester had gone out with Jen and Trina and ended up crashing out at their place.

In fact, it made absolute sense.

Any minute now, she could arrive home in a taxi.

He'd come this far, Nat reminded himself, a couple more hours wouldn't hurt.

He may as well wait.

Now he wished he hadn't. As Hester and the tall dark-haired stranger disappeared into the house, Nat glanced at the clock on the Renault's dashboard and realized that he could have reached the Bristol turn-off on the M5 by now. He also knew that some men in his situation would leap out of their car, hammer on the front door until it was opened, and throw a lightning punch at the stranger who had spent the night with their girlfriend. But Nat knew that wasn't the answer.

What good would that do? The other man wasn't to blame. From the way he and Hester had been laughing together, he clearly hadn't kidnapped her and forced her to spend the night with him against her will.

His heart knotted with pain, Nat turned the key in the ignition for the second time that morning and drove off down the road.

Feeling wretched and knowing she looked it, Millie almost jumped out of her skin when she heard activity on the front doorstep. For a split second her hopelessly optimistic imagination conjured up a happy-ending scenario. It was Hugh, complete with a massive, *massive* bouquet of flowers, coming back to beg her forgiveness and tell her that he hadn't meant a word of what he'd said earlier—

'Coo-eee! Wake up lazy bum, I've got a surprise for you!'

But it was only Con, Millie discovered when she stumbled out of bed and along the landing.

'And I've got a surprise for you,' she told Hester. 'Nat's been here.'

Silence. Hester's eyes widened.

'What?' Eventually she spoke. 'You mean… like a ghost?'

'No. It was the real Nat. He drove down to surprise you.' Millie pointed to the note scrawled on the back of the pizza flyer, now propped up on the hall table. 'But you weren't here, so he's gone back.'

Hester, her face crumpling in disbelief, wailed, 'Oh *God*!'

'Just as well I don't fancy you,' Millie grumbled, peering at her reflection in the Mercedes' rearview mirror. 'I look an absolute fright.'

'Just as well I don't fancy *you*,' Con cheerfully remarked. 'And what I don't understand is why you're looking so wrecked anyway. I mean, it's not as if you stayed up all night drinking and dancing on the tables.'

Millie only wished she had, it would have been a great improvement on staying up having a disastrous one-night stand.

But if there was one person she could safely confide in, it was Con.

'Someone came round,' Millie admitted, 'after the party. I made a fool of myself. I thought I meant something to him, but I was wrong. It wasn't a relationship he was after,' she said sadly. 'Just a quick shag.'

'Oh dear. Now you owe Hester two hundred pounds,' said Con.

Honestly, Hester was such a blabbermouth.

'I can't tell her. If I do, she'll want to know who it was.'

He looked entertained.

'Don't tell me you slept with her boyfriend.'

'No!'

'Lucas, then.'

'NO!!' Even more outraged, Millie gave him a thump.

'Ow!' Rubbing his arm, Con said with a grin, 'I don't know what's so terrible about that. I'd sleep with Lucas Kemp.'

'Where are we going anyway? I'm not up to anything energetic.' Millie gazed without enthusiasm at a couple of sturdily booted hikers striding past as he reversed the borrowed Mercedes into a space in the car park of the Ocean View Hotel.

'I thought we'd start with breakfast,' said Con. 'After that, we'll go down to the beach.' He nodded cheerfully at the curving stretch of golden sand below them.

Millie winced. The curving stretch of golden sand was two miles long.

'I'm definitely not up to walking.'

'In that case,' said Con, 'I'll just have to sit and ogle the surfers. While you catch up on some sleep.'

Hugh was having his worst day in months. Disgust and self-loathing were churning inside him like some volatile combination of chemicals. Sleep was out of the question. He hadn't been able to bring himself to sit down, or eat anything, or even drink a cup of coffee. Finally, out of sheer desperation, he had left his house and started walking, with no idea where he was headed. Maybe physical exhaustion would help.

Not that he deserved help, after what he'd done.

He hated himself.

He was no better than an animal.

He had betrayed Louisa.

It wasn't Millie's fault; Hugh knew that. And he felt bad about the way he had treated her. But if he was being honest here—and he was, brutally—Millie's hurt feelings weren't uppermost in his mind right now. All he could picture was Louisa's face, his beautiful wife's face, and she was no longer smiling back at him, because he had hurt her feelings a damn sight more than he'd hurt Millie's.

Eight months, thought Hugh, closing his eyes and failing to block out the image of Louisa. It had only been eight months since she'd died—God, eight months was *nothing*—and here he was, sleeping with another girl, carrying on as if his own wife had never existed.

Even the most cold-hearted husband, surely, would wait a year.

Hugh rubbed his aching temples. He'd never imagined he could be so callous, so unfeeling. As far as he was concerned, it was a betrayal of their entire marriage. All the old emotions, locked away for so long, had rushed back last night like clamoring hormonal teenage girls screaming with delight as they launched themselves at the latest boy band. He hadn't been able to think straight, let alone shoo them away. Millie had been all he'd wanted. And at the time it had been fantastic; guilt simply hadn't entered into the equation because he hadn't so much as *thought* about Louisa.

It had just been so great to feel normal again. Like a genuine, fully functioning member of the human race, instead of the emotionally frozen widower whose young wife had been so tragically killed.

And it *had* been great, Hugh admitted, until his conscience had kicked in like a whole truckload of mules. Moments after Millie's doorbell had rung, in fact, and she had hurried downstairs to answer it.

That was when it had suddenly occurred to him that the person at the door might be Louisa, come to challenge him and demanding to know what the bloody hell he thought he was playing at.

He hadn't seriously expected it to be Louisa; he wasn't completely mad. But the idea had been more than enough. Guilt had engulfed him like an icy tidal wave. Eight months—what was the *matter* with him? Eight months was nothing more than an insult.

He may as well have gone out straight after the funeral, picked up some girl in a bar, and taken her home for all the difference it made.

Actually, thought Hugh with renewed self-loathing, that might even have been an improvement, because then at least it would have been sex, pure and simple, with no emotions attached.

'Oi!' shouted a fat holidaymaker as Hugh cannoned into him. 'Watch where you're going, will you?'

Hugh hadn't been watching. In fact, he didn't have the faintest idea where he was going. It made no difference to him and he neither knew nor cared. All he wanted to do was keep on following the stony coastal path, until he walked himself into some kind of oblivion.

The next moment he spotted the sign saying 'Tresanter Point,' and realized that he'd reached the infamous section of cliff top so popular with would-be suicides.

Shaking his windswept hair out of his eyes, Hugh approached the edge and peered over at the angry mass of foam churning around the black jagged rocks below.

Well, not that kind of oblivion, obviously.

With a glimmer of amusement, Hugh decided he'd been rotten enough already to Millie without adding that one to her conscience. He imagined her discovering that the day he'd slept with her, he'd killed himself.

Hardly the ego-boost of the year.

Chapter 29

FISTRAL BEACH REALLY WAS *the* place to go if what you were after was a spot of ogling. Con Deveraux, leaning back on his elbows and enjoying himself immensely from behind the shield of his sunglasses, admired the taut, athletic bodies of the surfers in their licorice-slick wetsuits. There were hundreds of them, arranged in meandering rows just beyond the breakers, bobbing up and down like seals in the emerald green water, waiting for the next perfect wave to come along and sweep them away.

Rather like the boys at the gay clubs he occasionally frequented, all eyeing up the talent and wondering—when someone caught their eye—if he might turn out to be their Mr. Right.

Or, more likely, Mr. All Right for the Night.

Beside him on the dry sand, her head resting on his rolled-up, white Pernn sweatshirt, Millie slept. She was lying on her front, breathing deeply and evenly, and the lunchtime sun beating down out of a dazzling cobalt blue sky was having an effect on her bare shoulders. Already lightly tanned, they were starting to turn a delicate shade of peony pink.

As Con reached for the tube of suncream handily sticking out of her bag, his attention was caught by a familiar figure heading down the beach towards them. For a moment, Con couldn't place him, then he remembered. Orla's party, last night. Good-looking, definitely. Straight, sadly. And evidently not in the happiest of moods—in fact, from the expression on his face you'd think someone had died.

As the fellow guest approached, Con dolloped warm suncream into the palm of his hand, rolled it across Millie's exposed back, and began to massage it into her skin.

A guest of Orla's was, after all, a friend of Orla's, and it never did any harm to act in a convincingly heterosexual manner.

Furthermore, the Band-Aid on Millie's right thigh was beginning to intrigue him.

By the time Hugh spotted Con Deveraux it was too late; Con was already removing his dark glasses and beaming up at him.

'Hi! Saw you at Orla's party last night.'

It took less than a split second for Hugh to recognize the prone figure Con was languorously massaging with Ambre Solaire. Oh God, this was all he needed.

'Don't worry, she's asleep.' Con lifted a silver-blonde ringlet and let it fall back into place like a dead limb. 'See? Out for the count. This is the effect I have on the opposite sex,' he went on cheerfully. Then, recalling Millie's reaction last night when she had seen this man watching her in the helicopter, he added with an air of innocence, 'Know each other, do you?'

Hugh nodded.

I bet Millie wishes she didn't know me.

'So, any ideas about this little mystery?' As he spoke, Con Deveraux was running a playful finger along one edge of the square Band-Aid on Millie's leg, just visible beneath the frayed hem of her white cut-off shorts.

'You mean what's under there?' Hugh shook his head. 'Sorry, no.'

'The more I ask, the more she won't tell me.'

Me neither, thought Hugh, curious despite himself. The finger was easing beneath a corner of the bandage now, beginning to curl it away from the skin. Thanks to the suncream, the stickiness of the plaster was no longer one hundred per cent.

'Shark bite, that's what she said,' Con confided gleefully. 'Ha, it's a tattoo! Look, see that blue ink?'

He was loosening the Band-Aid millimeter by millimeter, with all the stealth of a safe-cracker. Realizing he was holding his breath, Hugh watched as—

'OUCH!' Con let out a yelp of pain as his wrist was seized in a vice-like grip. Millie, having rolled over and shot out an arm faster than a lizard's tongue, dug her nails in until he begged for mercy.

'OW! I'M SORRY I'M SORRY I'M SORRY God, that *hurts*.'

Millie was gladder than ever that she had, for once, covered the tattoo with a bandage prior to last night's party—simply because tattoos and abbreviated Dolce & Gabbana dresses didn't go together. Her blood ran cold at the thought that she had so nearly shown it to Hugh this morning.

'Never try that again,' she told Con. 'Never even *think* of trying that again. Otherwise,' with a pitying look, she increased the pressure on his wrist, 'I'm afraid I shall have to kill you.'

It hadn't been easy, lying there pretending to be asleep and mentally willing Hugh to leave. In the end, not wanting to face him had been overshadowed by the need to stop Con in his tracks. Now, glancing up at Hugh, she said briefly, 'Hi.'

'Hello, Millie.'

To his credit he looked ill at ease, but Millie wasn't in a credit-giving mood. You big, selfish bastard, she signaled—telepathically. What are you doing here anyway? This is our beach, not yours. Get back to poxy Padstow where you belong, pig.

Okay, so Padstow wasn't poxy, but the rest was spot-on.

Annoyed that he was still capable of getting her in a fluster, Millie elaborately patted down the edge of the Band-Aid and made a big production of brushing sand out of her hair.

Then, pointedly, she nudged Con.

'Time we were off.'

'Me too,' said Hugh.

So he could take a hint, that was something.

Good. Sod off then, you big *warthog*, said Millie.

Telepathically, of course.

'Look at them,' said Moira Deveraux, waving from the terrace as the orange Mercedes drew to a halt at the top of the drive and Con and Millie jumped out. 'Don't they make the perfect couple?'

Still struggling to take in Moira's devastating news, Orla simply nodded and gave her hand a squeeze. But Moira was right about Millie and Con; they really did seem perfect together. And it was all thanks to her.

'Bloody hell,' said Giles, watching in alarm as Orla's eyes began to swim with tears. 'I'm stuck in the middle of a Harlequin romance.'

'A happy ending,' said Moira, who didn't much like Orla's husband. She smiled blandly at Giles. 'What's wrong with that?'

Two hours later as the helicopter rose into the sky, Orla blurted out, 'She's got a brain tumor, you know. Just a few months to live… God, can you believe it? I had no *idea*. And she's such a lovely person!'

'I know. Con told me.' Millie carried on waving up at the sky as Giles, rolling his eyes, disappeared into the house.

'You and Con. This is *fantastic*.' Orla gave her a hug, then dragged a tissue out of her pocket and dabbed her cheeks. 'Look at me, blubbing like a baby. But you've made Moira *so* happy. Imagine being told you're going to die… it certainly puts your own life into perspective. There's me, getting twitchy and neurotic whenever Giles is late home because I'm so scared he might have found someone else… I mean, how utterly pathetic is that? When all the time JD and Moira are discussing funeral services… honestly, I'm so selfish I'm *ashamed* of myself, I've got a marvelous husband who loves me to bits and I don't *deserve* him!

Millie blinked. Was this a joke? But it seemed not; Orla was busy fumbling in her skirt pockets for her cigarettes and lighter and there wasn't a punchline in sight.

Having lit her cigarette, Orla tucked her free arm through Millie's. 'Come on, let's go up to my study and you can fill me in on everything that's happened. And I shall be wanting *all* the naughty details!'

Her eyes had by this time brightened at the prospect of lots of salacious gossip and plenty of material for her book. Millie sighed inwardly. The trouble with Orla was she couldn't keep quiet about something longer than she could hold back a sneeze. It was a physical impossibility for her—as she'd so ably demonstrated by blurting out the news of Moira's brain tumor practically before the helicopter had had a chance to get off the ground.

Millie definitely wasn't going to tell her about Con being gay.

Nor did she have any intention of mentioning any of last night's shenanigans with Hugh, not least because she wouldn't put it past Orla to decide that here was a situation ripe for a spot of meddling and to promptly start meddling for all she was worth.

Or more likely, giving her the mother of all lectures and shrieking, 'For heaven's sake, only a complete *twerp* would fall for a line like that… how could you be so *stupid*?'

Either prospect sent shivers of mortification down her spine.

Five thousand pounds, thought Millie, painfully aware that Orla wasn't getting her money's worth. Once again she was editing her own life. Actually, there was an idea. Wouldn't it be great if you could go back and edit to your heart's content, gaily snipping out and discarding any bits that made you shudder and cringe…? Somebody should definitely invent that.

❖❖❖

'Con's brilliant company. We get on really well together. We had breakfast at the Ocean View Hotel, then spent a few hours mucking about on the beach.'

This much had been true. Millie, swinging her legs against the side of Orla's desk, glanced out of the upstairs window at the lovingly tended rose garden. 'Oh, and Richard-the-gardener kissed me last night. He kisses like an Aquavac!'

Excitedly, Orla scribbled on one of the charts pinned up to the left of the filing cabinet, then searched for a different colored felt-tipped pen and dashed to another chart above the desk.

'Fabulous! Did Con see him kissing you? Was he madly jealous?'

'It wasn't the kind of kiss anyone would be jealous of.' Millie pulled a face, just recalling it was enough to make her feel queasy. 'Richard was very drunk.'

'He really likes you, it's sooo obvious. Oh, I *knew* this party would get things moving.' Orla sounded triumphant. Here, clearly, were the beginnings of an entertaining little subplot. 'So how did you feel when he kissed you?'

Honestly, she sounded like a psychiatrist.

'Wet.' Millie watched the felt-tipped pen flying over the chart; Orla's handwriting really was beyond belief.

'And what about Hester?'

'I've never tried kissing Hester. She'd probably bite me.'

'I meant did she get anywhere with Lucas last night? You could tell she was pretty smitten.' Orla paused, her greeny gold eyes dancing at the possibility of intrigue. 'But this falling-asleep-by-the-pool business sounds pretty suspicious to me.'

'And her boyfriend drove down from Glasgow to see her,' said Millie.

'No! When?'

'Last night. He slept in his car outside our house.'

'Oh good grief! And Hester didn't come home! But that's… *dreadful*." Orla, who had been about to say it was fantastic, stopped herself in the nick of time. 'Nat, isn't it? So what did he say when Hester finally turned up?'

'Nothing. He'd gone by then. Driven back to Scotland. Not thrilled.' Millie pulled a face. 'Still, look on the bright side. At least he wasn't still there when Hester rolled up in your Mercedes with Con.'

Chapter 30

Hester was on the sofa shivering like a beaten whippet when Millie arrived home at seven-thirty. Orla, who had given her a lift back, had been clamoring to come in for an update. Glad she'd managed to fend her off, Millie said gently, 'Spoken to him yet?'

Hester nodded, her lower lip beginning to wobble. Her duvet was wrapped around her, a sure sign of emotional upset. The phone squatted on the carpet amid a scattering of Cadbury Twiglets. A party-sized Twiglet drum poked out from beneath the sofa. Picking it up, Millie saw that the drum was empty. Plus, the Twiglets had been a month past their sell-by date. They must have tasted awful but Hester had plowed her way through them anyway, because this was what she did in times of stress. Demolished whole treeloads of Twiglets.

'I've been phoning and phoning all day. Leaving messages for Nat to ring me. He called ten minutes ago. Oh Millie, it was awful.' Hester gasped and shuddered, clawing pitifully at the duvet in search of leftover bits of Twiglet. 'He sounded like… like an android. All calm and polite, as if he didn't even know me. And I told him the truth—that I went to the party with you and fell asleep in the garden—but I just *know* he didn't believe me! Oh God, oh God,' she wailed, rocking backwards and forwards, 'what am I going to *do*?'

Compared with Hester, Millie felt she was coping with her own emotional catastrophe remarkably well. Actually, the Nat thing had done a good job of taking her mind off… what was his name? Oh yes, Hugh.

'Right.' Striding up and down the living room, she forced Hester's head to swivel from side to side like a spectator at Wimbledon. Then, slipping into scary-businesswoman mode, she began ticking points off on her fingers. 'Number one, okay, he's not very happy right now, but that's because he's just driven a thousand miles and didn't get to see you. Number two, he might think you've spent the night having riotous sex with some other bloke, but he's wrong. You didn't. Number three, so all we have to do is convince him. Proof, that's what Nat needs. So what I'll do is get Orla to ring him up and tell him the truth, that nothing went on, you just fell asleep in her garden.'

Hester was looking torn, as if half of her wanted to leap at this idea—which was, frankly, brilliant—while the other half was digging its heels in and whining, Yes, but what if he doesn't *believe* Orla?

'Yes, but—' began Hester.

'No, no buts about it.' Millie was brisk. 'You're acting like the guilty party here, but you aren't guilty, are you? Don't you see, you didn't do anything wrong!'

Silence.

'Oh God.' Millie stared at her as if she'd just sprouted two horns and a pointy tail. Orla had been right after all. 'You *did*. You spent the night having riotous sex with somebody else. Holy mackerel—not Lucas!'

Hester shook her head and looked utterly miserable.

'No.'

'WHO WITH, THEN?' bellowed Millie.

'Nobody. I mean, it was Lucas, but we didn't have sex.' Her shoulders slumped in defeat. 'I tried my best, but he refused. He just wasn't interested.'

'Good grief.' Forgetting all about being brisk and businesslike, Millie plonked herself down on the sofa next to Hester. 'You mean you actually offered yourself to him?'

'Ripped off all my clothes, jumped into the pool, and *launched* myself at him,' Hester groaned. 'And he still turned me down. I mean, there I was, *naked*, and Lucas Kemp didn't want to have sex with me! Can you think of anything more humiliating? Because I can't.'

Millie was stunned. It certainly didn't sound like Lucas.

'Did he, um, say why?'

'Some utter crap about me having a boyfriend already and him actually possessing some scruples.'

Oh dear. More and more unlikely.

Scruples? Lucas? Surely not.

Millie pulled a sympathetic face, because if ever there was a ridiculous excuse, this had to be it. Clearly, as far as Lucas was concerned, the prospect of intimate physical contact with Hester was too horrible for words.

'Still, look on the bright side.' Millie's tone was soothing. 'Nothing happened.'

'I wanted it to happen.'

Patience, patience.

'Yes, I know that, but it still didn't. So you don't have to give me two hundred pounds!'

'It would have been worth it.' Hester bunked and looked desolate.

Déjà vu. For a second, Millie was tempted to confess about Hugh. But only for a very brief second, because a) she didn't *want* Hester to know about it, and b) what good would it do?

Instead she said, 'But at least you can forget about Lucas now, put it down to experience, and stop fantasizing about him.'

'Right.' Unearthing a lone Twiglet from a folded-over bit of duvet, Hester ate it and looked more wretched than ever.

'And you can concentrate on getting Nat back! Not that he's gone anywhere,' Millie added. Then, because of course Nat *had* gone somewhere—left the country, in fact—she went on, 'I mean, it's not as if he's dumped you.'

'He might, though.' Wearily, Hester rubbed her face. 'He could be building up to it.'

'Well then, we have to make sure that doesn't happen! Convince him that you're innocent. I still think Orla's our best bet,' Millie declared. 'She'll vouch for you, no problem, and you know how persuasive Orla can be, she'll just keep going on and on until Nat sees sense, she's brilliant at that kind of thing… gosh, by the time she's finished, you'll have Nat on his knees groveling and apologizing and begging you to forgive *him*—'

Millie stopped abruptly. Hester was crying.

'Why are you crying?'

'Because I hate myself. Because I would have been unfaithful to Nat if only bloody Lucas had let me, and Nat doesn't deserve to be treated like that. I love him so much. How could I even try to do what I did? I'm disgusting,' sobbed Hester, 'just a complete trollop.'

'So you want Nat to finish with you?'

'I deserve to be finished with.'

'And would that make you happy?'

'Noooo!'

Hester was in the grip of a major guilt trip, Millie realized. Time to be brisk and businesslike again.

'You're going to pull yourself together,' she announced very firmly indeed, 'and salvage the only thing that matters, which is your relationship with Nat. Because if you let him go, I'm telling you, you'll regret it for the rest of your life.'

'I'm such an idiot,' Hester moaned softly.

'No you aren't, you just made a mistake. Everyone makes mistakes.' Millie forced herself not to think about Hugh. 'But it doesn't have to be the end of the world, okay?'

'What are you doing?'

Millie slithered off the sofa and reached for the phone.

'Ringing Orla.'

❖❖❖

Hugh looked at the *Yellow Pages*, lying open at F for florists. He couldn't decide whether sending Millie flowers would be a good thing to do or a bad thing.

Would it make matters better? Or worse?

The next morning as Millie emerged from the shower her dearest fantasy came true. Hearing activity outside, she wrapped an orange towel around herself and peered out of the bedroom window. A florist's van was double-parked in the street below.

As she watched, Millie saw a young skinny lad leap out of the driver's seat, lope round to the back of the van, pull open the doors, and lift out the most stunning basket of flowers she'd ever seen in her life. As her heart began to race, the young lad double-checked the address on the delivery slip and made straight for her front door.

Oh yes, yes, yes, thank you God, thank you, thought Millie, galloping joyfully downstairs. It was actually happening, which in her experience was an unusual thing for fantasies to do. But never mind, who cared, because Hugh had come to his senses and realized he hadn't meant all those awful hurtful things he'd said, hooray, hooray, oh what a beautiful morning, oh what a beautiful dayyy—

Urrgh.

Unless the flowers were for Hester.

In which case, it would go back to being a decidedly un-beautiful day.

Orange towel firmly in place and heart equally firmly in mouth, Millie opened the front door.

The young boy peered at her through the jungle of blooms.

'Millie Brady?'

YES, YES, YES!!!

'That's me,' said Millie, only just managing to stop herself leaping three feet off the ground and punching the air with glee.

'Delivery for you.'

'Really?' Millie limited herself to a modest smile. 'For *me*? Gosh, I wonder who they could be from?'

Oh well, it never did any harm to give the impression you were awash with fervent admirers.

'Dunno. Card's in the basket.' Bored, the boy shoved the massive arrangement into Millie's arms. 'Try opening it and you might find out.'

He was probably jealous because nobody ever sent him flowers, Millie decided. Endlessly having to deliver them to other people and never getting any himself had caused him to become bitter and twisted.

Still, he wasn't going to spoil *her* day. Nothing could do that, not now. Because Hugh had decided he loved her after all and he was begging her forgiveness, tra-la. Everything was going to be all right, diddly-dee, in fact from now on the entire rest of her life was going to be *perfect.*

Millie lowered the basket carefully on to the kitchen table—crikey, it was almost as *big* as the table—and rooted around until she found, in its midst, the all-important white envelope attached to a plastic prong.

Emerging from the undergrowth with her prize—and pollen all over her nose—Millie tore open the envelope and pulled out the card:

Dear Millie,

I'm so sorry, my behavior on Saturday night was appalling. I do hope you can forgive me.

Richard.

Millie frowned. She turned the card over, found nothing on the other side, then turned it back again.

It *still* said Richard.

Right message, wrong name. Surely there was some mistake here? The flowers had to be from Hugh, they *had* to be. After all, he was the one she'd slept with on Saturday night, not Richard-the-gardener. Richard-the-gardener didn't even know where she lived, for pity's sake.

Unless of course…

Chapter 31

'DARLING, HI, HOW *ARE* you? More thrilling news to report? Hang on, let me just grab a pen… okay, got one… right, fire away!'

'Orla.' Gripping the phone, Millie kept her voice even. 'Has anyone asked you for my address?'

'Hmm, darling?'

'I've been sent some flowers.'

'Really? Oh, that's fantastic! Gosh, that was quick.' Orla laughed. 'Poor boy, he turned up here this morning absolutely mortified… I've never seen anyone look so sheepish. He even groveled and apologized to me!'

'Richard-the-gardener?' Millie couldn't help it, she had to be six hundred percent sure.

'Well of course Richard-the-gardener, silly! Bless his cotton socks, he's the clean-living type, not used to drinking at all. After a few glasses of wine, he was up, up, and away, and from then on there was just no stopping him. All his inhibitions went for a burton—I told him that was what parties were all about!' Orla laughed and paused in mid-flow to light a cigarette. 'But of course when the poor lamb woke up yesterday morning and realized what he'd done he was absolutely mortified.'

Join the club, thought Millie. In fact, the club membership was expanding by the minute.

'He can't believe he behaved so dreadfully,' Orla gabbled on merrily, 'although I promised him he hadn't done anything dreadful as far as we were concerned. But he said he'd grabbed you and mauled you like an animal and he'd never been so ashamed in his life, he couldn't imagine what you must think of him now.'

'Did you tell him I thought he kissed like an Aquavac?'

'Of course not! Heavens, the poor boy might have committed hara-kiri in my kitchen with his pruning shears. Anyway, the point is, he doesn't *really* kiss like an Aquavac, it was only like that on Saturday night because he was so incredibly drunk. I bet he kisses perfectly normally when he's sober.'

'In that case,' said Millie, 'why don't you give him a try?'

'Heavens, I'm miles too old for him—he doesn't want a wrinkled old geriatric like me! Anyway, you're the one he's mad about.' Orla was sounding pleased with herself. 'He told me so this morning—although of course I already knew that.'

Millie blinked.

'How?'

'Darling, it's my job to know these things! And guess what?'

'What?' Millie was beginning to feel like a parrot.

'He's going to phone you up and ask you out to dinner!'

Never mind pleased with herself, thought Millie. Orla was, by this time, sounding positively gleeful.

In fact, she was fizzing with glee. Like Alka Seltzers dropped into a glass of water.

Millie said faintly, 'He doesn't have to do that. Really, one slobbery kiss, that's all it was. I forgive him, I promise.'

'Don't be silly,' Orla chided, 'that's not why he's doing it. He's wooing you, sweetie. Wooing you!'

Deeply suspicious, Millie said, 'Was this your idea?'

'No it was not.' Orla sounded shocked. 'That would be cheating. Inviting certain people to my party is one thing, but ordering them about and telling them what to do next... absolutely not. I'm not Machiavelli, darling!'

Except she was, in a way, Millie thought later as she made her way across town to Lucas's house. Because thanks to the five thousand pounds Orla had paid her, she hadn't felt able to tell Orla that she had absolutely no intention of going out on a date with Richard-the-gardener.

'There's no point,' she'd protested feebly, 'it won't come to anything.'

But Orla had said, 'Oh come on, darling, you don't know that for sure. You hardly know him for a start! At least give the poor fellow the benefit of the doubt.' Her eyes sparkling with mischief, she had added, 'If nothing else, it'll keep Con on his toes. Might even make him the teensiest bit jealous.'

So, reluctantly, Millie had found herself going along with it. When Richard phoned her she would be perfectly lovely and charming and when he invited her out to dinner she would agree to go.

Because, for five thousand pounds, basically, it was the least she could do.

Anyway, one date, that was all they were talking about here. It wasn't as if Orla was expecting her to bear his children.

Crikey, thought Millie, at least I hope not.

'Hang on a second,' Lucas complained when Millie had finished bringing him up to date on the Hester-front. 'I don't seem to be able to do anything right, here. There I was, thinking I was being Mr. Totally Heroic, doing the decent thing for once in my life, and now here you are, getting all het up and giving me grief about it!'

'I'm not giving you grief, I'm just saying you hurt her feelings,' Millie argued. 'And now I've got a flatmate to contend with who's convinced she's about as sexually attractive as a polecat.'

Sighing, Lucas leaned across the desk to check the bookings diary. 'Fine. So next time a naked girl throws herself at me, I'll just give her one. No more Mr. Nice Guy for me.'

'You've never been nice in your life,' Millie protested as he flicked through the pages.

'Hester's got a boyfriend. That's why I turned her down. How can you say I'm not nice?'

'Yes, well, he's probably going to dump her anyway. And it's all your fault.'

Lucas laughed. 'How?'

'If you hadn't turned Hester down on Saturday night, she wouldn't have drunk herself into oblivion and spent the night asleep in Orla's garden. Ten minutes with you, that's all it would have taken. Then she'd have been safely back home by the time Nat knocked on our front door.'

'Ten minutes? Thanks a lot,' said Lucas dryly. 'Anyway, you don't mean that.'

'Oh, I don't know what I mean anymore.' Exasperated, Millie shook her head. 'I'm just saying it's no fun at all. Having to share a house with a moping, sniveling wreck. Anyway, forget it, let's change the subject. What's this new booking you've got for me?'

'Thursday night, nine o'clock at the Castle Hotel in Truro. Name of Drew.' Lucas consulted his diary. 'The wife booked it. You're there to surprise her husband while they're having dinner in the hotel restaurant. Here's the poem she wants you to recite.' He handed her the fax that had been paper-clipped to the page in the diary. 'It's their anniversary apparently.'

Millie glanced at the poem—typical slush-bucket stuff about loving each other till the end of time, I'll be yours and you'll be mine, etc., etc. Nauseating of course, but easy enough to learn.

Oh dear, maybe I only think it's nauseating because I don't have a man of my own. Nobody loves me so I've become all sour and cynical.

Folding up the sheet of paper and stuffing it into her jeans pocket, Millie turned to leave.

'Oh, one other thing before you go,' said Lucas.

'What?'

'That question you asked me the other day. Remember, about being able to tell when people fancy you?'

Of course she remembered.

'Sort of.' Millie shrugged. 'So?'

'Your new friend.' Lucas gave her a knowing wink. 'The one you were with at the party on Saturday night. Con Deveraux.'

Mystified, Millie said, 'What about him?'

'Just thought you might like to know. He definitely fancied me.'

Sylvia Fleetwood's lips pursed like a cat's bottom when the door to the travel agency clanged open at twenty-nine minutes past five. She and Tim had some supermarket shopping to pick up on the way home from work. Tonight they had decided on salmon fillets poached with dill and new potatoes with baby broad beans, and there was nothing more annoying than being held up at work then discovering when you arrived at the supermarket that they'd sold out of salmon.

'You deal with it,' Sylvia told her husband, loudly enough for the customer to hear—honestly, some people were *so* inconsiderate. 'I'll start locking up. We don't want to be late, do we?'

'Sorry, hello, don't worry about the time.' Recognizing the customer, Tim Fleetwood flapped an apologetic arm in the direction of one of the chairs. 'Sit down, take as long as you like. How are you anyway? Looking very well, I must say.'

'You're too kind,' declared Adele, arranging herself on the chair and smiling vivaciously at the compliment because she knew it was true; she'd spent the entire afternoon being pampered in Deluxe, Newquay's premier beauty salon. 'But I need a holiday.' Leaning forward, she confided, 'Not to mention your expert guidance. I want you to tell me everything you know about Tuscany!'

Tim Fleetwood rubbed his hands together in delight; this was the kind of request he most enjoyed. For twenty years he'd been besotted with Tuscany, which had to rate as his all-time favorite holiday destination. Even if, these days, they tended to venture further afield because this was what Sylvia preferred.

'Ah ha, well now, you've come to the right place.' Swiveling round, breathing in the scent of Adele Brady's exotic perfume, he sifted through the rows of brochures on the shelves behind him. 'Let me show you this one… and this one… and these three…'

At the door, carrying her bag and ostentatiously jangling her keys, Sylvia said, 'We really mustn't be late, darling. Remember, squash court's booked for seven-thirty.'

'Oh look, I'm being a nuisance, I can tell!' Adele exclaimed. 'Why don't I take these brochures home with me and pop back tomorrow?'

'No, no, no need for that.' Bravely, Tim adjusted his spectacles, glanced across at his wife and said, 'Why don't you pick up whatever we need from the supermarket while I finish up here. I'll be home by half past six.'

By this time Sylvia's whole face was pursed. She recognized the client now, from her previous visit to the shop.

'Surely you don't need a whole hour.' What are you planning to do, for God's sake? Have sex with her?

'Not for this.' Tim tapped the brochures on the desk. 'But there is something else I need to arrange.' He smiled across at his twitching wife and hinted, 'Something to do with a birthday…?'

Short of dragging him out by his thinning sandy hair, Sylvia realized there was nothing more she could do.

Well, almost nothing.

'Fine, then.' She deliberately didn't look at Millie Brady's done-up mother. 'Just so long as you weren't planning on getting me one of those ghastly, common singing-telegram affairs.'

❖❖❖

'You're a hero,' Adele declared warmly forty minutes later. 'No, I mean it, this has been marvelous, *so* helpful. Really, above and beyond the call of duty.'

Tim Fleetwood flushed fiery red. 'It's been a pleasure.'

It had, too.

'But I mustn't take up any more of your precious time. And you,' Adele tapped a manicured fingernail playfully against his arm, 'must get on home. We don't want you to miss your game of squash.'

Tim hadn't been flirted with for years; married to the ferocious Sylvia, nobody had ever had the courage to give it a try. Now he experienced a sudden violent urge to play a different kind of squash. And he strongly suspected he wasn't the only one.

The words came tumbling out in a rush.

'There's a wine bar around the corner. Would we have time for a quick drink?'

They had been having the most heavenly discussion about Renaissance art and opera. Tim Fleetwood was utterly charming and clearly a man after her own heart. Patting her ash-blonde chignon, Adele said, 'I'd love to, but what about your wife?'

Wife? Or jailer? With a dizzying rush of blood to the head, Tim Fleetwood realized that there could be so much more to life than hobbling through it shackled to Sylvia, who was pathologically jealous and a vicious henpecker to boot.

And wasn't it about time he was eligible for parole?

'She'll be at home by now, cooking the dinner.' He smiled recklessly at Adele. 'She won't want to come for a drink.'

'He says he believes me but I know he doesn't.' Panicky tears seeped out of the corners of Hester's eyes as she clutched the phone to her chest. Having rung Nat three times today, she knew she had only succeeded in irritating him. But, catch-22, the more quietly irritated Nat had become, the more desperately she had needed to phone him again. Now, in despair, she thrust the phone at Millie.

'Here, keep it away from me. Hide it somewhere I'll never find it.'

Having come home and blanched at the state of the kitchen, which was piled high with washing-up, Millie said, 'That would be in the sink, then.'

'You're my friend,' wailed Hester. 'It's your job to be sympathetic.'

But I'm not in a sympathetic mood, Millie longed to yell back, because you're only scared you're about to be dumped, but I've already *been* dumped, thank you very much, and it wasn't very nice at all, and I still don't know what I did to deserve it.

Apart from behaving like a great big trollopy tart, of course, and leaping into bed with some bloke just because he fancied a meaningless quickie.

No frills, no fuss, and absolutely no emotional involvement, thought Millie. Basically, she'd been the human equivalent of a Pamela Anderson centerfold.

Only with smaller boobs.

Oh God, *how* could I have been so stupid?

'Haven't we got any more Twiglets?' Hester whined.

'No. You've caused a national shortage. The Twiglet factory is working twenty-four hours a day, trying to keep up. We've got salt'n'vinegar chipsticks,' said Millie. 'Have some of those instead.'

She knew she was being heartless. Chipsticks weren't nearly so comforting, not the same thing at all.

'You don't understand,' Hester fretted. 'You *can't* understand. How long is it since you had a proper boyfriend? And don't say Neil,' she added meanly, before Millie had a chance to open her mouth, 'because Neil was a prize pillock and he doesn't count.'

Millie briefly considered killing Hester. If she smothered her with a pillow, would that count?

Luckily, at that moment the phone rang in her hands.

'I'll get it!' Catapulting off the sofa, Hester launched herself at Millie's chest and wrestled the phone away. 'Hello? Hello? What? *Who?*'

It was completely pathetic, but Millie *still* found herself mentally crossing her fingers and praying it was Hugh, come to his senses at last and ready to lick her boots—maybe even the carpet—if only she'd forgive him.

'Here, it's for you.' Hester chucked the phone back at her in disgust. 'Some smarmy-sounding bloke trying to flog us a conservatory. Play your cards right, chat him up, and who knows, he could end up being your next prize pillock.'

Chapter 32

'BUGGER... OH *BUGGER*... NO, no, NO!'

Giles, who had been in the bedroom next door, poked his head around the door of Orla's office.

'What's wrong?'

'This bloody machine,' Orla wailed, her fingers flying over the keyboard as she punched one key after another like a demented pianist. 'I was doing so well and now I can't retrieve my file... in fact, I can't find the sodding thing anywhere. It's completely *vanished*.'

'Come on now, calm down. It must be there somewhere.' Giles didn't have a clue whether it was or not, he just knew what Orla was like when she flew into a blind panic.

'But it isn't, it's gone! Oh buggering hell, I don't *believe* this, I *knew* I should have stuck to my old typewriter. Eleven chapters, I've lost eleven pissing, bollocking chapters and I'm NEVER GOING TO GET THEM BACK AGAIN.'

'Stop it,' said Giles, because every bellowed-out word was accompanied by Orla banging the mouse down on the mouse pad. 'Smashing your computer up isn't going to help, is it? There there,' he crooned, massaging her rigid shoulders. 'We'll get this sorted out. What's the name of the fellow who set all this up for you? Hugh someone-or-other?'

'Hugh Emerson.' Orla fumbled frantically in her desk drawer for a cigarette.

'That's the one. Just give him a ring, get him over here. He's the expert, isn't he?'

Orla stuck a Marlboro in her mouth, flicked her lighter, and inhaled.

'What if he's busy and can't get over here for weeks?'

'He won't be.'

'Yes, but what if he *is*?' Orla was gabbling now, puffing smoke in all directions, and slipping into drama queen mode.

'Sweetheart, you're Orla Hart. Of course he'll get over here. Let me have his number,' Giles announced, 'and I'll ring him myself.'

Every now and again he did that *Me Tarzan, You Jane* thing. Jumping up, Orla spun round and threw her arms around him.

'I *love* it when you go all masterful on me… oh sweetheart, I'm so lucky to have you! Don't we make the best team ever?'

'There, sorted,' Giles announced, coming into the kitchen five minutes later.

Orla could easily have made the call herself, but she was wallowing in the all-too-rare sensation of feeling cossetted and looked after. In return, she poured Giles a cup of coffee, like a good wife.

'My knight in shining armor. I don't know what I'd do without you. So when's Hugh coming over to fix it?'

'Three o'clock this afternoon.' Giles sounded pleased with himself. 'Tried to put me off at first, but I wasn't having any of that nonsense. I *insisted*.'

Orla looked dismayed.

'Bugger, and I've got a hair appointment at two. Oh well, just have to cancel it…'

'No need. I'll stay here and deal with him,' said Giles with an easy shrug.

'But…?' Orla blinked, by this time truly astonished. 'Aren't you playing golf this afternoon?'

'What's more important, your computer or my game of golf? It won't kill me to miss an afternoon.'

'Oh, you!' Orla hugged him again, with a mixture of joy and relief. 'You have no idea how much I love you.'

'Actually, there's a tournament on in St. Ives tomorrow. Bit of a long day, but it sounds good fun…'

The joy and relief abruptly crumbled like a bouillon cube.

God, thought Orla, I'm really losing it. How ridiculous to be so insecure, just because he'll be away for a day.

Anyway, hadn't he just volunteered to cancel this afternoon's game?

'Of course you must go tomorrow.' She kept her smile determinedly bright and brave. 'You deserve to enjoy yourself.'

'Only if you're sure,' said Giles.

'Of *course* I'm sure.'

If it hadn't been Orla, Hugh wouldn't have agreed to do it. He was a software developer, not a call-out engineer. But since his concentration had gone for a burton anyway, work on his latest project for an American motor company had—appropriately—hit something of a brick wall. The prospect of getting out of the house, driving over to Newquay, and sorting out a relatively minor technical problem was actually an enticing one. And he'd be doing a friend a favor at the same time.

Orla, that was. Not Giles, who had made the call, and whom Hugh didn't trust at all.

As he drove, Hugh's thoughts strayed back—inexorably—to Millie. She was the reason he hadn't been able to concentrate on work for longer than thirty seconds at a time. Having finally decided against sending flowers by way of an apology, his conscience was nevertheless still nagging away at him, triumphantly reminding him over and over again what a complete hash he'd made of things.

Before, guilt at having betrayed Louisa had been uppermost in his mind, swamping all else. But now, like a fickle floating voter, his guilt was showing signs of changing sides. He had treated Millie appallingly and his conscience wasn't letting him forget it.

Millie deserved better. And an explanation, at the very least.

As he pulled up outside Orla's house, Hugh saw Giles on the drive talking into a mobile phone.

'Okay, I'll pick you up tomorrow morning, eight o'clock sharp.' Hugh caught the end of the conversation as he climbed out of the car. 'Have to go now, chap's arrived to fix the computer. Yes, yes, me too. Bye. Hello there!' Giles called over, beaming broadly as he switched off the phone. 'Come to sort out the mess, fantastic. Orla's not here, urgent appointment in town. I'll show you up to her office, shall I?'

Hugh hid his disappointment. When he had first installed the new system in this house, he and Orla had got to know each other pretty well. Not even bothering to pretend to be interested in how computers actually functioned, Orla had spent hours perched on the window seat in her office, smoking like a maniac, swinging her legs, drinking coffee, and chattering away endlessly about pretty much any subject under the sun. By the time everything was up and running, he knew more about Orla than he knew about some of his closest friends. And, since she was a compulsive questioner as well as a wickedly indiscreet gossip, he'd found himself telling her more than he'd meant to tell her about himself.

Without even knowing it, Hugh now realized, he had been hoping to continue their chat today. Orla knew about his former life in London, and why he had moved down to Cornwall. She also knew all about Louisa. Maybe she could give him some down-to-earth advice, or reassurance, or even a damn good talking-to to make him realize that life went on, that he was actually *allowed* to fall in love with other women…

Love?

Hang on, where had that sprung from?

Well, whatever. Hugh frowned, dismissing the word from his mind.

Except Orla couldn't do that anyway. Because she wasn't here.

And he certainly wasn't about to start confiding in Giles Hart.

'When d'you expect Orla back?'

'Hmm? Oh, hours, I should think. Hair appointment, emergency cover-up job,' Giles continued over his shoulder as he led the way upstairs. 'Found her first grey hair last night—*major* panic. You know what women are like, always on the hunt for some new thing to be neurotic about.'

Definitely no danger of being tempted to confide in Giles. Shaking his head, Hugh wondered what on earth Orla could have been thinking of when she'd married him.

'Here we are. She's lost eleven chapters.' Pushing open the door, Giles gestured towards the still-humming computer. 'For all our sakes, let's hope you can find them.'

The last time Hugh had been here, Orla and Giles had only recently moved in. The plain white walls had been bare, the shelves empty, and the floor piled high with countless cardboard boxes. Now, the cobalt blue carpet was visible, the shelves bulged with books and files, and the walls were entirely covered with multicolored charts.

Ignoring them, Hugh pulled out the swivel chair in front of the computer, reached for the mouse, and set to work unraveling the chaos Orla had caused with her frantic key-battering. Only when that was done could he begin the search for the missing chapters.

'Get you a beer?' asked Giles behind him.

'Great.'

⯐⯐⯐

It took less than five minutes to locate the fault, fix it, and retrieve the crucial file. Simple, when you knew what you were doing. And satisfying at the same time to know that—despite her best efforts—Orla hadn't accidentally managed to delete the first two hundred pages of her new book.

Swiveling the chair round in job-done fashion, Hugh leaned back, clasped his hands behind his head, and gazed idly at the handwritten charts lining the walls. Minutes earlier a phone had rung downstairs, delaying Giles's return with the beer. Maybe when he left here he'd head on down to Fistral Beach, hire a wetsuit and board, and catch some waves—

Hester Tresilian/Annie Jameson, 26, short dark hair—like ruffled feathers—curvy figure, tight-fitting clothes, mad shoes, major unrequited crush on Lucas Kemp, lovely boyfriend Nat (chef) working away.

Slowly, Hugh sat forward in the swivel chair as the significance of the words began to sink in. The potted biography of Hester had been scrawled in orange felt-tipped pen across the chart closest to him. There was more, but his gaze had already shifted to the adjoining chart…

Lucas Kemp/Dan Anders, 30, hunk in leather trousers, green eyes, longish v. *dark hair, charmer extraordinaire*, Orla had scribbled in violet felt-tip.

Hugh, his heart lurching around like a drunk inside his rib cage, ignored the rest of the Lucas chart and switched his attention to the next one along, larger and containing far more detail than the others.

Millie Brady/Cazzy Jackson, 25, angelic, rippling silver-blonde hair, wicked blue eyes, that *tattoo, impulsive, incident-prone, looking for adventure… ex-travel agent (Ref: Fleetwood's), now working as a singing telegram (Ref: Lucas Kemp). Mother Adele (Ref: A. Brady). Father Lloyd (Ref: L. Brady and Judy Forbes-Adams).*

There was much, much more, surrounded by a profusion of multi-colored arrows leading from Millie's chart to the others pinned up around the room. In the split second before the door to the office swung open, Hugh registered an explosion of asterisks and exclamation marks and the name Con Deveraux, followed by an excitedly scribbled, *This could be it!*

'How's it going?' Giles handed him a bottle of Labatt's, bringing him back to earth with a bump.

'Sorry? Oh, right.' Forcing himself to concentrate, Hugh spun back round to the flickering screen. 'No problem, found the file. Eleven chapters, all present and correct.'

'Good news, good news.'

'Although, hang on, I'd better just scroll through a chapter or two, make sure no paragraphs have slipped through the net.'

This was impossible, of course, but Giles clearly didn't have much of a grasp on information technology. Speed reading, Hugh skimmed the lines in silence. Within thirty seconds his suspicions had been confirmed. He knew exactly what he was reading, even if the names of the characters had been changed.

Unbelievable.

He scrolled back to the beginning and closed the file.

'Seems fine.'

'Brilliant. Send us an invoice,' said Giles.

Truly unbelievable.

Closing down the computer, swinging back round on his chair, Hugh nodded casually at the charts covering the walls.

'What's all this about, then?'

'Oh, Orla's latest plan. Fiction based on fact.' Giles shrugged and took a swig of his own beer. 'The critics slaughtered her last book—well, one critic in particular—so she's basing the next one on an actual person, someone she's got to know since we moved down here. Girl called Millie, she was at the party last week. You probably saw her—in fact, she was the main reason Orla decided to throw the party in the first place.'

What?

'Isn't that a bit risky?' Hugh marveled at Orla's cheek. 'How's this… girl going to react, d'you suppose, when she finds out she's the central character in the next Orla Hart mega-seller? What if she goes ballistic and threatens to sue?'

Giles laughed.

'Don't worry, Orla's not that stupid. Millie knows all about it, she's been in on the idea from the start. And Orla paid her up-front, so there won't be any problems there.'

Hugh blinked. Surely this couldn't be true; Millie had never so much as mentioned any of this to him.

He felt numb.

'Paid her, did you say?'

'A pretty good whack, considering she didn't even have a job at the time. Five grand,' Giles explained breezily, 'in exchange for the lowdown on everything that's going on in her life. I mean, I don't pay much attention—I've never even read any of my wife's books—but Orla seems to be enjoying herself, encouraging the girl to get up to all sorts. The two of them meet up once a week and Millie updates her on the latest goings-on… work, men, sex… you name it! And last week's party worked a treat, evidently. It might have cost a bomb but according to Orla it paid dividends. She changes the names of course, but otherwise it all goes in, down to the last sordid detail. Word for word,' Giles concluded with leery relish. 'No holds barred!' Waggling his empty Labatt's bottle at Hugh, he raised his blond eyebrows. 'Get you another?'

Paid dividends.

Orla encouraged the girl to get up to all sorts.

Down to the last sordid detail.

Hugh shook his head; if he didn't get out of here, he thought, he might explode.

'No thanks.'

Chapter 33

Orla had been woken the next morning by Giles bounding out of bed at six o'clock. He'd sung to himself in the shower, selected his favorite golfing outfit—pink cashmere Pringle sweater, orange and pink checked trousers—and brought Orla breakfast in bed before setting off for the tournament in St. Ives.

Agony aunts were always warning women to suspect their other halves might be having an affair when, out of the blue, they started showering more often, wearing aftershave, and buying themselves designer underpants. It wasn't so easy, thought Orla, when you had a husband who'd always taken immense pride in his personal appearance. Giles couldn't bring himself to so much as answer the door to the postman without first slapping on the cologne.

Not to mention the Clarins tinted moisturizer for that flattering, sun-kissed glow. Giles never stopped wanting to look his best.

Still, he'd planted a loving, Hugo Boss-scented kiss on her forehead before leaving at seven-thirty. And brought her toast (cut in triangles) with grapefruit marmalade *and* orange juice *and* coffee and even her cigarettes and lighter, all on a silver tray.

So he either loved her very much indeed or was feeling incredibly guilty about the fact that, once again, he was up to his old—

Stop it, stop it, *stop it*. Despairingly, Orla stubbed out her seventh cigarette of the morning—it was still only ten o'clock—and forced herself to concentrate on Chapter Twelve. Hugh had fixed her computer. She hadn't lost the first two hundred pages after all. With no interruptions, this was the perfect opportunity to crack on with the story. Giles was playing golf, it was as simple as that. She had to get a grip and stop being so hopelessly paranoid. What could be more innocent than a couple of rounds of golf?

At eleven o'clock, Orla tried ringing Giles on his mobile but it was switched off. Oh well, it would be switched off, you couldn't have phones trilling away all over the course while a tournament was in progress, that wouldn't win you any popularity contests.

Downstairs, the house phone rang for the third time that morning. Orla ignored it. When she was working in her office she routinely let the answering machine pick up the calls.

Lighting yet another cigarette—her standard reaction to the anxiety churning away like a cement mixer in the pit of her stomach—Orla stared at the computer screen in front of her, willing herself to stop obsessing about Giles and press on with Chapter Twelve.

By seven o'clock she'd finished it. Chapter Twelve was done and dusted. All in all, a good day's work, Orla decided with satisfaction as she wandered downstairs in her nightie because she hadn't quite got around to getting dressed. Still, never mind. Something to eat, followed by a long bath, and a change into a fresh nightie, then maybe a glass or two of red wine while watching something suitably trashy on television.

I'm turning into Hugh Hefner, bleeugh, scary thought.

Although imagining Hugh Hefner in a nightie was an even scarier one.

Having rummaged around in the freezer, Orla pulled out a Fogarty and Phelps pasta *puttanesca*. She stabbed the cellophane artistically with a fork, bunged the pasta into the microwave, and wrestled the cork out of a bottle of Valpolicella.

There were seven messages on the answering machine. While she slurped wine and lit a cigarette, Orla listened to a brief call from her agent about Spanish translation rights, two calls from the editorial director at her publishers, and a message from the opticians in Newquay letting Giles know his Bausch and Lomb sunglasses had been repaired and were ready for collection.

There had also been two silent calls, with no message left.

As the microwave went ding, the final message began to play. For a moment Orla thought it was going to be another no-show, then her heart leapt into her throat as she heard a stifled sob.

'Giles? Giles? It's me. Martine.'

The voice was husky with grief. Rooted to the spot, Orla listened to the girl struggling to retain some control.

'Oh Giles, it's been so long... I know it's all over but I just wanted to hear your voice... I'm so s-s-sorry.' Martine was weeping openly now. 'I know you love Orla, I accept that, truly I do. It's just so hard to think I'm never going to see you again. Please don't be cross with me for phoning you at home, but what else could I do? You changed the number of your mobile. Anyway, just to let you know, I've moved back to London and I hope you and Orla will be very h-h-happy together. Okay, that's it. B-bye.'

After a few more seconds of unrestrained sobbing, the line went dead.

Orla closed her eyes, breathing out at last. Hot tears of happiness slid down her cheeks. The relief was indescribable. It really was all over between Giles and Martine, she'd spent the last few weeks worrying herself sick over nothing. Not to mention the last twelve hours with a churning, knotted-up stomach, terrified that Giles may have been lying about the golf tournament and had in fact sloped off somewhere with Martine instead.

And all the time Martine had already been back in London, pining for the man she loved. The man who was *no longer interested in her*.

Slopping red wine on to the telephone table as she took another joyful swig, Orla wiped her wet eyes and smiled to herself.

Poor Giles, how could she ever have doubted him?

Oh God, this was the best news *ever.*

'Stay a bit longer,' Martine urged playfully, as Giles emerged from the shower and began to dress.

'Better not. We've had the whole day together.' Grinning, he dodged away from the bed as she made a grab for him.

'Coward.'

Giles tapped his watch; it would take him another fifteen minutes to drive from Martine's cottage in Perranporth back to Newquay.

'It's ten o'clock. I'm being sensible. Why push our luck?'

Martine reached across the bed for the phone and held it teasingly to her ear.

'I could always give Orla another ring, sob a bit, beg her to let me speak to you.' Martine slipped effortlessly into distraught mode: 'H-hello, could I have a word with G-G-Giles, please?'

Giles chuckled but shook his head.

'Once was enough. She'll be happy with that.' He was happy with it too; Orla had become increasingly twitchy over the last couple of weeks. The phone call earlier had been a master-stroke.

'D'you think she'll tell you I rang?' Martine ran her tongue over her upper lip as she watched him finish dressing. The great thing about Giles's pink cashmere sweater and truly appalling pink and orange checked trousers was that she hadn't been able to wait to get him out of them.

'Who knows?' He leaned over the rumpled bed and kissed her. 'Probably not. It'll be Orla's little secret.'

'I thought she couldn't keep secrets.'

'Ha, she can't. She'll tell the rest of the world. Everyone but me.'

'Good thing we're better at keeping things to ourselves than she is.' Martine smirked. 'And you'll still definitely be able to make it tomorrow? You'd *better* be able to,' she added, her tone mock-threatening. A lot of effort had gone into making Thursday special, an evening he wouldn't forget.

Giles already had his excuse mapped out; he'd told Orla he'd been invited to join the local branch of the Masons.

'No problem.' He kissed Martine again then straightened up, pleased with himself. 'I wouldn't miss it for the world.'

Hester was forced to acknowledge that the Twiglets had taken their toll. Then again, the custard creams, the chipsticks, the Bounty ice-cream bars, and the endless plates of lettuce may have had something to do with it as well.

Only joking about the lettuce, obviously.

Hester marveled at her ability to make any kind of joke. What with her life being over, Nat thinking she was a trollop, and the fact that in less than a week she'd apparently managed to put on half a stone.

Still, that was the thing about comfort-eating to cure your abject misery. Lettuce simply didn't hit the spot.

'God, I'm *gross*,' Hester blurted out, scaring away a couple of wealthy tourists who had been about to buy fifty pairs of earrings. Ha, *as if*.

Danielle, who ran the candle stall next to Hester's, switched off her mp3 player and said, 'What?'

'Me. Gross.' Hester plucked in disgust at the straining waistband of her jeans. 'Look at this flab, it's all *wibbly*.'

Danielle perked up at once; there was nothing she enjoyed more than a cozy putting-on-weight story. Particularly when it was somebody else's putting-on-weight story.

'Well, you have been eating a bit more than usual.' Glancing at the scrumpled-up family-sized Swiss roll wrapper in the bin behind Hester's chair she said brightly, 'Maybe you're pregnant.'

'Huh, that would be too much to hope for. I haven't had sex for the last fifteen years, remember.' Gloomily Hester shook her head. 'Let's face it, I'm just fat because I'm eating too much.'

'So stop eating.'

'I can't, I'm too *miserable.*' Hester thumped her thighs. 'And eating's the only thing that cheers me *up.*'

'Not doing a very good job then, is it?' Danielle shrugged. 'Losing a bit of weight, that's what' d really cheer you up.'

'But I'm too depressed to go on a diet!'

Danielle suppressed a sigh; Hester was being a pain, but she'd also been extremely kind in the past, patiently listening for hours on end to Danielle's own tales of fat-related woe.

The next moment, inspiration struck.

'I know! That new beauty salon on Cavendish Street!'

Hester wrinkled her nose.

'A beauty salon? What, eyebrow tints and facial scrubs? How's that meant to make me happy?'

'They do mud wraps,' Danielle explained eagerly. 'My sister-in-law had one last week, they've got it on special offer at the moment. It'll make you thin!'

'How?'

'They draw all the impurities out of you.' As she spoke, Danielle made extravagant drawing-out gestures with her hands. 'It firms you up and makes your skin feel fantastic, and you lose inches *all over.* My sister-in-law said it was brilliant, she can't wait to go again… she said she walked out of that salon feeling like Elle MacPherson.'

Hester blinked. Danielle's sister-in-law?

'Is this Margaret we're talking about?'

'Yes!'

Since Margaret was five feet tall and built like a cottage loaf, she'd either been taking hallucinogenic drugs, was an out-and-out liar, or the treatment had truly worked miracles.

A squiggle of hope stirred in the pit of Hester's rounded stomach.

'How much of a special offer?'

'Buy one, get one free.'

'What?'

'You pay for one leg wrap, they do the other one for nothing. Bargain!'

It was starting to sound like one.

'You know what?' said Hester. 'I might just give it a try.'

By half past six, Hester found herself lying on a bench being comprehensively mud-wrapped. Having taken a detour after work to Cavendish Street on the off-chance that the Deluxe Beauty Salon might be able to fit her in, she had been delighted to discover they could.

'We call it miracle mud,' confided the beauty therapist, who had introduced herself as Zelda. Energetically, she slathered great dollops of greenish-brown gunk over Hester's stomach and thighs. 'It really does the business.'

It smelled a bit funny, but Hester didn't mind; she knew you had to suffer in order to get results. She was also glad Zelda had given her a pair of paper knickers to change into, even if they were one-size-fits-all and less than glamorous. As Zelda carried on slapping and spreading, the gunk was going everywhere. Like a five-year-old icing a cake.

Hester sniffed.

'What's that smell?'

'Just the mud, don't worry about it. So are you down here on holiday?' Zelda set about getting the conversational ball rolling in true beauty-therapist style.

'I meant the other smell. Like cooking.'

'Oh, that'll be my supper! Cheese on toast!' Zelda had a tinkly, beauty therapist's laugh. 'When I'm on my own here in the salon I do myself a little snack to keep me going. We've got a kitchen through there.' Nodding at the door to their left, she slathered the rest of the mud briskly on to Hester's upper arms and midriff, then reached for a giant roll of plastic wrap. 'Okay, now lift that right leg for me, here's where we start wrapping you up… and round, and round, and round… so which part of the country did you say you were from?'

Hester's stomach rumbled loudly, she was starving and the cheese on toast smelled fantastic.

'Newquay.'

'Really? That's a lovely place. Oh, Newquay! You mean you actually live here? That's *great*.''

Who Wants to be a Millionaire? thought Hester. Not Zelda, that was for sure. Still, what she lacked in concentration she made up for with dexterity; she was actually doing a brilliant job of trussing her up like a plastic-wrapped spatchcock chicken.

Setting a timer, Zelda crooned, 'Is it starting to feel warm now?'

It was, actually. Hester nodded.

'Good, good. That's the minerals in the mud beginning to work, drawing out all those nasty toxins. It actually heats up to sixty degrees centigrade, you know.'

Hester tried to sit up. '*What?*'

'Oh sorry, is that wrong?' Zelda started tinkling again. 'Maybe I mean Fahrenheit, I'm always getting those two muddled up! I can assure you, our miracle mud only becomes pleasantly warm, it won't cause you any pain whatsoever.'

Now that she was enveloped in it, the smell of the mud had invaded Hester's nostrils. So this was how it felt to be a hippo. Lying back, she gazed out of the window as Zelda finished plastic wrapping her right arm. Outside, the sky was blue, the sun was blazing down and Hester could hear the chatter and laughter of the punters sitting outside the bars and pavement cafés that stretched the length of Cavendish Street.

'How long's it going to take?'

'Hmm? Ooh, half an hour. Then I'll unwrap you and you can have a lovely warm shower.' Zelda's tone was soothing. 'In the meantime, why don't you have a little nap?'

Closing her eyes, Hester pictured herself emerging from the salon, possibly to the sound of audible gasps of admiration and a spontaneous round of applause from the assembled crowds. The extra inches having mysteriously melted away, she would be sleek and sinuous and as lump-free as a Delia Smith sauce.

Frustratingly, Millie was working tonight—she had some job on in Truro—otherwise they could have gone out together. With me looking ravishing, Hester thought smugly, and attracting all the attention for once.

Danielle had been right: coming here and getting mud-wrapped had been a fabulous idea. She was feeling better about herself already.

'Could you open the window?' said Hester. I'm feeling quite hot now.'

'It is warm, isn't it?' Zelda fanned herself as she reached up to open the window. 'There, that's better.'

Puzzled, Hester gazed down at her supine body.

'Am I smoking?'

'Ooh no, you shouldn't smoke, cigarettes are bad for you, you'll get terrible facial wrinkles.'

'No, I meant the mud on my body. I know it heats up but does it actually produce smoke?'

Zelda looked baffled.

But now that the window had been opened, it became clear there was smoke in the treatment room. It was eddying around in the breeze, slithering out of the window like ectoplasm…

'Oh Jesus!' squawked Hester, suddenly realizing where it was coming from. Jack-knifing into a sitting position, she pointed to the kitchen door, beneath which grey smoke was beginning to billow.

'Shit, my cheese on toast!'

Zelda let out a decidedly untinkly screech, ran to the door, yanked it open—and promptly slammed it shut again as she was enveloped in a thick black cloud of smoke. 'Aaargh, we're on fire, the kitchen's on fire, help, help, HELP!'

Chapter 34

HESTER WAS OFF THE treatment table in a flash—no mean feat considering her trussed-up condition.

'Where are my clothes?'

'Ohmigod, ohmigod, my boss is going to kill me,' shrieked Zelda, her eyes wide with terror. 'Help, police, *ohmigod*—OW!'

'Sorry,' said Hester, who had slapped her, 'but you have to listen to me. WHERE ARE MY CLOTHES?'

'I p-put them in the k-kitchen.' Zelda whimpered and clutched her reddened cheek. 'So they wouldn't smell of m-m-mud.'

The smoke was everywhere now. Hester grabbed Zelda and propelled her out of the treatment room. Maybe in the front section of the salon there would be blankets or towels or a handily left-behind coat.

There weren't.

The door of the salon crashed open and two holidaymakers masquerading as have-a-go heroes burst in. Hester knew they were holidaymakers because they were wearing gaudy shorts and sandals, their backs were white, and their fronts were burned traffic-light red.

'This place is on fire! You have to get out,' yelled the first holidaymaker, stumbling to a halt at the sight of Hester in all her muddy plastic-wrapped glory. 'Blimey darlin,' what happened to you?'

'I'm going to get the sack for this!' wailed Zelda, grabbing her handbag from the desk drawer and shooting out of the salon.

'Anyone else in here?' demanded the second holidaymaker.

Miserably Hester shook her head. Somebody must have already

dialled 999—in the distance she could hear the nee-naw sound of a fire engine edging its way through the choked-up streets. She knew she couldn't stay in here, but it was like plucking up the courage to bungee jump out of a helicopter.

The next moment, seeing her fear, the first holidaymaker did it for her. Only instead of pushing her out of the helicopter, he grabbed her in a clumsy attempt at a fireman's lift.

Before Hester knew what was happening, she found herself hoisted over his shoulder. Her legs were bouncing off his beer belly, his sweaty arms were clutching her thighs, and her big bottom was stuck up in the air like a… well, like a big bottom stuck up in the air.

And then they were outside the salon, where everyone had gathered to watch. The pavement cafés and bars were packed and all eyes were fixed on Hester and her rescuer.

'Blimey love, you weigh a ton,' grunted fatbloke, lowering her to the ground. He was sweating profusely but looking ridiculously pleased with himself. Almost as if he expected her to be grateful.

Hester's eyes prickled with smoke and shame. In her fantasy less than ten minutes earlier, she had imagined the crowd gasping with admiration at the sight of her.

But this was real life and instead here she was, slathered from neck to knees in what looked like the stuff that shoots out of cows' backsides.

And miles and miles of plastic wrapped sausage-tight around her arms, legs, and midriff.

And a gunk-splattered orange bra.

And baggy, Sumo-sized disposable paper pants.

Needless to say, nobody was gasping with admiration.

The so-called adults were sniggering like schoolchildren. The schoolchildren themselves were pointing and shrieking with laughter. There were even babies whimpering and hiding their faces in their mothers' skirts.

Hester winced as someone let out a piercing wolf-whistle. It was now, officially, time to die of embarrassment.

There was nowhere to hide.

Nothing to cover herself up with.

She didn't even have her handbag, because Zelda had thoughtfully left it in the kitchen along with her clothes.

And nobody had even offered her so much as a T-shirt to cover her shame.

The road cleared and the fire engine eased its way through at last. Firemen leapt out and into action, unraveling hoses at a rate of knots. Within seconds, the hoses snaked furiously as torrents of water were aimed at the smoking salon. But even as the firemen did their job, they couldn't help sneaking incredulous glances in Hester's direction.

Just when she thought it couldn't get any worse, there was a tap on her shoulder. Swinging round, puce with mortification, Hester saw that it was Lucas.

Oh God.

'Here.' Having taken off his cream linen jacket, he gently draped it around her shoulders. 'Let's cover you up.'

Hester knew she should be thanking him. Profusely, no doubt. Instead she muttered, 'What are you doing here?'

'I was having a drink with a friend.' He indicated one of the bars with tables outside, further down the road. 'Didn't recognize you at first. My car's just round the corner.'

Hester said rudely, 'So?'

'Well, we could unwrap you now, stand you in front of the salon, and ask a nice fireman to hose you down. Or,' offered Lucas, dangling his car keys in front of her, 'I could give you a lift home.'

Of all the people to see her looking like this.

'What about your friend?'

'Who?' Lucas smiled. 'Oh, no problem. She'll wait.'

They headed for Lucas's car, leaving a tearful Zelda to help the police with their inquiries. Aware that his jacket wasn't completely covering Hester's cow-poo-and-plastic-wrap look, Lucas waved a twenty-pound note at the gawping owner of a beachwear shop and selected a pink and white fringed sarong from the revolving stand on the pavement outside.

'I can't pay you back,' whispered Hester. 'My purse is in the salon.'

'Don't be daft.' He put his arm around her, giving her waist a reassuring squeeze. When the plastic wrap squeaked he added, 'And cheer up. One day you'll look back at this and smile.'

This was such a ridiculous thing to say that Hester didn't even deign to reply.

The journey back to the house took less than ten minutes. The spare key, thank God, was still in its fiendishly clever hiding place under the doormat.

Hester turned the key in the lock and wondered if she was supposed to invite Lucas in for a coffee. Would that be the polite thing to do? All she wanted was to be on her own. Damn, why did life have to be so complicated?

Why did she have to be wrapped in plastic wrap and cow poo?

And why, why, *why* had she jumped naked into Orla's swimming pool the other night and begged Lucas for sex?

'I'll head back, leave you to it,' said Lucas. 'You have a nice shower, wash off all that muck.' He paused. 'Tell me, why *do* women do this mud thing?'

He'd been really kind to her. If he hadn't turned up, she'd still be trudging home now. With a Pied Piper trail of sniggering children in her wake.

'It's to make us more beautiful,' said Hester. 'More attractive to men.'

'Ah. Right. But you're already attractive.'

'Of course I am. I mean, look at me.' She spread her plastic-wrapped arms. 'Completely gorgeous.'

Lucas grinned and pecked her on the cheek. It was the kind of peck you'd give a five-year-old.

'Go and have that shower. I'll see you around.'

'Yeah.' Hester mustered a weak smile. 'Thanks.'

The mud had dried on her skin. It took ages to wash off. After twenty minutes of energetic scrubbing, Hester stepped out of the shower and surveyed her naked body in the mirror. Pinker than usual, but otherwise exactly the same as before. There was a lesson to be learned from this somewhere. Nestling at the bottom of a Twiglet box, probably.

Millie wouldn't be home before ten at the earliest. Wrapped in her dressing gown, Hester made a cup of tea and settled herself on the sofa with the remote control and the phone.

She punched out the code for Glasgow, then the number of the restaurant. Nat would be busy but even hearing his voice for a few seconds would cheer her up.

'Nat?' said a hassled-sounding male when Hester asked to speak to him. 'He's not working tonight, it's his night off.'

Pleased, because this meant Nat wouldn't be too busy to speak to her properly, Hester rang the pay phone at his lodging house.

'Nat? He's not here.' It was another young male voice, one she didn't recognize. 'He's out with Annie.'

Annie?

Annie?

'Who?' said Hester.

'Anastasia.'

Anastasia?

Ana-bloody-stasia?

There was the sound of muffled voices in the background before the boy, clearly worried, said, 'Sorry, look, I don't know who

Nat's out with. Maybe he's gone for a drink with some of the lads. Okay, bye.'

The line went dead. Hester stared at the receiver, as stunned as if the boy had told her that Nat wasn't there right now, he was in hospital having his sex-change.

It had simply never occurred to her that Nat might do this. He wasn't the type. He worked too hard. He loved *her*.

Except maybe now he'd changed his mind and decided he'd be better off loving someone else instead.

EastEnders was on television. Hester watched without taking in a word of it. Annie Annie Annie, that was a name that was almost bearable, rival-wise. It conjured up a picture of someone plump and a bit scruffy, with bitten nails, a friendly smile, and no dress sense.

But Anastasia… that was the kind of name that sent shivers of terror down your spine, because you just knew she'd be tall and exotic and ruthlessly chic, with Russian cheekbones and a wolfhound on a diamond-encrusted lead.

Hester buried her face in her hands. Nat had gone and found himself a Disney heroine.

Oh God, and it's all my fault.

Chapter 35

The Castle Hotel in Truro was floodlit and impressive, the car park packed with sleek, top-of-the-range specimens that put Millie's lime green Mini to shame. Having learned her lesson from the supermarket fiasco, she hauled her gorilla suit—stuffed into a black trash bag—out of the boot of the car and carried it through to reception.

The girl behind the desk was expecting her.

'This is brilliant,' she giggled. 'We don't get many gorillas here. We're just not that kind of hotel.'

'Okay if I change in the ladies' loo?' Millie held up her trash bag. 'Then I'll head on through and do my bit.'

'I'll come with you. I wouldn't miss this for the world. The Drews are on table fifteen, bang in the middle of the restaurant.' The receptionist reached beneath the desk and pulled out a disposable camera. 'And it's my job to record the happy event—Mrs. Drew gave me this and asked me to take loads of pictures. Oh, her husband's going to get the surprise of his life!'

In the plush loos, Millie changed into the gorilla suit, fastened on her roller skates, and practiced reciting the fantastically naff poem Mrs. Drew had written in praise of her husband. As she was lowering the gorilla's head into place, the receptionist pulled the door open and said, 'Ready? This is going to be so great!'

'Ready.' Millie seized the bottle of cheap sparkling wine and the 'You've Been Kemped' T-shirt, and roller-skated over to the door. 'Lead the way.'

The dining room was vast, high-ceilinged, and glittering with chandeliers. It was also packed with diners. Millie, glad she had the receptionist with her, heard the girl whisper, 'There they are, at that table for two, dead ahead. She's the one in the green sparkly dress, he's wearing a dark blue suit.'

As they navigated their way between the tables, the tinkle of cutlery and hum of polite conversation petered out. Spotting them, the other diners stared and began to whisper furiously to each other. Laughter broke out. Millie, who loved this bit, prayed her skates wouldn't slip on the highly polished oak floor, either sending her clattering to the ground or—more messily—pitching head first into a bowl of trifle.

Then the man who had his back to her at table fifteen turned around and Millie found herself with something completely different to worry about.

Because Mr. Drew wasn't Mr. Drew at all.

He was Giles Hart.

And the girl sitting with him in her green sparkly outfit was the girl with sleek magenta hair who had been at the party on Saturday night. The one Giles had introduced as Anna, the dressmaker from Perranporth, newcomer to the area, and a member of the golf club.

In a flash Millie knew the truth. The poem she'd memorized said it all.

Three years ago today we met,
Three years of utter bliss,
I never knew one perfect man
Could make me as happy as this.

The girl was Martine Drew.

Next moment there was another kind of flash as the receptionist took a photo with the disposable camera.

How could he?

How could he do this? How could he have the utter gall to invite his mistress along to Orla's party and introduce her to his own wife?

Martine, meanwhile, was beaming with happiness, thrilled with the success of her surprise, and waiting expectantly for Millie to launch into her poem. Unlike Giles, she clearly had no idea that the person inside the gorilla suit might be someone acquainted with Orla.

Giles, who knew what Millie did for a living, was less sure. It might be her under all that fur. Then again it might not.

Millie watched him hesitate, redden, then decide to bluff it out.

'Well well, what have we here?' boomed Giles, sitting back in his chair. Spotting the bottle of sparkling wine in Millie's paw, he added jovially, 'Are you the wine waiter?'

'Sshh.' Reaching across the table, Martine gave his hand a loving squeeze. 'Wait until you hear this.' She nodded at Millie, indicating that it was time for the poem.

Click, flash, went the disposable camera.

Quivering with outrage, Millie took a step back and announced in a clear, carrying voice:

'Why don't you get yourself a life
And stop this cheating on your wife?'

Improvisation wasn't really her forte. It wasn't great, but on the spur of the moment it was the best she could manage. Anyway, it did the trick. Giles, purple in the face, knocked over a glass as he leapt up from his chair. Everyone else in the room gasped audibly and held their breath.

Martine, staring at Millie in alarm, hissed, 'What the hell's going on? What are you *talking about*?'

Millie ducked as Giles's arm shot out. For a scary moment she thought he was about to punch her. But Giles grabbed the gorilla head and, with brutal disregard for Millie's ears, wrenched it off.

Pale eyes bulging, he roared, 'Who put you up to this?'

'I did,' said Martine, groaning as she recognized Millie. 'Oh God, it was meant to be a fantastic *surprise*.'

Click, flash, went the camera behind them, the receptionist really getting into her stride now.

'I think it's definitely been that,' Millie announced, aware that the rest of the restaurant was in uproar around her. The other diners were either shrieking with laughter or rigid with disgust. This was probably a good moment to leave. Plonking the bottle of sparkling wine and the cellophane-wrapped T-shirt down on the table, Millie said cheerfully, 'Enjoy the rest of your meal,' and skated out of the room with the gorilla head tucked under her arm.

Rather gratifyingly, she got a round of applause.

'Something tells me they're not going to want these photos,' sighed the receptionist, who had followed her out.

'I'll take it.' Millie reached for the disposable camera.

'Will you get into trouble over this?'

Millie unzipped the side of the gorilla suit and discreetly retrieved her car keys, which were tucked into her bra. That was the nice thing about Lucas: she knew he wouldn't bawl her out or sack her when he heard why she'd done it. With a smile, she said, 'Don't worry, I've got an understanding boss.'

The receptionist, whose own boss was a complete pig, looked envious.

'God, you're so lucky.'

Millie nodded. Lucas might be a womanizer but he undoubtedly had his good points.

'I know.'

❖❖❖

Giles caught up with her in the car park as she was unfastening her roller skates. Martine hung back in the shadows beneath the trees, allowing him to deal with Millie in his own way.

'Does Orla know about this?' He spoke without preamble.

'No.' Millie was glad she'd already stuffed the camera into the glove compartment.

'Are you going to tell her?'

'I don't know. I haven't decided yet.'

Oh, and did I mention my middle name was Pinocchio?

'Now you just listen to me.' Giles was breathing heavily. 'You wouldn't be doing Orla any favors if you told her. You'd break her heart.'

I'd break her heart? Millie boggled.

'Right.' Sweat glistened on his brow as he drew out his wallet. 'I'll make out a check. Five grand, how about that?'

Millie stared at him. Slowly, she unfastened the second roller skate and dropped it on to the passenger seat.

'Okay, ten grand,' said Giles. 'Ten thousand pounds not to say anything to Orla.'

He was trying to bribe her! Best of all, he was trying to bribe her with his wife's money! Then again, Orla's money and the lifestyle it afforded him were, of course, the reasons he was so keen to keep the marriage going.

'Go on then,' said Millie.

Giles's hands shook with relief as he scribbled out the check. Taking it from him, Millie fitted the key into the Mini's ignition.

'Thanks. If I cash it, you'll be safe.' She smiled briefly. 'If I decide to tell Orla, I'll give it back.'

He stared at her, the expression on his face one of fury mixed with fear.

'Are you going to tell her?'

'Who knows? I haven't decided yet.' Millie shrugged and gazed innocently up at him. 'Although if you ask me, life's too short to spend it being married to a tosspot.'

Giles gritted his teeth. He was clearly dying to call her a bitch.

'But will you?'

'Let's make it a surprise.' Smiling to herself, Millie started the engine. 'You'll just have to wait and see.'

'One o'clock?' said Orla cheerfully, phoning the next day to check when Millie would be turning up for her regular debriefing session. 'Then we can chat over a gorgeous lunch.'

'Actually, my car's broken down,' Millie lied. 'Would it be a pain for you to drive over to me?'

She watched from the bedroom window as Orla pulled up outside, jumped out of the gleaming, burnt orange Mercedes, and exchanged a joke with one of the neighbors. She was clearly in high spirits and looking radiant in a long turquoise strapless summer dress, flat silver sandals, and armfuls of bracelets.

Millie's heart sank at the prospect of erasing all that radiance. She felt like a doctor having to tell someone their leg needed to come off.

Even if, in the end, you knew they'd be better off without it.

'Okay, off we go.' Orla was sitting on the floor with her elbows on the coffee table. She had a notebook open, her pen at the ready, and the ever-present packet of Marlboros within grabbing distance. She was wearing her favorite Ghost perfume, a pretty, shimmery bronze lipstick, and her hair fastened up in a giant tortoiseshell barrette. She was also looking *happy*, as if she didn't have a care in the world.

'I'll start with Hester,' said Millie. 'She had the most awful thing happen to her yesterday.'

'This is perfect,' Orla declared, scribbling down the mud-wrap story.

'Although I don't know if she'll want you using it.' Millie felt it only fair to warn her. 'It's pretty embarrassing.'

'People love being written about.' Orla's smile was reassuring. 'I'll show it to her when it's finished. I bet you she won't mind.'

'It gets worse. When she got home last night, she rang Nat. But he wasn't there.' Millie ran through the details of Hester's phone call. 'So it looks as if he's got himself involved with this Anastasia, whoever she is.'

Orla flipped over the page of her notebook and carried on furiously scribbling.

'So Hester suspects he's playing around, but she doesn't know for sure?'

Millie nodded, her mouth suddenly dry.

'Right, now here's where I need your advice,' she told Orla. 'If you had a friend and you found out their other half was seeing someone else, would you tell her? Or would you keep it to yourself?'

Orla looked up, entranced.

'You mean if you had absolute proof? Are you saying you *do* have proof?'

'Um, yes.'

'Oh well, no question about it. You have to tell her.'

'She'll be upset. She might not want to know.'

'Come on! If she's a good friend, it's your duty to tell her.' Orla's eyes lit up as she reached for her cigarettes. 'You can't possibly keep something like that to yourself.'

Millie's heart began to pound. 'Yes, but are you saying that because you think it would be a good story line for the book or because you really mean it?'

'Oh please,' Orla declared indignantly. 'I'm not that mean! Hester deserves to know. You *have* to tell her. It's for her own good!'

'Okay.' Millie looked away, feeling sicker than ever.

'But what intrigues me is how you found out.' Avidly, Orla leaned closer. 'Did Nat actually tell you himself?'

Deep breath.

'This isn't about Hester and Nat.'

Chapter 36

THERE WAS A HORRIBLE sensation in Millie's mouth, as if she'd licked a battery. This is it, she thought unhappily, her gaze fixed on the carpet. No going back now. I am The Dark Destroyer.

She was startled to hear Orla laughing. Then came the sound of frenzied scribbling-out.

'You tricked me! I really thought you meant you had proof about Nat. Now look at the mess I've made of my notes! So who is it then, this other friend of yours?'

Prevaricating, Millie said, 'Maybe I shouldn't tell her.'

'Darling, you're being ridiculous. You know you have to.'

Slowly Millie raised her eyes, her gaze locking with Orla's.

'Oh.'

Orla stared back at her. As Millie watched, recognition gradually dawned.

'Oh,' whispered Orla, all the color sliding from her face. 'Oh. Oh. Oh God, nooo.'

Even her lips were white. She looked as if she'd just been drained of blood by a vampire.

'I'm so sorry.' Millie wished she could be somewhere else. 'I didn't know whether or not to say anything. But you just told me I should.'

'Giles?' It came out as a croak.

'Yes.'

'But he promised me he wouldn't do it again. Never ever again. He *promised* me that.'

And you actually believed him?

Instead, Millie said sympathetically, 'I know.'

Cra-aack, went Orla's pen, snapping in two between her fingers.

'Martine Drew?'

'Yes.'

'Really? I thought it might have been that girl who was at the party last week. Anna the dressmaker.' The words tumbled jerkily out of Orla's mouth. 'The one who recently joined the golf club? Remember her?'

Millie nodded, bracing herself yet again.

'That was Martine.'

Orla blinked.

'What are you talking about?'

'That was Martine Drew.'

'What?'

Millie wondered how else she could possibly say it.

'Last time, when the press found out about Giles and Martine… well, you didn't meet her, did you?'

Dazed, Orla shook her head.

'You just saw pictures in the papers. Not very clear photos, when she was trying to hide her face.'

'But she had blonde hair. Long blonde hair.' Orla's hand shook as she took a drag of her cigarette. Then her shoulders sagged as she realized the stupidity of what she'd just said.

'It's called going to the hairdresser,' said Millie.

'But… she rang, just the other day… she's living back in London,' Orla whispered. 'Except I suppose she isn't. It was just another lie, to put me off the scent.' She frowned, crumpling the cigarette into the ashtray, then looked up. 'How did you find out?'

'She hired me to turn up last night. They were in a restaurant, celebrating their anniversary. I thought she meant wedding anniversary.'

'Last night. Giles told me he was with the Freemasons. Look,' Orla blurted out hopelessly, 'are you sure this is true?'

'Here.' Millie slid the envelope containing the just-developed photos across the coffee table. 'There's something else in there too. The check Giles tried to bribe me with, to keep my mouth shut. I'll make us a cup of tea.'

Wine was a big temptation but getting roaring drunk wouldn't help Orla right now.

Ten minutes later she returned from the kitchen with two mugs of tea and—in the absence of Twiglets—a plate of nutella sandwiches.

Orla was pale and dry-eyed, and the ripped-up photographs were scattered over the coffee table.

'He promised,' she told Millie, her voice calm. 'He promised faithfully.'

Faithfully. That was a good one.

'Do you wish I hadn't told you now?' Millie held her breath.

'No. He brought her along to our party. All these months he's been lying to me. Seeing her, and cheating on me. I want to kill him. I do.' Orla's jaw was clenched. 'I do, I really want to kill him.'

Feeling brave, Millie said the unsayable. 'So long as you don't want to kill yourself.'

'God, no. I don't deserve this.' Shaking her head, Orla lit another cigarette. 'I really don't. I deserve better. He's got a fucking nerve. It's all over, you know. This is the last bollocking straw. I *won't* spend the rest of my life forgiving him and forgiving him and always wondering when it'll happen again… I mean, what kind of marriage *is* that?'

'The rotten miserable lousy kind,' said Millie.

'Giles is a rotten miserable lousy husband! He's a complete and utter shit.' Orla thumped the table for emphasis. 'And I'm just not going to take it any more. I'm going to go home and kick him out and divorce him faster than you can say… divorce.'

'Well, good.' Although Millie privately wondered if she'd go through with it. When push came to shove, Orla might chicken out.

'You don't think I will, do you?' As she rose to her feet, shaking the creases out of her turquoise dress, Orla smiled slightly at Millie. 'But I'm going to. I am. I can promise you that.'

At five o'clock, the first fat raindrops began to plop out of the sky.

Good, thought Orla, watching with satisfaction as the thick, charcoal grey clouds rolled overhead. She wanted it to rain. The harder the better. A thunderstorm would be fine. A typhoon would be perfect.

Twenty minutes later, Giles's car came into view. Her arms folded tightly across her chest, Orla followed his progress through the open gates and up the drive.

When the car braked, she knew he'd seen them. His clothes, strewn across the lawn, sodden with rain.

Not just *some* clothes, either. All of them. Every single thing he owned, right down to his underpants.

What with Giles being so vain, the lawn was actually pretty crowded.

Orla, who had thrown the lot out of the bedroom window, was feeling pleased with herself. Giles had always been so persnickety about his clothes, insisting that each shirt was precision-ironed, each handmade shoe flawlessly polished.

Except they weren't looking quite so flawless now, with the rain pelting down and his best dinner jacket dangling like a hanged man from the mulberry tree.

He knew the game was up, of course, the moment he saw what

she'd done. Glancing over her shoulder at the empty wardrobes—so *many* empty wardrobes—Orla unfolded her arms and pushed open the bedroom window. She watched Giles climb out of the car and gaze up at her.

He looked like a cornered animal.

'What's all this about?'

'Oh, I think you've probably got a rough idea.'

'That *bitch*!' shouted Giles, his sandy hair already darkening in the rain. He shook his head in despair. 'I knew she'd tell you. Sweetheart, I can explain everything. It's not how it looked, I promise.'

'Déjà vu,' Orla bellowed down at him.

'What?'

'I've heard that line before. Except last time I was stupid enough to believe you.'

'But it's the *truth*. Look, let's sit down and talk about this over a drink.'

As he made his way to the front door, he stooped to retrieve a sodden Jaeger sweater of which he was particularly fond.

'The door's locked,' yelled Orla. 'In fact, all the doors are locked. And I've had the locks changed. Because you don't live here any more.'

'Orla. You're overreacting. This is ridiculous.' Giles shook his head sorrowfully. 'Look, I'm out here getting *wet*.'

'You're lucky you're not getting shot.'

'Open this front door.'

'I've got a much better idea. Why don't you move in with your mistress?'

'Martine means nothing to me!'

Orla looked bored.

'I really don't care. All I want is a divorce.'

'But my clothes… you can't do this!'

'Watch me,' Orla said pleasantly, as he bent to pick up an armful of sodden underwear. 'Oh, nearly forgot.' Reaching for the packet of black trash bags, she hurled it out of the window like a grenade. 'You're going to need these to put your clothes in. Don't say I never give you anything.'

Ha, that was a joke; she'd spent their entire married life giving him practically everything. It had been ten years since Giles had even had a job.

'You have to let me explain,' he shouted up, squinting as the torrential rain splashed into his eyes. 'I tried to get rid of her but she wouldn't let me go. She's been *stalking* me—'

'You've got a fantastic imagination.' As she prepared to slam the window shut, Orla said conversationally, 'Know what? You should write a book.'

Millie was asleep in bed when the phone rang at midnight. She heard Hester, who was still downstairs, answer it.

'It's for yooou,' Hester sang up the stairs and Millie's heart began to thud with fear.

'Orla.' Hester pulled a face as she handed over the receiver.

Millie had known it would be Orla. Tucking her Robbie Williams T-shirt over her knees, she sat down on the bottom step of the staircase.

Oh *please* don't be where I think you are…

'Hi, it's me. Did you tell him?'

'Hmm?' Orla sounded odd, distracted. 'Oh yes. I told him. I definitely told him.'

Millie pictured Orla in a distraught state, her long dress and hair whipping around her as she wandered in the pitch darkness and driving rain ever closer to the cliff edge.

'Orla? Now listen to me. Where are you?'

'Sorry? God, this is a terrible signal, I can hardly hear a thing.'

'Tell me where you are,' Millie shouted. 'And I'll come and get you.'

'Come and *get* me? Darling, what are you talking about? Ah, that's better,' said Orla as the line cleared. 'Must be the storm.'

'Where are you?' repeated Millie, her feet jiggling with agitation.

'In my office, of course! You daft thing, where else would I be at this time of night?'

Millie exhaled noisily. All the muscles in her legs relaxed. She felt as if a door had opened in her chest wall, allowing a flock of birds to whoosh out.

'So why are you phoning?'

'For my update! You told me about Hester but you forgot to tell me what's been happening with you!'

Forgot?

In a daze, Millie said, 'Nothing's been happening with me. Orla, are you *working*?'

She'd imagined Orla doing a lot of things—weeping and wailing, getting drunk, slashing her wrists—but not this.

'Of course I'm working! I want to crack on, and since I can't sleep I may as well make the most of it. So...?'

There was an expectant pause as she waited for Millie to start regaling her with all the latest gossip.

'I haven't got anything to tell you.' Millie couldn't believe they were having this conversation.

'What, nothing at all? Honestly, you're hopeless.' Orla tut-tutted. 'If things carry on the way they are, you're going to end up as a lowly subplot. Hester and I will just have to be the stars.'

She was in shock, Millie decided. In deep, deep denial.

Either that or Orla had decided—oh God—to forgive the lying cheating slimy little bogweasel.

Cautiously she said, 'Um, where's Giles?'

Perhaps he was dead. Floating face down in the swimming pool or sprawled on the floor of the conservatory with a kitchen knife stuck through his heart.

'Giles? Darling, he's gone! For good!'

Yikes, definitely dead, then.

'Martine's welcome to him,' Orla went on airily. 'Give it a couple of years and he'll be cheating on her as well. She's got it all to look forward to. Do you know, I actually feel sorry for the girl!'

Chapter 37

It wasn't all plain sailing. The initial state of giddy euphoria didn't last. The next fortnight had its rocky moments and in the privacy of her bedroom Orla had shed a few tears.

But not nearly as many as she'd imagined—which was basically her own body weight in tears—and the frequency of the outbursts was already dwindling fast.

'It's just such a relief,' she confided in Millie as they strolled together along the beach. 'Knowing I don't have to worry anymore. I honestly didn't realize how on edge I was the whole time. It's like being beaten up by your husband.' Her many silver bracelets jangled as she waved an arm. 'He swears he'll never do it again, and you *want* to believe him, but you can never truly relax because you're always mentally bracing yourself for the next punch.'

Millie picked up a pebble and skimmed it. If that was what being married to Giles had been like, no wonder Orla wasn't feeling too bad.

'You deserve someone better.'

'Ah, but what if there isn't anyone better? What if, one way or another, all men are pigs?'

'They can't *all* be,' Millie objected.

'You don't know that. Some men cheat, some men lie, some are mean, some are violent… the whole happy marriage thing could be a complete myth. Perpetuated by people like me, who write about them.' Orla shrugged and flashed her a careless smile. 'Anyway, I'm not going to think about that now. One day at a time, darling. For the moment I'm just concentrating on work, doing loads of writing, going for lovely long walks…'

'But not to Tresanter Point,' said Millie.

'Definitely not to Tresanter Point! My suicidal days are well and truly over.' Orla's green eyes sparkled. 'Apart from anything else, I want to know how my book's going to end—ooh, look at that wave!'

Millie looked. The wave was a beauty, curling and breaking at just the right moment. The waiting surfers, launching themselves on to it, cartwheeled in all directions as the wave effortlessly got the better of them. Out of a hundred or so surfers, less than half a dozen remained on their boards.

'That's sorted the men from the boys.' Crowing with delight, Orla shielded her eyes as she watched the survivors ride out the wave, the sun glinting off their black rubber wetsuits as they expertly snaked this way and that. 'It must feel fabulous, just like flying—ooh, and will you look at the body on that one!'

Watching as the wave crashed on to the beach and the surfer leapt off his board and deftly caught it, Millie experienced a lurch in her stomach. It was a body with which she was pretty familiar.

'I don't believe it!' Orla exclaimed as the surfer, flicking his wet blond hair out of his eyes, momentarily glanced across at them. 'It's Hugh Emerson! Hey, Hugh, over here!'

Oh good grief. Oh well. We can be adult about this, thought Millie, biting her lip as Orla waved delightedly at Hugh and beckoned him over. No need to get het up about it. In fact, a couple of minutes of easy conversation might be just the thing they both needed to break the ice and get them back to normal.

Hugh was less than forty feet away and Orla's arms were going like cartwheels, but the next moment he turned, tucked his surfboard under his arm and headed back into the sea.

'Oh.' Disappointed, Orla shrugged. 'He didn't see me.'

Wrong, thought Millie, who knew perfectly well that he had. He saw you all right. He just didn't want to see me.

'Nevermind.' Orla brightened. 'We can catch him when he comes in on the next wave.'

Catch him. Like a prize fish, Millie thought. Except Hugh was the one destined to get away.

'I'm hungry,' she lied. 'Couldn't we go and find somewhere to eat?'

Manchester, perhaps?

'Darling Hugh, I haven't even thanked him yet for coming over and putting my computer right.' Orla gazed fondly out across the glittering water, to where Hugh was lying on his surfboard, lazily paddling with his arms as he headed out beyond the breakers.

'Have you read that other book yet?' As she changed the subject, Millie began making her way towards the steps leading off the beach.

'You mean the poison leprechaun's?' Gathering the sea-soaked hem of her long violet dress in one hand, Orla hurried to catch up. 'Only about six times.'

Any mention of the poison leprechaun was a surefire way of distracting her attention from Hugh.

'Written your review?'

'Ha! I've written at least twenty of the things. Fabulously vile.' Orla spoke with relish. '*Really* sticking the knife in. It's so much fun, thinking up more and more hideous insults.'

Millie was bemused. 'I thought you were going to do a nice one.'

'Oh darling, I am. And I will, eventually. But in the meantime I'm getting all the bitterness out of my system, saying all the things I'd really like to say. I'm telling you, it's better than sex—which is just as well,' Orla pulled a face, 'seeing as I probably won't be having sex for the next fifty years. Ooh, that reminds me, bad news for you too.' Sympathetically, she clutched Millie's arm. 'I had a phone call yesterday from Richard. His father's died and he's had to go up to Carlisle. What with arranging the funeral and having to sort out the house, he thinks he's going to be tied up there for the next fortnight at least. He wanted me to let you know, so you won't wonder why he hasn't been in touch. Bless him, he was really apologetic, but he says as soon as he gets back he'll give you a ring about fixing up that dinner date.'

A reprieve. Phew.

Aloud, Millie said, 'Oh, that's a shame. Poor Richard.'

'Poor us!' Orla sounded disgusted. 'I was pinning all my hopes on this story line.'

'I wasn't actually planning on having sex with Richard,' Millie protested.

'But you can't plan these things. You might have done. All this celibacy's starting to get monotonous.'

As they climbed the steep road leading away from the beach, Millie glanced briefly over her shoulder. Now that they'd retreated, Hugh was surfing again. From this distance she shouldn't have been able to pick him out from among the hundreds of other wet-suited surfers, but she still could.

'We need some romance in your life,' Orla persisted. 'We need excitement and suspense. And we definitely need a lot more shagging.'

'I'm sorry. I'll do my best.' Millie grinned. 'Was there anyone in particular you had in mind?'

'Well, Con would be great, but the selfish sod's flown over to New York to talk to some producer chappie about a show they're putting together for Broadway.'

'Damn, that is selfish.'

'So we've just got to come up with an alternative.' Orla fixed her with a look that was half confident, half ultra-persuasive. 'Okay, and I know I've said this before, but are you sure you wouldn't fancy a bash at Lucas?'

◈◈◈

It was like trying to hold a conversation with a double-glazing salesman, Hester realized, after the job had been done. Initially they were charm personified, nothing was too much trouble, and they couldn't be nicer to you. But try contacting them a fortnight later to complain about the draughts whistling through your newly installed window frames and they couldn't get you off the phone fast enough.

This was exactly what it was like, these days, trying to talk to Nat.

No more Mr. Nice Guy, oh no. Then again, he wasn't being Mr. Downright Horrible Guy either. Just ultra-polite, perfunctory, and oh-so-distant. As if he would rather be anywhere but on the phone talking to her, but was too well-mannered to say so.

Hester, her head aching with the effort of pretending nothing was wrong, clutched the receiver and said, 'You sound tired. Are you sure you're okay?'

Was that a sigh?

'Of course I'm okay. We're just busy, that's all.'

Busy doing what?

'Look, maybe I could come up this weekend.'

'I'll be working. Not really much point.'

'Nat.' Hester closed her eyes and braced herself. 'Who's Annie?'

Pause.

Hopefully not a pregnant one.

'Annie who?'

'Anastasia.' There, she'd done it at last. Asked the question she'd been dreading asking for the last fortnight.

'Oh.' Nat sounded guilty. 'Nobody. I mean, just someone we know.'

'We? You might know her,' said Hester, 'but I'm fairly sure I don't.'

'No. Well, we met through the restaurant, that's all.' Guardedly he added, 'How did you hear about her?'

Tears began to roll down Hester's cheeks.

'I just heard. Is she pretty?'

Nat hesitated again. It was rapidly becoming his party trick.

Finally he said, 'I suppose so. Hess, I can't stand here chatting, I'm supposed to be at work.'

'Are you seeing her?'

'Seeing her? I see her when she comes into the restaurant…'

'I meant are you sleeping with her?' whispered Hester.

'No.'

Nat had always been a hopeless liar.

'That means you are.'

He sighed.

'Hess, she's an acquaintance, not a girlfriend. And I really have to go.'

Hester couldn't bear it any more. She hung up.

Two hours later she rang the restaurant again. One of the waitresses picked up the phone.

'Hello?' Hester pitched her voice an octave lower than usual. 'It's Anastasia here,' she purred. 'Could I have a quick word with Nat?'

Oh God, I don't believe I'm doing this.

Watching her bare toes curling into the carpet, she braced herself for the worst. Moments later there was a clunk as the phone was picked up.

'Annie, hi! I wasn't expecting to hear from you tonight. Does this mean you can come over later after all?'

Hester's toes were white and practically bent over double. She stared at them, unable to speak. This was it. The worst, the very worst had happened.

And it was all her own fault.

'Annie? Is something wrong? Is there a problem with tomorrow night?'

It was the tone of his voice more than anything. He was clearly overjoyed to be hearing from Anastasia. He sounded happy. Enthusiastic. Warm. All the things he had once been with her. She hadn't heard him sound this loving for weeks.

And it hurt. It really, really hurt.

'Annie? Are you still there?'

For the second time that evening, Hester hung up.

There wasn't enough wine in the house to get drunk, only half a bottle of cheap Soave in the fridge. By the time Hester had finished it, she'd cried so much her eyes looked—and felt—like boiled lychees.

Desperate though she was for more alcohol to numb the pain, Hester was aware she looked too much of a sight to risk venturing down to the off-license. Thanks to Millie's selfishness in drinking the other half of the bottle the night before, she was still sober enough to know that inflicting her hideous appearance on the general public was both unfair to them and, more importantly, humiliating for herself.

The Tourist Board would probably have her arrested.

She needed more wine but she was too much of a cowardy custard to go out and get it.

She'd even run out of Twiglets.

When the doorbell went at half past nine it didn't occur to her that it could be anyone other than Millie, having forgotten her keys.

'Oh shit,' Hester wailed, when she realized it wasn't.

Chapter 38

'WHAT?' LAUGHED LUCAS, THE picture of injured innocence.

'You. Turning up at the worst possible moment.' Hester sagged miserably against the wall. 'I'm beginning to think it's your specialist subject.'

To add insult to injury he was wearing his *Officer and a Gentleman* outfit. Opening her front door and finding the Newquay equivalent to Richard Gere framed in the doorway had always been one of her most cherished fantasies.

'I just called by to drop off Millie's roller skate. I've had the broken wheel fixed.' Lucas held out the roller skate, hesitated, then said, 'Oh Hess, every time I see you these days you're unhappy. What's going on?'

'Didn't you know? Being unhappy is my specialist subject.' The mere fact that he cared enough to ask brought fresh tears to Hester's eyes. Shaking her head, she mumbled, 'My rotten old life isn't your problem. And you've got a job to get to. I'm fine, really I am.'

'I'm on my way home from a job. And how can you say you're fine?' Lightly, he touched her tear-stained cheek. 'Look, tell me to push off if you want to. But if you feel like talking about it, well, I'm a pretty good listener.'

Kindness only made Hester cry harder. It always had. She rubbed her hands in desperation over her salty, swollen eyelids.

'Sshh, come on.' Gently, Lucas guided her backwards into the house and kicked the front door shut behind him. 'Tell me everything. If there's anything I can do to help, I'll do it. There now, sit down, wipe your eyes,' he passed her a box of tissues, 'and give me the whole story. And don't worry about the time,' he added firmly, intercepting Hester's glance at the clock. 'I don't have to be anywhere. If you want, I can stay all night.'

Promises, promises, thought Hester.

'... so that's about it,' she concluded twenty minutes later, having brought Lucas up to date with the whole sorry saga. 'Nat's found someone else. And there's nothing I can do about it. Basically, it's all my own fault.'

'According to Millie, it's actually all *my* fault.' Raising a humorous eyebrow, Lucas said, 'For not sleeping with you on the night of Orla's party. And there was me thinking I was doing the honorable thing.'

'Story of my life.' Hester tried to smile. 'Making a big show of myself in that swimming pool. Getting turned down by you, then ending up being dumped by Nat anyway. Basically, I'm just an all-round loser.'

'I'm sorry.'

'Too late to worry about it now. It's happened. Shit happens,' she added with a fatalistic shrug. 'Especially to me.'

Lucas shook his head.

'You'll get over Nat. Meet someone else.'

Raising her gaze, Hester looked at him. Sitting there on the sofa in his crisp, white officer's uniform.

He genuinely didn't have a clue.

'What?' said Lucas.

'Nothing. You wouldn't understand.'

'Try me.'

Hester stared at the carpet.

'No.'

'Hester, what *is* it?'

In a flash, she knew she had to tell him.

'Okay, if you must know, it's you. Thanks to you, I messed up with Nat. And if I ever *do* get over him and meet someone else, I'll probably mess that up as well because I'll still be comparing them with you. There, you see? Now I've said it. I'm sorry if it's embarrassing, but you did ask. And this is me being cringe-makingly honest. You're the one I've had a crush on for years and I've never managed to grow out of it. I've tried to make it go away but it just won't, it's still in here,' Hester pressed her hand hard against her breastbone, 'and I *know* it's stupid and pointless but I really can't help how I feel. I really liked you and then you went away. It was all so… so… *unfinished*.'

Lucas looked at her.

Hester rubbed her forehead.

'Sorry, sorry, I did warn you it was embarrassing.'

And now he was standing up, preparing to leave. Desperate to be out of here, probably, away from the madwoman who—

The next moment Hester found herself being hauled to her feet. Lucas put his arms around her.

'I had no idea,' he murmured.

'Oh come on, you must have. Millie always says I'm about as subtle as a brick.'

'I knew you had a bit of a crush on me,' Lucas admitted, 'but I thought it was a small one. The kind that would just naturally fade away. I never realized it was… well, like you just described.'

'A great big out-of-control monster crush with bells on, you mean? And flashing lights and horns and miles and miles of ticker-tape?' Hester rolled her eyes as she spoke, but this time it was relatively easy to smile. That was the great thing about having not even an iota of pride left. Once you'd hit rock-bottom, there was no longer any need to pretend.

Actually, it was quite liberating.

'And this crush,' Lucas said slowly. 'Is it still there?'

'Of course it's still there! Even being miserable about Nat hasn't made it go away,' Hester confessed. 'It's like a completely separate thing, quietly burning away…'

'Like the Olympic flame?' suggested Lucas.

Hester shot him a suspicious glance.

'Are you making fun of me?'

'Absolutely not, I'm flattered. So if I were to do this,' he ran his fingertips lightly down the side of her face, 'what happens?'

She flinched away. 'Lucas! You're supposed to be being *sympathetic*.'

His voice low and insistent, he repeated, 'What happens?'

'It makes me go fizzy and all squirmy.' Hester heard her own breathing quicken, like a panting dog's. Oh brilliant, now she was turning into Scooby Doo. 'Lucas, stop it. I don't know what you think you're doing, but it's really not fair.'

'Your boyfriend's seeing someone else. How fair do you call that?'

Closing her eyes, leaning her head against his shirtfront in defeat, Hester mumbled, 'Not very fair at all.'

'So why should I stop?' Lucas paused, but his hand continued to stroke her face. 'Unless of course you don't *want* anything to happen.'

What? Was he serious?

Hester lifted her head slowly away from his chest.

'You were the one who didn't want to, last time.'

He shrugged.

'That was then. This is now.'

Ohmygod, thought Hester, every nerve ending in her body jumping up and down and squealing like a teenager. Ohmygod, ohmygod, whaaaah!

'Don't read too much into this, okay?' Lucas murmured the words against her ear, his mouth sending her body haywire. 'You know me, Hess. All that lovey-dovey stuff isn't my thing. But hey, there's more to life than relationships. What you need right now is some serious cheering up, and I know just the way to do it.'

'Oh yes,' Hester whispered as he pressed the length of his hard, muscled body against her, then masterfully swept her up into his arms, *just* like Richard Gere. 'Yes, yes, yes!'

Hester lay back on the bed amongst the tangle of sheets, panting for breath. It had happened, the miracle she had been yearning for all these years. It had actually happened at last.

She still couldn't believe it.

Tilting her head to one side and shaking her hair out of her eyes, Hester glanced at the alarm clock for confirmation. When Lucas had swept her off her feet and up the stairs she had noticed the time—10:07 p.m.—and known then that she would never forget it. After all, this was a momentous occasion. When you'd dreamed about something for as long as she'd been dreaming about this, you wanted to remember every last tiny detail.

And yes, there it was, just as she had suspected. The hands of her clock, arranged in a perfect V-shape. The time was now 10:10 p.m.

They had been in bed together for, ooh, all of three minutes.

No wonder she was in a daze. Since carrying her into the bedroom Lucas had stripped naked, launched himself at her, had sex, and then rolled over with a groan of contentment.

In one hundred and eighty seconds flat.

Oh, and he had told her she was great.

Unbelievable.

Hester, gazing up at the ceiling, wondered if this was how it felt to have your handbag snatched in the street. A flurry of activity catching you by surprise, then before you knew what was going on, it was all over. Your mugger was pelting hell for leather up the pavement, leaving you wondering what the hell *that* had been all about.

Except Lucas, her own personal mugger, wasn't pelting anywhere. He was right next to her, sprawled face-down across three quarters of the bed.

Snoring.

Too stunned to laugh, Hester replayed every moment in her brain in case she had somehow managed to miss a bit. Like when you settled down to watch a film and the next thing you knew you were waking up two hours later with the credits scrolling up the screen.

But that hadn't happened. There were no excuses. Three minutes had been the sum of it, from start to finish.

And it hadn't just been mind-bogglingly speedy either. It had been so… so *bad.* So unskilled, so completely lacking in prowess. Okay, Lucas might possess the necessary equipment, but he didn't have the foggiest idea how to use it. He'd been clumsy, jerky, and uncoordinated. As incompetent as a frenzied fourteen-year-old, marveled Hester, spectacularly lacking in both rhythm and finesse.

There was no getting away from the truth, however hard it was to comprehend. For all his sex appeal and reputation as a Lothario, the fact of the matter was that Lucas Kemp was *completely hopeless in bed.*

A huge snore shook his sleeping frame, a grunting snore loud enough to wake the neighbors. It was an ugly, piggy snort, so repulsive and undignified it was embarrassing. Hester jammed her elbow into his ribs and he let out a groan of protest.

'Wha? Whassa matter?'

'You're snoring.'

Like a big fat *hog.*

'Oh. Sorry.' Shaking his head and blearily opening his eyes as if he'd been asleep for hours, Lucas broke into a lazy, self-satisfied smile. 'Hey, that was brilliant. You were sensational, Hess. God, I'm shattered. What's the time?'

Pointedly, Hester said, 'Twelve minutes past ten.'

'Yeah? Just as well you woke me up, I'd better be making a move.'

Yawning, he hauled himself out of bed and reached for his Richard Gere suit. 'I really enjoyed that. We must do it again some time.'

Not on your life, thought Hester. But he had been so kind to her earlier, she couldn't bring herself to say it aloud. Instead, smiling slightly, she pulled the duvet further over herself and watched Lucas climb back into the clothes he had discarded at such lightning speed less than ten minutes ago.

'Um, yes. We must.'

Fully dressed once more, Lucas bent over the bed and planted a brief kiss on her forehead.

'Bye, sweetheart. You were fantastic.'

'Thanks.' Hester fought a wild urge to giggle.

'Was it good for you too?' Lucas was looking ridiculously pleased with himself.

'Oh yes. Definitely.' Hester somehow managed to nod and keep a straight face. Truthfully, she added, 'It was perfect for me.'

'No!' gasped Millie, totally agog. 'I don't believe it! Not Lucas. *Surely* not Lucas.'

'I'm telling the truth, the whole truth, I swear.' Hester, sitting cross-legged on the living room rug, shook her head. 'I can still hardly believe it myself.'

Millie was so stunned she didn't even notice the dunked end of her chocolate biscuit splash into her mug of tea. When she'd walked through the front door at eleven o'clock she definitely hadn't been expecting this.

To be on the safe side she said, 'Are you sure you didn't dream the whole thing?'

'I tried wondering that. I wish I *had* dreamed it. Millie, three *minutes*.' Starting to giggle, Hester said, 'I bet this didn't happen to Debra Winger in *An Officer and a Gentleman*.'

'What a letdown. Who'd have thought it?' Millie marveled. 'Lucas Kemp, rubbish in bed.'

'Major rubbish. All this time I thought he was such a sex god. And he's useless, a total fraud! What I really don't understand is how he's managed to get away with it for so long.'

'Then again,' Millie pointed out, 'you don't actually know anyone who has slept with him.'

'True.'

'And you didn't tell him he was a disaster.'

Hester pulled a face.

'I couldn't. Poor Lucas, he thinks he's terrific. How could I shatter his illusions after he'd been so nice to me? That would be like telling a five-year-old the painting he'd just done for you was rubbish. I couldn't be that cruel.'

Millie looked at her.

'You know, I thought you'd be more upset than this.'

'Are you kidding?' Leaning across, Hester helped herself to another biscuit. 'It's the best thing that could have happened. I'm cured, don't you see? There's no need to lust after Lucas anymore. I can get on with the rest of my life. *I'm free.*'

Well, that was a relief.

'And Nat?'

'Oh well, I'm still upset about Nat. Of course I am. But that all came about because he was convinced I'd slept with someone else. And I knew I hadn't.' She shrugged and said, 'That's what got to me more than anything, being found guilty when I knew I was innocent.'

'So having sex with Lucas actually helped?'

'God, yes. At least now when Nat finally finishes with me I'll know I've done something to deserve it.'

'Oh well,' said Millie, lifting her cup and clanking it against Hester's, 'in that case, cheers. Here's to Lucas.'

Chapter 39

'It's your mother,' Lloyd Brady said with a sigh.

Millie had wondered why she had been invited over to join him and Judy for lunch.

'What's the problem?'

'You mean apart from the fact that she's still here?' Lloyd raised his eyebrows in despair. 'A few days, she said. And it's already been a month. It's like being married to the bloody woman all over again!'

'Well, I did warn you.' Millie was sympathetic, but not that sympathetic. 'You should never have agreed to let her stay in the first place. That smells gorgeous.' She beamed up at Judy as a huge plate of shepherd's pie was laid in front of her. 'Can't you just tell her she has to go?'

'I tried that. She laughed and told me not to be so silly.' Lloyd heaved another sigh as he piled broad beans and baby carrots on to his own plate. 'She said how could she possibly leave while she was having so much fun.'

Millie looked astonished.

'Your mum's got herself a gentleman friend,' Judy explained.

'What? You're kidding! Is it serious?'

'Who can tell? She spends hours on the phone, giggling like a teenager. And most evenings she slopes off with him.'

Neither of them were looking thrilled.

'But that's great,' Millie protested. 'Isn't it? This is what she's been so desperate for, all these years. If she's finally found someone she really likes, it has to be brilliant news!' Eagerly she leaned forwards. 'Come on now, tell me everything about him. What's he like?'

Lloyd and Judy exchanged glances.

'We don't know what he's like,' said Lloyd, 'because we haven't met him. And it might not be brilliant news either.'

'Why on earth not?'

'We think he's married,' Judy said bluntly.

'What?'

'He has to be. It's the only explanation.' Lloyd shrugged. 'Why else would she be so secretive?'

'Oh God,' wailed Millie, her hopes dashed. 'This is all we need. My mother's turned into a marriage-wrecking hussy and it's all going to end in tears. How could she do something so stupid? More to the point,' Millie squeaked, 'how could she be so *embarrassing*!'

'I'm sorry, darling.' Lloyd gave the back of her hand a consoling pat. 'But we thought you ought to know. And maybe you could have a word with her. Find out a bit more about this fellow of hers, see if you can't persuade her to see sense.'

'Get out of it while she still can,' Judy chimed in teasingly, 'make a clean break, maybe catch the next train back to London.'

'You want me to do your dirty work? You pair of cowards!' Despite everything, Millie started to laugh. 'Why can't *you* tell her?'

'Since when did an ex-wife take a blind bit of notice of her ex-husband?' said Lloyd with a grin. 'The last thing Adele's going to do is listen to my advice and say, "You know, darling, you're absolutely right." But you're her daughter,' he reminded Millie.

'Ha. For my sins.'

'She's far more likely to listen to you.'

'Now you're really clutching at straws,' Millie warned.

'Well. Worth a try, eh?'

'Oh, no question. Tell you what, I'll buy a lottery ticket as well.

There's more chance of winning the jackpot than there is of persuading my mother to see sense.'

'Leave the poor girl alone,' Judy scolded. 'You aren't even giving her a chance to eat. Besides, there's something else I want to ask her about.'

Millie, busy tucking into possibly the best shepherd's pie in the world, said, 'What's that then?'

'Your own love life, of course. I'm dying to hear about all the thrilling things that have been happening to you!'

'Oh no, that's not fair.' Millie flung her arms possessively around her plate. 'I *have* no love life. Promise me you won't take my food away.'

'Sweetheart, I don't know what you're talking about. Of course I'm not seeing a married man!'

Adele was looking so outraged that Millie knew at once she was lying. But then again, had she seriously expected any other kind of response? Confession and remorse had never been her mother's thing.

Oh well, all she had to do was say her piece.

'So why haven't you introduced him to anyone?'

'Like your father and Judy, you mean?' Adele's laugh tinkled like a chandelier in the breeze. 'Why on earth should I? Is it so wrong to want a bit of privacy?'

'I'd like to meet him,' said Millie.

'Well you can't.'

'Why not?'

'Excuse me?' Adele raised her plucked eyebrows at the ridiculousness of the question. 'Because you'd probably start lecturing him.'

'So he is married.'

'Millie, you're in danger of becoming *very* boring.'

'I just don't want you to get hurt.'

'Oh poppycock, I'm not going to get hurt! I've never been happier in my life.'

'But Mum, do you seriously imagine he'll leave his wife?'

'I'm not answering that. You're my daughter, for heaven's sake. Could we please change the subject?'

'Okay. Dad was wondering how much longer you were going to be staying down here.'

'Really? Well, you can tell your father it's none of his business.'

'Mother!' Exasperated, Millie said, 'You're living in his house!'

'And why shouldn't I? He deserves it. What you don't seem to realize, Millie, is that this is exactly why I divorced him in the first place.' Sorrowfully, Adele shook her head. 'That father of yours is just plain *selfish*.'

'They really suit you,' lied Hester, angling the mirror so the pimply teenager could get a better view of herself. Holding the sequin-and-feather earrings up to her ears she swung her pudgy neck this way and that.

'They really look great,' Hester assured her. 'Not everyone can get away with earrings like that.' But those red sequins exactly match your spots, she didn't add.

Not out loud, anyway. Thinking up mean insults was pretty much all that kept her going these days. It was one of the few—pathetically few—remaining pleasures in her life.

'I can't decide.' The girl studied her reflection, then gazed longingly at the other pair she had picked out. 'I love those ones with the yellow beads as well.'

Ah, the yellow beads that go so well with your yellow teeth, thought Hester with an encouraging smile. Oh God, what's the *matter* with me? I'm turning into a nasty, mean, spiteful witch! At this rate I may never be able to think nice things about anyone ever again.

By this time next week I'll be reduced to yelling obscenities at complete strangers in the street.

'I tell you what.' Ashamed of herself for being so horrible, Hester said, 'They're seven pounds a pair, but you can have both pairs for a tenner.'

'Really?' The girl's plump chin quivered with delight.

'Really. When you go out tonight you'll knock the boys dead.' This time Hester's smile was genuine. See? I can still be nice when I want to be.

'It's my birthday today.' Overcoming her shyness, the girl confided happily, 'I'm having a party. There's this boy I've invited... he's so cool...'

How old was she? Sixteen, Hester guessed. Maybe seventeen. At that age she hadn't exactly been Claudia Schiffer herself but it hadn't stopped her chasing after Lucas with all the energy of a Energizer bunny.

'Have a brilliant time,' she told the girl as she wrapped up the earrings, 'and I hope things work out with this boy of yours.'

Take my advice, she added silently, and find out what he's like now. For God's sake don't waste the next ten years lusting after someone who shags like Mr. Bean. Because by the time you've actually made this earth-shattering discovery, you could have messed up your *whole life*.

Danielle was busy pulling a face at the back of a potential punter as he moved away from her stall without buying so much as a single candle. 'Miserable git,' she jeered when he was out of earshot. 'I hope all his hair falls out. And you're going soft in your old age. That girl would have bought both pairs anyway,' she went on, tearing the cellophane on her packet of Chelsea buns. 'You just did yourself out of four quid. Here, catch.'

Hester caught the Chelsea bun.

'I was just seeing if I could still be nice.'

'And that's the way you go about being nice?' Danielle tut-tutted. 'Try feeding stale bread to the ducks next time. It's cheaper.'

'I wanted to be nice to a person. I thought it might cheer me up.' Miserably, Hester bit into the Chelsea bun, giving herself a confectioner's sugar moustache in the process.

'In that case, throw stale bread at me.' Danielle made swimming movements with her hands and loud quacking noises. 'Go on, try me. Bet you I can catch it in my beak.'

Hester began to feel a bit less miserable. Tearing off a corner of Chelsea bun, she lobbed it at Danielle, who leapt off her stool and almost managed to get her mouth to it.

'Quack, bugger! That was *so* close. Do it again!'

This time the chunk of bun sailed over Danielle's head and bounced off a large silver candle carved into the shape of St. Michael's Mount.

'My turn!' Hester scrambled eagerly to her feet, bracing herself like a goalkeeper facing a penalty shoot-out. 'Let me have a go.'

'Only if you honk like a goose,' Danielle demanded.

'Honk! Honk! HONNKKK!' bellowed Hester, flapping her wings and waggling her tail. Nodding with approval, Danielle ripped off another bit of bun, took careful aim, and…

'MMPHHH!' Punching the air with delight, Hester did an ecstatic little dance on the spot. Half the bun was sticking out of her mouth and there was confectioner's sugar all over her face but she just didn't care, because she'd caught the bun first go, she'd *leapt* at it like a gazelle…

After all these years, I've finally found something I'm really, really good at!

'She did it,' Danielle whooped, equally thrilled, 'She actually did it! Ladies and gentlemen, a round of applause for—'

Hester gave her an encouraging nod. Why had she stopped? Had she forgotten her name? To help Danielle over her embarrassing memory lapse, she hurriedly removed the wodge of bun from her mouth, spread her arms wide, and declaimed, 'A *huge* round of applause, please, for… me!'

A fair-sized group of tourists had by this time gathered around the stall. Easily entertained, they laughed and clapped. As she smiled and curtsied, acknowledging their appreciation, Hester wondered why Danielle was doing that thing with her eyebrows. For heaven's sake, it was like two caterpillars wiggling across her forehead, she was making herself look completely *stupid*—

'Hello, Hester.'

Hester, her sugar-moustached mouth dropping open, swung round. Not looking stupid at all, she stared gormlessly at Nat.

'Nat?'

Was it *really* him?

'And there I was, thinking you'd be pining away in a corner,' Nat told her, 'because you missed me so much.'

'Wh-what are you doing here?' stammered Hester.

'I'm back.' Nat was watching her carefully. 'The question is, is that good news as far as you're concerned? Or not?'

It was really odd, not knowing. As she struggled to get her act back together, Hester brushed a shower of sugar granules from her mouth.

Finally, she said, 'That all depends. If you're here to tell me you've just got married to Anastasia, it's not good news at all.'

Chapter 40

Like a trooper, Danielle volunteered to look after the stall for the rest of the afternoon. In a daze, Hester allowed Nat to lead her outside. When he took her to one of the crowded pavement cafés on Cassell Street, she wondered if he'd chosen it because he thought dumping her in public would be safer, that she'd be less likely to wail like a banshee and cause an embarrassing scene.

Ha, as if embarrassing scenes weren't her specialty.

'Right,' said Nat, when their drinks had arrived. 'We need to talk.'

'That's what I've been trying to do for the last few weeks. But you've been doing your best to avoid me.' Hester didn't mean to sound bitter, but it was hard to be chirpy when your knees were clacking away like castanets under the table. It wasn't helping, either, that Nat was looking so serious.

It's three months since I last saw him, Hester realized with a stab of longing. He's had his hair cut shorter than ever, he's wearing a yellow shirt I've never seen before, there's even a new scar on the back of his hand... all these things happened while he was up in Glasgow and I was down here panting after Lucas.

Don't think about Lucas.

'I'm sorry,' Nat said finally.

Oh God.

'About what?' Hester clamped her clattering knees together. 'Sorry it's all over between us? Sorry you've found someone else?

Sorry you were never there when I phoned because you were too busy shagging Anastasia?'

Nat didn't flinch.

'It's not like that. I was never involved with Anastasia. Not in the way you mean.' He waited. 'But I'm sorry I made you think I was.'

Hester's hands were shaking. She didn't dare pick up her drink because she knew she'd only spill it down her front.

'So what are you doing here now?'

'I told you. I've come home. For good,' said Nat.

For good?

'Why?'

He shrugged.

'Why not?'

Stunned, Hester gasped, 'Did they sack you?'

'No. I handed in my notice.'

'Why?'

'Because I missed you.' Nat sounded calm but she sensed he wasn't. 'And me being up there wasn't doing either of us any favors. But of course the rest is up to you,' he went on slowly. 'You might not want me back. I saw the chap who drove you home the morning after that party, remember? For all I know, you two could still be seeing each other.'

'Me and Con Deveraux? Are you serious? I *told* you,' wailed Hester. 'He gave me a lift. Nothing happened between us, that's the God's honest truth. How can I make you believe me?'

'I believe you.' Nat nodded to show he meant it.

'And now you have to tell me about Anastasia,' Hester blurted out. Oh help, this was like instructing the dentist to rip out all your wisdom teeth without anaesthetic. Did she really want to be doing this?

'Annie's a TV producer,' said Nat.

Jealousy rose up in Hester like a wave. Oh brilliant, so not the least bit glamorous then. Just your humdrum, ordinary, everyday TV producer. Fine, fine.

Swallowing, she croaked, 'Go on.'

'Her company's been filming one of those fly-on-the-wall documentaries in the restaurant.'

'Wouldn't that be a fly-in-the-soup documentary?' Hester couldn't help it; when she was nervous she had a habit of saying stupid things.

'Anyway.' Nat ignored her feeble stab at humor. 'They began filming three weeks ago. Jacques was in his element, throwing tantrums, playing to the camera, chucking saucepans at the junior staff and making them cry... well, you know what he's like.'

Hester nodded. She'd never met the famously temperamental Michelin-starred chef, but she'd heard about him from Nat. Jacques made Gordon Ramsay look like Terry Gilliam in a wimple.

'The rest of us let Jacques get on with it. He was the star of the show, after all. I just kept my mouth shut and stayed in the background. Anastasia was too scared of getting her head bitten off to ask Jacques any questions. So every time she needed to find out something or have some tricky technique demonstrated, she came to me. And after a while she started telling me I was such a natural in front of the camera, she could see me with my own TV show.'

Ha! Hester bristled. I'll bet she could! And did she by any chance happen to have her lithe body pressed against yours and her hand plunged meaningfully down the front of your trousers at the time?

Desperate not to picture the scene—at least, not in any more shudder-making detail than she was already doing—Hester said accusingly, 'You never mentioned *any* of this to me.'

'It all happened after Orla Hart's party. I needed time to think things through.' Nat gave her a pointed look. 'Annie was getting keener and keener on the idea, pressing me for a decision, and I needed to think about that too. It would mean moving down to

London. Throwing myself into the whole media scene, doing endless PR to sell the program. I didn't tell you,' he went on, 'because I didn't want it to be a factor in how you felt about me.'

Thanks a lot, Hester thought indignantly, but a small, shameful corner of her knew he'd been right not to. Cringing inwardly like a slug showered in salt, she reminded herself that the reason she'd been so enraptured by Lucas in the first place had been the fact that he was a DJ with his very own show on ritzy, racy Radio Cornwall.

Worse still, Nat knew this. Oh God, she was as bad as those girls whose ambition in life was to sleep with a premier-league footballer. No wonder he didn't trust her an inch.

'Okay,' Hester whispered. 'So what happens next?'

He was back for a few days, at a guess. Then off to London to begin his glitzy new life as a celebrity chef.

Nat's gaze was unwavering.

'I decided against it.'

'What! *Why*?' Hester's head jerked up in astonishment.

'I want to cook, not show other people how to cook. I'm a chef. Slaving away in a kitchen is what I do. It's what I love doing. As for all that "it's-not-what-you-know, it's-who-you-know" business and being seen out at all the right parties… well, that's just not me.'

Hester pictured Nat on TV. There was a lump the size of a kiwi fruit in her throat.

'Well, I'm glad you're not going. But you could have done it, you know. You'd be great on TV.'

She meant it. He would have been fantastic. Nat had an easy way about him that inspired confidence. He possessed massive enthusiasm for his subject, endless patience, and wonderful flashes of humor that made you feel as if the sun had just come out. Remembering the time he'd spent an entire afternoon teaching her how to make faultless mayonnaise—they'd ended up using seventeen eggs—tears sprang unexpectedly into Hester's eyes.

If you rolled Jamie Oliver and Delia Smith together—into a mille-feuille, perhaps—you'd get Nat.

'Well, thanks. But I decided against it.' Nat smiled briefly. 'And as it turned out, I made the right choice. I hadn't realized there was a hidden agenda.'

'Oh.' Hester guessed at once. 'You mean Anastasia…?'

'Had a massive crush on me. I was completely in the dark about it.' Bemused, Nat ruffled his short spiky hair. 'I hadn't a clue what was going on. Until she tried to get me into bed and I turned her down.' He raised his expressive eyebrows in despair. 'She ended up going completely mental.'

This was absolutely typical of Nat. He had no idea how attractive he was to the opposite sex. If a woman stood in front of him and peeled off all her clothes, Hester thought, he'd simply assume she must be feeling a bit hot.

'What kind of mental?'

'Furious. Jesus, more than furious. She couldn't believe I wasn't interested. God, she even accused me of leading her on.' Nat hunched his broad, rugby-player's shoulders in disbelief. '*And* she told me I was an ungrateful little shit. She said I could forget about moving down to London, she'd find someone else to launch into the big-time. Launch,' he repeated, shaking his head. 'Like a ship. Can you credit it?'

'Plenty more chefs in the sea,' said Hester.

'So anyway, that was that. I handed in my notice and now here I am.'

Idiotically, Hester said, 'And now here you are.'

God, sparkling conversationalist or what? Look out, Jonathan Ross.

'My sister's offered to put me up until I find a place of my own. And finding another job—any old job—shouldn't be a problem.'

'Right, well, no, you're absolutely right,' gabbled Hester, 'it shouldn't. I mean, a man with your talents.'

'So the only other thing that needs sorting out is… us.'

Hester's heart began to flap like a panicky pigeon. Oo-er, this is it, make-or-break time.

'I know I put pressure on you when I took the job in Glasgow. Things haven't been easy,' said Nat. 'For either of us.'

Blimey, you can say that again.

'Um, well… you know.'

'Look, if you've found someone else, I'll understand. But if you haven't and you think we still have a chance… well, it's up to you. Your decision.'

Was this a joke? He'd jacked in his stinking rotten job in Scotland and come back to Newquay—which was, basically, the answer to *all* her prayers—and now he was asking her if she still *wanted* him?

Stumbling to her feet, cracking her knees painfully against the edge of the table, Hester let out a wail of pain. 'You complete *idiot*,' she bellowed, 'how can you even think I wouldn't want you? I loved you when you went away and I've never stopped loving you, not for a single moment! I thought you didn't want me any more and you can't even *begin* to imagine how completely miserable I've been!'

Red-faced, wild-eyed, and ranting on like… well, probably like Anastasia, Hester realized belatedly that her arms were windmilling with abandon and she was yelling at the top of her voice. Everyone else in the café was by this time paying rapt attention.

And Nat hated scenes.

Oh bugger it, what the hell.

Launching herself across the table, Hester kissed and kissed him until she couldn't breathe any more.

Finally, light-headed with joy, she mumbled, 'I've never loved anyone else in my life. Only you, I promise. Why would I even *want* anyone else when I've got you?'

Nat smiled, visibly relieved.

'I'm so glad you said that. You wouldn't believe how scared I've been. I had visions of arriving down here and finding you shacked up with some new bloke.'

More tears threatened, pricking the backs of her eyes, but Hester refused point blank to cry. She was too happy for all that nonsense.

'No new bloke. Just the same old gorgeous one.' Ecstatically, she plastered his mouth with butterfly kisses. 'And you have no idea how glad I am to have you back!'

Chapter 41

Lucas was busy on the phone when Millie pushed open the door to his office.

'Right, that's fine, all booked for Friday evening.' Glancing up, he winked at Millie as he scribbled the relevant details in the diary. 'Eight o'clock at the King George pub—don't worry, I know where that is. I'll be there at eight on the dot.' Listening to the voice at the other end of the line, he grinned broadly. 'Sweetheart, of course you won't be disappointed. When you book me, I can promise you,' he lowered his voice to a sexy purr, 'satisfaction is very much guaranteed.'

Millie didn't know where to look. She was having more and more trouble these days keeping a straight face in front of Lucas. Every time she saw him, all she could do was picture him naked in bed, being comically incompetent. And every time she conjured up the picture, she was forced to bite her lip so hard it hurt, in a desperate attempt to stave off a full-blown fit of the girly-giggles.

She hadn't been able to mention Hester to him, hadn't dared. If Lucas knew she knew about their one-night stand, he wouldn't be able to resist boasting about it and Millie knew this would be her undoing. If that were to happen, she definitely wouldn't be able to stop herself laughing out loud.

She still found it utterly astounding that someone who looked so good, acted so cool, and stripped so brilliantly (no one else was able to grind their hips like Lucas) could turn out to be so abysmal in bed.

No, mustn't think about that now, blank it out, get a grip, you are not *not* going to start sniggering like—

'Okay, see you there, bye.' Hanging up, Lucas swiveled his chair around and let out a low whistle. 'Hen night, Friday. Those girls are *so* up for it, I'm telling you. Outrageous. What can you do with them?'

Phew, I don't know, thought Millie. Have mind-bogglingly bad sex with them in about thirty seconds flat, probably. And jolly well serve them right.

Shrugging, composing her face with care, she said, 'Why did you want to see me?'

Lucas winked and reached across the desk for his car keys.

'I've got something special to show you.'

Aaagh, not the something special you keep in your trousers, I hope!

'Really?' said Millie. 'What?'

'It's a surprise.' Jumping up, Lucas led the way to the door. 'Come on, off we go.' Raising a playful eyebrow, he added, 'I think you're going to like this.'

Millie heroically stifled the urge to giggle. So, definitely not sex.

'Oh brilliant!' she exclaimed ten minutes later when Lucas pulled up outside the Pear Tree restaurant overlooking Watergate Bay. 'This is the story of my life. I'm such a brilliant employee you've decided the least you can do is bring me out here and treat me to a fabulous four-course lunch. Lucas, couldn't you at least have rung them first to check they were still open for business? This place closed down weeks ago!'

He laughed.

'Oh dear, you don't have a very high opinion of me, do you?'

Certainly not in the bedroom department, thought Millie.

Damn, she wasn't supposed to be thinking along these lines at all. Change the subject, quick.

'So you knew the restaurant was shut but you still brought me here,' she gabbled. 'That's an even meaner thing to do. Can't you hear my stomach rumbling? You're a sadist, Lucas Kemp. It's like promising to take a dog for a run on the beach then locking it in the car and only letting it look at the beach through the window.'

'Come on now, don't be so hard on yourself.' Lucas patted her arm. 'You're not a dog, and I'm not going to leave you locked up in the car. See?' Leaning across, he flicked open the passenger door. 'You're allowed out.'

Humoring him, Millie did as she was told. Well, it was hot in the car and there was always the chance he might bring her a bowl of water and a couple of dog biscuits.

'What's more,' Lucas went on, pulling a set of keys from his shirt pocket, 'you're also allowed in.'

'Why?' Millie demanded as he unlocked the door of the restaurant. 'Why would they give you the keys? Good grief, don't tell me you're thinking of buying this place!'

'Actually,' Lucas was looking pleased with himself, 'I've already bought it.'

The dining area was spacious and—not to put too fine a point on it—completely hideous. Ruffles and flounces abounded. The room had been Laura Ashleyed to within an inch of its life.

Dismayed, Millie said, 'My mother bought me a dress exactly like this when I was fourteen.'

'The decorators move in tomorrow.' Lucas laughed at the look of horror on her face. 'By the time they've finished, you won't recognize the place.'

Hmm.

'I don't get it. What brought this on?'

'It's a fantastic location. I got it for a good price. The last owner wasn't a businessman, that's why he went bust. But I'm a great businessman and I know I can make it work. Plus,' Lucas added with a crooked smile, 'it's always been my dream. To own and run a top-class restaurant.'

Millie was stunned. He could do it, too. Charming the birds from the trees was Lucas's forte. Having him run front-of-house operations would pull in the punters like nobody's business.

So long as he didn't sleep with too many of them, of course.

'But what about the kissograms?'

Solemnly, Lucas said, 'Can't do both. It's tragic, I know, but I'm afraid the time has come to hang up my leopardskin jockstrap.'

Quick, delete that mental image!

The next moment, Millie's face fell as she realized what he was telling her.

'You're jacking in the business? But you only set it up three months ago and I thought we were doing pretty well.'

Bugger. So that was it, she was out of a job—one she really enjoyed. And so too were Eric and Sasha. Although Eric had his day job as a history teacher and only did it to boost his income. Plus, Sasha would doubtless still be working for Lucas here at the restaurant in some capacity or other.

So it's just me, thought Millie with a huff of resignation, because the pay might not be that great, but she did actually love being a gorilla. Everyone else is going to be just fine, thanks very much. I'm the only one actually being kicked on to the unemployment scrap heap. Unless Lucas takes pity on me and offers me some grisly part-time work scrubbing out the restaurant loos or hoiking slimy old potato peelings out of the plughole in the kitchen sink—

'Ha! Your face!' said Lucas. 'You should see yourself.'

I am seeing myself, Millie thought glumly. That's the problem.

Feeling cross, she said, 'I'm just wondering how you can possibly have thought bringing me here and telling me this would be something I might *like*.'

'Millie, calm down. The kissograms *are* doing well. I'm just not going to have the time to be involved any more. It occurred to me that you might like to take over the running of the business.'

Millie boggled at him.

'Me?'

'You.' Lucas smiled briefly. 'And there's no need to look so stunned. It's hardly MI-6.'

Her eyes narrowed. 'Is this a joke?'

'No joke. It would still be Kemp's, of course, but you'd be in charge.' He waited. 'Well? What do you think?'

Duh?

'I think it's the most fantastic idea you've ever had,' squealed Millie, throwing her arms around him. 'I think you're a *lot* nicer now than I thought you were two minutes ago. And I think you've definitely got yourself a deal!'

After an hour exploring every inch of the restaurant, listening to Lucas's plans and realizing how very serious he was about this new venture, Millie was so impressed she'd completely forgotten about his embarrassing lack of sexual prowess.

Until Lucas dropped her at her car, when it all came back to her in a whoosh. As she was about to open the passenger door and climb out, he said casually, 'Um, how's Hester?'

Eek, don't splutter, don't smirk, don't *snigger*.

'Hess? Ooh, she's… okay.' Millie shrugged, extra casually. 'Well, you know. Considering.'

Considering she had sex with *you*, you big hopeless failure, you smooth sex-god impersonator, you fraud!

'Right. Well.' Lucas hesitated for a moment, then said extra, extra casually, 'Tell her I said hi.'

Why? Because you think she might be interested in a repeat performance, you completely incompetent fornicator? Lucas, you cannot be serious!

Millie nodded vigorously, desperate to get out of the car before the uncontrollable torrent of laughter bubbled up and out.

'Oh, I will.'

This was why sharing a house with a friend—even a currently glum and droopy one—was so much nicer than living alone. Bursting into the kitchen at five o'clock and realizing that Hester was home early, Millie shouted, 'Fantastic news!'

Hester, oddly, was wearing her pink silk dressing gown and just-got-out-of-bed hair. Letting out an ear-splitting shriek of delight she spun round—all signs of glum droopiness miraculously banished—and yelled, 'I know!'

Hang on. Er…

'What?' Taken aback, Millie frowned. '*How* do you know?'

Hester looked at her as if she was crazy.

'What are you *talking* about!'

'My fantastic news. How can you possibly know about it?' Mystified, Millie said, 'Did Lucas tell you?'

'I'm not talking about your fantastic news, I'm talking about *my* fantastic news!' Hester's eyes were ablaze with triumph. 'So you don't already know about it? Oh please, pleeease let me tell you mine first!'

Feeling very grown up—because, to be fair, Hester had been going through an extra-miserable time recently—Millie said generously, 'Well, okay then, if—'

'It's Nat! He's back! Nat's back and everything's *perfect*,' Hester joyfully blurted out. 'He's here and he's never going to go away again and he loves me and the Anastasia thing was all a bluff to make me jealous and we're going to live happily ever after... oh God, I can't believe it, I'm so happy happy *happy*.'

She did a little dance of joy to prove it. Millie was suitably stunned.

'Truly? He's here? Right now?' Since it seemed the obvious place for Nat to be, she pointed at the ceiling, in the general direction of Hester's bedroom.

No wonder her hair was looking so manic.

'Not right now. Although we have of course been doing a bit of that.' Pink-cheeked and unable to stop the triumphant smirk spreading from one ear to the other, Hester said, 'Well actually, quite a lot of that. All afternoon in fact. Oh, and it was such heaven, I'd honestly forgotten just how fabulous Nat is in bed! When you compare him with Lucas—my God, you can't *believe* the difference!'

Hester's dreamy expression said it all. She'd never been happier. Millie, giving her a hug, tried hard not to picture Hugh, who had been equally heavenly and fabulous in bed.

'I'm so glad. So where is he now?'

'Gone off to find a job! You know what Nat's like—he doesn't hang around.' Leading the way through to the living room, Hester pointed to the *Yellow Pages* lying open on the table. 'He made a big list of restaurants, rang round the first dozen or so, and set off half an hour ago to check them out. Of course, he won't be doing the kind of thing he's used to—not too many Michelin stars floating around this neck of the woods—but Nat doesn't mind. He says as long as he's down here with me he'll be happy working in Burgers'R'Us. Oh will you listen to me!' Hester exclaimed suddenly. 'Wittering on and on, and you're dying to tell me *your* fantastic news. Well?' She raised her eyebrows and looked suitably agog. 'What is it?'

Sadly, nothing to do with my love life, thought Millie. Oh stop it, stop it, don't even *think* about Hugh.

'Well, Lucas is giving up the kissograms. He's handing the reins over to me... I'm going to be in charge of running the business.'

'You're kidding, that's *brilliant*.' Hester's eyes lit up with a mixture of delight and relief. 'You mean Lucas is leaving Newquay? Hooray, even more brilliant!'

As far as Hester and her guilty conscience were concerned, it was the best thing that could happen. The further away he moved, the happier she would be.

'Actually, he's not.' Millie hesitated. 'He's, um, bought a new business.'

'Damn. Oh well. What kind of new business?' Hester smirked and suggestively wiggled her hips, 'Rent-a-Stud?'

'Ah... well... um... a restaurant, actually. It's going to serve really high-class food. Give Rick Stein a run for his money, according to Lucas.' Millie watched the expression on Hester's face change from joyous to appalled.

'You mean... oh *bum*! Have the staff been hired yet?'

Apologetically, Millie shook her head. 'He's placed an advert in next week's *Caterer*. But you said Nat had gone out this afternoon to find a job. And anyway, the chances are he won't even *see* the ad.'

Hester pulled a face, the who-are-you-kidding kind. The *Caterer* was Nat's bible; he read it from cover to cover every week. Plus, Newquay was hardly the kind of place where you could fail to notice the opening of a top-quality restaurant. Apart from anything else, kitchen staff were famed for their ability to gossip.

'He'll see it,' sighed Hester. 'And he'll be knocking on Lucas's door faster than you can say Sabatier. Rick Stein's place over in Padstow was the first number he rang,' she said with gloomy resignation, 'but they didn't have any vacancies. I suppose I could always sneak over there in the dead of night and poison their head chef.'

'So you didn't tell Nat about Lucas.'

'Good grief, of course I didn't tell Nat about Lucas! Picture it,' Hester demanded. 'The love of my life arrives back in Cornwall. He's given up his job to be with me. He's finally accepted that I wasn't unfaithful to him on the night of Orla's party. He's spent the last month being lusted after by Anastasia, and by refusing to sleep with her, he threw away the chance of a fantastic new career in London. And what do I say to him?' Hester spread her arms wide. 'Oh by the way, darling, I did actually have sex with Lucas Kemp a little while back, but don't worry, he wasn't a patch on you.'

'Hmm,' said Millie. 'I see your point. Well, we'll just have to make sure Lucas keeps his mouth shut.'

'How?' wailed Hester.

Good question.

'Appeal to his better nature, I suppose.'

'Excuse me, this is Lucas Kemp we're talking about! He *doesn't* have a better nature *and* he's a big blabbermouth. That man wouldn't know a scruple if it stuck its tongue down his throat—if I asked Lucas not to say anything he'd just laugh.'

Also true.

'Well,' Millie sighed, because there weren't that many options to choose from, 'you'll have to tell Nat and hope he forgives you.'

'I CAN'T DO THAT,' roared Hester.

'Hess, you've got to talk to one of them.'

'No, I can't, I really can't. But you could.' Hester gave her a pleading look. 'You could warn Lucas not to hire him, tell him Nat's a lousy chef.'

Excuse-wise, they both knew this was taking flimsiness to extremes. Nat held a fistful of glittering references and his reputation was flawless. Furthermore, as a businessman, Lucas was only interested in hiring the best possible staff.

And Nat was inescapably one of the best.

'Maybe he'll find another job somewhere else,' said Millie. 'If he doesn't, I'll have a word with Lucas. See if I can persuade him to keep quiet.'

'I need a drink.' Hester pressed her hand to her chest. 'My heart's doing that Skippy-the-Bush-Kangaroo thing, I'm all of a jitter. Oh, this is *so* unfair,' she cried. 'Why does this kind of stuff always have to happen to me? I was perfectly happy until you came home!'

Chapter 42

Millie called on Lucas four days later. Having spotted the advert in the *Caterer* that morning, Nat had wasted no time in phoning the number and fixing up an appointment.

'He's seeing Lucas at three o'clock,' Hester had hissed through the bathroom door while Millie was brushing her teeth. 'You'll have to get to him before then.'

It was all very MI5.

'Millie!' Grinning broadly, Lucas opened the front door to her at one o'clock. 'What a surprise, I wasn't expecting to see you today.' He looked as though he'd just come out of the shower. His hair was wet and, apart from a dark red towel fastened around his hips, he didn't have a stitch on.

Millie swallowed and tried not to let her gaze drop.

'We need to talk.'

'So serious.' Following her through to his office, Lucas combed his fingers carelessly through his dripping hair. 'Not to mention a bit flushed. What's this all about then? Or can I guess?'

It was hard to concentrate when the man you were trying to have a conversation with was, effectively, naked.

'Why?' she countered. 'What do you think it's about?'

Maybe he had guessed; that would make things easier.

Lucas shrugged, a playful smile lifting the corners of his mouth.

'You and me, perhaps? I think you're trying to pluck up the courage to tell me you've got a bit of a crush on me. Am I right?'

Millie opened her mouth to let out a shriek of denial. Too late, she realized he was laughing at her.

'Just teasing.' Lucas made calm-down movements with his hands. 'No need to burst my eardrums. Come on now, sit down and tell me why you're really here.'

'This *is* serious,' Millie warned, when he'd passed her an icy can of Coke and opened another for himself. 'You have to pay attention. It's about Hester.'

Paying attention and looking suitably serious, Lucas nodded. 'Hester.'

'You and Hester,' Millie expanded. 'And the… um, thing that happened between you two the other week.'

Lucas raised an eyebrow.

'So she told you about that. I wasn't sure whether or not she had.'

Oh yes, every last detail—and it didn't take her long either, speedy boy!

'The thing is, her boyfriend's come back. Everything's been sorted out and they're blissfully happy together. Which is why I've come here to ask you to promise never to breathe a word about what happened. Not to *anyone*.'

'Well, I'll do my best.' Lucas shrugged.

'No.' Vigorously, Millie shook her head. 'Not good enough. This is important, Lucas. You have to promise.'

'Okay, okay.' His eyes bright with laughter, he held up his hands. 'I promise I'll try really hard not to accidentally let slip.'

'Lucas, I mean it, you *mustn't* say anything, this is Hester's—'

'Boyfriend, yes, you already told me. Well, I'm happy for them both. Hester and...'

'Nat.'

'Nat, that's the one.' Lucas nodded in recognition. 'She told me all about him. So, a happy ending. That's great.'

'Yes, but it's only going to be great if you promise faithfully never to breathe a word about it to *anyone*.' Millie's teeth were by this time irretrievably gritted; it was obvious Lucas wasn't taking this seriously. She longed to reach over and grab hold of him and shake his head violently like a maraca.

Lucas, suddenly interested, said, 'This chap of Hester's, isn't he a chef?'

Exasperated, Millie bounced out of her chair, crossed to the desk and seized Lucas's navy leather-bound diary.

'I say, steady on.' Grinning broadly as her arm brushed against his naked torso, he said, 'For a moment there I thought you were about to rip off my towel.'

'*Yes*, Nat's a chef.' Millie really wished Lucas was dressed more appropriately. 'And he's coming here this afternoon to see you about a job. Look.' Finding the page at last, she stabbed at the entry in Lucas's handwriting. 'Three o'clock. N. Kenyon. That's Nat. *Now* do you understand why this is so important?'

You complete *numbskull*.

'Oh, riiight.' Slowly Lucas nodded. 'N. Kenyon is Hester's boyfriend. Fancy that.' After a moment he added, 'He isn't coming at three o'clock. He changed his appointment.'

'Oh.' Absolutely typical. All this subterfuge and rushing around for nothing.

'I saw him at ten o'clock this morning,' Lucas went on.

Millie blinked.

'And?'

'He's got the job.'

'Just like that?' It came out as a squeak.

'Why not? He's perfect. Fantastic references. Enthusiasm. Innovative ideas.' Lucas looked pleased with himself. 'And best of all, he feels exactly the same way as I do about the direction the restaurant should take, what we should be aiming for. We actually have a great deal in common.'

'You've got a bit too much in common,' Millie pointed out. 'That's your problem.'

'Not my problem. Hester's. Anyway, I rang Nat's last restaurant and spoke to his boss there, who had nothing but praise for him. Then I took him over to the Pear Tree and explained the ideas I had for the place. The more we talked, the more I realized he was the person I was looking for. I didn't hire him "just like that,"' Lucas patiently explained. 'He was here for over two hours. Nat and I are going to make a perfect team.'

Nat.

'So you did know who he was.' Millie's eyes narrowed accusingly.

'Millie, I'm not stupid. Of course I knew who he was. Apart from anything else,' Lucas added with a flicker of amusement, 'there's a framed photo of him on the chest of drawers next to Hester's bed.'

Millie winced.

'More to the point,' Lucas went on, 'Nat knew who I was.'

'Oh God. Well, I suppose he was bound to.' During the last three years Nat could hardly have escaped hearing about Lucas, the heartthrob DJ who had made such an impact on Hester's teenage hormones. As well as the not-so-teenage ones.

'You seem a bit agitated.'

'I *am* agitated,' Millie shot back. 'I'm very *very* agitated.'

Lucas shrugged easily. 'No need.'

Oh phew. She clutched her chest with relief.

'So you didn't say anything about you and Hester, and cross-your-heart-and-hope-to-die you absolutely promise never to breathe a word about it to Nat.'

'Oh no.' Lucas looked surprised. 'I've already told him.'

'WHAAAT??'

'Millie, calm down. I had to. If we're going to be working together it's best to get everything out in the open. So I told him. And when I'd finished explaining what had happened, Nat agreed that it was the best thing I could have done. He thanked me. We shook hands. No problem. So you see, honesty is the best policy. You should try it some time,' Lucas added with a wink. 'You never know, you might like it.'

Millie's brain was in a whirl. Nat had actually shaken Lucas's hand and *thanked* him?

'Hang on.' She braced herself. 'Does this mean Nat's going to dump Hester?'

'Not at all. Like I explained to Nat, they were going through a bad patch and she thought he was seeing someone else.'

'Right,' said Millie cautiously.

'And we all know Hester's had a crush on me for God knows how long. I realized the only way to put a stop to that was by sleeping with her.'

Which you did, after having sex with her for less time than it takes to poach an egg.

Aloud, Millie argued, 'But it could have gone the other way! Sleeping with Hester could have made it worse, she might have ended up more besotted than ever!'

'What, after the performance I put up?' Lucas flashed a wicked grin. 'No chance.'

Millie went pink.

'I don't know what you mean.'

'Come on, look at your face. Of course you do.' Enjoying himself now, Lucas raised a playful eyebrow. 'I wasn't sure before whether or not Hester had told you, but now I know she did. No need to blush, Millie. You didn't seriously think I was that useless, did you?'

This was too much. Millie couldn't believe what she was hearing.

'You mean…?'

'No foreplay. No rhythm. No comprehension of the female body. Just get it over with, roll over, and fall asleep within seconds.

Well, pretend to fall asleep within seconds. And snore like an elephant seal,' Lucas gave her a jaunty wink. 'And you can't tell me it didn't do the trick.'

'Lucas, are you *serious*?'

He looked suitably modest.

'If I say so myself, it was a brilliant performance. Best of all, Hester fell for it. And now she doesn't have a crush on me anymore.'

Millie rubbed her aching temples.

'So you told Nat all of this?'

'Oh yes.'

'And is Nat going to tell Hester that you were rubbish in bed with her on purpose?'

'We agreed that he shouldn't.'

'So much for honesty being the best policy,' Millie retorted.

'I know, but Hester's perfectly happy with things as they are. If she thought I'd short-changed her, she might demand a rematch.'

'Mr. Bean,' giggled Millie. 'That's what she called you.'

'Exactly. I was Nerdy Norris, getting lucky for the first time in my life.' There was a twinkle in Lucas's eye.

'This is incredible, I still can't believe it.' In a strange way, she was discovering, he did have some scruples after all.

'No? Want me to prove it?' Lucas gave her an encouraging look. 'Would you like me to show you how great I really am in bed?'

Hmm. Then again, maybe he didn't.

'So kind of you to offer,' said Millie, 'but actually I'd better be making a move. And you should think about putting some clothes on.'

'Hardly worth the bother.' Lucas tapped the open diary, in which another name was scrawled above Nat's. 'Only twenty minutes before the next interview.' Winking at Millie he said, 'Pretty little sous chef called Nadine.'

Millie managed to keep a straight face.

'You're a disgrace.'

'I'm not. Just honest.' Lucas was laughing at her. 'You should try it, sweetheart. Find yourself a man, have a bit of fun.'

Ha.

To keep busy, Nat assembled a peppered gazpacho and calamari with linguini and sauce nero.

He needed to be occupied, but he was happy too. And when he was happy he liked to cook.

Nat knew that if he were being completely honest with himself, there had been a moment back there when he'd been sorely tempted to land a punch on Lucas Kemp's big, handsome nose. But it had, literally, only lasted a moment. Lucas had been so upfront, so completely matter-of-fact about the Hester situation that almost before his hands had had the chance to curl themselves into fists, Nat had come to see the sense in what he was saying.

Furthermore, the truth had turned out to be a lot easier to bear than the endless awful scenarios his fevered imagination had been busily conjuring up. This had been dealable with, the best possible solution all round.

To his amazement, Nat found he didn't hold even a vestige of a grudge.

In a funny way, he would always be grateful to Lucas for what he had done.

'I got the job,' he told Hester when she arrived home from work.

'You did?' Encouraged by the glorious cooking smells emanating from the kitchen—good news, surely?—Hester's face lit up. 'Oh, *that's fantastic*, that's so—'

'And Lucas told me everything.'

Hester's rib cage contracted with terror. How, how could Lucas have done this to her? It simply wasn't fair.

'Wh-what did he tell you?'

'That you slept with him. Once.' Nat shrugged slightly and turned down the heat on the pan of furiously bubbling linguini. 'That it didn't mean anything and that it's never going to happen again.'

The color drained from Hester's face. This was it, Nat was bound to finish with her now.

'It's true.' As she nodded, a tear slid down one cheek. To her shame, Hester realized she'd been busy mentally piling all the blame on to Lucas, which wasn't fair at all. Hastily brushing the tear away—because whatever happened now was entirely her own fault—she said, 'It's all true, especially the last bit. As long as I live, I'll never be tempted to sleep with Lucas again. Not that it makes much difference to you.' Nodding her head jerkily in the direction of the food already laid out on the kitchen table, Hester added, 'What's this, the last supper?'

Forgiving a girlfriend who had been unfaithful wasn't something Nat had ever imagined himself capable of doing. But in the past few months, he had grown up a lot. Furthermore, he may have managed to resist the charms of Anastasia in Glasgow, but only by the skin of his teeth. It had so very nearly happened, that final night in her flat.

Oh yes, thought Nat, it could have been me. It really could have been me.

'Out of interest, what was Lucas like?' asked Nat, already knowing perfectly well.

'Diabolical. Awful. Pathetic.'

'Really? So is that why you wouldn't bother again?' Nat raised an eyebrow. 'How about if he'd been fantastic?'

It was over now; she could say whatever she liked. In despair, Hester retaliated, 'Don't you get it? It wouldn't have made a blind bit of difference, because he still wouldn't have been you! Oh, this is ridiculous, why are we even having this conversation?' In a rush to get out before Nat could see that she was crying again, she made a furious dash for the door.

'It's okay, it's okay.' Swiftly Nat intercepted her, grabbing her by the elbows. 'I can handle it. We're going to put this behind us. Okay, so maybe we can't forget it ever happened, but it's in the past now. We don't have to let it spoil everything.'

'T-truly?' stammered Hester, her knees almost giving way.

'That's why Lucas told me. So that we can realize how unimportant some things are and get on with the rest of our lives.' A glimmer of a smile lifted the corners of Nat's mouth. 'Seems a shame not to, now that he's given me the chance to prove myself in this restaurant of his.'

'Are you sure?' Nat had always been so straight, so proud. Hester needed to be convinced.

'Sure I'm sure. So long as you never do anything like it again. Not with anyone,' warned Nat. 'Because I'm telling you now, I'm only human. Once is enough.'

Hester flung her arms around his broad shoulders, so deliriously happy she could have burst into tears all over again.

'Believe me,' she said with feeling, 'once was more than enough.'

Chapter 43

'OOF! GOD, SORRY, ALL my fault... oh Hugh, it's *you*!'

It was absolutely typical of Orla, Hugh thought, that the reason she had cannoned into him was because she was too busy waving over her shoulder and chattering away to watch where she was going as she made her way out of the shop.

'How lovely to bump into you again!' Still clutching her Fogarty & Phelps carriers, Orla kissed him with enthusiasm on both cheeks. 'And you're looking so *well*. Actually, Millie and I saw you the other week doing a spot of surfing, but you didn't notice us. I must say, we were most impressed—I had no idea you were so skilled with a board!'

As she spoke, Orla's green eyes sparkled with laughter and spirals of red-gold hair bounced like springs around her bare shoulders. She was wearing a long silver and white squiggly-patterned dress with a purple felt-pen mark just below her left breast.

The trouble was, Hugh decided, you could disapprove of the unscrupulous way Orla went about her work, but it didn't stop you actually liking her as a person. Her information-gathering techniques might be underhanded, but she was such a warm, impulsive character you couldn't *not* like her.

'Oh yes, hugely skilled.' He nodded seriously. 'In fact, I'm odds-on favorite to win the title this year at the world surfing championships.'

'Nooo!' Orla let out a shriek of delight.

'No,' agreed Hugh, his mouth twitching. 'So how's your computer? Behaving itself?'

'Absolutely. Unlike my pig of a husband. Did you hear about Giles moving out?'

'I read about it in the papers. I'm really sorry.'

'Don't be.' Orla rolled her eyes dramatically. 'I'm not. God, listen to me, I can't believe I'm even saying this, but it's true! I did my level best to make our marriage work, but it wasn't enough for Giles. In the end, I just snapped and thought sod it, he's treated me like a bit of old rubbish and I really don't deserve it. Not that it's all been plain sailing since he left, of course. I've had my miserable moments.'

Orla was glossing over the gloom and doom, Hugh realized, putting on a brave face for his sake. But there was an air of genuine optimism about her all the same.

'You'll be fine,' he said, and meant it.

'I know. And that's half the battle, isn't it?' Her smile was determinedly bright. 'My friend Millie keeps telling me I deserve better. Actually, I don't know how I'd have managed without her. She's been fantastic.'

Hugh wondered if this was a dig, a pointed reminder that he'd not been in touch with Millie for weeks. This too was absolutely typical of Orla; even in the middle of telling him about the break-up of her marriage she was unable to pass up the opportunity to drop a hint.

He had spent the last couple of weeks doing his best not to think about Millie. And failing utterly.

'Lord, is that my stomach?' Orla placed her hand apologetically over her stomach and laughed. 'Rumbling away like an old tractor! I've been working since six o'clock this morning—I only popped down here because I'd run out of coffee. Of course, as soon as I walked into the shop I went completely mad.' Holding up the bulging carriers she said impulsively, 'I've got tons of stuff, enough to feed an army. Are you terribly busy or can I persuade you to come back with me and let me give you lunch?'

Hugh hesitated. He'd only called into the delicatessen on his way home to pick up a couple of sandwiches. He had no other pressing engagements this afternoon. Then again, was Orla only inviting him because she was desperate to pump him for information about his one-night stand with Millie? Because she needed to hear his side of things in order to include it in her book?

'Oh please,' Orla cried, suddenly aghast. 'I really hope you're not thinking what I think you're thinking!'

Exercising caution—because somebody had to—Hugh said, 'What's that?'

'You don't know if you dare risk coming back to the house, because I'm single and lonely and a desperate old bat, and you're terrified I might make an embarrassing pass at you!' Silver bracelets dangling, Orla clutched her throat in horror. 'I won't, I promise!'

'Right.' Hugh nodded slowly, his expression deadpan. 'The thing is, what *if I wanted* you to make an embarrassing pass at me?'

'This time,' Orla was triumphant, 'I know you're joking. Can't catch me out twice. So, how about lunch?'

Hugh broke into a grin. 'Okay. I'll risk it.'

'You'll be safe.' Orla winked at him. 'Besides, I don't steal men who belong to someone else. And you're already taken.'

The World According to Orla, Hugh mused. Did she seriously think she could orchestrate people's entire lives? Did writing it all down and deciding what should happen to each character mean it actually *had* to happen?

You couldn't help admiring her nerve, he thought wryly as he followed Orla out into the street.

❖❖❖

Over lunch in the conservatory they talked mainly about Giles.

'There are good points,' Orla confided, twiddling a slice of wafer-thin Parma ham on to her fork. 'Not having to miss the programs I want to watch on the telly because he's glued to Sky Sports. And I don't have to listen to him going on and on and on about bloody golf. I don't have to pretend to be interested anymore, when he tells me how he decided to use his eight iron on the seventeenth hole, instead of a six iron like Dougie Plumley-Pemberton. And there's nobody to tell me off if I eat crisps in bed, or leave the top off the shampoo bottle, or accidentally get marmalade on the *Sunday Times*—' Abruptly, Orla stopped herself. Reaching across the table to clasp Hugh's hand, she shook her head, mortified. 'God, you must want to slap me. Talk about insensitive. I'm *so* sorry.'

Smiling, Hugh moved the bowl of tarragon mayonnaise to a place of safety, before Orla's elbow ended up in it.

'Don't be daft. You're just saying what we've all said at some time. It used to drive Louisa demented, always having to clear a pile of CDs off the passenger seat before she could climb into my car. And the way she used to leave mascara splattered all over the bathroom mirror drove *me* mad.' He spread his hands in amazement. 'I'm serious. Every single day! I'd clean it off the mirror, and the next morning it'd be back again. I mean, how can that happen?'

'Oh, easy, you just kind of flick the end of the brush. Putting your mascara on with a flourish makes your eyelashes feel longer. It's a girl thing,' Orla consoled him.

'Either that or Louisa was doing it on purpose because she knew it would wind me up.'

'Maybe it did at the time,' said Orla. 'But I bet you'd give anything for the chance to wipe that mascara off the mirror again now.'

There were sympathetic tears in her eyes.

'Actually, no.' Hugh smiled. 'You love someone despite their faults. But I can't honestly say I miss cleaning our bathroom mirror.'

Orla topped up their glasses of wine.

'Anyway, I want to hear what you've been up to.'

I'll bet you do, thought Hugh.

'You know how nosy I am,' Orla went on.

I certainly know that.

'So how *are* things?'

'Well, you know, improving.' To tease her, Hugh said, 'Making a start, at least.'

'Well I know that, of course! And I couldn't be happier for you.' Orla nodded encouragingly. 'I must say, I did wonder if she was quite your type, but then again, what does it matter? You're just having a practice run, getting back into the swing of things for heaven's sake. Having a bit of fun!'

Hugh hid his surprise. This wasn't the kind of reaction he'd been expecting. Then again, maybe Orla was the mistress of the double-bluff.

'Exactly.' He shrugged and helped himself to more prosciutto.

'Oh phew, for a moment there I thought I'd put my foot in it again.' Orla fanned herself with relief. 'But you're doing the right thing. I mean, it's not as if she's the kind of girl you'd be remotely interested in settling down with!' Lowering her voice, she added, 'The only thing that worries me slightly is, does *she* realize that?'

Carefully, Hugh tore off a chunk of baguette. Wasn't Orla being a bit unkind here, singing Millie's praises one minute and criticizing her the next?

Feeling incensed on Millie's behalf—and heaven only knew why, after the way she had used him—he shrugged. 'Never say never. You can't plan these things. By this time next year we could be married with… well, anything could have happened.'

'Married with a *baby*?' Pouncing like a panther on the unspoken words, Orla's eyebrows shot up. 'That's what you were about to say, isn't it?!'

Hugh shrugged. Honestly, it was a wonder she didn't have a tape recorder whirring on the table between them to make sure no detail was lost.

'I'm just saying anything can happen.' He kept a straight face; no doubt this entire conversation would be relayed back to Millie before nightfall.

'Hugh, now listen to me, I may not be the world's greatest expert on happy marriages, but I can tell you now that would be a *disaster*.' Orla's earrings jangled with agitation. 'You have to promise me you won't do that! Okay, she's a sweet enough girl, but let's face it, she's simply not in your league!'

'How can you say that?'

'Because I've got *eyes* in my head.' Vigorously, Orla poked her fingers at her eyes. 'I've seen the way she looks at you. And the way you look at her. For heaven's sake, you could have any girl you wanted.'

'Maybe I've found the girl I want.'

'I'm sorry, but you're wrong.' Orla was getting really worked up now, the food on her plate forgotten. 'She isn't good enough for you. A pretty face isn't everything, you know. There has to be more to it than that. And let's face it, she's *so* immature.'

Coldly Hugh said, 'In what way, exactly?'

'Oh God, now you're really cross with me. I don't mean immature in the derogatory sense.' Orla flapped her hands in an attempt to appease him. 'I'm just saying she's so much younger than you. I mean, how old *is* she? Sixteen? Seventeen?'

Click click click, the cogs slipped into place. Orla wasn't describing Millie. As far as she was concerned, Hugh belatedly deduced, this entire conversation had been about his next-door neighbor, Kate.

The relief, for some reason, was indescribable.

'Sixteen,' said Hugh, pushing his plate away.

'And now I've made you hate me.' Orla looked at him with a

mixture of determination and regret. 'Darling, I'm sorry, but someone had to say it, and I won't take it back.'

'You're entitled to your opinion.' Hugh's tone softened. 'We'll just have to see what happens, won't we?'

Rather like reading one of your novels.

Click click click…

'What's wrong?' Alarmed by his air of distraction, Orla said, 'We're still friends, aren't we?' Jumping to her feet, she blurted out, 'There's a lemon tart for pudding!'

Hugh frowned, deep in thought.

'And pomegranate ice cream!'

He shook his head.

'It's not that. I was wondering about your hard drive.'

'What?' The abrupt change of subject completely wrong-footed Orla.

'The hard drive in your computer. It just occurred to me. If you've been doing as much work as you say you have, it must be getting pretty cluttered.'

'Oh.'

Computer talk was something of a no-go area, as far as Orla was concerned. Technology wasn't her forte.

'Well?' Hugh prompted. 'Is it?'

Orla looked blank; she hadn't the least idea. Crikey, she didn't even understand the question. This was like being asked to stand up and explain the inner workings of a carburetor.

'I don't know.'

'Well, is the provider taking a long time to connect?'

Mystified, Orla shrugged.

'It's not a good idea to overload the system. The hard drive probably needs clearing.' Hugh added kindly, 'Would you like me to take a look while I'm here? Sort it out for you, before…?'

He didn't say so, but the implication was clear. Before it crashed, basically. Taking her entire manuscript with it.

'Heavens, would you?' Orla's feet jiggled with anxiety. 'I had no idea this could happen.'

'I did mention it when I installed the system,' said Hugh.

'I didn't listen! It's not the kind of thing I listen to!'

'Never mind. I'm here now.'

Oh, those reassuring words, like Batman swooping to the rescue.

'Thank goodness I bumped into you today!' Orla exclaimed. 'This is so kind of you.'

Hugh broke into a smile as he pushed back his chair.

'I know.'

Chapter 44

Upstairs in her office, from the safety of the window seat, Orla watched him with the kind of awe generally reserved for army experts detonating an unexploded bomb.

Hugh, working in silence to access the hard drive, determinedly didn't feel mean.

Ten minutes later, Orla reached for her cigarettes. Without looking up, Hugh said, 'You shouldn't smoke around computers. It buggers them up.'

She pulled a face; this was definitely something he'd told her before. Not that she'd taken a blind bit of notice.

'I don't know what this world's coming to, I really don't.' Orla heaved a sigh and fiddled with her necklaces instead. 'Can't smoke in front of children or pregnant women *or* computers. If I went back to writing by hand, I'd probably be had up for cruelty to felt-tips.'

'Look.' Hugh pointed to the screen. 'Forty megabytes of memory. Everything shoved in, willy-nilly. It's taking up too much space, like bundling clothes into a chest of drawers. You have to throw out the stuff you don't need and put the rest into some kind of order.'

Orla rolled her eyes like a teenager being nagged to tidy her room.

'And you need backup on an external hard drive.'

'What I need is a cigarette.' Defiantly, Orla slid a Marlboro out of the packet. 'Darling, don't look at me like that. You can manage all this external hard drive business without me, can't you? I'll just be in the garden getting some fresh air.'

Hugh forced himself to wait until the backing-up was in progress before studying the various charts pinned up around the office. This time Orla had had no idea that he would be coming in here and no opportunity to take down the relevant sections.

The ones with his name on them.

As the computer busily clicked and whirred behind him, Hugh checked each chart in turn.

His name wasn't there. It wasn't *anywhere*.

The sense of relief was incredible. Orla hadn't been lying to him after all. Millie hadn't used him. She hadn't breathed so much as a word to Orla about their night together.

Then again, this might have less to do with sparing his feelings and more with being too embarrassed to admit to Orla that she'd slept with someone who'd run out on her with no rational explanation.

At least, not one that he'd been able to put across.

Hugh pushed his fingers through his hair and gazed out of the window. He'd treated Millie abysmally and she hadn't done anything to deserve it.

Something she did deserve was an apology.

Then again, how much of a success was that likely to be? Absently fiddling with the loose button on the cuff of his white cotton shirt, he ran swiftly through the dialogue in his mind. Oh Millie, by the way, sorry if I've been keeping my distance lately, but a couple of things happened that I needed to sort out. First, I panicked after our night together. It was guilt, pure and simple. I felt like I was betraying Louisa… well, I *was* betraying Louisa… anyway, it hit me for six. And then the next thing was, I thought you'd been relaying every detail of our relationship back to Orla to give her book a bit of a boost. Except now, I realize you weren't telling her about us at all. So, well done you!

Bugger. Hugh cursed under his breath as the button came off his shirt. Apologizing was all very well, but what was he supposed to do after that? More to the point, what was Millie likely to do? Because if she flung her arms around him crying, 'Oh thank God, I knew you loved me really,' he was going to be faced with the horrid task of disentangling himself and explaining that no, no, sorry, she'd got hold of completely the wrong end of the stick here. This was an apology, pure and simple. It didn't mean he wanted them to be together. In fact, that was the last thing he wanted. She really shouldn't jump to conclusions.

Hugh shuddered at the thought of actually saying the words. Basically, he knew he couldn't.

But that was the situation. If Millie had been upset when he'd done his runner—if she really had liked him a lot—then getting her hopes up and dashing them again would be cruel. Not to mention awkward.

Then again, maybe he was flattering himself. She might not have given him a second thought. As far as she was concerned, it could simply have been a no-strings one-night stand.

In which case, there was no need to even bring the subject up. She would have moved on by now, consigned it to the past and embarked on new adventures.

With the likes of Con Deveraux.

By the time Orla returned, several chain-smoked cigarettes later, he had finished backing-up her files and clearing space on the hard drive. He had also learnt from the chaotically scrawled charts pinned up around the office that Con Deveraux was currently in New York, that Hester's boyfriend Nat was back from Glasgow, and that, having in the meantime slept with Lucas Kemp, Hester had discovered that he was staggeringly inept in bed.

He found this last snippet of information hard to believe but curiously comforting.

'All done?' Orla, reeking of smoke, flashed him a bright smile.

'All done.' Hugh switched off the computer, then nodded casually at the charts on the walls. 'These to do with the new book?'

'Yes! I'm having a complete change of direction—this is my fly-on-the-wall, coming-of-age, *literary* novel.' Orla beamed, as proud as any new mother.

Hugh nodded. 'And how's it going?'

'Really well! I'm actually enjoying the discipline of writing properly, after all these years of churning out mindless pap. Apart from the fact that it's supposed to be about sex and relationships and my main character's being completely hopeless and leading the life of an agoraphobic nun.' Orla pulled a face and laughed. 'Still, we'll soon snap her out of that. It's my friend Millie,' she explained as an afterthought. 'She was at my party the other week, but I'm fairly sure I didn't introduce you.'

Truthfully, Hugh replied, 'No, you didn't.'

'Anyway, I've been doing a spot of matchmaking, so things are starting to look up.' Orla's green eyes sparkled with mischief. 'In fact, she's got a date tomorrow night with a lovely chap and I just *know* they're going to get on.'

Hugh's faint smile concealed the involuntary tightening of the muscles in his jaw. 'Really?'

'Oh yes. See for yourself.' Kneeling up on the window seat, Orla excitedly beckoned him over. 'There he is, down there!'

The man trimming the edges of the lawn was stripped to the waist, with broad, tanned shoulders and a capable air about him. He was also instantly recognizable as the drunk at Orla's party who had grabbed hold of Millie and—in her own words—kissed like an Aquavac.

'Your gardener.' Hugh felt the muscles in his jaw relax.

'He's very well educated,' Orla announced with pride. 'His favorite author is Salman Rushdie.'

Moving away from the window so she wouldn't see the expression on his face, Hugh said idly, 'And how can you be sure that this girl...' he searched for the name '... Millie, tells you about everything she's been up to?'

Orla burst out laughing.

'Honestly, that is such a typical man thing to say! I've already told you, Millie's my friend. I *trust* her.'

'How do you know you can trust her?' Hugh was enjoying himself.

The look Orla gave him was full of pity.

'Because, Mr. Doubting Thomas, I *know* her. And she wouldn't dream of lying to me. Millie Brady is as honest as the day is long.'

Just so long as it's a day in the middle of winter in Greenland, thought Hugh.

'Anyway, we have to keep our fingers crossed for them.' Crossing her own with a dazzle of diamonds, Orla wagged them gaily under his nose. 'Because I'm telling you, I have *very* high hopes for tomorrow night.'

'Oh come on, cheer up, you're not *that* ugly.'

Millie, gazing without enthusiasm at her reflection in the mirror above the fireplace, said, 'I don't want to do this.'

'Don't do it then.' Hester shrugged, as if it were that simple.

'I have to. I feel sorry for him. You can't be mean to someone whose dad's just died.'

'Fine. I was only trying to help. You go off out to dinner with Richard-the-gardener-whose-dad's-just-died. Just try not to have *too* much fun, okay? We don't want you keeling over with the excitement of it all!'

A happy Hester was almost as unbearable as a suicidal one, Millie decided as the front door swung open heralding Nat's return. Until Lucas's new restaurant was up and running, Nat was working in a tapas bar on the promenade. Squealing with delight, Hester wound herself around him and covered him with kisses. In the mirror, Millie saw Nat grin and murmur something naughty in Hester's ear. Then, catching Millie's eye, he made an effort to control himself. Clearing his throat, he gave Hester a nudge. Because that was the kind of person Nat was, Millie reminded herself. Thoughtful. Kind and considerate. He wouldn't want her to feel awkward.

Taking several steps back, Millie surveyed her outfit in the mirror. Nothing dazzling, just a light green strappy dress and matching fluffy angora cardigan in case she was chilly later. A bit boring, to be honest, but somehow appropriate for dinner with a horticulturist.

Waiting patiently for Hester to finish canoodling with Nat, she said, 'How do I look?'

Sensitivity and consideration for other people's feelings had never been Hester's big thing. She beamed at Millie.

'Like a gooseberry.'

Richard turned up, as Millie had known he would, bang on time and looking like every mother's dream son-in-law. Muscly, but not too muscly. Clean-cut and handsome, but not *too* handsome. Wearing a navy polo shirt, crisply ironed beige chinos, and—most important—a pair of well-polished tan brogues. He was also wearing aftershave, but not too much of it. Short, clean nails. And one of those nice, honest, crinkly-eyed smiles so beloved of prospective mothers-in-law the world over.

Millie's heart sank into her bronze sandals. Here was exactly the kind of man she should be settling down with, the faithful, hard-working kind who'd treat you like a princess and bring you breakfast in bed.

And he did absolutely nothing for her.

It was so unfair.

'You look fantastic.' Richard's cheeks promptly reddened, in a clean-cut, healthy way.

'Thanks. Um, so do you.'

Doh!

'Ready to go?'

Millie smiled brightly and reached for her bag. 'All ready!' Turning, she yelled, 'Hess? We're off now. See you later.'

Hester appeared at the top of the stairs clutching an empty Evian bottle.

'I've just spilt water all over my bedroom carpet.' Innocently raising her eyebrows, she said, 'Okay if I borrow your Aquavac?'

Twenty-seven hours later, Richard went to the gents', leaving Millie alone at their table. Actually, it wasn't twenty-seven hours, it was only two, but it felt like twenty-seven.

He had brought her to Vincenzo's, a popular Italian harborside restaurant with candles flickering on every table, fishing nets slung authentically from the ceiling, and Just-One-Cornetto-type music oozing sensually from the rickety speakers above the bar. Nobody could accuse Vincenzo of failing to provide potential young lovers with lots and *lots* of atmosphere.

Poor old Vincenzo, thought Millie, it certainly wasn't his fault their evening wasn't going with a swing.

The problem was Richard, who had all the charisma of a party political broadcast. Her earlier fears that he might talk non-stop about his father hadn't materialized. Instead, he'd gone on and on about something far worse.

Gardening.

With the occasional dollop of Salman Rushdie thrown in for light relief.

Feeling mean, but not mean enough to stop, Millie fantasized about the toilet door getting stuck shut, forcing Richard to spend the rest of the evening in the gents'. She was bored, bored, bored. Not to mention horribly sober.

Terrified of repeating his performance at Orla's party, Richard was sticking resolutely to mineral water. When he had asked Millie earlier if she'd like some wine, she had nodded eagerly, expecting him to order a bottle. Richard, in turn, had smiled his true-blue, crinkly-eyed smile at the waitress and announced with pride, 'And a small glass of white wine for the lady.'

To be fair, he'd ordered her another, fifty-five minutes later. Forty-five minutes after she'd finished the first.

Feeling wicked—why, *why?*—Millie resolved to take advantage of his absence. Reaching for her empty glass, she attempted, valiantly, to gain the attention of a waiter.

He whisked past without noticing the pleading tilt of her eyebrows. Bugger, so much for subtlety. Nat had always told her it was the height of rudeness to click your fingers for attention, but it had worked for that fat bloke over by the window. Maybe if she stood on her chair, pointed, and bawled, 'Oi, you!' that might do the trick.

Millie's shoulders were in the process of slumping in defeat when a voice murmured in her ear, 'If there's one thing I can't stand, it's a damsel in distress.'

Chapter 45

The tables at Vincenzo's were squashed together—to make it more atmospheric, Millie presumed. Startled, she watched one of the men at the adjoining table whisk her glass from her hand and fill it to the brim with red wine. With a flourish, he presented it to her, his chair still tilted back on its hind legs, and added, 'There you go, you look as if you need it.'

He was in his late twenties, Millie guessed, and he was laughing at her. But in a nice way. And he'd certainly done a kind thing, even if he did appear to think she was an alcoholic.

'Thanks. But I'm not a damsel in distress.'

'Ha, could have fooled us.' The other one grinned at her.

'Really, I'm not!' Even as she was protesting her innocence, Millie couldn't resist glugging back the wine.

'My dear girl, you can't fool us. We've been sitting here eavesdropping for the last forty minutes. And you are not having a happy time of it,' the first one solemnly pronounced. 'Furthermore, as doctors, we are in complete agreement. Our diagnosis is acute distress.' He refilled her glass as he spoke. 'Triggered by terminal boredom and talk of rhododendrons.'

'And deciduous seedlings,' monotoned his friend.

'And rockeries and nasturtiums and the importance of mulching your grass cuttings.'

'Although, to be fair, we did find the bit about cross-fertilization techniques *almost* interesting.'

'Only because you thought he was leading the conversation around to sex,' the other one chided. He shook his head at Millie in sorrowful fashion. 'We're right though, aren't we? You're in the middle of the date from hell and you need rescuing.'

Oh I do, I do!

'He's a nice person,' Millie feebly protested.

'Treatment is simple. A good brisk walk. I'm Jed, by the way.' He winked and nodded in the direction of the propped-open front door.

'I can't. His father just died.'

'Probably from boredom, having to sit and listen to his son droning on and on about potting compost and adequate drainage and the importance of pruning—'

'He's coming back,' squeaked Millie as Richard reappeared, threading his way between the packed-together tables.

As he sat down, Richard said with enthusiasm, 'Sorry I've been a while. There's a pot of pelargoniums on the window ledge in the gents', about to expire! I've just been explaining to the owner of the restaurant that it needs regular watering and its tips pinched out if it's going to have any chance of flourishing back there.'

'Really?' Out of the comer of her eye Millie could see Jed's shoulders shaking. Cradling her glass so Richard couldn't see the dregs of red in it, she said bravely, 'I'd love another drink.'

Ten minutes later, Jed and his friend finished their meal and asked for the bill. When they'd paid, Jed stood up and announced, 'Right, we're off. Actually, I need the loo first. You go on ahead.'

As he moved away he glanced over his shoulder, catching Millie's eye for a fraction of a second. Waiting until he had disappeared through the swing doors, she reached for her bag and pushed back her own chair.

'Excuse me for a moment.'

Jed was waiting for her in the narrow corridor leading to the loos.

'I couldn't go without checking on that pelargonium,' he told Millie. 'I've been worried sick about it.'

'Me too,' said Millie. 'I just hope Vincenzo remembers to pinch those tips out.'

'I knew I knew you from somewhere. Couldn't figure it out before.' Jed grinned at her. 'You're the gorillagram.'

'Fame at last!' Millie was delighted. 'Where did you see me?'

'At the hospital. You were great. And all the more reason to rescue you,' he declared. 'After all, gorillas are an endangered species.'

'I can't just climb out of the toilet window.' Millie shook her head. 'His—'

'Dad's just died. I hadn't forgotten.' Drawing a mobile phone out of his jacket pocket, Jed dropped it into her unfastened bag. 'I'm not completely insensitive, you know.'

'I'm sorry.'

He flashed her a wicked grin.

'Maybe you could tell him it's nature's way of pruning the tree of life.'

The next moment, like Superman, he was gone.

Except he wasn't wearing his underpants over his trousers.

To pass the time, Millie went into the loo and redid her lipstick. The windows, she noticed, were too small to squeeze through anyway. Her bottom would have got stuck and she'd have been stranded there like a wolfhound wedged in a cat flap.

Her bag began to trill five minutes later, interrupting Richard's in-depth lecture on water features just as he was getting to a really exciting bit.

Joke.

'Sorry about this. Excuse me.' Reaching for the phone, Millie pressed it tight to her ear. 'Yes, hello?'

'We're outside.'

'What do you mean, where am I? I'm having dinner with a friend,' Millie replied indignantly.

'In a dirty, D-reg Toyota with a dented front wing.'

'But I'm not supposed to be working tonight! Oh God!' Millie exclaimed, the look on her face changing to one of horror, 'I completely forgot!'

'Oh dear me, that'll never do,' Jed tut-tutted.

'So you've told them I'm on my way? Okay, okay. I'm at Vincenzo's. Lucas, I'm *so* sorry about this... you're where? Just around the corner? And you've got my costume in the car? That's fantastic, okay, see you outside in thirty seconds. And listen, I really *really* owe you one.'

'Don't mention it,' said Jed cheerfully, before hanging up.

'What's happened?' said Richard. As if a five-year-old couldn't have worked it out.

'I can't believe it.' Millie banged the side of her head. 'I'm supposed to be doing a wedding reception tonight, in Truro. I wrote down all the details and forgot to transfer them to my diary. The mother of the bride just rang Lucas to find out why I hadn't turned up. God, I'm such an *idiot*. And Lucas is on his way here now to pick me up... look, I'm sorry, I'm going to have to go.' Shaking her head and reaching for her purse, Millie pulled out a twenty-pound note.

'You don't have to do that.' Richard looked astonished.

I do, I do, because I'm running away from you!

'Please. Let me.' Hastily she squashed the money into his hand. 'I'd rather pay my half, I'd feel terrible otherwise. Right, Lucas is probably here by now, I'd better shoot off! Bye!'

◈◈◈

A piercing whistle from across the street rang out as Millie emerged from the restaurant.

'This is like doing a bank job,' Jed whooped as she ran over to the filthy silver Toyota. 'I always wanted to be a getaway driver. Come on, jump in!'

Millie hesitated.

'I'm not supposed to jump into cars with strange men.'

'Oh that's good, coming from the girl who earns a living impersonating a gorilla. Anyway, we're not strange, we're surgical registrars.' Jed flashed his hospital ID card as he spoke. 'What's more, we've just rescued you from the gardener who's about as much fun as compost. And you've still got my phone,' he reminded her. 'Still, it's your call. We're off to the Mandrake Club. If you want to come along, you're more than welcome. But I have to warn you, in case you fancy me rotten, I never sleep with strange girls on the first night.'

Millie glanced back at the lit-up entrance to Vincenzo's. Then she checked her watch. Ten-fifteen. If she went home now, she'd have to sit in the armchair while Hester and Nat canoodled together on the sofa.

Hopping into the back seat of the car—and landing on a stethoscope—Millie said, 'The Mandrake sounds good to me.'

The club was packed and there wasn't an inch of space on the dance floor, but that didn't stop Jed and Warren—his co-conspirator—dragging Millie into the fray. Their enthusiasm knew no bounds and they danced like boisterous Labradors, until thirst and exhaustion drove them in the direction of the bar. As soon as they'd downed their pints of lager, they piled back onto the dance floor to trample on yet more people's feet. Millie found herself being flung between the pair of them like a frisbee. It was fraught but it was fun. Jed and Warren weren't out to impress anyone—just as well, really—they were simply enjoying themselves, making the most of their precious night off. Neither of them had allowed her to buy a single round of drinks. And—best of all—nobody had so much as mentioned gardening.

This is more like it, Millie thought, panting as she was hurled from Warren to Jed and back again—this time less like a frisbee, more like a grenade. Getting out and having fun, this is what I need to stop me thinking about…

Well, other stuff.

Other people.

Other people who shall remain nameless and who, no doubt, hadn't wasted a moment of their precious time thinking about *her*.

What was his name again? Gosh, wasn't that strange, she couldn't remember.

'Knackered!' bellowed Warren in her ear. 'Tell Jed it's his round!'

Ker-plaaang! Millie spun across the dance floor and ricocheted off Jed's broad chest.

'Warren says it's your round,' she yelled above the music.

Jed lifted her up and spun her round like a top. When he lowered her to the ground Millie was forced to steady herself against his arms. Clutching her to his side, he grinned and steered her in the direction of the bar.

'Ready for another pint? Down in one, mind. Last one to finish is a nancy.'

Millie's bladder was at bursting point. The glasses of wine earlier plus three pints of lager in the last hour were making their presence felt.

'Just a half,' she pleaded.

'A half?' Jed's eyebrows rose in dismay. 'What are you, some kind of *girl*?'

'And my name is Nancy.' She gave his arm an apologetic squeeze. 'What can I say? I'm a weak and feeble female, I can't keep up.'

As the music died down for a moment, the phone in her bag began to ring again. Millie, who had forgotten she still had it, looked around to see where the noise was coming from.

Amused, Jed slid his arm casually around her waist and lifted it from her bag.

'Yes? Hey, where are you lot? No, we're at the Mandrake,' he bawled above the resurgent thud of music. 'Coming down? Great! See you in a bit.' Switching off, he grinned at Millie. 'The late shift have just come off duty. They're on their way.'

'Fine.' Millie crossed her legs.

'Look, can I ask you something? Um, it's pretty personal.'

'Go ahead. Only be quick,' Millie said romantically, 'because I'm desperate for a wee.'

Jed hesitated. Already flushed and perspiring from their recent exertions on the dance floor, he now turned a deeper shade of crimson.

'The thing is, do you like me?'

Millie looked shocked. 'Of course I like you! You rescued me, didn't you? I was the damsel in distress and you were my heroic knight! Plus, you bought me loads of drinks, which always helps—'

'I mean,' Jed cut through her babbling, 'do you fancy me?'

Millie fell silent.

'You don't, do you?' He looked anxious.

'Um… well, no.'

'Brilliant.' Jed heaved a sigh of relief and gave her shoulder a clumsy pat. 'Phew. I mean, I was pretty sure you didn't, but I thought I'd better double-check.'

His ears had by this time gone bright red. Grinning, because it was actually pretty obvious, Millie said, 'Why?'

Jed shrugged and looked bashful, resembling a gauche young farmer more than a dashing surgeon.

'There's this nurse I'm quite keen on, and she's one of the crowd from the hospital on their way down. I just wanted to make sure you wouldn't be upset if I—'

'Had a crack at her,' smirked Warren, having just joined them at the bar. 'This is Jenny we're talking about, I take it? He's been psyching himself up for this for weeks.'

'If you're sure you don't mind.' Jed ignored him. 'I mean we did drag you here. I don't want you to feel—'

'You big pillock, of course I don't mind!' Millie laughed at the expression on his face. 'Go for it.'

Relieved, he planted a damp kiss on her forehead.

'Cheers, I'll introduce you to the rest of the crew when they get here. You never know, one of them might take your fancy,' he added with a wink. 'There's Raoul, one of the orthopods, he's a bit of a catch by all accounts.'

'Thanks, but I'm really not looking for a… you know…'

'Hey,' Warren interrupted with a groan of impatience, 'we're losing valuable drinking time here.' He gave Jed a hefty nudge. 'Are you getting this round in or not? I need another drink.'

Millie, whose legs had by this time wound themselves around each other all the way down to her ankles, said, 'And I need the loo. Back in a sec.'

Chapter 46

The air in the ladies' was thick with cigarette smoke, hairspray, perfume, and gossip. Leaning against the cool tiled wall, waiting her turn, Millie closed her eyes and concentrated on the snatches of conversation buzzing around her. Basically, because anything was better than thinking how desperate she was for a wee.

'… I'm telling you, it's like kissing a camel.'

'… Oh shit, one of my bra-fillers is missing… bloody thing must've fallen out on the dance floor.'

'… How can he fancy her? The girl's a walking bag of cellulite.'

'… I'm telling you, he's gorgeous. He can access my system any day.'

'… We've got to find it, they cost forty quid in La Senza!'

'… But I love him and he said he loved me and now he's all over that fat cow and I just don't know what I'm going to do-hoo-hooo…'

'… He got it caught in her belly-button ring. They had to dial nine-nine-nine and be lifted on to the stretcher together.'

'… His wife died last year.'

Millie's eyes snapped open. Her toes stiffened. This last remark had come from a tall brunette over by the sinks, busy slapping powder on to her cheeks. Next to her, her dumpy friend was overdoing the lilac eyeshadow.

The door of the toilet cubicle opened. It was Millie's turn to pee.

I'm overreacting, thought Millie. They could be talking about anyone, I need to pull myself together, I really do.

But she peed as slowly and quietly as she could, in order not to miss a word.

'How d'you know?'

'I asked him, dumbo! He was working in the café yesterday and Jerry was yakking on as usual about his girlfriend—God, that man is a complete wet lettuce—and I said, "So how about you? Do you have a girlfriend?" and he said "No," and I thought, Yay. So I went, "Why not? What's wrong with you—too ugly?" and he kind of smiled and went, "I think that's probably it." Then Jerry gave me a big kick and dragged me into the kitchen and hissed, "He was married, you idiot. His wife died last year." And I was like, Ohmygod, that is sooo sad. That is, like, *tragic*.'

Millie, having finished her excruciatingly slow, silent wee, pulled the chain and emerged from the cubicle. Sooo Sad was now vigorously brushing her hair, flicking it back over her shoulders, and grimacing at herself in the mirror, making sure she didn't have lipstick on her teeth.

'Then again, tragic for him,' she went on happily, 'but luck-luck-lucky for me. I'm definitely going to have a crack at him tonight.'

'Yeah.' Dumbo sounded doubtful. 'But how d'you know he fancies you?'

Sooo Sad snorted with derision.

'Come on. Who wouldn't fancy me?'

Dumbo, who was much less attractive and clearly jealous, said, 'You might not be his type.'

Having adjusted her fluorescent pink bra strap and squirted breath freshener into her mouth, Sooo Sad stepped back to admire her reflection. Satisfied, she smiled and said, 'I'm a girl, aren't I? And a thirty-six double D. Of course I'm his type.'

Millie was none the wiser. They could have been talking about anyone. And since the object of their attention worked in a café, it was unlikely to be Hugh. But she was still seized by a terrible urge to launch herself at Sooo Sad, pin her against the sink, and scribble all over her face with eyebrow pencil.

She could definitely do with a Groucho Marx moustache.

Anyway, it wouldn't be Hugh.

Damn, and she'd been doing so brilliantly earlier, not thinking about him. Practically not even being able to remember his name.

And if you believe that, you'll believe anything.

Stomach lurching, Millie scrabbled around in her bag for her apricot lip gloss.

Just to be on the safe side.

Although of course, it wouldn't be Hugh.

It was Hugh.

Spotting him at once, Millie realized she'd known, deep down, all along. Just from the predatory way Sooo Sad had been talking about him. Because, let's face it, there might be plenty of other widowers in Newquay, but in all honesty, how many would a nubile twenty-something describe as gorgeous?

And there she was, talking to him now, having wasted no time and homed in like a heat-seeking missile.

A fountain of jealousy welled up inside Millie, lurking like a peeping Tom at the back of the club. Sooo Sad was standing inches away from him, leaning closer still as she murmured something in his ear then tossed back her long hair and laughed.

Hugh laughed too. The bastard.

What was he doing here anyway? This was a nightclub, a place where men went to pick up women and women went to pick up men. Why would Hugh *want* to come here? He wasn't supposed to be interested in this kind of thing.

Bastard.

Her mouth dry, Millie watched him talking and smiling as

though he hadn't a care in the world. Sooo Sad was nodding and gesturing and angling her body provocatively towards his as she shifted from one spiky high-heel to the other. Her 36DD breasts spilt over the top of her minuscule, electric blue camisole and her legs, encased in microscopic white shorts, were endless.

Glancing down at her own gooseberry-green jersey dress, Millie felt like a bowl of left-out, dried-up cat food. By contrast—and offering herself up on the proverbial plate—Sooo Sad was an enticing mound of plump, juicy prawns.

Millie's blood curdled with envy. By now it wasn't just her dress that was green. Sooo Sad was fluttering her long fingers against the front of Hugh's dark blue shirt. It was practically foreplay. And he was standing there, *letting her do it.*

I know why he's here tonight. Hugh tried me once and walked away. Actually, ran away. But now he's being promised fresh prawns…

'There you are! We thought you'd run out on us!'

Jed materialized through the haze of smoke like a genie, clutching two slopped-about pints of lager and perspiring more dramatically than ever. His shirt had come untucked and his hair was sticking up like dandelion fluff. Touched that he'd come in search of her, Millie smiled.

'Is she here yet?'

'Who, Madonna? Nah.' He grinned and patted the pocket containing his mobile. 'She rang and said she'd be late. I told her if she couldn't be bothered to turn up on time, she could take a running jump.'

'Well done you. Don't take any nonsense from half-baked C-list celebrities.' Millie nodded her approval. 'How about your nurse?'

'No sign so far. D'you think I smell of garlic?'

He was breathing anxiously into his cupped hand. Honestly, these medical types, brains as sharp as custard.

'You ate spaghetti marinara in an Italian restaurant,' Millie pointed out. 'Of course you smell of garlic.'

'Oh God.'

'Here.' Delving into her bag, she slid a couple of peppermint TicTacs into his hand—probably the equivalent of the mouse scratching the elephant's ear, but every little helped. Jed took them and gave her shoulder a grateful squeeze as she popped a TicTac into her own mouth.

'Thanks. Hey, "Chumbawumba"!' His eyes lit up as the thumping beat started up. 'I *love* this song!'

Millie winced but she had no choice; her pint glass was whisked from her grasp—*again*—and she was carted onto the dance floor. Happily bawling along to the song—'I take a lager drink, And then a lager drink, And then a lager drink, And then a lager drink'—Jed bounced her around like a ping pong ball.

Agonizingly aware of Hugh's presence less than ten feet away, Millie pretended she hadn't seen him there. All she could do was be a good sport and act like she was having the time of her life. Then again, who was to say Hugh had even noticed her? Sooo Sad was still preening in front of him, doing her Pantene impression and giving him her undivided attention. Why would he even bother to glance at the lunatics pogoing across the dance floor?

'Wa-hey, she's here!' yelled Jed, screeching to a halt. 'Quick, got any more of those things?'

Rummaging in her bag once more, Millie found a loose TicTac in the side pocket—bit fluffy but still edible—and popped it into his mouth. Jed was all of a quiver, like an overgrown greyhound itching to race after a hare.

'Off you go.'

'Are you sure?'

'Don't be daft. I need to sit down anyway. Best of luck.'

It was like firing a starting pistol. With a huge grin of relief—

and a blast of garlicky-minty breath—Jed shot off in the direction of the bar and the girl of his dreams. Leaving her stranded alone in the middle of the seething dance floor.

Bugger, now I look as if I've been dumped.

This time—although her eyes didn't so much as flicker in his direction—Millie just knew Hugh was watching her. Attempting an air of nonchalance—and overdoing it horribly, as usual—she glanced at her watch (why?), patted her handbag (pointless), fiddled with her hair (still there), and sauntered casually back to where Jed had abandoned their drinks.

There was a small empty table right in the corner, out of sight of the dance floor. Feeling safe, but still stupid, Millie sat down and started riffling through her bag. She had the number of a taxi firm in there somewhere. Jed had already explained that in view of the astounding amount of alcohol they planned on drinking tonight, they were leaving the car and cabbing it home. He'd offered to drop her off en route. But that wouldn't be for hours yet, and she was ready to go now. Where was that card anyway? Unless it had decided to run off and abandon her, just like everyone else in this—

'Millie.'

Her head jerked up, and there he was.

Chapter 47

Oh Lord, thought Millie, and there was her stomach, off again, squirming like that pit of snakes in *Indiana Jones*.

Praying that Hugh couldn't actually *see* her stomach squirming, she mustered a bright, nonchalant smile and said, 'Oh, hi, I didn't know you were here.'

He look amused.

'Oh, I think you did.'

'I didn't!'

'Yes you did.'

This was ridiculous.

'Okay.' Millie gave him a humor-the-lunatic nod. 'What makes you think I knew you were here?'

'You weren't looking at me. When you were on the dance floor just now, with that friend of yours.' Hugh paused. 'You were looking everywhere except at me. Which can only mean you'd spotted me earlier and were deliberately avoiding looking at me. Should you be drinking that, by the way?' He nodded at her half-empty lager glass.

For an earth-tilting moment, Millie wondered if he thought she was pregnant.

'It's allowed. I'm over eighteen.'

'I saw you taking something earlier. A tablet.' His tone was even. 'And you gave one to your boyfriend.'

Millie smothered a grin. No wonder he sounded so disapproving.

'And you thought it was Ecstasy. For heaven's sake, do I *look* ecstatic?'

'The pair of you were dancing as if you were on drugs,' Hugh pointed out reasonably.

'Actually, we were on TicTacs.' Millie took a gulp of her drink. 'And I was only dancing like that to keep Jed company.'

'Hmm. Shame your boyfriend couldn't return the compliment. He's over by the bar chatting up some other girl now.'

'Jed isn't my boyfriend. Just a friend.' Craning her neck, Millie was able to see Jed at the bar, making his long-awaited play for the nurse he'd secretly fancied for months. She was tall, with mad frizzy hair and a Julia Roberts mouth. 'Anyway, what are you doing here? I mean, I know what you're doing here,' she amended, flapping her free hand, 'but I wouldn't have thought this was your kind of place.'

As the words came tumbling clumsily out, Millie realized she was being watched. It was her turn now. Through a gap in the crowd, Sooo Sad was staring across at them both, completely ignoring the man who was standing next to her whispering into her ear.

'It isn't. I was dragged here against my better judgment.' Hugh followed the direction of Millie's gaze. 'I've been designing a website for a new company. They opened for business last week and insisted I came out with them tonight to celebrate.'

'Really? I'd heard you were working in a café these days.' Millie's insides were still squirming but she felt she was doing a pretty good job of hiding it. Gosh, they were practically having a normal, polite conversation.

'That's the business.' Hugh smiled slightly. 'It's an Internet café on Wardour Street. I've been overseeing the technical side.'

Oh. Not washing up then.

'Her name's Anita,' he went on. 'She's one of the waitresses.'

'She's going to have a crack at you tonight.' Millie didn't know whether or not she should be saying this, so she said it anyway. Well, what the hell.

Hugh laughed and pulled up a chair.

'I'd gathered that much.'

'I heard her talking about you in the loo. She's a thirty-six double D,' Millie added recklessly. God, what was she, some kind of masochist?

'I knew that too. She told me.'

'Shouldn't you be over there with her?'

'Come on,' Hugh said dryly. 'The whole point of coming over here was to get away from Anita.'

How deeply flattering. Miffed, Millie wondered if he had any more tricks up his sleeve. Like asking her to dance with him to something slow and smoochy, perhaps. Not because he fancied her or anything; just to get Sooo Sad off his back.

This was a scenario familiar from her teenage years, an effective way of letting someone know you weren't interested in them. The trouble was, when you secretly fancied the boy who was using you to get the message across, it hurt like anything when the music stopped and he declared with satisfaction, 'Right, that's her sorted out, you can go now.'

Or even—ugh—'Cheers Millie, you're a sport.'

Not the kind of words you could forget in a hurry. Especially when you were fifteen.

'Actually, that's not true,' said Hugh.

'It is true! That's what he called me! *And* he clapped me on the back as he said it.'

Hugh gave her an odd look.

'What?'

Too late, Millie realized that they hadn't actually been talking about the ritual humiliations of her teenage years. Now he was going to think she was completely loopy.

As well as the girl you wouldn't want to sleep with twice.

Shaking her head, trying to appear sane, she said, 'Sorry, sorry. What isn't true?'

Thankfully, he decided to overlook her moment of madness.

'I mean I didn't just come over here to get away from Anita. There's something we need to talk about.' Hugh hesitated, searching for the right words. 'I owe you an apology.'

Damn right you do, matey!

'Look, there's no need,' Millie lied. 'Really. It's fine.'

'It isn't. I have to explain why—'

'Hugh?' Anita, clearly tired of waiting, had materialized in front of them. 'Will you dance with me?'

Just like that, Millie marveled. No hesitation, no shilly-shallying about. Sooo Sad wanted him back, so she'd come to get him. Like a three-year-old bluntly demanding the return of her favorite toy.

'Actually,' Hugh replied, 'I was—'

'*Please?* This is my favorite song.'

The DJ, who prided himself on his quirkiness, had replaced pounding techno-rap with Celine Dion warbling that her heart must go onnnnnn.

'Actually,' Hugh repeated, 'I was about to ask Millie if she'd like to dance.'

The years fell away; all at once, she was fifteen again. With braces on her teeth and a whopping crush on Andy Trent. Millie knew she didn't mean a thing to Andy—he was only asking her to dance to make Stefanie Chambers jealous—but turning him down was easier said than done. If she said no to Andy, he'd simply shrug and laugh and ask someone else. If she said yes, she'd have three minutes of bliss to hug to herself for weeks to come, three minutes of heavenly physical contact before the music ended and he gave her a matey clap on the back before heading back to his friends.

Which was why she never had been able to bring herself to say no. Who cared about pride anyway? Three minutes of unimaginable bliss were better than none. Saying no was simply cutting off your nose to spite your face.

Stop it, stop it, I'm not fifteen any more. I'm twenty-five. I'm a mature adult with buckets of pride *and* metal-free teeth.

'Okay,' Millie blurted out.

'Sorry.' Hugh shrugged and smiled up at Sooo Sad.

Sooo Sad shot a withering glance in Millie's direction and stalked off.

'We'll have to go through with it now,' murmured Hugh, which boosted her self-esteem no end.

'No need. In fact, I'd rather stay here.'

'Don't be daft.'

Millie was no longer sure she wanted to dance.

'I thought you had something you needed to tell me.'

Smiling fractionally as he reached for her clammy hand, Hugh pulled her to her feet.

'It can wait.'

Oh dear, was there any form of torture more exquisite than this? As they danced together every cell in Millie's body clamored for more, shamelessly urging her to move her thigh against his thigh, allow her hand to slide over his back, tilt her head an inch closer to his shoulder... and then another inch... and another...

Come on, squealed her overexcited hormones, let's get this show on the road! It's him, isn't it? Don't try and pretend you've forgotten! This is the one we had so much fun with last time, so what are we waiting for?

They were only hormones; they didn't understand. Millie, employing every last ounce of willpower, concentrated on the music instead. When she'd gone to see *Titanic* with Hester, the manager of the cinema had been forced to ask them to cry more quietly. Apparently other members of the audience were complaining that they couldn't hear the film. Don't think about Hugh, don't think about

Hugh, it'll be over soon, just keep going and don't think about Hugh. Oh good grief, he just pinched my bum!

'What?' said Hugh, all innocence.

'Why did you *do* that?'

'Do what?' he teased.

'That!' It was such an inappropriate, unromantic thing to do. He hadn't even been gentle.

Outraged, Millie pinched his backside—hard—in return.

'Ow, that hurt.'

'Good.'

A split-second later she felt it happen again. Twisting round, Millie saw Jed happily smooching away behind her with the nurse of his dreams. He gave her a broad wink and a deeply inappropriate and unromantic double-thumbs-up.

For his sake, Millie hoped he was gentler with his patients.

'Sorry. Thought it was you.' Mumbling the words, she avoided Hugh's dark eyes. She had a horrid feeling he was laughing at her. She also wished Celine Dion would hurry up and finish; this song was dragging on for longer than it had taken the *Titanic* to sink.

More than anything else though, she wished Hugh didn't have to be wearing that aftershave, the one he always wore. It reminded her so strongly of their night in bed together that she knew the rest of her life would be haunted by it. Her body was programmed to react to that particular smell.

It wasn't funny, Millie gloomily decided, realizing you were at the mercy of a bottle of aftershave. Not funny and not fair. If she could drag Hugh through to the cloakroom, strip off his clothes, and scrub him all over with a stiff-bristled brush, she would do it in a flash.

Then again, there was always the possibility that she might complete the first two tasks and then… oh gosh… get distracted…

'Are you all right?'

'What?'

'Your breathing's gone a bit funny,' said Hugh.

Oh crikey, it had too. Realizing she'd been getting carried away, practically hyperventilating into his ear, Millie took an abrupt step backwards.

'I'm okay. Just feeling a bit, um, faint.'

He looked alarmed. 'You idiot! Why didn't you say something?'

'I'm saying it now.' Millie swayed on her feet for added authenticity, then let out a shriek as they abruptly lost contact with the ground. 'Jesus, what are you *doing*?'

'Getting you out of here before you keel over.' Having lifted her into his arms, Hugh moved swiftly through the crowds on the dance floor and headed towards the exit. Behind her, Millie heard an ear-splitting wolf-whistle and a raucous—inappropriate, even—whoop of approval.

Aware of her handbag dangling from its strap and bashing less than glamorously against her bottom, Millie wailed, 'Put me *down*. I didn't mean I *was going* to faint—I'm not a fainty person!'

'This place is enough to make anyone pass out. It's okay,' Hugh told the smirking bouncers on the door, 'I'm not kidnapping her. She just needs some fresh air.'

Chapter 48

OUTSIDE, HE SAT MILLIE down on a bench and tried to persuade her to put her head between her knees. Feeling this was undignified—and not wanting to look any sillier than he'd already made her look—Millie flatly refused.

'I'm fine, really. See?' She waggled her head at him like a top-heavy sunflower. 'Never felt better.'

'Give yourself a couple of minutes. Then you can go back in.'

Millie thought this was an unenticing prospect. Jed had his nurse to occupy him now. And Sooo Sad, no doubt, was in there waiting to reclaim Hugh. Glancing up the street, she saw a taxi slow down and disgorge a gaggle of rowdy clubgoers.

'Actually, I think I'll call it a night. Catch a cab home.'

'I'd give you a lift, but I don't have my car,' said Hugh. 'No, don't.' He placed a hand on Millie's arm as she made a move to flag down the cab. 'Don't go yet. We still need to talk.'

Millie winced. She wasn't really in the mood just now for one of those you're-a-great-girl-but lectures.

Let's face it, she never was going to be in the mood.

Watching the cab sail past, she said flippantly, 'I've got a better idea. Let's not talk about it.'

Hugh ignored this suggestion.

'The reason I didn't contact you after that night is because I felt guilty about my wife. Then, before I had the chance to apologize, I found out about your arrangement with Orla.' He paused. 'I assumed you'd told her about us.'

'I didn't.'

'I know that now.'

He was sitting next to her on the bench, his elbows resting on his knees and his hands loosely clasped. Was this what it had all been about? Millie held her breath and allowed her hopes to rise, by the tiniest of notches.

'You could have asked me.'

'I know that too. Look, I'm sorry.'

'Okay. Apology accepted.' Millie's stomach was off again, squirming away. Was Hugh going to kiss her now? She shifted round, just a fraction, to make it easier for him if he did. Ever the optimist, her hopes rose another semi-notch. But he wasn't looking as if he was about to sweep her into his arms and kiss her. His gaze was still fixed on the pavement.

When he spoke, it was clearly with some difficulty.

'I'm sorry about the other thing as well. That night. It shouldn't have happened.'

What? What are you *talking* about?

Aloud, she murmured, 'Oh.'

'It's all my fault. I should never have turned up at your house like that. I don't know what made me do it. You see—'

'No, no, that's fine, it really doesn't matter.' Millie blurted the words out before he could get on to the bit about her being a great girl—possibly even a sport. 'I know what you're trying to say, and there's absolutely no need. It was one of those spur-of-the-moment things, that's all. A complete one-off. I'd practically forgotten it ever happened!'

'Really?'

'Really! Gosh, it couldn't matter less. Now could we please change the subject? Talk about something else?'

Something easier to handle maybe, like quantum physics?

Hugh shot her a sidelong, crooked smile; there was no disguising his relief.

'Could we change the subject,' he echoed thoughtfully. 'I usually hate it when people say that.'

'Do you? I hate it when people say they're off to a swanky restaurant.' Millie knew she was babbling but she didn't care. Babbling was a damn sight better than having to listen to someone explain just how much they didn't fancy you. 'I mean, *swanky*. I can't bear that word! And going for a *slap-up* meal... what's that all about? How can a meal be slap-up?'

'Munching a biscuit,' said Hugh. 'There's an expression I can't stand. Munching's a hideous word. You just know it means really noisy.'

Delighted that he could play this game, Millie yelped, 'And I hate it when people say, "Ooh, Blossom's playing up today," and you realize they're talking about their car. They actually think it's cute to give their car a pet name—and they always choose really nauseating names like Flossie or FunBun or Eric.'

'Men don't do that,' Hugh pointed out. 'Only girls.'

'Go on,' Millie urged. 'Your turn.'

'Mensa members,' he said promptly. 'People who slide the fact that they have an IQ of two hundred and fifty into the conversation to prove how intelligent they are. Because otherwise you might think they're thick.'

'I joined Mensa last year,' said Millie. 'Actually, I've got an IQ of over sixteen thousand.'

'And my car's called Tinkerbell,' Hugh riposted.

'I always want to slap people who go: Oh. My. God.'

'I cringe when someone says, "The world is your lobster."'

'In fact,' Millie said happily, 'between the two of us, we hate pretty much everyone.'

'I know, isn't it great?'

They grinned at each other. Hugh stood up and held out his hand.

'We're more likely to find a cab in the square, if you're up to walking that far.'

'Know what I really hate? People who make a big fuss of you when you're feeling absolutely fine.' To prove how fine she was, Millie pointedly ignored his outstretched hand.

'Next time you collapse in a nightclub I'll leave you in a heap on the floor.' Glancing behind her, he added casually, 'By the way, I'm not wild about walking down the street with a girl whose dress is tucked into her knickers.'

'Nooo!' Millie clapped her hands to her bottom in dismay. When she realized her dress wasn't tucked into her knickers she gave Hugh a whack on the arm.

'Two more things I can't stand,' said Hugh. 'Violent women. And girls who can't take a joke.'

'I hate men who wear nasty, cheap aftershave.'

'What really annoys me is getting phone calls from people putting on ridiculous accents, asking me the answer to crossword clues.'

'That isn't true!' Millie exclaimed. 'You asked me to give you the clues. You were bursting to show off how clever you were. And that's something I really can't stand in a man.'

'I was trying to help you out. I felt sorry for you because you were obviously thick. Anyway, it's a man thing. We can't resist showing off our superior knowledge. Through here,' Hugh gestured as they reached the entrance to the park. 'It's a shortcut to the square.'

'What I *also* hate is someone new to the area thinking they know more about the shortcuts than somebody who's lived here all her life.'

He laughed; she saw his teeth gleaming dazzlingly white in the darkness.

'Fine. We'll do whatever you say. You tell me the best way to get to the square.'

'Through the park, dipstick.'

'Now that,' Hugh announced, 'is something I do like. A girl who can admit when she's in the wrong.'

'I didn't say I was wrong.' Millie was in her element now. 'I'm just saying this time you happened to be right, but don't assume you'll always know best. Because I am, in fact, the shortcut Queen of Newquay. Trying to out-shortcut me would be like offering to show Delia Smith the best way to bake a cake. It's like demonstrating to Michael Schumacher how he should be taking his corners.'

'Like teaching your grandmother to suck eggs.' Hugh nodded gravely.

'Oh yeeuch, I hate that saying. Makes me feel sick.'

'You mean you try not to, but you can't help picturing it? And you just know she's going to have bits of broken egg shell around her wrinkled mouth and raw yolk dribbling down her whiskery old chin?'

Millie started to laugh. How could he possibly know that?

'Exactly! You too?'

'Oh yes,' said Hugh. 'Every time.'

Swooooosh…

It was one of those moments, Millie realized, that she would remember for ever. Captured in her mind as efficiently as a butterfly in a box. Every sense was heightened; she could feel the blades of grass tickling her feet, the warm night breeze on her bare shoulders. The silhouettes of the trees shifted in the darkness. She could hear the rustling of the leaves and shouts of revelry in the far distance and the sound of Hugh's breathing. She could smell his aftershave and the sweet green scent of the just-cut grass. His blond hair glistened in the reflected moonlight. His dark eyes were—for the moment—completely serious, as if he too had realized what was happening.

Millie's body felt like a buzzing bundle of electricity. It was at this precise moment that she realized just how in love with this man she was.

Completely and utterly and helplessly.

Not to mention pointlessly, seeing as he'd made it abundantly clear to her that what had happened before would never ever happen again.

Millie closed her eyes in defeat. She may have thought she'd known it before, but now she truly knew it. This was so much more than mere physical attraction and the realization that here was someone you got on fantastically well with.

This was the man with whom she knew she could spend the rest of her life.

He was The One for her. There couldn't be anyone else.

And who did she have to thank for this discovery? Some toothless old egg-sucking grandmother.

'Hear that?' said Hugh, turning his head.

Oh, don't worry, it's just my heart breaking, shattering into a zillion pieces.

'If I'm not mistaken,' Millie pronounced, 'it's the mating call of the greater-spotted, swallow-tailed, ring-necked redwing.'

Obligingly, at that moment, a bird sang out from one of the trees overhead.

Hugh gave her a pitying look.

'If there's one thing I can't stand, it's a smug intellectual. And if you listen again I think you'll find that's the call of the *lesser-spotted*, swallow-tailed, ring-necked redwing.'

'Tell you what,' said Millie, 'let's just shoot it anyway.' Peering ahead into the darkness, she glimpsed movement. 'There's somebody over there.'

'That's the noise I heard. Two people talking. I can see them now,' Hugh added as they followed the curve of the path and drew nearer. 'Over there on that bench.'

The bench was close to the park's exit gates; to get out they had to pass it. As they approached, Millie saw that the couple were entwined in a pretty intimate embrace.

'I hope they aren't having sex,' whispered Millie.

Sounding amused, Hugh whispered back, 'Why? They're the ones who'll be embarrassed.'

Yes, you big nitwit, but I'll be jealous!

They had almost reached the park bench now. The couple on it were kissing passionately… and audibly.

'Yuk,' Millie murmured. 'I hate noisy kissers.'

'They haven't seen us. They don't know we're here.' Hugh spoke in an undertone. 'Otherwise I'm sure they'd do it more quietly.'

Millie was tempted to clear her throat and startle them out of their passion-fueled snog. Thankfully, it appeared to be no more than a snog, although the two of them were by this time practically horizontal on the bench. It couldn't be comfortable either—those narrow wooden slats had no give in them—and from the look of the couple they weren't what you'd call spring chickens. Not that Millie could see their faces, but the man's shoes and trousers weren't the kind anyone under the age of thirty would be seen dead in, and it stood to reason that no female under thirty would be seen dead with the kind of man who went out in public dressed like that.

The next moment two things happened more or less simultaneously. The man who was lying almost on top of the woman stopped kissing her noisily for just long enough to let out a groan of longing. Cupping her face in his hands, he sighed passionately, 'Oh God, you drive me *insane*.'

'It drives me insane when people say that,' Hugh whispered in Millie's ear.

But Millie didn't hear him; she was too busy being in shock.

Surely not. It couldn't really be her ex-boss, could it? Tim Fleetwood? It sounded exactly like him, but how could it be?

Because apart from anything else, the woman lying underneath him sure as hell wasn't his wife, scary Sylvia.

A split-second later the woman's shoe, which had been dangling from her toes, slid off and fell to the ground. It was an elegant lime green stiletto with a leather bow on the heel and a gold lining.

Millie promptly went into triple shock. The shoe was a size three and a half. She knew this because she had tried it on last week. Or, at least, had tried to try it on. Being a size five herself, it hadn't fit.

'Oh darling, you look just like one of the ugly sisters,' the owner of the expensive new shoes had trilled with her customary lack of tact.

Millie closed her eyes but it was too late, she'd already recognized the slender stockinged leg now minus its shoe. There was surely no mistaking that leg, nor the hands that were entwined in Tim Fleetwood's hair—although maybe entwined was putting it a bit strongly, considering there wasn't actually that much of it.

But the clincher, the absolute clincher, was the jewelry. Those rings, that bracelet, the narrow gold watch.

Chapter 49

'WHAT WAS THAT ALL about?' demanded Hugh thirty seconds later. He rubbed his arm where Millie's fingers had dug in so hard she'd left a series of nail-shaped indentations. One minute they'd been wandering at a leisurely pace through the park; the next, she had seized his arm and with superhuman strength practically dragged him out through the gates.

Millie didn't reply. Seemingly unaware of her surroundings, she was heading away from the square at a rate of knots, her spine rigid and her arms folded tightly across her chest. Hurrying to catch up, Hugh marveled at the pace she was setting.

'Millie? Slow down a minute. Tell me what's going on.'

When she turned to look at him, he saw that her face was white.

'I can't tell you.'

'You have to.' Seeing her like this, Hugh's chest tightened with concern. He wanted to protect Millie from whatever had upset her. Put his arms around her and make everything better. He couldn't bear the thought of anyone hurting her.

As if I haven't hurt her enough myself.

Millie was trembling violently. Her green angora cardigan was tied around her waist. Gently, Hugh untied the sleeves and helped her into it as if she were a child.

'That man on the bench back there.' The words came out jerkily, between chattering teeth. 'I know him. It's Tim Fleetwood, my old boss.'

'Okay.' Hugh nodded slowly, wondering what all the fuss was about. He knew why Millie had left the travel agency; she'd told him all about the downtrodden husband and his possessive, wildly jealous wife. But why would seeing him now—

'I know the woman too, the one he was with,' Millie blurted out. 'Oh Hugh, this is awful, I'm so ashamed. It's my mother.'

Down on the beach, the tide was in. An almost-full moon lit up the inky water. Millie sat on the dry sand above the high-tide line and hugged her knees. Hugh, sitting next to her, allowed her to talk.

'I mean, we knew she was seeing someone and we'd guessed he was married. In theory I could cope with that. It's just the shock of actually seeing them together, your own mother kissing some man… it's so gross… and in *public*, where anyone could have seen them! And to cap it all she had to choose Tim Fleetwood!'

'At least she didn't see you,' said Hugh.

'Of course she didn't see me, she was too busy sticking her tongue down her hideous old boyfriend's throat… ugh, double-gross! Just the thought of it makes me feel *sick*.' Repulsed, Millie covered her face with her hands. 'I wanted to yell at them, throw a bucket of water over them, anything to make them stop pawing each other like that!'

Hugh hid a smile. Poor Millie, she was upset, but actually there was a funny side to this. Picturing her flinging a bucket of cold water over her mother and her ex-boss, he struggled to keep a straight face.

Lucky, really, that there hadn't been any buckets lying about.

'Why didn't you yell at them?' In fact, he was surprised she hadn't; it would have been a Millie thing to do.

'I couldn't. I couldn't. It would have been too embarrassing for you.' Her voice rose again. 'I'm so ashamed—God, my own mother! How would that have made *you* feel?'

Touched, Hugh put his arm around her.

'You idiot. You know, I think I could probably have coped.'

'Tuh,' Millie retorted. 'You might have been able to, but I couldn't.'

His mouth twitched.

'Why not? What did you think I'd say? Ugh, get away from me, Millie Brady, I don't want anything to do with a girl whose mother cavorts shamelessly on park benches with married men?'

Millie picked up a pale grey pebble and lobbed it—plop—into the sea. Funnily enough, this was almost exactly what she had expected Hugh to say. Well, maybe not *say*, because he simply wasn't that rude. But she could picture him thinking it, which was just as bad.

Still, he had his arm around her waist, which wasn't bad at all. In fact, it was extremely nice, even if she knew it didn't mean anything. It was a cheer-up-and-don't-worry-about-your-delinquent-mother gesture rather than a romantic one. Then again, beggars can't be choosers, and right now any friendly gesture was better than none, especially when the merest physical contact was making her go zingy all over and want to writhe helplessly with pleasure like a puppy having its stomach tickled.

Millie's breathing grew shallower and more rapid as Hugh's fingers, idly stroking her hypersensitive skin, began to head in a direction they really shouldn't have been heading.

Oh, but he was doing it so seductively she didn't know if she could bring herself to stop him.

'Please don't,' croaked Millie.

'I want to. I have to,' Hugh whispered back, his breath warm on her ear. 'You've kept me in suspense long enough. I can't stand it any longer.'

'No. You mustn't.' Summoning all her mental strength, Millie clamped her hand over his fingers and peeled them away from her leg. She took a deep breath. 'No, no, *no*.'

Hugh grinned.

'Spoilsport.'

'I promise you,' Millie said with feeling, 'you don't want to know.'

She kept the flat of her hand firmly over the tattoo as she spoke. To her relief Hugh didn't persist.

'Okay, fair enough. But there's something else I'm curious about. Why didn't you tell Orla about us?'

Actually, not that relieved.

'Because it was a one-off. It didn't mean anything,' Millie lied—since it had, of course, meant the exact opposite. 'It wasn't… relevant,' she floundered on, 'and I knew you wouldn't want to be included, no matter how much Orla disguised your identity. Anyway, I'm allowed to keep some stuff private.' Especially stuff that makes me look like a wally and a complete pushover. 'I didn't happen to think that was any of Orla's business.'

Hugh raised an eyebrow.

'I thought she paid you to tell her everything.'

'Look, what Orla doesn't know won't hurt her.' Shifting uncomfortably on the sand—her bottom was going numb—Millie retorted, 'You aren't going to tell her, are you? And neither am I. So basically, Orla's never going to find out.'

'You're sure that's not cheating?'

'Of course I'm sure!' Honestly, what was he suggesting, that she gave the five thousand pounds back to Orla? 'She's got heaps of stuff to write about.' Getting huffy, Millie tugged the gooseberry-green angora cardigan up over her shoulders. 'The thing is, you're acting as though what happened between us that one night was important, and it wasn't. Compared with all the other stuff that's been going on, crikey, it was nothing! It *meant* nothing. It was just a… blip.'

Silence. Millie wondered if she'd gone too far. It was, after all, the kind of declaration at which a man could take offense.

Finally, slowly, after studying her face for what seemed like an hour, Hugh tilted his head to one side.

'A blip. Of course it was. You're absolutely right.'

The taxi drew to a halt outside Millie's house. Hugh, who was traveling on to Padstow, said, 'I'll move to the front.'

It was an excuse to get out of the cab and say good night to Millie. This evening's events had shaken him more than he cared to admit, even to himself, and he was fighting to keep his feelings under control.

First, seeing Millie at the club with Jed, assuming that he was a new boyfriend, and not liking it one bit. Then, dancing with Millie and wondering if it was affecting her as profoundly as it had affected him.

He truly hadn't known the answer to this until she had called him a blip. That was when he'd known for sure that he wasn't a blip.

Guilt had mingled with relief. There was no easy answer. He didn't want to feel this way about anyone, but he just couldn't help it.

Standing on the pavement together while the taxi driver lit a cigarette, they gazed into each other's eyes.

'Gosh, it's late,' said Millie, shivering. 'Two o'clock.'

He wanted to kiss her so badly but knew he mustn't. It wasn't fair on Millie. He knew what else he wanted to do, but that wouldn't be fair either.

Instead, smiling slightly, he said, 'Thanks for rescuing me this evening.'

'Any time.'

She was either shivering or trembling. Hugh couldn't tell which.

He didn't want to go.

But he must.

'I ended up enjoying myself more than I'd expected.'

'Me too.' Millie pulled a face. 'Apart from the bit where we bumped into my mother.'

'And the bit where you called me a blip.' Jesus, what am I doing? Why am I saying this? Do I want her to tell me it isn't true?

'I love that word,' said Millie. 'Actually, it's one of my all-time favorites.' Slowly, she repeated it. 'Blip.'

Hugh nodded. 'I'm very fond of Tombola.'

'Lozenge.'

'Jinx.'

'Swizzlestick.' She twirled the syllables around her tongue with relish.

'Yodel.'

'Fandango. Although,' Millie confessed, 'I don't really know what it means.'

She was smiling and still shivering, stumbling slightly over the words. Hugh shivered too; there it was, happening again, just as it had happened on the beach. Some indefinable chemistry was at work, zapping between them. Millie had this effect on him. He wished she didn't, but she did. There was no escaping it.

He really liked the word testosterone, but it hardly seemed appropriate to say so.

He mustn't weaken, he *mustn't*. If the guilt came flooding back, as it had last time, that would be it. He would hate himself and Millie would certainly never forgive him.

Not again.

Hugh tilted his head slightly to avoid the glare of an approaching car's headlights. Misconstruing the movement, clearly thinking he was about to kiss her, Millie angled her own cheek towards his. Awkwardly, because a decorous peck on the cheek was so far removed from the kiss he wanted to give her, but knew he couldn't risk, he did the gentlemanly thing. Fleeting contact, two inches from the corner of her mouth.

They gazed at each other with silent, throbbing longing as the car moved steadily past them.

Millie cleared her throat as she fumbled in her bag for her front-door key.

'Doppelgänger's a gorgeous word.'

'It's German. That's cheating.' A tiny insect was dancing just in front of her face and he brushed it gently away with the back of his hand. 'No foreign words allowed. Otherwise you just end up reciting types of pasta. *Pappardella. Conchiglia. Vermicelli.* See?' He shrugged. 'Those Italians have all the best words. Who can compete with that?'

'*Vermicelli* means little worms.'

'Exactly. That's why they win every time.'

The taxi driver, having finished his cigarette and begun fiddling with the dial on his radio, located some sad local DJ with a penchant for country and western. Tammy Wynette yodelling, 'Staaayaand by your maaayaaan,' made them both jump.

'God, now I'm definitely going,' said Millie.

Hugh smiled; she'd once told him she'd rather knit her own intestines into a vest than listen to country and western.

'Let me know what happens with your mother,' he said as Millie unlocked the front door.

Now that they were several feet apart, it was easier to pretend they were just good friends.

'Don't worry.' Millie waved over her shoulder as he climbed back into the cab. 'First thing tomorrow morning, she's going to get the talking-to of her life.'

Lucas had reached the end of the road and stopped. There was no other traffic about but he waited at the junction anyway, watching the goings-on in his rearview mirror with deepening interest.

Nobody was more of an expert than Lucas when it came to body language. Interpreting those barely there, seemingly insignificant signals was what he did best; it was a particular talent, like possessing perfect pitch or the ability to paint like Degas.

Not that there had been anything insignificant about the signals being given out back down the road outside Millie's house. But whereas anyone else seeing them might simply have assumed that here was a couple who fancied each other, Lucas was able to read far more into the situation than that.

This was Millie as he had never seen her before, caught up in the grip of emotions he seriously doubted she had ever experienced before. Lucas recognized the tall blond guy she was with—he'd bumped into them once, months ago, in a bar. But Millie had barely seemed to know him herself back then; there had been no atmosphere of intimacy between them. Lucas also recalled seeing him at Orla's party but was fairly sure he'd been there with someone else. Nor did he recall there being any contact between him and Millie.

But there was no mistaking the situation now. This was serious. As he'd driven slowly past, they had been oblivious to anything but each other; the air around them had practically been vibrating with mutual longing. Pure *Brief Encounter*. Minus the railway platform, of course, and the billowing clouds of steam. If Lucas had tooted his horn they wouldn't have heard it. If he'd leapt out of his car and danced naked on the hood they wouldn't have noticed him.

Interesting that Millie hadn't mentioned this new development in her life.

But what intrigued Lucas most of all was the fact that they were saying goodbye to each other on the doorstep, rather than taking the evening to its logical conclusion.

When it was so clearly what both of them wanted to do.

As he watched in the rearview mirror, Millie stepped back and the blond guy climbed into the passenger seat of the waiting taxi. Lucas was too far away to see the expression on her face, but he guessed she wasn't wearing one of her phew-that's-got-rid-of-him smiles.

The next moment, the taxi pulled away and Millie disappeared inside the house.

Very interesting indeed, thought Lucas. Millie had found herself a man at last, one she was evidently head over heels in love with.

And for some reason he wasn't able to spend the night with her.

Plus, she was keeping their relationship a secret.

Ha! thought Lucas, entertained to recall all the times Millie had had a hissy fit and lectured him about his own sex life.

No doubt about it. Millie's new man was married.

Chapter 50

Millie didn't get the chance to speak to her mother about Tim Fleetwood. When the front doorbell rang at eight o'clock the next morning she was still upstairs, asleep.

Nat, answering the door in his striped boxer shorts, found a middle-aged woman in a severe navy jacket and grey knife-pleated skirt on the doorstep.

'Hello. Does Millie Brady still live here?'

'Um, hi.' Nat wondered if the woman was a probation officer. 'Yes, yes she does. But she's not up yet.'

'Don't worry, it isn't Millie I'm after.' The woman smiled tightly and gestured towards her briefcase. 'I was actually looking for Adele Brady, Millie's mother. I know she was down here visiting her daughter, but—'

'Oh, right. No, Millie's mum's not here,' Nat explained. 'She's staying with Millie's dad.'

'Really?' The woman's eyebrows rose. 'I thought they were divorced.'

'They are. She's staying with Millie's dad and his ladyfriend.' With a grin, Nat added, 'Millie's mum's still young, free, and single.'

'I see.' Another chilly smile. 'Well, I wonder if you could give me the address.'

Nat scratched his head, 'I haven't got a clue where they live. Hess? Hess?' he yelled. The next moment, wrapped in a towel and still dripping from her shower, Hester appeared at the top of the stairs.

'Hello. So sorry to trouble you. My name's Sylvia Fleetwood. Millie used to work for my husband and me.' Flipping open her briefcase, Sylvia withdrew a handful of glossy brochures. 'The thing is, Millie's mother is a client of ours and she's been desperate to get hold of some brochures. These were delivered to the office yesterday afternoon, so I thought I'd drop them off this morning on my way to work.'

'Oh, right.' Hester had heard all about Sylvia Fleetwood from Millie. Obsessively jealous and paranoid that other women were after her henpecked husband. As if any woman in her right mind would be interested in the kind of man who allowed himself to be henpecked. 'Well, you can leave the brochures here. Millie'll make sure her mum gets them.'

'Mrs Brady is extremely anxious to see the brochures,' Sylvia insisted. 'It'll be quicker if I take them to her now.'

Hester shrugged; it made no difference to her.

'Okay, if you're sure.' She told Sylvia Fleetwood the address and helpfully gave her directions to Lloyd and Judy's hard-to-find house at the end of a narrow lane off the main road leading from Newquay to Padstow.

'Thank you. You've been most helpful.' Sylvia Fleetwood headed briskly back towards her car.

'Bit keen, isn't she?' said Nat when they had closed the front door. 'All that way, just to drop off a few holiday brochures?'

Hester squirmed with pleasure as he caught hold of her and began to kiss her neck.

'That woman's so paranoid, she's probably doing it to keep Adele away from the office and out of her husband's sight. One glimpse of him and she's worried Millie's mum will be consumed with uncontrollable lust…'

'Speaking of being consumed with lust.' Nat's hands began to wander teasingly over her damp, towel-clad body.

'Nooo! I'll be late for work,' Hester protested unconvincingly.

'Tell the boss you'll be half an hour late. Actually, don't bother, I'll tell your boss.' His expression solemn, Nat removed her towel and let it fall to the floor. 'Hester, you're going to be half an hour late.'

She grinned. That was the blissful thing about being self-employed.

'Oh, okay then. Thanks for letting me know.'

'My pleasure,' said Nat.

'In fact, just to be on the safe side, maybe we should say an hour.'

As she took his hand and led him upstairs, Hester wondered if she'd ever been happier in her life. How could she ever have thought Lucas was more of a catch than Nat?

'You'd think that woman from the travel agency would have Millie's mother's address on their computer files,' she mused idly.

Nat, pushing her gently backwards through the bedroom door and on to the rumpled bed, murmured, 'Sshh. You talk too much.'

When Millie emerged from her own bedroom forty minutes later, Hester was by the front door hurriedly dragging a brush through her hair and jamming her feet into a pair of pink Reeboks.

'You're late for work.' Millie pretended she didn't know why.

Hester winked. 'Some things are more important.'

Frowning, Millie said, 'Did I hear the doorbell earlier?'

'Oh, yeah. Your mum's off to Trinidad.'

WHAT?

Millie blinked. 'Excuse me?'

'Or Tobago. One of the two. Trinidad and Tobago, that's what it said on the front of the brochure.'

'Are you *serious*? My mother came round to tell me she's off to Trinidad and it didn't even occur to you to wake me *up*?'

Hester's eyes widened with astonishment as Millie's voice spiraled up through several octaves.

'Blimey, keep your knickers on. You sound like Bjork when you do that squeaky dolphin thing. And it wasn't your mother who was here, anyway. It was that truly lovely ex-boss of yours.'

Faintly, Millie said, 'You mean Tim Fleetwood?'

'No, you twit. That bunny-boiler wife of his.'

Oh God. Sylvia.

'What was she doing here?' squeaked Millie.

'Honestly, you aren't paying attention at all, are you? She had these brochures your mum wanted. For Trinidad and Tobago.' Hester enunciated the words slowly and carefully, since Millie was clearly having trouble keeping up. 'She needed your mum's address so she could drop them round to her, that's all. And now, thanks to you, I really am late for work. I'm off.'

As the front door slammed shut, Millie clutched her head and murmured, 'Oh shit.'

With Lloyd and Judy out of the house—having disappeared on one of their long, early-morning walks—Adele had the kitchen to herself and was enjoying a breakfast of Earl Grey tea, buttery croissants, and blackcurrant preserves. Keeping the sleeves of her lemon satin peignoir hitched up so they wouldn't trail in the butter dish, she helped herself to more tea from the pot and idly admired her new French-manicured fingernails. The phone began to ring again, but since Adele knew it wouldn't be for her at this hour of the morning, she didn't bother to answer it. She had better things to do—like think about darling Tim—than spend all her time taking down messages for Lloyd and Judy like some downtrodden secretary.

The moment the phone stopped ringing, the doorbell started. Heaving a sigh of irritation—and *almost* dropping a jammy blackcurrant down the front of her satin robe—Adele pushed her chair back and rose slowly to her feet. If it was that frightful old farmer-neighbor of Lloyd's, calling round for one of his dreary chats, she would just have to pretend not to understand a word he was saying—which, with his impenetrable Cornish accent, wasn't difficult—and shoo him away. Preferably before he trod cow muck from his dirt-encrusted wellies into the house.

Her nostrils pinched in readiness against the farmyard stench, as well as the thought of having to converse with a man who kept his trousers up with blue nylon baler twine, Adele braced herself and opened the front door.

'Are you having an affair with my husband?' demanded Sylvia Fleetwood.

Stunned, Adele took a step backwards.

'I beg your pardon?'

'You heard.'

'I'm sorry, this is ridiculous.' Adele shook her head. 'You can't turn up on someone's doorstep and start accusing them of—'

'Fine, let's put it another way. I know you're having an affair with my husband, and I'm here to tell you it's over. God, the smell of you,' spat Sylvia, her face wrinkling with revulsion. 'I searched Tim's car this morning, and it stank of your cheap scent.'

This was too much; this was insupportable. Quivering with outrage, Adele snapped back, 'It is *not* cheap, it's by Giorgio Armani.'

'And it makes me want to be sick,' sneered Sylvia. 'How dare you try and steal another woman's husband? We have a happy marriage—'

'Oh come off it,' Adele laughed mirthlessly, since the cat appeared to be well and truly out of the bag. 'He's been miserable for years.'

Sylvia shifted from one sensibly shod foot to the other, her eyes narrowing like a snake's.

'I've come to tell you that it's time you left Cornwall. If you stay, I'll make *your* life a misery, and that's a promise.'

'But I'm quite happy here. And you can't order me to leave. Just as you can't order Tim to stop seeing me,' Adele continued smoothly. 'You see, you may have spent the last twenty years bossing him around and generally treating him like some little lapdog, but he is actually a grown man capable of making his own decisions, and I think you'll find he doesn't actually *want* to stop seeing—AAARRGH!'

Adele sprang back as the liquid hurtled towards her, spraying her face before she had the chance to throw up her hands. Jesus! Jesus! Tim's wife was a madwoman! If this was bleach… or some kind of acid… oh God, this couldn't be *happening*…

Stumbling backwards, fumbling blindly for the phone in the hall, Adele whimpered, 'Dial nine-nine-nine, oh please, not my face… just dial nine-nine-nine…'

Sylvia laughed at her distress.

'You stupid bitch, look at yourself. Go on, you can open your eyes. It's not acid.'

'AAAAARRRGGH!' screamed Adele twice as loudly when she had peeled her hands away from her face. The front of her yellow satin robe was splattered with dense black liquid. It was dripping from her arms, her hands, her face, her hair. 'WHAT THE HELL HAVE YOU DONE TO ME?' she bellowed, shaking her head furiously and spraying black droplets like a wet dog.

'Given you something to think about.' Sylvia smiled with grim satisfaction. 'Not looking quite so gorgeous now, are you?'

Triumphantly she held up an empty bottle. 'Don't worry, it's only indelible ink.'

'Indelible ink? Are you MAD?' shrieked Adele, clapping her hands to her chest in horror. 'This peignoir cost two hundred and fifty *pounds*.'

◈◈◈

By the time Millie reached the house, Adele had gone.

'Your car,' Millie spluttered, as Lloyd and Judy came out to greet her.

'I know. I've never been called a whore before.' Lloyd chuckled, taking the situation in his usual easygoing stride. 'I shall be the talk of the town.'

His beautiful red Audi, parked on the driveway, had been dramatically graffitied with the words, 'TART,' 'SLUT,' and 'WHORE.'

'Your father was too lazy to walk down to the beach this morning so we set out in my car,' Judy explained. 'We saw a woman in a grey Renault as we pulled out of our lane. She must have assumed Lloyd's car belonged to Adele.'

'So Sylvia did all this before knocking on the door. Crikey, Mum must have been in a complete state.'

'By the time we got back she'd been scrubbing away in the shower for a good forty minutes. That ink isn't going to be coming off in a hurry. I can't imagine what the other people on the train back to London are going to make of your mother.' Lloyd was doing his best to keep a straight face. 'It's the hottest day of the year and she's done up like a beekeeper… black veil, long-sleeved gloves, and a hat the size of a sombrero.'

'This is all my fault,' Millie fretted. 'If I'd been awake this morning when Sylvia came round, I'd never have given her your address.'

'Oh please, will you listen to yourself?' Lloyd shook his head and tut-tutted. 'It's your mother's fault for getting herself involved with a married man in the first place.'

'So what's going to happen now? Is it all over between them?'

'She was on the phone to Tim Fleetwood before she left,' Judy said easily. 'Reading out train times and basically telling him he had twenty-four hours to leave Sylvia and join her in London.'

Millie was wide-eyed.

'Blimey, d'you think he will?'

'Well, we could only hear Adele's side of the conversation.' Judy shrugged. 'But I have to say she sounded like a mother ordering a sulky teenager to tidy his room.'

'I still can't believe it,' Millie marveled, polishing her sunglasses on the hem of her polka-dotted skirt. 'Of all the men to have an affair with. How did he ever get away from Sylvia for long enough to see my mother? I thought she had him electronically tagged.'

'He joined an evening class,' said Judy. 'Adele told me while she was packing.'

'And Sylvia didn't join up with him?' This was astounding. Every year they had enrolled for some course or other, always as a couple.

'He joined a men-only discussion group: The Role of the Male in the Twenty-First Century: Exploring Repressed Emotions.' Heroically, Judy managed to keep a straight face. 'Apparently, he told Sylvia he needed to discover his inner self. And it worked a treat, until Sylvia caught on last week. She turned up at the community center as the rest of the class was leaving and found out that Tim hadn't actually bothered to attend any of the meetings.'

Millie still felt as if she were in some way to blame. She watched as her father licked an index finger and gave the indelible felt-pen graffiti on the bonnet of his car an experimental rub.

It wasn't coming off.

'Are you going to call the police?'

'What, and have the poor woman arrested for a spot of grievous car-bodily harm?' Lloyd laughed. 'I don't think there's any need for that.'

Millie nodded at the graffiti—hardly the kind you'd want to flaunt as you drove around Cornwall.

'It's going to need a respray. That'll cost a bit.'

'My darling, look at it from my point of view.' Lloyd placed a genial arm around her shoulders. 'Thanks to Sylvia Fleetwood, my ex-wife has upped sticks and moved out, gone back to London for good. Sylvia provided the answer to my prayers. She has removed the thorn from my side.' His grey eyes crinkling at the corners, he lowered his voice and confided, 'My darling, getting the car resprayed is a small price to pay, believe me. That woman has done me a massive favor. In fact, I should probably send her red roses and a crate of champagne.'

Chapter 51

MILLIE WAS IN THE kitchen being taught by Nat how to create the perfect souffle omelette when the phone rang the following afternoon.

'... and then you fold the egg whites into the beaten yolks with a metal spoon—no, *not* a wooden one...'

'Millie, it's for you.' Hester appeared in the doorway with a ph-woarh expression on her face. 'Some gorgeous-sounding French guy, says it's très importante.'

'Excuse me.' Nat feigned despair. 'What's more très importante: some gorgeous-sounding French guy or my omelette-making masterclass?'

'Ask a silly question.' Briskly, Millie seized the phone. 'Hello?'

'Ah mademoiselle, bon soir. Per'aps you could eenform your charming friend that I am not only gorgeous-soundeeng but gorgeous-lookeeng also.'

Oh! Millie's heart began to flap about inside her rib cage like a landed haddock. This was definitely a turn-up for the books.

'He says he makes Olivier Martinez look like Quasimodo,' she told Hester, without covering the receiver. 'Then again, we only have his word for it. He could look like Quasimodo's ugly brother.'

'Ze thing ees, I need some 'elp wiz a crossword,' said Hugh. 'Seex-teen across, two words, six and three letters, cricketer found guilty.'

'D'you know what I think?' said Millie. 'I think all men should speak all the time with a French accent. It ought to be compulsory.' Shivering happily, she added, 'Caught out.'

'Hey, excellente, merci beaucoup mademoiselle. Actually,' Hugh reverted to his normal voice, 'the reason I rang was because—'

'Don't tell me, you're dying to know what I said to my mother.' Clutching the cordless phone, Millie sidled past Nat out of the kitchen. In the living room, she told Hugh what had happened.

'So there you have it,' she concluded several minutes later. 'Mum's back in London scrubbing away at her face with Comet and a Brillo pad. My dad's busy celebrating. And my mother's lover has decided not to join her because he's too much of a wet lettuce to leave his wife.'

At that moment a shriek echoed through from the kitchen, followed by a volley of giggles. 'Excuse my flatmate,' Millie sighed. 'Sounds like she's being ravished. Again.'

'How's it going with those two?'

'Oh, they're still sickeningly happy, like a couple of newlyweds. Which I'm pleased about, *of course*, but…'

'Still thinking of moving out?'

Why? Are you going to invite me to move in with you? *Really?* Wow, that'd be great!

Wisely, Millie kept this rogue fantasy to herself. Instead, she said, 'Probably. Well, it makes sense.'

'Where will you live?' said Hugh.

Huh, so not with you, obviously.

'Well, Lucas has offered me a room at his place. He says I'm welcome to stay as long as I like.'

There was a brief pause.

'And will you go?'

'I don't know.' Millie heaved another gusty sigh. 'Seems a bit ridiculous, moving out of here to get away from all the sex that's going on… and ending up at Lucas's house. Talk about jumping out of the frying pan. Still, it was kind of him to offer.'

Unlike you, Mr. Can't-take-a-hint.

'He might expect you to sleep with him.' Hugh sounded disapproving. 'As a way of saying thank you.'

'Suppose he might,' Millie agreed.

'You'd be another notch on his bedpost.'

'I'll let you in on a secret,' said Millie. 'Lucas has carved so many notches there's no actual bedpost left.'

When she hung up five minutes later, she wondered what the phone call had really been about. Was it her overactive imagination or had Hugh sounded as if he were biting his tongue, willing himself not to tell her she mustn't sleep with Lucas?

Actually, it probably was her imagination. If Hugh had something he wanted to say, in Millie's experience he generally said it.

And it wasn't as if he could be jealous, that just wasn't possible, because he'd already made it abundantly clear that he wasn't interested in being any more than friends.

Oh well, forget it. As if she'd be even remotely tempted to sleep with Lucas Kemp anyway.

Recalling the rest of their conversation yesterday, Millie marveled at Lucas's ability to get hold of completely the wrong end of the stick. Having dropped a casual inquiry about her love life into the conversation, he had shot her a knowing grin when she'd told him—perfectly truthfully—that she had no love life.

'Come on, you can tell me.' The grin had broadened and he had given Millie a persuasive nod. Gosh, he could be annoying when he wanted to be.

'I just have,' Millie repeated patiently. 'I promise you, there's nothing to tell.'

'Not what it looked like last night.' Lucas was busy proving it was possible to be both annoying and persistent. Lightly he added, 'I saw you.'

'You did? Who was I with?'

He raised a teasing eyebrow. 'You mean you can't remember?'

He could have seen her with Richard at the restaurant… Jed at the club…

'What time?' said Millie.

'Late.'

Ah. Millie felt herself going pink.

'You can trust me, you know,' Lucas went on. 'I'm very discreet.'

'Oh right, of course you are. So discreet that you announced to Hester's boyfriend that you'd slept with Hester.'

Lucas shrugged, unperturbed.

'That was just common sense. No point trying to keep something like that a secret, not when Nat's going to be working for me. Better out than in, that's what I say.'

Millie marveled at his reasoning. She vowed never *ever* to tell Lucas anything remotely private.

'Anyway. He's nobody,' she announced.

Lucas gave her a playful smile.

'So I was right.'

'About what?'

'He's married.'

Millie had looked flustered and hurriedly changed the subject, letting him think he'd hit the nail on the head. Basically, it had been the easy option.

Plus, of course, it was a lot less humiliating than having to admit the truth. That Hugh wasn't married, he simply didn't fancy her.

Come to think of it, even Jed hadn't been interested.

God, I must have as much sex appeal as soggy shredded wheat.

The kitchen was empty, the beaten egg whites slowly deflating in their glass bowl. Hester and Nat had evidently sloped off while she'd been on the phone; she could hear scuffling noises and whoops of laughter filtering down from Hester's bedroom.

Honestly, those two were a disgrace. They should be ashamed of themselves. Didn't they realize there was such a thing as too much sex?

Seeing as her masterclass in omelette making appeared to have been abandoned—thanks to the chef being made an offer he couldn't refuse—Millie found a slice of lemon cheesecake in the fridge and ate that instead. Then she picked up her car keys.

'I'm going out,' she yelled up the stairs.

The scuffling and squeals abruptly stopped.

'Okay,' Hester bawled back. 'Have fun!'

Tuh.

Orla was sunbathing by the pool when Millie arrived. Thankfully, there was no sign of Richard-the-gardener.

'Come and sit down.' Eager to hear the latest, Orla patted the indigo padded recliner next to her own. Judging by the amount of paraphernalia surrounding her, she had been out there for some time. As well as piles of glossy magazines, various notebooks, and discarded newspapers, the grass was littered with empty Coke cans, ice cream sandwich wrappers, a scattering of opened post, and several packets of chewing gum.

Orla, her red-gold hair piled up and fastened with an assortment of combs, was wearing a crocus yellow bikini and generous quantities of Ambre Solaire to protect her pale, freckled skin. Clutching her pen-top between her teeth, she balanced a notebook on her knees and scribbled down all the details as Millie relayed them.

'I'm so disappointed about Richard.' Mournfully, she shook her head. 'I really thought you two would be great together.'

'He's boring.' Slowly, Millie intoned, 'Very very very very very very very boring indeed.'

'But such a fantastic body!'

'Maybe, but having a conversation with Richard is about as interesting as watching grass grow.'

Regretfully, Orla spat out her pen-top and began chewing the arm of her sunglasses instead.

'I suppose Richard would think watching grass grow is interesting, poor lamb.'

Millie carried on bringing Orla up to date. She told her all about the flight from the restaurant with Jed and Warren—which Orla loved—and about Jed's nurse turning up at the club—which made her tut with disappointment. Orla whooped with delight upon hearing about Millie's mother and Tim Fleetwood, but not about the incident in the park, because Millie left that bit out. Then she whooped even louder when Millie mentioned in passing that Lucas had offered her a room in his house.

'Oh that would be *fantastic*.' Orla did a triumphant little jiggle on her recliner. 'Heaps of potential there, just imagine! You and Lucas—this is so great—darling, you *have* to do it.'

'I don't know.' Millie pulled a face. 'I'm not sure.'

'Come on! I've got a book to write here… stuff needs to start happening,' Orla protested. 'At this rate, all my readers are going to die of boredom. They need a will-she-won't-she situation to capture their interest, they want a man they can drool over—and let's face it, Lucas fits the bill perfectly. He is a bit of a god!'

'He's a wicked, unscrupulous ex-DJ with no morals and a one-track mind.' Since he also had a sense of humor, Millie felt sure Lucas wouldn't object to this description of him. 'He's incapable of staying faithful to one woman,' she went on, 'and he doesn't care who he hurts. All Lucas cares about is no-strings sex.'

'All the better.' Orla flashed a naughty smile. Just because she was writing a 'proper' novel to impress the critics didn't mean it couldn't have any shenanigans going on in it. Even reviewers as plug-ugly as Christie Carson were entitled to some form of love life.

Not much of one. Just a bit.

'But I don't *want* to have sex with Lucas,' Millie protested.

'Darling, the trouble with you is, you don't want to have sex with anyone.'

Oh I do, I do, Millie thought with a stab of longing.

'Not even Con Deveraux,' Orla went on despairingly. 'I mean, how could you not like Con? What was *wrong* with him?'

You mean apart from the fact that he fancied Lucas?

'Nothing,' Millie sighed. 'Except he's in America. Look, I'm really sorry, I did warn you I was boring.'

But Orla wasn't listening, she had already swung her legs over the edge of the recliner and was busy rummaging amongst the assorted letters and discarded envelopes on the grass. Having found what she was looking for, she seized a stiff, white card and waved it triumphantly at Millie.

Millie flinched out of sheer habit. God, what had Orla done now—signed her up for membership of some singles club?

She wouldn't put anything past her.

'Sorted.' Orla was looking smug.

Peering at the card with suspicion, Millie said, 'What is it?'

'Next weekend. A big book awards ceremony in London. Great fun and extremely glitzy. See?' Orla pointed to the embossed lettering. 'It says Orla Hart plus guest. Of course Giles always used to be my "plus guest," but this time I can invite you instead. We'll have the most fabulous time, I promise! I'll introduce you to everyone I know and, out of eight hundred or so guests, you're bound to see someone who takes your fancy. Plus,' Orla rattled on, as excited as a child by her brilliant plan, 'you never know, I may even have an extra surprise for you!'

Her eyes had lit up as she rejoiced in her own cleverness. It didn't take a genius to work out that Orla had flipped through her mental file of eligible males and come up with another contender in the make-it-happen-for-Millie stakes. She was evidently going to matchmake successfully if it killed her.

'I don't want to be a party pooper,' said Millie, 'but I'm working next weekend. Retirement do for one of the keepers at Paignton Zoo. Honestly,' she protested, as Orla's eyes narrowed with suspicion. Scrabbling in her bag, she hauled out her diary. 'See? Sunday afternoon, three o'clock sharp outside the monkey house.'

Having snatched the diary from her, Orla broke into a broad smile.

'No problem, Cinders, you shall go to the book awards. I was referring to the weekend in its broadest sense—they're actually being held on Thursday night. And on Thursday night,' she jabbed triumphantly at the relevant empty page, 'you are free.'

Millie gave in with good grace. A trip to London might be just what she needed to take her mind off Hugh. Looking on the bright side, it wasn't beyond the realms of possibility that she might meet her perfect man at a book awards ceremony in a top London hotel.

A *swanky* hotel, even.

While they were enjoying a *slap-up* meal.

Maybe even *munching* it.

Hmm. Taking her mind off Hugh was evidently going to be easier said than done.

'So that's a date,' Orla announced, pleased with herself. 'I'll book us into the hotel. In fact, no time like the present…'

'Something's missing.' Millie found herself peering suspiciously at Orla as she made the call. It wasn't until the rooms had been booked and Orla had leaned over to slide the mobile phone back under the sun-lounger that she suddenly twigged. 'You *smell* different.'

It sounded mad, but it was true. Orla smelt of Ambre Solaire and minty chewing gum, mingled with a dash of Rive Gauche.

She didn't reek of stale cigarettes.

Millie, her tone accusing, said, 'You've given up smoking!' As she spoke, her gaze dropped instinctively to the grass, which would normally be littered with Marlboro packets, a couple of lighters, and numerous stubbed-out fag ends. 'I don't believe it—when did this happen?'

'Five days ago.' Orla's eyes glittered with pride. 'Isn't it amazing? And I'm feeling fantastic! The first day was pretty hellish of course, but it's so much easier already, I can't understand why I didn't do it years ago. Well,' she amended with a lopsided smile, 'actually, I can.'

Millie could too.

'Let me guess. You were married to Giles.'

'That's it! I really think that was it,' Orla exclaimed. 'I mean, I know he didn't physically force me to smoke, but I was just so on-edge all the time, having another cigarette was the only way of calming myself down.' She spread her arms wide, clearly dazzled by the simplicity of the solution. 'Now I don't have Giles any more, I'm a million times more relaxed, and I don't even *need* a cigarette. Honestly, it's like being a born-again Christian, I just want to run up to people in the street and tell them how completely brilliant it is not to smoke. In fact, every time I even *see* someone smoking I want to rip the cigarette out of their fingers and tell them how disgusting and pathetic they are!'

Orla was in the grip of acute post-nicotine euphoria, where the novelty of not smoking hadn't yet worn off. Millie, who had seen it all before, dutifully nodded and pretended to be impressed. She recognized the symptoms only too well. Throughout her growing-up years, her father had been the same, binning his cigarettes with a flourish and waxing evangelical on the evils of addiction for... ooh, about a fortnight, generally, before getting bored and taking up smoking once more.

It had taken him fifteen goes at least before he'd finally managed to give up for good.

'... and sometimes I just want to bury their faces in a filthy old ashtray and say, "See? See? *That's* what you smell like!" I know I mustn't,' Orla conceded with reluctance, 'because I'd probably end up getting arrested or punched on the nose or something, but honestly, these people have no idea how much damage they're doing to their bodies—'

'What's this doing here?' Hastily, Millie picked up the proof copy of Christie Carson's novel. Anything to get Orla off the subject of cigarettes. 'I thought you'd written your review.'

The paperback proof copy was now dog-eared and distinctly battered, and she was baffled as to why Orla would have brought it out to the garden. Unless she'd been using it to kill wasps.

'I know, I know. I just felt like reading it again.' Orla looked shamefaced. 'Christie Carson might be a complete pig, but his book's actually quite good.'

Chapter 52

'OH, HI, COME ON in. He isn't here,' said Sasha when Millie arrived at Lucas's house the next morning. 'He's gone over to the restaurant to bully the electricians. Stick the kettle on if you fancy a cup of tea.'

Millie followed her into the kitchen, trying not to stare at Sasha's glorious curves. A statuesque platinum blonde in a white bikini was an arresting sight under any circumstances. The fact that Sasha was carefully ironing her nun's habit made it even more of a showstopper.

'I just popped over to check the bookings for next week.' Millie filled the kettle as she spoke. While her future living arrangements remained undecided, the business was still being run from Lucas's house.

'They're fine. See for yourself.' Sasha jerked her head in the direction of the pine dresser, where the bookings diary lay open. 'I've been manning the phone. I checked that Eric could manage Truro on Monday. I've drafted an ad to go in the local paper for someone to replace Lucas. Now there's an audition to look forward to,' she deadpanned. 'Oh, and I've fitted in another booking for you as well.'

Contrary to appearances, Sasha was fantastically efficient. Marveling at the way she flipped the immaculately pressed nun's habit off the ironing board and on to a padded hanger, Millie said, 'Doesn't it bother you that Lucas sleeps with other women?'

Heavens, she hadn't meant it to come out quite that abruptly. But it was something that had been puzzling her for months. And it wasn't as if Lucas made any secret of the fact; he often discussed his exploits in front of Sasha.

'No.' Sasha looked amused. 'Why?'

'Well, look at you! You could have anyone you want. And here you are living with Lucas who *does* have anyone he wants. I mean, don't you think you deserve better?'

'Millie, are you serious? Lucas and I aren't a couple! I have my own room here.' Sasha gestured at the ceiling. 'I pay him rent. Okay, we slept together a few times when we first met, but it didn't take long for both of us to realize we were better off as friends. Nowadays Lucas does his thing and I do mine. In fact,' she added with a grin, 'there's someone I've been seeing quite a lot of recently. He's a lawyer in Truro. And Lucas is fine about it. But I can't believe that all this time you actually thought we were an item. That's just too funny for words!'

Millie couldn't believe it either. Yet again, she'd managed to get hold of the wrong end of the stick. Sasha had looked the part and she'd simply jumped to conclusions, assumed they were living together like a proper couple.

'I'm such an idiot,' she said humbly.

'And you've spent all this time feeling sorry for me. That is so sweet of you! Although I daresay Lucas perpetuated the myth—he does like to uphold this image he has of himself.'

'Well, yes, he did drop the occasional hint.'

'Shall I let you into a secret?' The comers of Sasha's generous mouth twitched with mischief. 'Lucas doesn't sleep with nearly as many girls as he makes out. He's actually far pickier than you'd imagine.'

'You're kidding!' Now this *was* hard to believe.

'I'm not. It's true.' Sasha raised an eyebrow. 'Of course, his bad-boy reputation would be in tatters if this got out, so you mustn't breathe a word to anyone. But in his own way, our Lucas is quite a gentleman.'

'Gentleman,' Millie echoed faintly.

'He has more morals than most men I know.'

'Morals.' Fainter still.

'I know it's come as a terrible shock. Why don't you sit down?' said Sasha kindly. 'You're looking pale.'

Clutching the appointments diary, Millie slumped on to one of the high kitchen stools.

'It's like discovering that Father Christmas doesn't exist.'

'I'm sorry I've shattered your illusions. I'll make us that cup of tea.'

'Oh bum,' cried Millie as Sasha flung teabags into mugs and broke open a fresh packet of custard creams. 'You've booked me in for Thursday.'

'Hmm? Is that a problem?' Humming happily to herself, Sasha glanced over her shoulder. Millie had been checking through the diary.

'I can't do Thursday. I'm in London.'

'Oh. Doesn't say that anywhere. You should have let me know.'

She was absolutely right. Gloomily Millie said, 'I only found out yesterday.'

The booking was for her to appear at Polperro village hall at eight o'clock on Thursday evening, where a local family were holding a surprise party to celebrate the return of a brother who had emigrated years before to Australia. For a change, they'd composed a poem that was actually witty.

Mentally crossing her fingers, Millie looked up.

'You couldn't do it, could you?'

Sasha plonked a mug of tea down on the table and flicked the attached poem-sheet with a magenta fingernail, revealing the rest of the writing on the page beneath.

'Sorry, big Royal National Lifeboat Institution bash on Thursday night. I'm booked to do my naughty nun.' She winked, lit a cigarette, and did a lascivious wiggle by way of demonstration. 'And I can't let down our brave lifeboatmen, can I?'

Millie groaned.

'You could always ask Eric,' Sasha suggested.

Millie pulled a face. Eric the history teacher specialized in comedy kissograms. His Full Monty went down a storm with raucous women of a certain age who enjoyed a good laugh. Which was just as well, seeing as Eric—bless him—weighed fifteen stone and, minus his clothes, looked like a gyrating strawberry blancmange.

Millie, who weighed half that, sighed and said, 'They want a gorilla. He'd never fit into the suit.'

'In that case, you'll just have to cancel the booking.' Unconcerned, Sasha blew a smoke ring and slid the phone across the counter.

The contact number was there in the diary. To her shame, Millie realized that a fortnight ago she would have rung and canceled without a qualm. But now that Lucas had offered her the job of running the business, her conscience wouldn't allow it. Letting people down smacked of inefficiency. It was deeply unprofessional.

Which meant, basically, that she was left with two choices. Either find someone else to step into the breach on Thursday night or cancel her own plans and do the job herself.

'Do you want me to phone them?' offered Sasha. 'I could tell them you've been rushed to hospital with appendicitis.'

Decisions, decisions. It was still tempting.

'No, it's okay.' Millie pushed the phone firmly out of reach. 'I'll sort something out.'

At six o'clock that evening, half-way round the supermarket, Millie heard a voice she recognized and promptly stopped dead in her tracks.

'No no *no*, you've picked up the quick-cook pasta by mistake. We prefer the normal kind, remember?'

It was Sylvia Fleetwood's voice, coming from the next aisle along. Unable to resist it, Millie skulked to the end of her own aisle and prepared to peer round into Sylvia's.

'Now, olive oil. Virgin, darling? Or extra-virgin? Which do you think we should go for? Ooh, and we mustn't forget the ciabatta.'

Feeling very *Charlie's Angels*, Millie sidled past a towering display of tinned tomato puree and spied on Sylvia and Tim, whose backs were towards her.

'The extra-virgin, I think,' Tim decided, having carefully weighed up the merits of each in turn. 'It costs more, but the flavor's infinitely superior.'

Sylvia was nodding in agreement. 'You're right, Timmy. Definitely the extra-virgin. We do prefer the flavor, don't we?'

'We do, darling, we do. Right, bread next. Are you sure about the ciabatta or shall we try the focaccia for a change?'

'Focaccia's fine by me,' Sylvia crooned happily. 'Infact, we may as well get a large one, you know how hungry we always are after our round of golf.'

Millie slipped away before they turned and saw her. Sylvia and Tim were back in the old routine, as if the hiccup that had been her mother had never happened. A dash of excitement had been more than enough for Tim, it seemed. He would never leave Sylvia and the endless comforting routines of their marriage.

Nat gazed with satisfaction around him at the gleaming kitchen, now freshly repainted and fully equipped with the tools of his trade. The pristine white walls were hung with aluminum pans and every cooking implement known to man. The pale grey tiled floor was spotless, as were the stainless-steel ovens. Within the next day or two they would begin stocking up the glass-fronted cupboards with supplies. The first menus, both set and à la carte, had already been agreed upon. In less than a fortnight, Kemp's would open for business.

You had to give Lucas his due—when it came to getting things done, he didn't hang about.

Opening the linen cupboard and running his hand down over the neatly stacked piles of marigold orange tablecloths and napkins, Nat wondered if he'd ever been happier in his life. And basically, he hadn't. Everything was coming together now; he had the job of his dreams and the girl of his dreams. He also knew—without a shadow of a doubt—that he and Lucas were going to make a terrific team.

Through the swing doors, propped open to dispel the smell of fresh paint, Nat heard Hester laughing at some comment Lucas had made. They got on like a house on fire nowadays. Smiling to himself, Nat marveled at the irony of the situation.

Lucas Kemp was a man you could trust.

Nat made his way through to the dining room to find Hester wobbling on top of a stepladder, tweaking the last of the curtain pelmets into place.

'Excellent,' Lucas pronounced, turning to grin at Nat. 'I'll say this, your girlfriend knows how to hang a mean curtain.'

Proudly, Hester took a bow.

'I am the queen of curtain-hanging. So, what's the verdict?'

'Fantastic.' Having helped her down from the stepladder, Nat moved back to take a proper look. The room had been transformed in the past week. Out had gone the atrocious flower prints and hideous ruffles and flounces. In their place, the walls had been painted marigold orange and amethyst blue, great swathes of color glowing jewel-like against a white background. The patterned carpet had been ripped out too, revealing scuffed floorboards beneath. Now, thanks to an industrial sander and several coats of honey varnish, the wood gleamed with a life of its own. The paintings on the wall were modern, individual, and expertly lit. A talking-point chandelier by a local artist hung from the ceiling, chunks of violet and orange glass swaying and glittering in the sunlight. The marigold curtains needed tie-backs to stop them flapping about in the breeze from the open sash-windows.

'Completely fantastic,' Nat amended.

'Especially the curtains.' Hester gave him an encouraging prod.

'Oh, goes without saying. Especially the curtains.'

'Doesn't matter how great the place looks,' Lucas pronounced. 'The food's the important thing. Not too many people are going to say, "Ooh, I know, let's go back to that place where the food was rubbish but they had those really great curtains."'

Nat grinned. 'The food in this restaurant is going to be even better than the curtains.'

Having heard a car drawing up outside, Lucas glanced at his watch. Great, the computer chap was here on time.

Chapter 53

As he pulled open the front door, Lucas recognized him in an instant. Well, well. He smiled his easiest smile and stuck out his hand.

'Hi. I'm Lucas Kemp. Thanks for coming over.'

This was going to be interesting. Quite a coincidence too, the computer expert Fogarty and Phelps had recommended to him turning out to be Millie's bloke. The one she so vehemently denied being involved with.

'Hugh Emerson.' He was smiling too, looking completely relaxed as he shook hands. Lucas checked for a wedding ring. There wasn't one, but that didn't mean anything. Privately, he was still convinced Hugh Emerson had to be married.

Lucas didn't approve of extra-marital affairs. Why bother to get married if all you were interested in doing was cheating on your wife? And what did Millie think she was playing at? How could she have been silly enough to get involved with someone else's husband in the first place?

He had, nevertheless, been struck by the evident strength of feeling between the two of them. No doubt about it, this was no casual fling.

Basically, Millie was in big trouble. One way or another it would end in—

'Hugh! Good grief, what are *you* doing here?' Hester let out a high-pitched shriek of delight and Lucas found himself barreled out of the way as she greeted Millie's lover with an enthusiastic hug and a kiss.

Even Hugh Emerson looked momentarily taken aback.

'He's going to be designing the restaurant's website.' Casually Lucas added, 'So you two know each other?'

It was a rhetorical question, obviously.

'We certainly do! Millie and I both know Hugh.' Hester gave Hugh Emerson's arm a squeeze as she spoke. 'We're great friends, aren't we?'

More and more interesting, thought Lucas, observing the flicker of reaction in Hugh's dark eyes at the mention of Millie's name. Interesting that Hester hadn't added, 'And of course, Hugh and Millie are having *the* most rip-roaring affair.'

More to the point, Hester didn't even appear to be *thinking* it. Millie had evidently chosen not to confide in her best friend.

Which in turn made Lucas wonder whether, maybe, Hester was on friendly terms with Hugh's wife.

Jesus, this was like being trapped in an episode of *Coronation Street.*

'Why d'you want a website?' said Hester, as Hugh and Lucas sat down at the computer.

'Customers like to be able to see a restaurant before they use it for the first time.' Hugh was rolling up the sleeves of his white shirt and loosening his tie. He slid a CD into the machine. 'We can give them all the information they need, from a list of available tables to that day's specials. They can book online and read the reviews posted up by other diners. Fogarty and Phelps have increased their turnover by four hundred and fifty percent since setting up their website. Okay now, I'll just run through a few of my preliminary ideas. I don't think a webcam's viable, by the way.' He glanced briefly at Lucas. 'Too many men scared stiff of getting caught out having dinner with their secretaries. Anyone up to no good would avoid the place like the plague.'

He was right, of course. Lucas, who hadn't thought of that,

decided that this was because he, unlike Hugh Emerson, wasn't a cheating husband.

Correction: a lying, cheating, no-good *bastard.*

Leaning back on his chair he said casually, 'Are you married?'

Behind them, Lucas heard Hester's speedy intake of breath. Hmm, evidently a touchy subject.

Hugh's dark eyes remained fixed on the flickering computer screen.

'Me? No.'

So why had Hester gasped?

Shaking his head in self-deprecating fashion, Lucas said lightly, 'I must be losing my touch. I'd have bet money you were a married man.'

Hester didn't suck in her breath this time, she let out a wail of dismay.

'God, Lucas, you're such a pillock sometimes! How can you be so *insensitive*? Hugh was married but his wife died, okay? And the last thing he needs is to be interrogated by a complete dumbbell asking *stupid* questions!'

Twisting round, amused by the expression of outrage on Hester's face, Hugh said, 'It's fine, really.'

'It's not fine, it must be *awful* for you,' Hester protested.

'Look, all he did was ask if I was married. It's a reasonable question. He didn't know. And if it makes you feel better, I promise I'm not about to burst into tears. Which,' Hugh added, 'is what most people are terrified might happen should they accidentally mention anything to do with death or dying.' He broke into a grin, as if remembering something. 'In fact, Millie did it, the first time we met. She worked herself up into a complete state and I hadn't even noticed what she'd been saying.'

Lucas wasn't slow. It had taken him less than a second, following Hester's outburst, to make the connection. Hugh Emerson was Millie's Dropped-Wallet-man. It all fit together now.

Or rather, most of it did.

'I'm sorry about your wife. How long ago?'

'Ten months.' Hugh was getting into the files, his hand expertly whisking the mouse to and fro, clicking on various icons.

'Something like that must knock you for six,' Lucas remarked. 'I can't imagine how you begin to get through it.' He paused. 'If it's not a rude question, are you involved with anyone else yet?'

'Oh for God's sake,' Hester exploded, incensed by such monumental lack of tact. 'Just because you can't imagine going without a shag for more than a week! Lucas, you moron, not everyone else is as obsessed as you are with sex. Hugh was *happily married*, can't you understand that? Of course he isn't involved with anyone else yet!'

Lucas was listening to Hester's outburst—actually, she was magnificent when she was angry—but he kept his gaze fixed on Hugh's profile. Blink and you would have missed it, but Lucas hadn't blinked.

And the brief, giveaway flicker in his eyes told him all he needed to know.

'It's too soon,' Hugh agreed, before pointing at the screen. 'Right, here we are. See what you think about the layout of what I've done so far.'

They spent an hour going over all aspects of the proposed website. Nat had disappeared back into his beloved kitchen and Hester, press-ganged into helping out, was hunched over a sunny window table busily compiling a list of must-haves to attend the opening night. Around two hundred guests were being invited for canapes, champagne, and maximum press coverage.

By the time Hugh closed down the computer, Hester had scribbled down a hundred or so names.

'Your old boss from the radio station—I can't remember his name,' she announced, tapping her pen against the list.

Lucas winked.

'Shouldn't think he can either, the amount of white powder he's shoveled up his nose. We'll ask his secretary instead—Gloria pretty much runs the station these days.' Taking the list from Hester, he swiftly added a few more names. 'Orla Hart, Fogarty and Phelps. And Hugh, of course.'

'Excellent decision,' said Hugh. 'Otherwise, I'd be forced to completely sabotage your appointments system.'

'Representatives from all the local papers,' Lucas went on. 'The president of the golf club and his fat wife.' He paused. 'My grandparents.'

Hester burst out laughing.

'Fancy you having grandparents! What are they like?'

'Brilliant.'

'And how do they feel about having you as a grandson?' Hester glanced mischievously at his black leather trousers. 'I bet your sweet little old granny spends all her time knitting, desperately trying to convert you to Fair Isle tank tops.'

'My sweet little old granny,' said Lucas, 'could drink you under the table. She can also ski better than any of us, drive faster than us, and fly her own plane.'

It was Hugh's turn to laugh.

'I'm serious. And she's a crack shot. They're incredible, the pair of them,' Lucas told him. 'She still paints professionally. My grandfather's retired from the RAF but he's rebuilding an old Spitfire in a hangar in the back garden. Actually, theirs is a great story,' he went on. 'Grandad's first wife was killed in a bombing raid during the war. He was devastated. Five months later he met this dazzling eighteen-year-old, Zillah, and fell head over heels in love with her. He was appalled, disgusted with himself, thought everyone would accuse him of never having really loved his wife—no respect for the dead, and all that—so he finished with Zillah and went back to flying Spitfires. This was nineteen forty-four and you didn't know what would happen from one day to the next. Anyway, he came back from a mission several weeks later, drove up to a party at the Savoy, saw Zillah dancing with another officer, and realized there and then that she was the girl for him. Sod what anyone else might think. He had to marry her. And two weeks later,' Lucas concluded with a brief smile, 'he did.'

'And Zillah was your grandmother?' Hester was enthralled.

'She still is. That was fifty-six years ago and theirs is the happiest marriage I know. In fact,' Lucas said dryly, 'they're entirely to blame for the fact that I'm still single. I vowed years ago that until I felt like that about somebody, I wouldn't get married. And here I am,' he shrugged, 'still trawling my way through the female population in search of the perfect wife. Ah well, it's a tough job but somebody has to do it.'

Hester's eyes were bright. 'It's like one of those old black and white films, so romantic it makes you want to cry. Lucas, that is a fantastic story.'

Certainly is, thought Lucas. It'd be even more fantastic if it was true.

Glancing at Hugh, who was sliding a CD back into its sleeve, he announced, 'Films that make you cry are strictly a girl thing. Give me a decent thriller any day. Now, you haven't even seen over the rest of the place yet. Why don't we give you the guided tour?'

Hugh couldn't believe he was about to do what he was about to do. After visiting Kemp's restaurant yesterday evening, he had been seized by a compulsion to rush straight over to Millie's house and tell her how he felt about her. Just turn up and blurt it all out.

But common sense had taken him to one side and warned him that this was something he needed to think through. Very thoroughly indeed. Common sense had also told him that Lucas Kemp hadn't been entirely truthful with them; Hester might have fallen for it, but

Hugh suspected the majority of the touching story they'd been told was pure fiction.

Nevertheless, he was grateful. It had taken him long enough to arrive at the same conclusion. It was nice to know that Lucas agreed, and approved.

But this time, Hugh knew he had to be absolutely sure he was doing the right thing. As a result, he had spent a sleepless night, tossing and turning, examining his conscience, playing over and over in his mind the events of the past months, planning what he would say to Millie *should* he decide to do it. At least he'd overcome the fear that lightning could strike twice. Before, he had been determined never to fall in love again because the prospect of losing someone else would be too much to bear. But as time had passed, he'd realized this was no way to live. There was an element of risk—however small—in everything. You just had to accept that and get on with it. Besides, it was no longer an issue because he simply couldn't imagine life without Millie...

At six o'clock in the morning he had finally fallen asleep. In fact, he had slept until four o'clock in the afternoon, which was one of the advantages of being self-employed, but bad news for those clients waiting for him to come up with the work they were paying him to do.

By five-thirty Hugh's mind was made up. Irrevocably. This was it. No going back. Lucas had been right; when it happened, it happened. You couldn't risk losing something this important. Even if the thought of doing it—and possibly being rejected—was scarier than he had imagined possible.

And now it was six-thirty and he was actually here, turning into the road where Millie lived. Pulling up outside Millie's house.

Switching off the engine, Hugh observed his hands shaking. This was definitely scary. Worse than sitting finals. Worse than preparing to bungee jump off a tower block. Worse than... well, pretty much anything.

Feeling sick, he checked his appearance in the rearview mirror. Jesus, *just like a girl.* Still, it gave him something to do. And this was one of those moments that could only be improved by the knowledge that you didn't have a bit of spinach caught between your front teeth.

Okay. Hair, same as ever.

Face, still there.

Teeth, no spinach. Which wasn't altogether surprising, seeing as he never ate the filthy stuff.

Aftershave, yes.

Too much aftershave? Hope not.

Deep breath.

Another deep breath.

All this gearing himself up, and Millie might not even be at home.

But she was, he knew she was. There, parked just across the street, was her lime green Mini with its almost-expired tax disc and a jaunty pink sun hat perched on the back shelf.

Right. You can either sit here all evening like a complete dickhead or get on with it.

Hugh opened the car and stepped out on to the dusty pavement.

Remember the last time you were here, standing outside Millie's front door, wanting more than anything to kiss her and telling yourself you mustn't?

Well, now he knew he must.

Raising his hand, he knocked on the door.

Moments later, the door swung open.

Millie was wearing her gorilla suit; she must be on her way out to a job. Hugh realized that he was glad; saying what he had to say to a girl dressed as a gorilla might be unconventional, but not being able to see the expression on her face actually made it easier.

Not easy. But easier. Just a bit.

'Okay, let me just say this.' Hugh held up his hands because Millie was breaking into a little dance and this was the kind of distraction he didn't need.

Obediently she stopped and tilted her head inquiringly to one side.

Here we go.

'Right then. The thing is, I've been a complete idiot. I panicked after that night when we… you know. I panicked because I realized how I felt about you and that wasn't supposed to happen. I knew I couldn't *let* it happen. I've treated you so badly and I didn't mean to… dammit, you wouldn't believe how many times I've rehearsed this, and it's coming out all wrong.' Hugh shook his head, sweat prickling the back of his neck. 'Look, I just want to say sorry for everything and… I love you. I mean, really love you. If you think you can forgive me for everything I've put you through, maybe we can try again. Properly, this time.' Shit, this wasn't easy at all. Raking back his hair, he concluded, 'And if you can't forgive me, please feel free to slam the door in my face.'

There, he'd done it. Told a gorilla he loved her. It was all out in the open now. In her hands.

Well, hairy paws.

Filled with trepidation, Hugh watched as the paws went up to remove the gorilla's head. There was a ripping sound as the velcro attaching it to the neck of the suit was wrenched apart.

The head came off and he was greeted with a broad smile.

'This is really great, and I can't tell you how flattered I am,' Hester said cheerfully, 'but I'm actually very happy with Nat.'

Chapter 54

'You'd better come in,' Hester said kindly. 'Before you pass out on the pavement.'

Having just crammed fifty years' worth of mortification into five seconds, it occurred to Hugh that passing out on the pavement might be the most desirable option. Seeing as there was no sign of a big hole conveniently opening up.

But since passing out clearly wasn't going to happen either, he followed Hester into the living room.

'Sit down.' Solicitously, she patted the back of the sofa. 'Now, can I get you something? Cup of tea, glass of nice cold lemonade?' Fractional pause. 'Great big bucket of Scotch?'

Hester was struggling hard to keep a straight face. She was having the time of her life, Hugh realized, extracting maximum enjoyment from the situation.

In other words, taking the piss. To be fair, he couldn't blame her.

'Come on, cheer up.' Hester broke into a huge, irreverent grin. 'In years to come, we'll be able to laugh about this. Well, you will,' she happily amended. 'I'm laughing about it already.'

All the buckets of Scotch in the world weren't going to help him now.

'Can I ask you something?' Hugh gestured to her costume. 'Why are you wearing Millie's gorilla suit?'

'I'm her stand-in. Millie had a job booked for tonight. She couldn't make it, so she asked me to do it instead. Can I ask you a question now? How long has this thing between you and Millie been going on? And why haven't I heard a word about it? And what *did* you do, exactly, that was so terrible?'

Hugh sighed. 'That's three questions.'

'No problem. I don't have to be at Polperro until eight, so we've got plenty of time.' As she spoke, Hester unzipped the suit and wiggled out of it, brushed a few moulting nylon hairs from her Faith No More T-shirt, and plonked herself companionably down beside him on the sofa. 'I was only trying it on to get the feel of it. When the doorbell went I thought I'd give Nat a surprise. Now, take a deep breath and relax.' Her tone was soothing but her eyes danced with glee. 'You'll feel a million times better once you've told me everything, I promise.'

Hugh ignored this blatant lie.

'Where's Millie?'

'In the kitchen.'

'*What?*'

'Only joking.' Triumphantly, Hester mimicked his look of horror. 'Up in London. Orla was invited to some big party. She didn't want to go on her own, apparently, so she dragged Millie along with her.'

'What kind of big party?'

'God knows. Some kind of awards ceremony, I think Millie said. They're staying up there for a couple of days, but she'll definitely be back by Sunday lunchtime because she's got a booking on Sunday afternoon. Anyway, that's enough about that.' In schoolmistressy fashion, Hester tapped his arm. 'You still have some serious explaining to do. And what I especially want to know is when did all this start?'

Hugh closed his eyes; he was in an impossible situation here. If he told Hester to mind her own business, she could spoil everything for him. With Millie away for the next three nights, she was bound to phone Hester from London at some stage. And Hester would take ghoulish delight in telling her what had happened here this evening.

No, no, he couldn't let that happen. He'd messed up enough of this relationship already. Okay, it might not *literally* be the end of the world if Hester spoke to Millie first, but after so much had gone wrong, it was important to at least get this part right.

I should be the one to tell her, not Hester. Dammit, thought Hugh, I *have* to be the one to tell her.

Shit, he needed to get Hester on his side. He was going to have to appeal to her better nature.

If she had one.

This was definitely one of life's major dilemmas, Hugh decided. Like being confronted by a ravenous grizzly bear and wondering if throwing it one of your arms would be enough.

'The night of Orla's party,' he finally admitted.

'You're kidding! And did you and Millie sleep together?'

Oh now, this was outrageous. Ravenous grizzly bear or no grizzly bear, he wasn't going to answer that question.

Unfortunately, not answering told Hester all she needed to know.

'You DID,' she whooped, bouncing around on the sofa like a two-year-old. 'You really did! So *that's* why she said I needn't pay her two hundred pounds for losing our Celibet. By the time I had sex with Lucas she'd already done it with you… and I thought she was being so nice, letting me off. Can you believe I actually thanked her? Honestly, that girl is a complete tart!'

'It only happened once.'

'Doesn't matter. A bet's a bet.'

'And then I panicked. Thinking of my wife. After Louisa died, I swore I'd never get involved with anyone again.'

Hester stopped gloating and gave him a sympathetic look.

'But that's not realistic.'

'I can see that now. But there are certain unwritten rules.' Hugh shrugged. 'Like yesterday at the restaurant when you got mad with Lucas, just because he asked me if I was involved with anyone else. You were outraged at the very idea, remember?'

'I was mad with Lucas because I thought *you'd* be outraged by the idea!' Hester exclaimed. 'That's not the same thing at all! Asking someone if they've met someone else yet when they haven't is horrible. But there's absolutely nothing wrong with it if they have.'

'Well, I was pretty disgusted with myself.' He shook his head. 'I thought it was too soon. Disrespectful and all that. I dropped Millie like a hot potato, couldn't even bring myself to explain why. And I tried my best to forget her. But I couldn't. The feelings just refused to go away. Basically, the last couple of months have been pretty hellish.'

'But you can't help how you feel!' Hester spoke with passion. 'Some people lose their partners and it takes them twenty years to find someone else. And there are others who find someone in twenty *weeks*. I mean, look at—'

'I know,' Hugh interjected with a brief smile. 'Lucas's grandparents.' He wasn't going to be the one to tell her Lucas had more than likely made the whole story up.

'*Exactly*. God, this is fantastic.' Hester clasped her hands together in delight. 'You and Millie. It's perfect! Ooh, and she said she'd probably ring me tomorrow—just wait until she hears about this!'

Shit.

He'd ripped his own arm off for nothing. The grizzly bear was going to eat him alive after all.

'No. *No!*' Hugh kept his voice level. 'Hester, you mustn't do that. This is between Millie and me. If she phones, you have to promise me you won't breathe a word.'

Hester's face fell. He watched it happen, like a lift with severed cables plummeting to earth.

'I'm serious,' he said. 'Very serious indeed.'

Finally, she managed a brave-little-soldier nod.

'Of course. I understand. You're absolutely right. I won't tell Millie anything.' She shook her head with such vigor her emerald green parrot earrings bounced off the sides of her neck. For added emphasis she mimed zipping her mouth shut.

Her great big blabbermouth, Hugh reminded himself, wondering if it might not be simpler to superglue it shut.

Illegal. But tempting.

He gave it one last shot. 'Do you promise?'

In reply, Hester gave him her most trustworthy—in other words, not trustworthy at all—Cheshire-cat smile.

'Absolutely. Definitely. You can rely on me, I *promise*.'

Hugh wondered why he wasn't reassured.

The Royal Lancaster was the poshest hotel Millie had ever stayed at. Actually, apart from a dreary little boarding house masquerading as a hotel in Blackpool where she'd once spent a dirty weekend with an accountant called Kevin, it was the only hotel she'd ever stayed at. And it was turning out to be a completely thrilling experience. Hot water shot out of the taps at such a rate that she'd had two baths already. Her room was vast, six times the size of her bedroom at home. And the view over Hyde Park and Kensington Gardens was stunning.

Feeling like a yokel up from the sticks—which, of course, she *was*—Millie pressed her nose to the window, marveling at the red double-decker buses trundling along the busy road below, as well as the sheer number of black cabs zipping past. It was so completely different from Cornwall. Apart from a few brief visits to her mother, she had never spent any real time here. Thanks to Adele, who regarded it as hopelessly common, she'd never even done any proper sightseeing.

Well, it was about time she did.

I might decide I love it enough to move here, thought Millie, feeling reckless. Maybe a change of scenery is just what I need.

Because basically, now that Hester was settled with Nat, she was going to have to find somewhere else to live anyway. And apart from her job—which was, after all, *only* a job—there was precious little to keep her in Newquay. It wasn't as if her father and Judy were likely to slip into a Victorian decline.

Plus, moving away would hopefully take her mind off Hugh. Because, let's face it, all this bumping into him and just-being-friends simply wasn't working out. It was hard to cope with. Falling in love with someone who didn't love you back was the pits. And if she stayed in Newquay, they would only keep bumping into each other.

Whereas if she moved up here, she could get on with making a new life for herself. With a bit of luck, her memory would be wiped clean of him, like turning the wheel on an Etch-a-Sketch. In a couple of months, she might wake up one morning and think, Hugh? Hugh *who*?

Ooh, look at that black cab doing a U-turn right in front of that truck! The taxi drivers in this city drove like demons, they just—

'Millie, it's me! Ready to go?'

Millie raced barefoot across the pale carpet—so thick and springy it was like bouncing on a trampoline—and flung open the door.

'My God!' she exclaimed. 'What happened? You look *awful*.'

Orla grinned, because she knew she didn't. Her eyes sparkled, her pre-Raphaelite curls tumbled past her shoulders, and she was poured into a memorably low-cut dress of sea green shot-silk that shimmered every time she moved.

'I know, I'm a complete disaster. They probably won't let me in.'

The message was clear. Orla was proving to the world that she was well and truly over Giles. Looking at her now, no one would doubt it. Millie had nothing but admiration for her.

'Honestly, someone's *smoking* in one of these rooms.' Lifting her head like an outraged bloodhound, Orla sniffed the air and glared at the many doors lining the broad corridor. 'It smells completely *repulsive*. People who smoke shouldn't be allowed to stay in hotels—as soon as we get downstairs I'm going to report them to the manager!'

Oh, and she was still off the cigarettes.

'Not looking so bad yourself,' Orla teased as they stepped into the lift. It was also the poshest lift Millie had ever been in in her life—to be fair, there weren't many buildings *with* lifts in Newquay—but she didn't mention this to Orla. There was such a thing as sounding too much like Crocodile Dundee.

Checking herself briefly in the mirror as they traveled downwards, Millie made sure her hair and make-up were okay. She was wearing the Dolce & Gabbana caramel suede dress. (If Orla was her matchmaking fairy godmother, this was her version of Cinderella's ballgown.) She'd even remembered to polish up the tiger's eye earrings Hester had given her last Christmas.

Well, as Orla kept gleefully pointing out, tonight could be the night that changed her whole life.

Then again, so could any night. If you were at home watching TV and a spider ran across your foot, you could panic and leap up on to the coffee table, lose your balance, topple over backwards, fracture your skull, and… well, die.

Which would also change your life.

With any luck, this evening wouldn't provoke anything quite so dramatic.

'Here we are,' Orla announced as the lift door slid noiselessly open. 'And we are going to enjoy ourselves. Smile, darling. It's showtime!'

Orla certainly knew a lot of people. Millie, incapable of remembering the names of everyone she was being introduced to, could only marvel as Orla worked her way through the throng. They were having drinks in the Lounge Bar before the ceremony itself got underway. More guests were arriving all the time. As the noise level rose, so did the perfume and smoke levels in the room.

Brightly, Orla called out, 'How are we doing so far? Spotted anyone *you* like the look of?'

It was like being injected with a giant dose of anti-aphrodisiac. Being ordered to find someone and chat them up simply wasn't natural. Especially not with Orla standing there avidly charting your progress.

Like having a wee, thought Millie. It was one of those things she just couldn't do in front of an audience.

'Why don't you introduce me to someone you like the look of?' she countered. 'Anyway, I thought you already had someone in mind.'

'Oh yes. My surprise.' Orla pulled a face. 'Except there's no sign of him so far. To be honest, I don't know if he's going to be able to make it. Okay, okay, my choice.' Keenly, she scanned the room. Moments later, her eyes lighting up, she said, 'There's someone you might like. Noel Blackwall. Writes horror novels, lives in Sussex, just sold the film rights to his last book for two mill.'

Millie dutifully looked over and her heart did… nothing. Noel Blackwall was of average height. Looks-wise, he was average. He appeared to be around thirty and was engaged in conversation with a slightly older woman sporting a towering blonde beehive.

'Is that his girlfriend?' said Millie.

'*Nooo*, only his agent.' Briskly, Orla nudged her forward. 'Come on, I'll do the honors.'

The trouble with Orla, Millie belatedly realized, was that she had extremely dodgy taste in men. Look at who she'd married, for a start.

'… So that was how I got the idea for my new book, *Crunching Cockroaches*.' Noel was still droning on in her ear. He'd barely paused for breath since Orla had foisted Millie on to him. Even his agent had looked relieved when Orla had dragged her away in order to give 'these two young people time to get to know each other.' Having heard enough stomach-churning detail in the last twenty minutes to put her off her food for life, Millie was now wondering if she was ever going to be able to escape. With his monotonous voice, complete absence of humor, and supercilious manner—he loathed and despised *everyone* in publishing—he was, officially, the most awful man she ever met.

Ever.

'Gosh, that's fantastic,' she lied. 'I wonder where Orla's got to, it's probably time I went and found her before—'

'No, you can't go yet.' Urgently, Noel placed a damp, pale hand on her arm, his eyes bulging with irritation. 'I haven't finished telling you about the book-signing session I did for *Crunching Cockroaches*. This weird guy turned up with a bucket and you'll never guess what was in it.'

Millie, her skin crawling from the contact with his hand, suppressed a shudder. Oh Hugh, where are you? Why can't I be with you now, instead of stuck here with this weirdo?

Except, depressingly, she knew the answer to that one. Because Hugh doesn't want to be with me, thought Millie. He probably thinks I'm a weirdo.

Aloud, she said, 'Um... cockroaches?'

Noel Blackwall stared at her, unblinking.

'How did you know that?'

Orla coughed and made pointed get-it-away-from-me gestures with her arm. Usually it had the desired effect; people apologized at once and moved their cigarettes away. This time she might as well have been invisible. The man carried on puffing and waving his own hands about as he spoke to his companion. Orla, standing less than two feet to his left, tsked and coughed again, more loudly, as the noxious fumes swirled around her head.

And still he seemed not to notice her.

'Excuse me.' Leaning over, bashing the clouds of smoke away like centuries-old cobwebs, she tapped him on the shoulder. 'Would you mind?'

Breaking off his conversation, the man appeared to see her for the first time.

'I'm sorry? Oh…' Realizing that Orla was looking at his cigarette, he smiled and pulled a packet of Marlboros from his jacket pocket. 'Of course not. Here you go, help yourself!'

Having geared herself up to get angry with him, Orla was now forced to be nicer than she'd planned.

'No, I don't *want* one. I was trying to tell you that your smoke is going in my eyes.'

'Ah, that's the trouble with smoke,' he confided comfortably. 'You have no control over it. It's like trying to be in charge of a field full of sheep—you do your best, but before you know it, they're bounding off all over the place.'

He had a seductive Irish accent and laughing eyes that crinkled up at the corners. Aware that she was sounding prissy and schoolteacherish, Orla said evenly, 'You could control it if you put it out.'

'What?' Feigning alarm, he held up the offending half-smoked cigarette. 'You mean before I've had all the goodness out of it? That's a terrible idea, and one that only an extremely successful and *wealthy* novelist could suggest.'

He was in his mid-thirties, Orla guessed. Tall, with cropped curly hair, a thin, tanned face, and a quirky smile.

'You really shouldn't smoke, you know. It's so bad for you. Stains your teeth, gives you wrinkles, makes you smell disgusting.'

'And causes cancer. Don't forget that one.'

'I don't know if you even realize this,' said Orla, getting into her stride now, 'but every single time you light up a cigarette, all the non-smokers in the room wish you wouldn't. They look at you and despise you for being so weak-willed and selfish. I mean, how would you like it if we spat in your food?'

He raised an eyebrow.

'You'd do that?'

'You see? As far as you're concerned, that's a terrible thing to do. Yet you're allowed to kill us with your secondhand smoke!'

'You're very... passionate about this,' he observed. 'May I ask how long it's been since you renounced the evil weed yourself?'

Orla sensed he was making fun of her.

'Quite a while.' As if that had anything to do with it, damn cheek! 'In fact, a *long* time ago.'

'Is that so? Truly?' Taking another pleasurable puff of his cigarette, her tormentor drawled innocently, 'Sure it's not just a couple of weeks?'

He had the most mischievous eyes Orla had ever seen, silvery-grey and narrowed with laughter. She knew she should be crosser with him than this.

'Look, how long ago I gave it up is irrelevant. I'm now a non-smoker.'

'I'm sorry. That's grand.' Acknowledging her superiority, he nodded in deferential fashion. 'Good for you. I'm deeply impressed. So how are you doing, on the vice-front? Any left, or was that the last?' A dimple appeared in his cheek. 'Are you now a vice-free zone?'

Heavens, what was going on here? Aware that goose pimples were breaking out all over her arms, Orla wondered if she could get away with blaming it on the air-conditioning.

It had been so long since anything like this had happened to her that for a moment she genuinely couldn't figure out what it was. Then it hit her like a football in the chest; she was actually experiencing sexual attraction.

Sexual attraction to a stranger, Orla amended. Not the married kind, where you somehow slipped into a comfortable routine of sleeping together. This was completely—*completely*—different. Heightened awareness fuelled by adrenalin. A kind of fizzy whoosh of anticipation, like Alka-Seltzer bubbling up in a glass. Tingling all over. A delicious eagerness to hear what he would say next.

How ironic to think that she spent her life writing about these sensations, yet it had actually been twenty-odd years since she'd last experienced them herself.

So long, frankly, that she'd had trouble recognizing them.

This is flirting, Orla realized in a haze of happiness. I'm standing here flirting with a complete stranger. And it feels... *fantastic.*

Hew liked her, she could tell. The spark was definitely mutual. Furthermore, it had been acknowledged by the man he'd been talking to earlier; he had moved discreetly away, leaving them alone together to get on with it.

It, thought Orla with a pleasurable shiver. Crikey, I can barely remember how *it* goes. Let's hope he's less out of practice than I am.

Belatedly she realized that he was still waiting for her to reply to the question he had put to her several hours ago. Well, thirty seconds.

What had the question been? Oh yes...

'Me? No vices left at all. I'm now one hundred percent flawless.' Orla smiled as she spoke, basically because it was impossible not to smile. 'A temple of perfection. And a very lovely person to boot.'

'I can tell. In fact, I already knew that. It must be great,' he added. 'There aren't all that many completely perfect people around.'

Orla had so many questions; she longed to know everything about him. She wanted to find out his name for a start, and how old he was, what he did, where he lived, and whether or not he was married.

But at the same time she was terrified of breaking the spell. What if he *was* happily married with five children? What if he turned out to be twenty-three and just over on a flying visit from Australia? What if he told her his name was Ernest?

To their right, a flashbulb went off. One of the photographers who had been circulating all evening called out, 'Orla, could you turn this way?'

Orla turned and smiled automatically for the next picture, then realized that it was no good, she simply had to ask.

Out of the corner of her mouth she murmured, 'Are you married?'

He didn't flinch or hesitate.

'No.'

'How old are you?'

'Thirty-seven.'

'Where do you live?'

'Just bought a place in Wimbledon.'

'*Lovely!*' exclaimed the photographer. 'Just move a bit closer together now, could you?'

My pleasure, thought Orla, doing as she was instructed and squirming with delight as, for the first time, their bodies brushed together. The sparks might not be visible but she could certainly feel them.

Anyway, next question.

'Do you work in publishing?'

'Me? I write a bit.' His shrug was modest, his mouth twitching playfully at the corners. 'Of course, I'm not in your league.'

'Great.' The photographer gave them an encouraging thumbs-up. 'Just one more. I want you looking really happy now!'

Orla had no trouble looking happy. In fact, she was finding it ludicrously easy.

'Would I have read any of your work?'

'Oh, I think you have.'

'Really?' Delighted, she clutched his arm. 'What's your name?'

Pause.

'Actually, it's Carson.'

Carson. Carson. Orla racked her brains; there was a thriller writer called Carson Phillips, but he was a born and bred New Yorker.

Slowly, slowly, she made the connection.

The Irish connection.

No wonder he hadn't introduced himself earlier.

'Oh, I get it now. You're related to Christie Carson.' She drew back slightly, studying his face. 'You don't look like him, but you must be. Who are you, his son?'

At that moment a big arm was flung around Orla's shoulder.

'Hello there, Christie,' JD boomed in her ear. 'Fancy bumping into you like this.' Giving Orla a bone-crunching squeeze he went on in his loud voice, 'And as for you, my darling, what *do* you think you're doing, consorting with the enemy?'

Chapter 55

'... It's no picnic, you know, being a millionaire. When you meet up with your old friends they expect you to buy every round.' Noel was still droning on, relating a seemingly endless list of grievances. 'They seem to think they're doing you a favor, just by coming out with you for a drink or a meal. And the moment you've picked up the tab, they're off. Jealousy, that's all it is. They resent the fact that I'm successful and they're just a bunch of losers. Are you listening to me?'

'What? Oh, sorry.' Millie had been peering round in search of Orla who was—typically—nowhere in sight. 'Why don't you ditch your friends if you don't like them? Make some new ones?'

Well, *try*.

Noel looked at her as if she was thick.

'I am. That's why I'm talking to you.'

Oh God. Definitely time to escape.

'We could meet up tomorrow,' he went on. 'Go out for lunch somewhere.'

Millie hesitated, wondering how best to convey the news that she would rather tip a bucket of live cockroaches over her head.

'Thanks, but—'

'I'd pay. Seeing as it'd be our first meal together.'

She broke into a light sweat. Where the bloody hell had Orla got to?

'Look, it's really nice of you to offer, but I can't.'

'Okay.' Noel shrugged. 'We'll go Dutch.'

Millie wished she was fifteen again; life had been so simple then. When you were pestered by a boy you didn't fancy, you just screeched with laughter and howled, 'Do I look desperate? Get lost, frogface, I'd rather die than go out with you! Just the thought of you makes me want to vomit!'

But she wasn't fifteen, she was a grown-up. It wasn't so easy now.

'I mean I can't meet you.' Inside her shoes, her toes were curling up with embarrassment; the fact that Noel Blackwall was so awful only made her feel more guilty. 'I have other plans.'

Noel said stolidly, 'Dinner, then.'

'I'll still be busy.'

For crying out loud! Take a *hint*, can't you?

'Are you sure?' Noel frowned, his eyebrows drawing together like curtains. 'Because—'

'She's sure,' a male voice announced behind Millie. 'She's absolutely sure. In fact, she's spending tomorrow and the rest of the weekend with me.'

'Con!' Millie let out a shriek of delight as he picked her up and whirled her around. Wrapping her arms tightly around his neck, she whispered into his ear, '*Keep whirling.*'

Finally, when they were twenty feet away from droning Noel, Con Deveraux put her down.

Millie kissed him, noisily, on both cheeks.

'You have *no* idea how glad I am to see you. I thought I was going to be trapped with that boring man all night.'

'I know. I was listening.' Mischievously Con added, 'I didn't like to interrupt at first, in case you were crazy about him.'

'As if. Orla made me talk to him. But what are *you* doing here? Oh my God!' Millie exclaimed, as realization dawned. 'Don't tell me. You're my surprise!'

Con broke into a grin.

'Got it in one. Good old Orla, up to her matchmaking tricks

again. She rang and persuaded me that all we needed was another chance. As it happened, I wasn't doing anything else, so I thought I may as well come along. Just as long as you aren't expecting rampant sex,' he added with a straight face.

'Poor Orla, you can't say she doesn't try. Still, never mind.' Thinking how handsome he looked in black tie, Millie gave him another ecstatic hug. 'It's lovely to see you again. I couldn't have asked for a nicer surprise.'

Well, maybe just one…

'Unlike Orla.' As he spoke, Con deftly spun her round and pointed across the room.

'Where is she? I can't even see her.'

'Left a bit, left a bit, behind the woman in purple with the huge backside.' Guiding Millie like a periscope, he whispered gleefully, 'There she is. Getting the biggest shock of her life.'

Millie saw. Orla was indeed looking dumbstruck. Her eyes were like saucers, her mouth a perfect O as she gazed at a good-looking man with something approaching horror.

'Why? What's he saying to her?' Millie couldn't work it out at all. JD was there, roaring with laughter, with his arm around Orla. A photographer was busy capturing her comical reaction for posterity.

'I think he's just told her who he is.' Admiringly, Con added, 'Brave chap.'

'Well, I've never seen him before. He's certainly not famous. How do you know him?'

'I don't. Dad was introduced to him as we arrived. This should be good.' Con looked amused. 'He could be about to experience a close encounter with Orla's glass of wine.'

'Crikey. Should we go over?'

'Absolutely not. I'd hate to get wet.'

'But who *is* he?'

'Christie Carson. The one who gave Orla that stinking review, remember?'

Millie remembered only too well; it was the review that had changed *her* life.

She also remembered the photograph of the author adorning the proof copy of his own book.

Shaking her head pityingly at Con, Millie said, 'No it isn't.'

Across the room, Orla declared, 'You can't be Christie Carson. You don't look anything like him.'

His eyes were twinkling but he was clearly on edge, ready to leap out of the way should any wine come hurtling in his direction.

'Actually, I do. We're astonishingly alike.'

Orla frowned.

'I saw your photo. Was that not you?'

'Oh yes, it was me.'

'You looked like the wild man of Borneo.'

'Ah well, that was taken while I was going through my wild man of Borneo phase,' he replied gravely. 'Long hair, beard, fierce expression, the works.'

'We thought you were about fifty.'

'I know. All that facial hair. Terribly aging.' Lightly, he added, 'Promise me you'll never grow a beard.'

'But why would you *want* people to think you look like that?'

'Okay. Your publicity photos.' Christie Carson fixed her with a steady gaze. 'You have a hairdresser in attendance, am I right? A make-up artist, maybe even a stylist. And a photographer angling his lights to capture you at your absolute best.'

This was true. Defensively, Orla said, 'So?'

'So, that's fine. Practically de rigueur for the kind of books you write. It's what your readers expect.' He shrugged. 'It's different for me. My style of writing is more—'

'Intellectual?' bristled Orla.

'Masculine. Anyway, if it's any comfort to you, my mother had an absolute fit when she saw that photo. She told me I looked a sight and ordered me to spruce myself up. So here I am.' He ran a hand briefly over his cropped curly hair and clean-shaven chin. 'Well and truly spruced.'

Orla was lost for words.

But not for long.

'You're supposed to be a recluse.' Her tone was accusing, her fingers tightly laced around her wine glass. 'You've never given an interview. So what are you doing here tonight?'

Orla had long ago convinced herself that Christie Carson lived the life of a hermit in an unheated, crumbling stone cottage in the wilds of Ireland. Any journalists daring to approach his hovel of a home would be met with a barrage of abuse and the business-end of a double-barrelled shotgun.

She couldn't help it. She was a novelist.

'I don't like giving interviews,' Christie Carson agreed, the laughter lines deepening around his eyes. 'But that doesn't make me a recluse. So anyhow, now we have the misunderstandings cleared up and the introductions out of the way. Maybe we could get down to the serious business of the evening.' Nodding at Orla's almost-full glass, he drawled, 'Are you going to throw that over me or not?'

Orla hesitated. The shock of discovering who he was had begun to wear off. The butterflies in her stomach were starting up again.

'I haven't decided yet.'

Oh, that smile! She was at a serious disadvantage here. Flinging wine into the horrid bearded face of the wild man of Borneo would have been easy—a positive *delight*, in fact—but this was a different matter altogether.

Somehow she knew her heart would no longer be in it.

Besides, the dinner jacket he was wearing was well cut and clearly expensive.

Watching her weigh up the options, he raised his eyebrows. 'Yes? No?'

'I'll keep you in suspense.'

The hovering photographer looked disappointed.

'They're going through to dinner,' JD announced, having heroically kept quiet throughout this exchange. 'Come along, darling, you're on my table.'

Orla felt like a two-year-old having her birthday present abruptly snatched away. Practically before she'd had a chance to unwrap it.

Everyone was moving away from the Lounge Bar, drifting towards the double doors at the far end of the corridor. Ahead, in the Nine Kings' Suite lay two hours—minimum—of eating and making polite conversation with your fellow diners, listening to a daunting number of speeches (some funny, some not), and watching the dozen or so awards being presented. Which, if you hadn't been nominated yourself, was frankly boring.

Plus, you were expected to applaud until your hands were sore.

Orla, who usually adored every minute, realized that she would only enjoy it this time if Christie Carson was on their table.

'Ready, darling?' Jovially, JD held out his arm. 'Let's go and find the rest of our gang.'

Of course, they weren't on the same table. Not even close. From her position at the back of the vast room, Orla saw that Christie Carson was occupying one of the tables close to the stage at the front. If she tilted her chair slightly, she had a clear view of him chatting easily to the woman on his left, a flirtatious actress who had just published her autobiography.

Wishing he could be chatting easily to *her*, Orla flushed as he glanced over at that moment and caught her looking at him. Hastily filling her glass, she beamed as Millie and Con joined them. Laughing and teasing each other, they really did make a perfect couple.

Pleased with herself, Orla said, 'How d'you like your surprise?'

'Brilliant. How do you like yours?' Millie beamed across at her. 'I couldn't believe it was actually him!'

'Me neither.' It was the kind of face a fifteen-year-old might pull, but Orla pulled it anyway. It was a yeeuch face, designed to prove that you loathed someone and definitely didn't secretly fancy them rotten.

'I thought they'd have to call security to drag you off him.' Con winked. 'Maybe even an ambulance.'

Modestly, Orla fluttered her hands. 'Oh, all in good time.'

'But how did he react when you had a go at him?' Millie was dying to hear all about it; to her frustration, Con hadn't allowed her within eavesdropping distance. 'What made him write that horrible review?'

'Haven't asked him yet.' Orla leaned back, allowing the waiter to serve their first course.

Millie was astounded. 'Why not?'

'No hurry. We've got all evening.' Once the awards had been dished out, the business of serious drinking and networking would begin. Orla could hardly wait. Aloud she added casually, 'Let him sweat.'

'She's playing it like a pro,' boasted JD. 'Reel him in, reel him in, then—*bam*. That lad won't know what's hit him.'

Her starter looked delicious but Orla's stomach was in too much of a tangle for her to eat it. Glancing across the room, she saw that Christie Carson had—oh God—caught her out once more.

Never mind him, thought Orla. What's hit *me*!

As if she didn't know.

'Are you okay?' said Millie.

Picking up her fork, Orla smiled brightly.

'I'm fine!'

For the next hour she forced herself to join in. Conversation whirled around the table and Orla bantered along with the best of them. Dinner came and went. As their plates were efficiently cleared, the speeches began. The first awards were announced and the winners mounted the stage to receive their trophies.

When her bladder began to protest at the unfairness of having been filled with wine and squashed within the confines of such a tight-fitting dress, Orla discreetly excused herself. The compere was announcing the shortlist for Best Travel Guide as she slipped out to the loo.

Five minutes later she was in the process of carefully re-powdering her nose in the gilded mirror above the basin when the door swung open and Christie Carson sauntered in.

Not walked. *Sauntered.*

Orla, her heart clanging away like a school bell, promptly doused her nose with far too much loose powder.

'Wrong loo. This is the ladies.''

'Right loo.' He broke into a slow, mesmerizing smile. 'It's actually a lady I'm looking for.'

Clang clang clang, went Orla's heart, clang clanggg.

Hastily brushing Estée Lauder's finest off her nose, she said, 'Are you following me?'

Christie Carson looked around the otherwise deserted cloakroom, then back at her.

'I'd say that's highly likely, wouldn't you?'

At least he'd allowed her enough time to go to the loo first. It showed he was thoughtful. Imagine if he'd interrupted her in mid-pee.

Aloud, Orla said, 'Why?'

'I missed you.' His tone good-humored, he moved closer. 'I was lonely without you. I didn't want to wait another whole hour before talking to you again.'

Phew.

'Why not?'

'Because sometimes you meet someone and… you just *know*.' Christie paused, then shrugged. 'Don't you agree?'

YES,YES!

'I'm not sure. Know what?'

'I haven't the foggiest. You just… know.'

He was Irish. It was blarney time. With those eyes and that lilting accent he could say pretty much anything and get away with it.

'Why did you write that review?' Helplessly, Orla blurted the words out.

'Why? Because it was the truth.' He faced her without flinching. 'Come on, you already knew that. There you were, churning out rubbish without even thinking about it. The lazy person's way to make a few million. You're actually a much better writer than you give yourself credit for. All you needed was a good shake-up. Look at me honestly and tell me I'm not right.'

'That review was way below the belt. You have no idea how much it hurt me.'

'It had to, if it was going to do its job. Tell me what you're working on now.'

'Something completely different.' Recklessly Orla added, 'Something that's going to knock your socks off.'

Not very modest, perhaps. But it was the truth.

Christie's eyes crinkled at the corners.

'See? It did the trick.'

As he moved closer still, Orla caught a waft of aftershave and cigarettes. All of a sudden, she discovered, the smell of smoke was no longer a turnoff.

'What are you doing?'

'I haven't thanked you yet, for the nice things you wrote about me. I must say,' he flashed a self-deprecating smile, 'I nearly wet my pants and ran away when I heard you were reviewing my book.'

'I didn't write nice things about you. Only your work.' He had the most beautiful mouth Orla had ever seen. Dimly, she heard cheering and wild applause drifting through from the ceremony in the Nine Kings' Suite.

'I thought you might retaliate.'

'I did. If you give me your address I'll send you copies of the first drafts I put together. There are two hundred and eighteen of them.' She forced herself to stop watching his magical mouth. 'But publicly, we decided to be gracious. Rise above it. Put you to shame.'

'And you did. Still, thank you anyway.' Closing the distance between them, Christie raised Orla's mouth to his and kissed her.

And kissed her, and kissed her, and kissed her.

Orla, almost dissolving on the spot, gasped, 'I don't believe this. Anyone could come in here. You have to stop it *now*.'

Embarrassingly, her fingers were still entwined in his silky dark curls as she panted out the words. They didn't appear to want to let go.

'I've got a better idea.' Smiling, Christie led her towards one of the open cubicles. As he drew her inside and kicked the door shut, another thunderous burst of applause rang out, accompanied by laughter and raucous whoops of delight.

'Just so long as this loo isn't bugged,' Orla shuddered with anticipation as his hand skillfully unzipped her mermaid dress, 'and they aren't all out there applauding *us*.'

Chapter 56

On the one hand, Millie felt it was probably just as well Orla was missing out on this part of the ceremony. On the other hand, she had been gone from their table for quite some time.

Almost fifteen minutes now.

Pushing her chair back, Millie leaned over to Con and said, 'I'm just going to find out where Orla's got to. Check she's okay.'

The ladies' loo appeared to be deserted when Millie pushed through the door. Pausing on the threshold, she wondered if Orla had been feeling ill and had made her way back to her room.

Then, hearing a slight noise, she saw that one of the cubicle doors was locked.

'Orla?'

No reply.

'Orla?'

Nothing. Had she fainted?

'Orla, is that you? Are you okay?'

A moment later, sounding distinctly strange, Orla's voice drifted out from the closed cubicle.

'It's okay, I'm fine. I'll be… um, out in a minute.'

Millie frowned.

'You don't sound fine. You've been gone for ages. What's up?'

This time she heard hastily stifled laughter. Followed by more shuffling around. Instinctively, Millie crouched down and peered through the narrow gap between the cubicle door and the green and black marble tiled floor.

Since she wasn't entirely stupid, she had actually worked it out for herself by now.

'Orla. Bad news. You've grown a couple of extra legs.'

More muffled laughter, this time bordering on the hysterical.

'Damn,' Orla gasped finally. 'Two extra legs. I hate it when that happens.'

'And I hate to be an old killjoy, but any minute now somebody else is going to walk in here and then you'll be stuck. I really think you'd better come out now.'

So that I can see who you're in there with, you shameless tramp!

At that moment, in the corridor outside, an agitated male voice could clearly be heard shouting, 'Has anyone seen Christie Carson?'

Inside the cubicle, much giggling and rustling accompanied the sound of a zip being done up. Then the door of the cubicle was unlocked and opened.

'... so you see, that's the basic principle of the flushing mechanism, it's all in the S-bend,' Christie Carson was earnestly explaining as he emerged behind a smirking, pink-cheeked Orla. Apparently surprised to find Millie there, he said, 'Oh, hi!'

'You may want to tuck the back of your shirt in before you go up on stage,' Millie solemnly informed him. 'They're waiting to present you with the award for Author of the Year.'

'Really?' Christie Carson grinned. 'That's the second-nicest thing to happen to me all night.'

After the ceremony was over, the serious business of drinking, table-hopping, celebrating, and gossiping began in earnest. Those who had been nominated for awards and failed to win them were commiserated with and told they deserved to have won. The winners were subjected to endless photos and interviews. Champagne bottles proliferated on the tables. JD was off boasting to journalists of his latest acquisition, a twenty-five-year-old milkman who had written a swords-and-sorcery blockbuster set to trounce Harry Potter into the ground.

'It's his way of coping with Mum's illness,' Con explained, as he refilled Millie's glass. Having no need to network, they were finally alone at their table.

'How is she?'

'Not so bad. At home, resting. She insisted on Dad coming tonight.' He paused. 'She's not in any pain, which is a relief.'

'And how are things with you?'

He smiled and sat back in his chair.

'Good. I've met someone.'

Delighted, Millie clutched his arm.

'That's fantastic! Is it serious?'

'Who can tell? Still, we're enjoying ourselves. He's a lighting technician. And his name's Joe, which is handy. My mother thinks it's short for Josephine. But he understands my situation, why we need to be discreet. We'll just have to see how things go.' He paused. 'How about you?'

Millie almost kissed him—she'd thought he'd never ask. Con was the only person she could truly confide in. Within minutes she had blurted out the whole depressing story.

'The one I talked to on the beach.' Con nodded, recalling the day after Orla's party. 'We tried to get a look at that tattoo of yours. Has it occurred to you that maybe your tattoo is jinxing your love life? If you'd have let us see it, everything might have turned out differently for you and Hugh. You could be blissfully happy together now. Like when a Catholic confesses his sins. Maybe if you showed me...'

He was laughing at her, his warm hand inching up her leg as he spoke.

'Sshh.' Millie slapped the hand away as it reached the hem of her dress. 'Change the subject. Here comes Orla.'

Orla, back from her table-hopping, was grinning uncontrollably.

Her green eyes were bright. If she'd had a tail, it would be a bushy one. She'd never looked happier or more vibrant in her life.

'Just came over to say good night. I'm absolutely shattered. Phew, what an evening—I can hardly stand up!'

'What a surprise,' Con murmured, *nearly* under his breath.

'Oh! She told you!' Orla pretended to be indignant.

'All that unaccustomed activity in a confined space, bound to take it out of you,' he teased. 'Of course she told me.'

'And tomorrow morning it'll be my turn—I'll want to hear everything you've been up to.' Still incapable of wiping the idiotic grin off her face, Orla pointed sternly—well, fairly sternly—at Millie. To Con, she added, 'And it had better be good.'

'What time would you like me to wake you?' Millie innocently inquired. 'Six? Seven?'

'Heavens no. I told you, I'm absolutely exhausted—*desperate* to catch up on some sleep!' Having gaily kissed them both, Orla feigned a huge yawn.

'The thing is, I've had my wallet nicked and I can't get home,' said Con. 'You couldn't put me up in your room for the night, could you? I'd be no trouble, I promise.'

'Sorry, no.' Orla smiled sweetly at him. 'Absolutely not.'

Christie Carson said his good-byes and slipped discreetly out of the room shortly afterwards. He winked at Millie as he left.

Millie, who had been timing him, murmured, 'Five minutes and twenty-three seconds. I won.'

'You can tell he's not gay,' Con sighed. 'If he were, he'd have been out of here and up those stairs in no time flat.' Shaking his dark head he added, 'I hope he isn't going to break Orla's heart.'

'Don't be such a pessimist. She's having the time of her life.' Sitting back, Millie twirled the stem of her champagne glass. 'Crikey, after putting up with Giles all these years she deserves it.'

'Like discovering Cottonelle after a lifetime of that awful scratchy, hard stuff.'

Millie hiccuped.

'I don't know how flattered Orla's going to be when she hears you've been comparing her lovers to loo rolls.'

'I'm tired. Blame it on the jet-lag.' Con stretched out and yawned, revealing a couple of gold fillings. 'God, sorry, it's just caught up with me.'

He yawned again. Unlike Orla, he really was shattered.

'You've done your duty.' Millie patted his arm. 'Time you went home.'

'What about you? Will you be okay?'

Across the crowded room Noel Blackwall was glancing over, the determined look on his face indicating—yuk—that he hadn't given up on her yet.

'I'll be fine, I'm pretty tired myself,' Millie lied. 'I think I'll call it a night.'

In her room, she changed out of the Dolce & Gabbana dress and into her second-best nightie. (No tatty old T-shirts for the Royal Lancaster, thank you very much.) Since it was only just gone midnight and she wasn't sleepy at all, Millie arranged herself comfortably on the bed with the TV remote control, one of the tooth mugs from the bathroom, and the almost-full bottle of champagne she had brought upstairs with her because it had looked so lonely all on its own on their empty table. Unsure whether or not this counted as stealing—and keen not to be arrested and forced to spend the rest of her long weekend in some smelly police cell—she had therefore stolen it discreetly, smuggling it out of the Nine Kings' Suite clasped between her hip and her handbag. The bottle, of course, had slipped sideways as she was stepping into the lift. By the time Millie had managed to straighten it back up, champagne was dripping and fizzing down the front of her dress. At least she' d been fast enough to catch the bottle before any more champagne could spill out. There was still plenty left.

Crikey, thought Millie as she filled her tooth mug, with reflexes like that I should be wicket-keeping for England.

Flip, flip, flip.

Glug.

Flip, flip, flip.

Slurp.

Alternately zapping through the many cable channels and guzzling Veuve Clicquot—lukewarm, but she'd never have got away with smuggling up an ice bucket—Millie watched a couple of minutes of some dire sci-fi drama before switching off the TV. There were more important things to think about, like what she wanted to do with the rest of her life.

Relocate to London?

Get a job in a travel agency?

Set about finding herself a new man, one she could fall in love with who might even love her in return?

In other words, *move on*?

Millie waggled her toes, briefly admiring the silvery-bronze polish on them. She gazed at the blank TV screen, then took another slurp of champagne and felt the bubbles pop on her tongue.

As the alcohol began to swirl through her bloodstream, she thought how nice it would be to hear Hugh's voice now, the light, sexy, amused drawl he used when he was teasing her.

The voice that made her shiver with longing.

The voice she craved, almost like a drug.

Ridiculous. Vigorously, Millie shook her head. No, no, *no*. It's almost half past midnight. You can't possibly ring him now. Not unless you've got a jolly good reason.

Oh, but that was the trouble with phones, they were just too tempting. They were… *there*.

A hundred years ago, if you were in London and you experienced a sudden, violent urge to speak to someone in, say, Cornwall, you had to jump on to a horse and gallop the three hundred-odd miles in order to do so. It probably took more than a week before you were able to reach the person and say what you wanted to say.

Millie, snatching up the phone and jabbing out the numbers, decided that it was all Alexander Graham Bell's fault. If he'd stuck to stamp collecting or train-spotting, she wouldn't be able to do this now.

Ha, if it weren't for Alexander Graham Know-it-all Cleverclogs Brainbox Bell, she'd never have got herself into this mess in the first place.

Oh well, too late, it was ringing.

Hugh picked up on the third ring. This was good, Millie decided. At least it meant he'd been awake.

'Allo? Allo? Ah, bonjour m'sieur, thees eez the *News of ze World*, yes? I 'ave a scoop for you! A beeg, *beeg* item of gossip you weel not believe!'

Chapter 57

In Cornwall, Hugh's heart began to pound. Unable to sleep himself, he had been lying in bed thinking about Millie. And now here she was, ringing him.

The question was, had Hester phoned her?

Feeling sick, forcing himself to sound normal, he replied gravely, 'Oui, mademoiselle, this is the *News of the World*. You are through to the Beeg Beeg Gossip department. May I ask what this is about?'

'Ah, mais oui! Ze beautiful bestselling novelist, Orla Hart! I tell you, you vill not *believe* zis!'

Hugh began to relax. He knew Millie well enough by now to know that she hadn't spoken to Hester.

He still had a chance to get this right.

'You're slipping into German,' he warned.

'Bugger, so I am.' In her hotel room, Millie took another slurp of champagne. 'Better give up on the accent.' She paused, then said, 'You still won't believe it when I tell you about Orla.'

'Where are you?'

'In London. In the poshest hotel you ever saw. Well, maybe not the poshest one *you* ever saw,' Millie conceded. 'But as far as I'm concerned, it's a palace.'

'The Ritz?'

'Nooo! The Royal Lancaster, overlooking Hyde Park *and* Kensington Gardens,' boasted Millie. 'Chandeliers like you wouldn't believe and carpet so thick you could hide a sniper in it. Orla brought me up here, we've been to an awards ceremony.' Unable to resist name-dropping, she added proudly, 'Michael Palin was there.'

'Don't tell me, Orla ripped off her clothes and did a streak across the stage.'

'Nope!'

'She ripped off Michael Palin's clothes and made *him* streak across the stage.'

'If only. Much worse than that,' Millie pronounced with relish. 'Oh dear, maybe I shouldn't tell you.'

'Millie. You have to.'

'Okay! Orla's been shagging! I caught her in the ladies' loo… you'll *never guess* who she was with.'

Hugh, clearly amused, said, 'Michael Palin?'

'Ha! Much much *much* worse. Christie Carson!'

'You mean the ugly old bloke with the beard?' Hugh was laughing now. 'Her sworn enemy? *That* Christie Carson?'

'I know, I know, but it turns out he isn't old and he isn't ugly. And they aren't sworn enemies anymore. In fact, they're probably in her suite right now, *still* doing it. Good thing Orla booked us into separate rooms!' Millie exclaimed. 'Otherwise I'd be spending the night curled up on one of the sofas in reception.'

Tucking her bare feet under her, she told Hugh everything. The longer they talked, the less she wanted to hang up the phone. She could happily carry on like this all night. Hearing his voice. Imagining his face. Picturing his dark eyes and the way his mouth curved up at the corners when he smiled…

Damn, getting tiddly now. The bottle of Veuve Clicquot was almost empty. And—completely pathetically—hot tears were beginning to well up in her eyes.

'By the way, I've come to a decision. I'm leaving Cornwall, moving up to London,' Millie blurted out. Tell him now, then you'll have to do it, you can't back down.

'What? Why?' Hugh sounded taken aback. 'Why would you want to leave?'

'I've just made up my mind. It's the best thing to do. Lots of people move to London.'

'Lots of people living in London wish they could move to Cornwall.'

Tears were now rolling down Millie's cheeks. Silently, they dripped on to the starched cotton sheets pulled up over her knees. When she was confident she could sound normal—and not as if she was blubbing like a big baby—she said, 'I just think I need a change. Nothing wrong with that. Oh, and there's something else I've decided.'

There was a long pause.

'What?'

'The next time we bump into each other, I'm going to show you something. My tattoo.'

'Why?'

'Because it doesn't matter anymore. I'll be moving away, won't I?' Draining the last dregs from the bottle into her tooth mug, Millie wiped her eyes. 'Anyway, it's no big deal. Only a stupid tattoo. If you want to see it, you can.'

This is ridiculous. He probably isn't even interested. So much for Con's brilliant suggestion.

Another, even longer pause.

'I'd like that.'

He was just being polite, she could tell.

Glancing at her watch, Millie saw that it was almost one o'clock. Now that she'd stopped crying, her swollen eyelids were beginning to droop.

'I suppose I'm keeping you up.'

Please don't agree with me! Don't say yes!

'It's getting pretty late,' Hugh agreed. *(Bastard. Wrong answer!)* 'Maybe you should get some sleep.'

He didn't want to talk to her anymore. Feeling rejected, Millie knocked back the last inch of flat champagne.

'I'm not tired. Are you tired?'

He sounded amused.

'Actually, I am. Exhausted. And I do have a busy day tomorrow.'

Millie blinked hard. Here it was again, the oh-so-familiar brush-off. He'd been listening to her patiently, pretending to be interested, and all the time wondering how much longer she was going to be on the phone.

She'd been endlessly prattling on and he'd indulged her. Because he simply wasn't the type to interrupt and retort, 'For Christ's sake woman, will you *listen* to yourself?' before slamming the phone down.

Oh God, I'm so *selfish*.

'That's fine!' Summoning up a carefree, cheerful voice, as opposed to a whiny, self-pitying, and somewhat-the-worse-for-drink one, Millie took a deep breath. 'You get some sleep now. Sorry I've kept you up. You really should have said.'

'No problem.' Hugh sounded equally cheerful. 'And I'm glad you rang. Bye, then.'

You pig, you just don't get it, do you? You don't understand me at all!

Aloud, Millie said, 'Bye.'

At eight-thirty the next morning the phone shrilled next to Millie's bed.

'What? What? Who is it?' Jolted into consciousness, she stared blankly around the room. A strange room, with the door on the wrong side and unfamiliar curtains.

Extremely *posh* curtains.

The phone carried on shrilling. Feeling stupid, Millie realized it hadn't been the doorbell after all. That was the trouble with waking up somewhere you weren't used to. The telephone didn't ring like the one at home. It caught you on the hop, deliberately confused you…

Shrill, shrill.

Answering it might be a good idea.

Millie seized the receiver and mumbled, 'Hello?'

If it was Con, she would kill him. It surely couldn't be Orla, who never woke before nine. Particularly when she'd spent a torrid night shagging with the enemy.

'Miss Brady? Good morning, it's reception here.' The voice clearly belonged to someone who had been up since six and had eaten a muesli-and-orange-juice-type breakfast before jogging three miles to work. She sounded disgustingly healthy.

'Oh, hi.' Eyeing last night's empty bottle of Veuve Clicquot on the bedside table, Millie briefly closed her eyes and waited for her hangover to kick in. Oh no, *and* she'd phoned Hugh last night. Droned on and on like one of those sad people who rang late-night radio phone-ins and stubbornly refused to get off the line.

I've turned into a nuisance caller. Any more hassle and he'll be forced to get one of those court order thingies to stop me harassing him—

'Miss Brady, I'm sorry, but there appears to be some kind of mix-up with your reservation.'

The sun was streaming through the curtains Millie had last night forgotten to close. Averting her eyes from its glare, she huddled into the pillows.

'Mix-up? What kind of mix-up?'

'I'm really sorry. Maybe if you could come down here to reception we can get it sorted out.'

'Now?' Millie was having trouble concentrating. 'You want me to come down *now*?'

The receptionist replied chirpily, 'If you could, that'd be great. See you in a mo!'

A mo?

This girl had to be joking.

The phone went dead in Millie's hand. Little Ms. Bright'n'Breezy had hung up.

Regular bowels. Millie would bet a month's wages the girl had regular bowels.

But was that actually such a great thing? What if you had a bowel movement at seven-thirty every morning without fail? What if you were on the Central Line surrounded by fellow commuters at the time?

Ha! Wouldn't be so great then, would it?

In the bathroom, Millie splashed cold water over her face, hurriedly brushed her teeth, and combed her morning-after-the-night-before hair into some kind of order.

Back in her room, she discovered the downside of not closing the curtains. Her suitcase, lying open on the floor next to the window, contained her white jeans. Sadly it also contained the Cadbury bar she had torn open and half eaten yesterday afternoon. The remaining half, having liquefied in the heat, had melted all over one leg of her jeans.

The moral of the story being, once you've started a Cadbury bar, always *always* finish it.

Wrecked trousers. Bugger. Champagne-stained suede dress. Bum. Bending down and rummaging through the extremely small case, Millie pulled out her best nightie—last year's Christmas present from Hester. Made of heavy lilac silk with a deeper lilac velvet trim, it really wasn't nightie-ish at all. In fact, with its spaghetti straps, fitted bodice and just-above-the-knee hemline it could easily pass as a summer dress.

Which was just as well, seeing as it was going to have to.

Making her way down in the lift, Millie tried to imagine how the mix-up could have come about. Had her room been double-booked? If the hotel was full, did that mean she was about to be turfed out into the street?

The lift doors slid open and Millie instantly spotted the receptionist in question. Everything about the girl was pert. She was even wearing her hair in pigtails. Her favorite film had to be, just *had* to be *The Sound of Music*.

'Millie Brady?' The receptionist flashed an apologetic smile. The badge she wore announced that her name was Wendi. With an i. 'I'm sorry about this. He made me do it.'

As her perfectly made-up eyes slid sideways, so did Millie's. Before, she had been concentrating on Wendi-with-an-i. Now she saw who was standing a few feet away and her stomach went DOINNGGG, like a Sumo wrestler crash-landing on a trampoline.

Hugh was leaning against the desk, watching her reaction.

'My God, I don't believe this!' Crazily, it occurred to her that maybe he had a twin brother he'd never told her about. Staring at him, Millie said carefully, '*Hugh?*'

'Is this okay?' Wendi looked as though she might be about to pounce on the nearest panic button. 'You do know him?'

In a daze, Millie said, 'Well, I thought I did.'

'You told me Orla had abandoned you.' Hugh's tone was conversational. 'I thought you might not be safe here all on your own. Also,' he added, 'you did say that the next time we bumped into each other you'd show me your tattoo.'

'You're certain this is all right?' Wendi needed reassurance. 'I mean, he seems normal enough, but he did ask me to do something pretty weird just now. I told him straight, there was *no way* I was doing that.'

Having somehow made it from Cornwall, Hugh now appeared to have forgotten what he was supposed to say next. Similarly, finding it easier to talk to Wendi-with-an-i than to him, Millie cleared her throat and said delicately, 'Um… did he by any chance want you to dress up in a gorilla suit and burst into my room on roller skates?'

'*What?* No!' Wendi's eyebrows rocketed into her fringe. Turning to Hugh, she gasped, 'My God, you really *are* weird.'

Hugh's tone was consoling. 'I'd never have asked you to do that.'

'What then?' prompted Millie.

'He wanted me to phone your room, put on a Dutch accent and ask you some kind of… well, here, I can't figure it out.' Wendi pushed a piece of paper across the desk. 'I mean, this is bizarre. He says he's driven up here from Cornwall overnight, but how can anyone be that desperate for the answer to some dumb riddle?'

Millie read what was written on the sheet of paper.

Clue: Idiot. Two words, four and seven letters. Last letter, N.

Wendi might be pert, but she wasn't the brightest fairy light on the Christmas tree.

'It's not a riddle. It's a crossword clue,' Millie explained. 'And I think I know the answer. Hugh Emerson.'

Hugh nodded.

'That's me. I am that idiot.' He paused, then added steadily, 'But I'm over it now, I promise.'

Millie began to tingle all over. Was he actually saying what she thought he was saying? Or, at least, trying to say?

Chapter 58

'WHERE ARE WE GOING?' Millie protested as he led her out of the hotel. 'I haven't got my handbag with me.'

Come to think of it, I'm not even wearing any knickers.

Oops.

'No problem. My treat.' Hugh nodded at the open-top double-decker across the road. It was one of those sightseeing buses, Millie realized, the kind that provided hour-long tours of the city.

'You don't want to live in London,' Hugh went on. 'It's dirty and crowded and horrible.'

The bus driver was leaning against the railings of Hyde Park, smoking a roll-up and waiting for the first tourists of the day.

'It's got Buckingham Palace.' Millie pointed to the board propped up against the side of the bus, depicting the delights on offer. 'Look, and Downing Street and the Millennium Wheel, Regent's Park and Kew Gardens,' she recited. 'Not to mention the Houses of Parliament, Tower Bridge, and much much more.'

'That's why I'm going to show them to you now. Get it out of your system. Once you've seen everything, the novelty will wear off.'

'It might not.'

'Newquay's better,' Hugh assured her. 'It has the sea, for a start. And beaches.'

Millie feigned horror.

'You mean London doesn't have a sea? It doesn't have *beaches*?'

'There's always the Thames. We might be able to rustle you up a few mudflats.'

'Will I not be able to surf?' gasped Millie, who had never surfed in her life.

'Two please,' Hugh told the bus driver, who was looking at them as if they were barmy.

Millie made sure she followed him up the narrow, curving staircase. She was also careful to keep her nightie tightly wrapped around her legs—accidentally coming out minus your knickers wasn't what you'd call restful.

'This is weird.' Millie shook her head when they'd chosen their seats. 'I still can't believe you drove up here. Have you any idea how cross I was with you, when you practically hung up on me last night?'

Hugh, looking amused, said, 'You did sound the teeniest bit pissed off.'

The Sumo wrestler was still trampolining away inside her stomach. Millie felt that, all in all, she was doing a pretty good job of sounding normal. What's more, considering the distance he'd driven, Hugh was looking pretty good himself. His white cotton shirt was crumpled, but that didn't matter one bit. His black trousers were gorgeous, her favorites. She longed to run her fingers through his hair, so sun-streaked by now it was practically honey blond. His humorous dark eyes were flecked with gold in the sunlight, as was the stubble on his tanned face. Millie was finding this stubble disturbingly attractive. She also liked the fact that he wasn't wearing aftershave; instead, he smelt clean and sexy and intensely Hugh-ish. Phew, so this was what they meant by pheromones. She could sit here and breathe in his heavenly smell all day.

'Anyway.' Hugh tapped her right thigh. 'You promised.'

They hadn't been alone together on the open top deck for long. It was filling up fast with chattering, camcorder-wielding tourists.

Bracing herself, Millie slowly raised the hem of her dress-cum-nightie to reveal the tattoo on her tanned thigh.

Hugh surveyed it in silence for several seconds.

Finally he spoke.

'When did this happen?'

For heaven's sake, when did he think she'd had it done—last week?

'Six years ago.'

'Are you serious?'

'You have to understand. I was only nineteen. I'd been going out with this boy for a couple of months and he persuaded me to have it done. I was mad about him, so I thought it was a great idea. Plus, I knew it would infuriate my mother. Of course,' Millie sighed, 'we split up ten days later when I found out he'd been seeing some other girl behind my back. So there you go,' she added dryly. 'My first ever love-rat.'

Sadly though, not my last.

The corners of Hugh's mouth began to twitch.

'And you've been stuck with this permanent reminder of him ever since. Still, he wasn't all bad.'

Millie gazed down at the neatly executed heart shape, with the name of her ex-boyfriend enclosed within it.

Hugh.

'So, don't tell me, you've been waiting all these years for the right man to come along,' Hugh deadpanned. 'Or at least some man with the right name. You must have been delighted when you found my wallet under that bush.'

'Ha ha,' said Millie.

'Were you never tempted to give Hugh Grant a ring?'

'Oh I did, loads of times. But he just kept saying, "Look, it's terribly nice of you to offer, but I'm just the teensiest bit busy right now... "'

'Bad luck,' Hugh sympathized.

'I was going to get the heart filled in,' said Millie. 'But it hurt so much having the stupid thing done in the first place I kept putting it off. Then I thought I'd just leave it there as a reminder never to do anything so completely ridiculous ever again.'

'And has it done the trick?' Hugh still looked as if he was trying hard not to laugh.

'Don't be daft, of course it hasn't. Doing ridiculous things is what I do best. Anyway, now you know.' Signaling that the show was over, Millie slid the hem of her dress-cum-nightie back down over her thigh.

'Well,' said Hugh, 'thanks for showing me.'

'Worth the trip?'

'Oh definitely. Every mile.'

At that moment the bus rumbled into life and began moving jerkily forwards. Everyone on the top deck obediently plugged themselves into the headphones that would enable them to listen to the tour guide's running commentary.

Millie didn't need to do this. She had Hugh.

'… and this is Buckingham Palace,' he said as the bus trundled up The Mall. 'What a dump. Damp, poky little place. Full of Ikea furniture and nasty modern prints in plastic frames.'

'I see what you mean.' Millie nodded. 'I certainly wouldn't want to live there.'

'That's Tower Bridge,' Hugh pointed out some time later. 'See the Thames? Told you it was manky.'

Followed by: 'Trafalgar Square. You can't move without treading on a pigeon. Did you ever see that Alfred Hitchcock film, *The Birds*?'

Millie leapt excitedly to her feet at one stage, convinced she'd just spotted Prince William emerging from a Burger King in Piccadilly Circus. Yanking her back down, Hugh said, 'You mustn't do that.'

'I only wanted to look at him!' Millie wondered if it was one of those London rules she didn't know about, where you could be prosecuted for hassling a Royal. Crikey, what did he imagine she'd been about to do—throw herself at their future king from the top of the bus?

'For a start, it wasn't Prince William. And for another start,' Hugh kept a straight face, 'everyone can see right through that nightie you're wearing.'

Luckily the tourists' camcorders were trained elsewhere, on some boring statue thing. Millie decided to brazen it out.

'It's not a nightie. It's a dress.'

'Really? I thought it might be a nightie. What with it being so transparent.'

'You know nothing about fashion. It's actually quite the thing this season… *What?*' Millie protested, all of a sudden finding it hard to breathe normally. 'Why are you looking at me like that?'

'You might be gorgeous,' Hugh shook his head good-naturedly, 'but you're a diabolical liar.'

Oh! He called me gorgeous!

'Thank you.' Lightly, Millie added, 'I think.'

'So what's the verdict?'

'On what?'

Hugh gestured with his arm. 'London.'

'Horrible.' She pulled a face. 'Like you said, not a patch on Cornwall.'

'Changed your mind about coming to live here?'

His tone was playful, but Millie no longer felt like playing along. She had to know what this was really all about.

'Why don't you tell me why you're here?' Her attempt to sound sophisticated and in control was spoilt somewhat by the fact that her teeth had begun to chatter.

Quite loudly, in fact.

Hugh nodded.

'Okay. Right. Remember the recurring dream I told you about? The one where the phone rings and I think it's Louisa.'

Of course I remember.

'Yes.'

'Well, that doesn't happen any more. It stopped.' He paused. 'After Orla's party.'

Millie held her breath.

'And?'

'And I know I swore I'd never fall in love again. But I did. And it's taken me a while to accept that, but now I have.'

'R-really?' Her teeth were still at it, like boisterous school children incapable of keeping still in assembly.

'In fact, I went to see her last night.' Hugh stopped, his dark eyes serious. 'I went to see her and I told her I loved her.'

'Wh-what?'

Millie felt sick. His face swam in and out of focus. Oh God, all of a sudden things were going horribly *horribly* wrong.

'She was wearing her gorilla suit at the time.' His tone was wry. 'Well, I *thought* she was wearing her gorilla suit. Turns out, she'd lent it to her best friend for the evening. So that's something I'm never going to live down.'

'No!' It came out as a shriek. Clapping her hands to her mouth, Millie spluttered with laughter.

'This is why I had to drive up here, to get to you before Hester did. I'm sure everyone already knows about it in Newquay.'

Millie, awash with happiness, said, 'Are you sure?'

'Are you kidding? Hester's probably driving around the town as we speak, broadcasting the news through a megaphone.'

This was undoubtedly true.

'I meant are you sure about… you know, the other stuff you just said?'

Hugh smiled slightly.

'Only if you're happy about it. I mean, I've pretty much put my neck on the line here. You might be about to tell me you aren't interested.'

Millie considered this. It might be fun. It would definitely give him a taste of his own medicine. Then again...

'I could,' she admitted. 'Except I'm a lousy liar. I've always been interested in you, and you've always known that.'

'The thing is,' Hugh's expression softened, 'can you forgive me for the way I treated you?'

'I don't know,' Millie lied. 'You'll have to persuade me first.'

It was ten o'clock; the tour was at an end. As the bus slowed to a halt outside the Royal Lancaster Hotel, Hugh drew her into his arms and kissed her until her head began to spin.

Then he kissed her some more.

Around them, the foreign tourists prepared to disembark. Chattering and giggling, they made their way past the two mad English people. When Millie finally opened her eyes, she saw a camcorder pointed at them, whirring away. A Japanese girl said something to her friend and they both went off into peals of laughter.

'What was that about?' Millie murmured, not really caring at all.

'Actually, I speak a bit of Japanese.' Hugh raised an eyebrow. 'She said, "That girl isn't wearing any knickers."'

He was joking, Millie told herself.

At least she hoped he was.

Then again, maybe they shouldn't get off the bus just yet.

Moments later they had the top deck to themselves once more, and Hugh kissed her again. Ecstatically, she closed her eyes and wound her arms around him.

'Millie Brady, what *do* you think you're doing?'

Millie's eyes snapped open. At the sound of the familiar voice she froze, then peered guiltily over Hugh's shoulder.

Orla was standing outside the entrance to the hotel. Next to her, still wearing his dinner jacket and dress shirt from last night, and with a lighted cigarette dangling from his fingers, was a rumpled but happy-looking Christie Carson.

Orla stared, transfixed, at the sight of Millie on the upper deck of the open-top tour bus, enthusiastically canoodling with a man who had his back to her but who certainly wasn't Con Deveraux.

The strumpet!

The shameless hussy!

And about time too, thought Orla, who had in recent weeks begun to inwardly despair at Millie's spectacular lack of progress on the man front.

'She must have picked him up at the party after we left last night.' Delighted, Orla gave Christie's hand a squeeze. 'Maybe he's a writer too.' Raising her voice to a bellow, she gestured wildly with her free arm. 'Hey, Millie! Come down here, this minute! Introduce us to your new friend.'

'She's going to go mental when she recognizes you,' said Millie.

'That's nothing.' Hugh grinned. 'You've been withholding vital information. She'll probably demand her money back. But,' he added consolingly, 'I'll still love you. Five grand or no five grand.'

'Okay. Here goes.' Millie took a deep breath, grabbed his hand for moral support, and stood up.

Hugh, rising to his feet, turned and waved at Orla.

Orla's mouth promptly dropped open.

'I don't… but… how can he be…?' she spluttered as Hugh, laughing now, blew her a kiss. 'This is completely… good grief, I don't *believe* this.'

'Neither do I.' Shielding his eyes from the sun in order to get a better look, Christie Carson let out a low, appreciative whistle. 'You can see right through that dress.'

Also by Jill Mansell,
available from Sourcebooks Landmark

An Offer You Can't Refuse

Miranda's Big Mistake

Perfect Timing

Reading Group Guides available at
www.sourcebooks.com

From

perfect timing

'If you want to dance, dance.' Dina looked smug. 'Don't mind me.'

The last record of the night was 'Lady in Red'.

'Thank God you aren't wearing something red,' said Tom. 'That really would have been too kitsch for words.'

Poppy, whose heart was going nineteen to the dozen, didn't tell him she had red knickers on.

She said, 'I thought you'd left.'

'I did. Then I came back. I had to.' Tilting his head he murmured into her ear, 'I want you to know I don't make a habit of this. It isn't some kind of bizarre hobby of mine, in case you were wondering.'

Over his shoulder Poppy saw Jen and one of the airline pilots cruising at low altitude towards them. Jen winked.

'Watch what you're doing with my future cousin-in-law,' she instructed Tom. 'By this time tomorrow she'll be an old married woman. We're under instruction to keep our eye on her tonight.'

This is awful, thought Poppy, beginning to panic as the song moved into its final chorus. Any minute now the night will be over, it'll be time to leave. How can this be happening to me? I need more time—

In a low voice Tom said, 'Will your friends miss you if we sneak out now?'

'Of course they will.' Close to despair Poppy felt her fingers dig helplessly into his arms. 'Dina's already phoned for a cab to take us home.'

'Okay, I'll leave it up to you.' He shook back a lock of curling dark hair, studying her face intently for a second. 'Delgado's, that all-night café on Milton Street. You know the one, directly opposite the university?'

Poppy nodded, unable to speak.

'I'll wait there. Until three o'clock. If you want to see me, that's where I'll be. If you don't… well, you won't turn up.'

'This isn't funny.' Poppy realized she was trembling. 'I'm not enjoying this. I'm hating it.'

'You mean you wish you hadn't met me?' Just for a second Tom traced a finger lightly down the side of her quivering face. 'Fine, if that's how you feel. If it's how you really feel. Go home. Get a good night's sleep. Carry on as if tonight never happened. Get married—'

'Our taxi,' Susie declared with a melodramatic flourish, 'is waiting.' She passed Poppy her handbag and began to steer her in the direction of the door. Glancing from Poppy to Tom and back again she chanted, 'Ladies and gentlemen, your time is up. No more flirting, no more smoochy dances with handsome strangers, no more scribbling your phone number in Biro on the back of his hand and praying it doesn't rain on the way home. The girl is no longer available. Tomorrow, she gets hitched.'

The journey from the center of Bristol back to Henbury at two in the morning normally took ten minutes. This time the trip was punctuated with a whole series of stops and starts.

It's worse than musical bloody chairs, thought Poppy, willing herself not to scream as Jen, spotting a still-open burger bar, begged the driver to pull up outside. Susie had already sent him on a convoluted tour of local cash dispensers in search of one that worked. If Dina announced that she needed to find yet another public loo, Poppy knew she would have a complete nervous breakdown. At this rate it would be four o'clock before they even arrived home.

But they made it, finally. Dina, with her stressed bladder, was dropped off first. Then Susie, then Jen. Kissing each of them goodbye in turn, Poppy wondered how they would react if they knew what was racing through her mind. Jen was Rob's cousin, Dina his sister-in-law. Only an hour or so ago Susie had confided tipsily, 'If I could meet and marry someone even half as nice as your Rob I'd be so happy.'

'Edgerton Close is it, love?' asked the taxi driver over his shoulder when only Poppy was left in the car.

Poppy looked at her watch for the fiftieth time. Quarter to three. She took a deep breath.

'Delgado's, Milton Street. Opposite the university. Hurry, please.'

Delgado's was a trendy post-nightclub hangout popular with students and diehard clubbers alike. Poppy, who had visited it a few times in the past, knew its atmosphere to be far more of a draw than the food.

But with its white painted exterior and glossy dark blue shutters it certainly looked the part. On a night like tonight Poppy knew it would be even busier than usual, packed with people showing off their tans, making the most of the perfect weather while it lasted and pretending they weren't in Bristol but in the south of France.

As her taxi drew up outside Poppy wondered just how stupid she would feel if she went inside and he wasn't there. She looked again at her watch. One minute to three.

Then she saw him, sitting alone at one of the sought-after tables in the window. He was lounging back on his chair idly stirring sugar into an espresso and smoking a cigarette.

Poppy's pulse began to race. Twelve hours from now she was due to walk down the aisle of St Mary's church on her father's arm. Twelve and a bit hours from now she would become Poppy McBride, wife of Robert and mother—in due course—to three, maybe four little McBrides. It was all planned, right down to the middle names and the color of the wallpaper in the nursery. Rob was a great one for thinking ahead.

'Here, love?' The taxi driver was showing signs of restlessness. When Poppy still didn't move he lit up a cigar and exhaled heavily, making smoke ricochet off the windscreen and into the back of the cab. This usually did the trick.

Poppy didn't even notice. She saw Tom look at his own watch then gaze out of the window. She knew, without a shadow of a doubt, that if she stepped out of the taxi now her life would be changed drastically and forever.

The taxi driver shifted round in his seat to look at her. 'Don't tell me you're dozing off back there.'

Hardly. Poppy, awash with adrenalin, wondered if she would ever sleep again. Her fingers crept towards the door handle.

'Look, love,' began the driver, 'we can't—'

'Edgerton Close.' Poppy blurted the words out, clenching her fists at her side and willing herself not to leap out of the cab. 'Please.'

'You mean back to Henbury?' The driver stared at her in disbelief. 'Are you sure about this?'

'No, but do it anyway.' She turned her face away from Delgado's and held her breath until the taxi reached the far end of Milton Street. It was no good; she couldn't go through with it.

The bad news was, she didn't think she could go through with the wedding either.

About the Author

Jill Mansell lives with her partner and children in Bristol, and writes full time. Actually, that's not true; she watches TV, eats gum drops, admires the rugby players training in the sports field behind her house, and spends hours on the internet marveling at how many other writers have blogs. Only when she's *completely* run out of ways to procrastinate does she write.